...king...
...g around th...

...cheloe has been writing stories ...
...member, and somehow they always
... Always a Kentucky girl at heart, she
...ennessee with her husband, children, and
...g menagerie of pets. Visit her on Twitter:
...Author.

Discover more at millsandboon.co.uk.

FLING WITH HER LONG-LOST SURGEON

SUE MacKAY

SAVING THE SINGLE MUM'S HEART

ALLIE KINCHELOE

MILLS & BOON

First Published in Great Britain 2022
by Mills & Boon, an imprint of HarperCollins*Publishers* Ltd,
1 London Bridge Street, London, SE1 9GF

www.harpercollins.co.uk

HarperCollins*Publishers*
1st Floor, Watermarque Building,
Ringsend Road, Dublin 4, Ireland

Fling with Her Long-Lost Surgeon © 2022 Sue MacKay

Saving the Single Mum's Heart © 2022 Allie Kincheloe

ISBN: 978-0-263-30130-4

06/22

MIX
Paper from
responsible sources
FSC™ C007454

This book is produced from independently certified FSC™ paper
to ensure responsible forest management.
For more information visit www.harpercollins.co.uk/green.

Printed and Bound in Spain using 100% Renewable Electricity
at CPI Black Print, Barcelona

FLING
WITH HER
LONG-LOST
SURGEON

SUE MacKAY

MILLS & BOON

To all my readers, thank you. I'd be lost without you.
Cheers, Sue MacKay.

CHAPTER ONE

GYNAECOLOGIST GEORGINA PRICE stepped out of her office at Scott's Women's Health and tried not to stare at the man pacing the small space between her and the waiting room. Wow. Had he grown up or what? She'd never looked twice at him before, but then she was four years older than Blake and when he and her brother were knocking around together the last thing she'd been interested in was some pain in the backside who needed to grow up and get a life. 'Hello, Blake. It's been a long time since we last caught up.'

Thirteen years had turned the boy into an outstanding-looking man. She couldn't help but observe how the skinny young guy she'd last seen when she was twenty-three had become almost unrecognisable. Almost. The long, too-lean body had filled out in all the right places to become that of an attractive man. Stunning said it all—even when his once open face was now shuttered with lines tugging at the corners of his mouth and eyes. Sadly those eyes had lost their cheeky twinkle, but on the good side, the riotous curls were as dark and thick as ever, and still wild despite an upmarket haircut. As though the wind had been blowing through his hair on the way here. Oh, to run her fingers over his scalp, to feel the softness of those shiny curls. Her mouth dried. Definitely gorgeous.

Georgie, get a grip. Blake's here because of Sarah, nothing else.

His mother was very ill and had been referred to this practice for surgery. She'd wanted Georgie to be her consultant but understood it wasn't possible for ethical reasons as they were family friends. Georgie had seen to it that Andrew, a senior partner here, stepped up for Sarah, and right now Blake's mother was in with him going over tomorrow's procedure.

'I wish we were catching up in better circumstances.' Blake had stepped closer and, with a glance in the direction of the office where his mother was sitting patiently waiting for him to join them, said quietly, 'Is Mum putting on a brave face? Or are you the one she tells all to? Downloads on? I know she's talked to you a lot about what's going on.' He was hurting, and worrying himself sick. It was there in the dark gaze now locked on her as though she could alleviate his pain with a few words.

Not possible, sorry, Blake.

But as a doctor, he knew that. Georgie sighed. Later, when this was over and hopefully Sarah was back on her feet, he could return to being her late brother's best friend whom she hadn't seen since the funeral, but for now his mother was ill and preparing for major surgery tomorrow morning to remove a massive fibroid, as well as have a full hysterectomy because of the possibility of cancer. 'She's being Sarah, resilient and quiet.' And worried sick, but Georgie wasn't putting that into words. Blake sounded apprehensive enough as it was. Something she understood too well. While logically she and Andrew were ninety per cent certain Sarah didn't have a malignancy, the family friend part of her mind was afraid she might be wrong. The thought of this family being hurt gripped her, making her almost relieved she wasn't the one doing the surgery. She now understood better why Blake had felt so guilty over Noah's death when he had no reason to.

Blake shook his head. 'What else did I expect?' he muttered almost to himself.

'It would be more upsetting if she was behaving any different.'

Dull eyes met her full on. Where was that twinkle when she needed it? Because she also felt out of sorts about what Sarah and her family were facing. 'You're right. But sometimes I want to be the strong one.'

'You were always strong, Blake.' He'd never faltered when his cricket team needed runs from him, when her brother wanted to try some outlandish feat like leaping out of a plane wearing nothing but a parachute. He'd stepped up and passed his exams with the highest scores ever seen at the medical school he was trying to get into while he'd been broken-hearted over Noah's passing. He was tough. Or he had been. What did she know these days? Anything could've changed within him. She only had his mother's take on things now and of course Sarah would be biased, or unwilling to talk about anything distressing about her son, but reading between the lines, Georgie had a feeling Blake had struggled at times over the intervening years since all their lives had been changed for ever.

'You don't know the half of it,' Blake said quietly,

verifying her own thoughts. 'But thanks for the vote of confidence.'

Andrew's door opened and he appeared. 'Like to join us, Blake?'

Blake swallowed. 'Sure.'

Georgie tapped his arm. 'Go on. You can do this. I'm available if you need to talk later.' Naturally she'd be there for this family that had been there for hers thirteen years ago.

He smiled tiredly. 'Thanks, Georgie. I might take you up on that.'

'Georgie,' Andrew called. 'Sarah would like you in on this too. As a friend,' he added pointedly. The direction of his gaze suggested that was more for Blake's sake than hers.

But Blake didn't hesitate. He held out his hand and gestured to the doorway. 'After you, Georgie.'

Ever the gentleman. 'Thanks.' It was easy to smile at him as she went past. Strange how right it felt being here with him.

Sitting down at his desk, Andrew quickly filled them in on details. 'I've explained the operation to Sarah, and also made it very clear that she has to take things easy for the following six weeks.'

'Good luck with that.' Blake squeezed his mother's shoulder, a grim look on his face. 'I'd like to see the X-ray and scans that were taken of this fibroid.'

Andrew nodded. 'Your mother said you'd want to do that. I totally understand, especially being a doctor.'

Standing by the door, Georgie glanced beyond the chair where Sarah sat to the man she hadn't seen for so long and once more took in his good looks, strong chin and the determination in those eyes that always used to be filled with laughter and fun. A lot like hers before her brother's accident. Now she saw pain and fear, presumably brought on by his mother's illness and knowing what it was like losing someone special. Had his life been all he'd once hoped for? From the little she'd heard from Sarah, apart from his medical career, he didn't seem to have followed through on anything else he might've dreamed about, like marrying and having a family. But maybe he hadn't found the right woman yet, or was too busy protecting his heart to get involved with someone who might cause him hurt again.

Sounded awfully familiar, she conceded. There'd been a few failures along the way for her. It was possibly the same with Blake. They'd both hurt badly over Noah, and she'd lost a lot of confidence and trust, so why wouldn't it be? She had tried to let go the pain of losing Noah, had even fallen in love and married, only to end up divorced and sorry for the pain she'd put her husband through. Afraid of the consequences if something terrible happened to him, she hadn't been able to give him enough love. Especially after she lost their baby at twelve weeks. That had been the final straw. More pain, more loss, and it made her feel guilty for even trying for happiness when Noah would never experience those things. She'd withdrawn from looking for love and a family, and got on with what she was good at by putting her heart and soul into it—medicine.

Which made the way she was noticing Blake as an attractive man rather odd. She hadn't felt any warm tingly sensations tickling her since her marriage fell apart. It had to be more to do with catching up with someone who'd known her brother so well and understood the pain of losing him than anything else.

Sarah was talking, reminding Georgie why she was here. 'Blake.' Sarah paused until she had her son's full attention. 'Andrew's my specialist and he doesn't need any input from you. You're not the doctor in this situation. You're my son.' She reached for his hand and gave him a mother's smile. Gentle, understanding and 'do as you're told' all rolled into one.

Georgie's heart expanded, and her eyes watered. Family love was so enveloping and got a person through the daily hits life sent. Her parents gave her strength and understanding, as well as acceptance: things she'd needed over the years, and still did occasionally. She thought of Sarah and knew Blake had been given all the support he needed, but had he accepted it?

'Andrew won't take the slightest bit of notice of anything Blake says anyway.' Georgie smiled at the woman she'd known for as long as she had Blake, which was since he and Noah met at the private school they'd attended here in Christchurch and became inseparable when it came to getting into mischief. Over time their families had got to know each other, but she hadn't had a lot to do with the boys as the age gap had seemed huge back then. But in the intervening years she had got to know Sarah and Alistair, Blake's dad, quite well over dinners at her parents' place.

'Nor would you.' Blake had found it in himself to smile at her for the first time since she'd set eyes on him. He did still appear uncomfortable with being here though. It was a scary time for him and his family with the cancer question hanging over them like a black cloud in an otherwise bright blue sky. Memories of pain from the past would up the stress levels and tighten those well-shaped shoulders even further.

Blake and Noah had been in their second year at university in Dunedin when tragedy struck, taking Noah from them. Blake had not coped with losing his best mate and blamed himself for the accident that killed him, when it couldn't be further from the truth. He'd believed if he'd been with Noah that night, he'd have prevented him from getting into the car with the drunk driver. Since then Blake had been notable by his absence in Christchurch, and rarely visited her parents on the few occasions he did spend a few days with his family. She knew Sarah and Alastair struggled with his absence but they also understood and supported him. It was as though they too had lost a son the same night her parents lost Noah.

'Yes, I still like to be in charge,' she admitted. 'I'm guessing you do too.' It was a way of surviving. But in this case Blake wasn't a gynaecologist or obstetrician so his mother's condition was out of his league. His strength was in orthopaedics—which would only make this more frightening. There was nothing he could do but wait and be there for his parents and sisters. Returning his smile, Georgie felt awkward. It was true they hadn't been close but he'd been around her family a lot as a teenager, like a part of the furniture, as had her brother with Blake's family. Now he was worried for his mother, and so was she, even when, from what she'd seen and talked through with Andrew, medically she believed Sarah did not have cancer. It would only be once the surgery was done and Andrew could say with some certainty there was no cancer would she begin to relax. Even then it would take a negative pathology report to take away any lingering doubts.

Sarah looked from her son to Georgie, and back. 'Even though I understood Georgie couldn't be my specialist I rang her the moment I knew I had to have this operation. I want her close to the action.'

Georgie nodded and smiled at Blake. 'Your mother rang me at home while I was enjoying a quiet meal after a busy day in Theatre,' she told him in an attempt to lighten his mood. Sarah had been calm and forthright when she explained how she'd ended up in the emergency department in extreme abdominal pain after a heavy fall while out walking in Hagley Park. 'She told me she'd been referred to the public system but that she wanted to go private with the practice I work at.'

'Relax, Georgie. I'm more than happy that you're here, especially as a friend.' His smile was looking less strained by the minute. Then it wavered. 'Dad's not pleased to be presiding over the trial of those two men caught bringing in ten million dollars' worth of cocaine last year. It's going to run for four weeks. He'd far rather be here with Mum.'

'Bad timing.' High court judge Alistair Newman had spoken to Georgie earlier that morning to once again say thanks for supporting them. He was worried sick about his wife having to undergo major surgery. As were they all. Looking at Blake, Georgie was surprised to see approval beaming out at her from those charcoal eyes. The grey used to be light and sparkly. So far today, she'd only seen the colour of wet tar. Until now. Though nowhere near sparkling, they were lighter.

Relieved even. 'I think we need to let Andrew get on with his job rather than listen to us yabbering.'

Andrew laughed. 'It's fine. I've got a few minutes to spare. But...' He shrugged. 'Blake, come here.' He indicated the screen on the desk. 'Look at the MRI. It shows the clearest image of what's causing Sarah so much pain.'

Blake crossed over and stared at the images, the colour draining from his face. The fibroid pressing on Sarah's uterus was so big it made her stomach extend outward, which she'd put down to eating too many sweet delicacies lately.

Georgie heard Blake suck in air at the sight of the fibroid mass, saw his hands tighten, but he didn't say a word. Probably didn't want to scare his mum.

But Sarah was a GP and understood her problem, including the swelling on the walls of the uterus. That was the bigger of the concerns here; it was an indicator of cancer, though so far Andrew hadn't seen anything to back that up. He tapped the screen. 'That's why we're doing a full hysterectomy.'

Blake winced. 'At least six weeks taking it easy, Mum.'

Georgie couldn't take her eyes off him. He was very attractive now that she was seeing him as a man. Like blood-warming, stomach-tightening attractive. Gone were the laughter lines and cheeky twinkle in those eyes, sure, but there was a strength in his face, and a maturity that hadn't been there when she'd known him all those years ago. Interesting that she was even noticing. She didn't get overly involved with men these days. Not after her marriage failed. Tommy, her husband, reckoned she didn't try hard enough to love him, and after one too many arguments he'd packed up and left, breaking her heart and making her more cautious than ever. She'd wanted to have a family with him, but after losing her baby it was too much to bear on top of Noah's death so she'd said she couldn't try again. Love hurt bad when it went wrong. Tommy had been right in that she had been afraid to open her heart too much because of her fear of her love going wrong. It had taken a while for her to see that, which kind of suggested his accusations were bang on. Which didn't bode well for any other relationship she might find herself in, so she was staying clear of love.

On the screen the X-ray taken at the emergency department two weeks ago when Sarah was admitted with severe abdominal pain appeared. 'This is what led to the scan showing the size of the fibroid and the other problem.' Andrew gave him a few minutes to take it in.

Blake nodded when he'd finished studying the image with an intensity that would've been scary if Georgie hadn't known he was thinking of his mother.

'We've done routine blood tests and everything's normal. A cross match has been done and bloods are on hold for tomorrow, in case a haemorrhage occurs, which isn't infrequent with this type of surgery. It helps Sarah's fit and otherwise healthy.' Andrew turned to Sarah. 'Anything else you would like to go over before tomorrow?'

'No, nothing. I just want it over with.'

Blake said to Andrew, 'I can't thank you enough for getting on to it so quickly.' Which implied he was even more worried than he'd shown so far, because there was nothing out of the ordinary about how soon the operation was being performed.

Andrew stood up and shook Blake's hand. 'No problem.'

Out in the corridor Blake's sombre eyes locked onto Georgie as though they were connected in all ways about this. Which, with the history of Noah there with them, they probably were.

Her stomach knotted. Touching his arm briefly, she said, 'We'll get through this.' Somehow she'd make sure of it. And she meant it when she'd said 'we.' They mightn't have stood by each other when Noah died because they'd both been struggling so much with their own grief to allow anyone else's in, but they had gone through the same pain and lived with the consequences in their own ways, and now could understand each other a little. Could understand the fear of losing Sarah.

'It's hard.' His voice was heavy.

'Yes.' He wouldn't have been expecting his mother to be undergoing surgery for a fibroid or possible cancer. No one ever did. She'd seen the shock in the faces of too many patients learning they had a serious problem so knew Blake was feeling it, if trying not to show his concerns. Turning away from that interesting but worried face, she drew a breath and calmly asked Sarah, 'You all right?' After the meeting with her surgeon about the procedure, it would feel more real than it had before. Very real.

'Pretty much as well as expected.' There was a waver in her voice.

'You can always ring me if you want to go over anything.'

And, Blake, try to stop worrying.

'I will.' Sarah gave her a hug. 'Thank you for being here. It makes everything easier somehow knowing you're looking out for me as a friend and doctor.'

Make me want to cry, why don't you?

This was why she didn't like getting close to people. Hadn't since Noah was taken from them. 'You couldn't keep me away.' She glanced at Blake and was surprised to see him nodding. He was happy she was here? When they'd not seen each other at all for so long? It did surprise her, though he used to try and get her attention when they were younger. When the boys finished high school and moved south to Dunedin and university where she was training to become a doctor she had caught up with them regularly. She'd been studying hard with a bit of partying on the side whenever possible. Blake had been partying hard and cramming his studies in between. It's how it was for students in their first couple of years before they settled into serious study.

Then the night of the phone call came and her world fell apart. Nothing was ever to be the same again. She didn't know how to grieve, how to move forward. Everyone had advice, but they hadn't been there and couldn't understand why she couldn't spend six months crying, then pack up her feelings and get on with her life. In the end she had done almost that, turned to study and training as hard as she could, focusing on her career and the goals she'd set before she'd even left school. No more parties, no more nights out with the girlfriends. But the pain never left, downsized, maybe, but it was always ready to roar to life whenever something else went wrong.

That was the past, and her future had been about being serious and careful so her mum and dad could rely on her to be there for them for ever. She'd even transferred back to Christchurch to finish her training so they could see her whenever they needed to, only leaving town for training stints in other hospitals up and down the country. Then she'd met Tommy and fallen in love and got married. Only she hadn't really given him her whole heart, had been afraid of being hurt again, and in the end *she'd* hurt Tommy, and herself as well.

'Sarah, I'll pop in to see you tomorrow morning in the pre-op room. You'll get to see me all glammed up in baggy scrubs.'

'Can't wait.' Sarah's face suddenly dropped.

Georgie reached for her hand. 'You'll be fine. We've got this.'

Don't break down. Not now.

Though if ever there was a moment for Sarah to fall apart it would be with Blake at her side. She adored her son even though he'd abandoned them for the most part. Until now when he was here to help and support his family.

'Come on, Mum, let's go home and wait for Dad to finish up for the day.' Blake gently took her arm to lead her away. Over his mother's head, he said, 'See you tomorrow?'

Georgie nodded. 'Of course. I'll drop by between surgeries.'

Bet Blake would be waiting when Sarah was wheeled into her room after recovery. He'd want to see for himself that she'd come through all right. More importantly, he'd want to hear what Andrew had to say about the surgery and what he'd found and if his mother had cancer or not. Until then, he wouldn't begin to relax. 'Catch you tomorrow.'

Watching him lead his mother out of the clinic, she drew a long, shaky breath. Strange how she was really looking forward to seeing him again, and it had nothing to do with talking about Sarah's condition. She'd never once thought of Blake Newman as anything but Noah's mate. Who'd have believed he'd grow up so damned good-looking?

There had been a drought of men lately but surely that had nothing to do with her reacting to Blake like he was necessary to her. She didn't have it in her to get deeply involved with men any more, or anyone, really. The few men she'd dated lately seemed to want the whole caboodle, almost before they took the time to get to know her very well. She didn't want to take another chance on finding happiness. She'd blown it twice before so didn't believe she'd be that lucky. The relationship she'd been in when Noah died had collapsed because she couldn't function properly, and then her marriage, which for all its faults could've been good if only she'd known how to let go the strings tying down her heart. She and Tommy would've doted on their child, if only—

'If only' was a mantra from her past.

There were barriers to lower before any relationship was likely to happen. Barriers that were now so ensconced in her makeup it would take a bulldozer to move them. Anyway, it was preferable to protect her heart, and concentrate on her career.

Georgie's eyes followed Blake's tall figure walking

at a slow pace matching his mother's weary one, his head on an angle as he listened to her. Now that she'd caught up with him Georgie felt he might be a man she'd always be aware of, if he was in town, which he hardly ever was.

Really? Why did she think that? She didn't usually just see a guy and go, 'He's the one for me.' Not that she'd had that decimating thought today, but there were tweaks going on in her body that spoke of interest and long-forgotten excitement over spending time with a virile man. 'Blake,' she called and headed after him. 'Blake, hold on a minute.' Why was she doing this? If he needed to contact her he'd find a way.

'Yes, Georgie?'

She shivered. Her name sounded different coming off his tongue. Softer. Sexier? How likely was that? She hadn't noticed she was getting desperate for a man, but perhaps that's what these unexplainable sensations he invoked were all about. Nah, hardly. This was all about Blake, and nothing, nobody, else.

'Georgie?' Now he sounded concerned. Next he'd be thinking she knew something he didn't about his mother.

'If you need to get in touch at any time, Sarah's got my private number.'

Sarah turned, a soft smile lighting up her eyes. 'I gave it to him already.'

Air whooshed out of her lungs. 'Right. Okay. That's fine.' Not that she expected Blake to be ringing to ask her about the operation. He'd get the details from Andrew. So was she expecting him to phone for the hell of it? To have a chat about the weather? Georgie swallowed the disappointment the idea of not hearing from him brought on. It wasn't as though she had any reason to expect him to be in touch. They were all but strangers after all, even though there was a sense of togetherness about Sarah and her op tripping through her at the moment. 'See you tomorrow.' Sometime. Maybe. If he was around when she dropped by. She turned back towards her office.

'Georgie, thank you for looking out for Mum. It's made it easier for her, having another medical mind to download with. I know Dad feels the same.'

Pausing, she stared up at Blake, who'd returned to stand close to her. For once she was seeing him as the guy she used to know, seeing his gentleness in battle with his determination to always be the best at everything. They'd got on as much as two young people with their age difference could. Noah had been their common denominator whenever they were in the same space, but they'd never been best friends or anywhere close. She'd felt grown up while thinking he had a way to go on that score. Regret filled her. What if they had known each other better? Would they have been able to help one another through the tragedy that struck? Would a friendship have softened the pain any? Probably not. Anyway, it hadn't been and nothing could change how they'd both managed to carry on with their individual lives. 'So has you being here for Sarah. She was thrilled when you told her you were coming home for this week.'

'Fortnight.' He seemed surprised he'd said that, as if he'd just had the thought. 'Talk later.' He turned to go back to his mother's side.

Georgie watched him walking purposefully, head

high, back straight. The new, grown-up, empathetic
Blake she'd never met before. The tip of her tongue
touched the centre of her top lip. Fifteen minutes and already she liked him as much as the younger, cheeky version. Oh, those dark curls. They were begging to have
her fingers run through them. But most of all, her heart
wanted to soften his worry, take away the fear that was
spilling out of his eyes whenever he looked at Sarah.

She'd be there if Blake should want to talk.

Hands behind his head, Blake lay on the bed in what
had been his room since he was a toddler, and stared at
the rafters. A vision of a certain gynaecologist startled
him, teasing him with its clarity.

Georgie had matured into an absolutely stunning
woman.

And that wasn't the half of what was stirring him up.
Her confidence and calmness was new. To him any rate.
Okay, maybe she'd always been confident in a do-as-I-
say kind of way. But calm? Not even close. A hurricane
on legs. And what legs they were. Still were from what
he'd seen highlighted by a fitted black skirt that barely
reached her knees. That had been Georgie when they
were growing up in the suburb of Fendalton. A hurricane that puttered out to a breeze when Noah died. Not
that he'd seen her since the funeral and she hadn't been
aware of him that day. He'd sat squeezed between his
father and mother, and deliberately refrained from talking to her for fear of increasing the pain she was suffering. The kind of fear that had lived with him ever since
the night Noah died, fear that dominated how he approached everything, especially getting close to others,

of hurting others. Yes, he was a bit of loner nowadays. A bit? Mostly a lone wolf, more like. He had friends, didn't he? Friends he did his best not to get too close to, though their offspring did make a mockery of that at times with their straightforward approach, the little ratbags.

He sighed. Georgie and those legs brought back other memories. In the past he'd seen them coming out of short shorts, from below tennis skirts that stretched across her thighs accentuating the muscles and curves and eating up the pavement when she went for a run. Georgie was Noah's older sister, not overly interested in what he and her brother were up to, though always there for advice when they moved to Dunedin to attend university. She was always on the go, studying, working, partying. Full of life. But yeah, as a horny eighteen-year-old he'd noticed Georgie far too much. And when he was nineteen. Then Noah was gone and so was the desire to get close to anyone.

Maybe Georgie was even more confident now. She had locked those stunning eyes on him whenever he spoke, tough as ever, but seeming bruised and a little withdrawn. She'd still take no prisoners, yet he felt that beneath the don't-mess-with-me exterior there was a woman who longed to be held, hugged, to be reassured she was still Georgie Price: daughter, sister, even a friend. He'd been told by his parents she was almost completely focused on her career now, especially since her marriage fell apart. Another blow to an already broken heart.

Feelings he understood too damned much. Nearly thirteen years since his life was abruptly flipped onto its back. Years of guilt and doubt, of starting over when it came to believing in himself, except he hadn't quite managed that yet. Sure, he'd done brilliantly in his training to become an orthopaedic surgeon and was now working in a private practice in Auckland. He had the perfect career, a small but reliable set of friends whom he kept at arm's length and an awesome family he did his best to keep away from because they got under his shield and into his heart far too easily. But he did miss love, the belonging, the cohesiveness of being a part of a loving environment. It was lonely at night when he was finished with work or socialising and headed home to his beautiful but empty house, the cold sheets on his bed, a glass of wine on the deck with no one to grump about his day with. Was he feeling sorry for himself? Good point. It was time to get over himself and look beyond his own fears. If he knew how, or had the courage to give it a go.

His mother was ill. How ill, no one would know until after tomorrow's operation, and even then, there would be no surety in the answer about cancer until the lab report come back. Andrew had hesitated when he said he was fairly certain Mum didn't have cancer, but that was doctor-speak for not laying it on the line without proof. His mum said Georgie doubted cancer was in the uterus after she'd seen the scan and MRI, and a part of him believed her. Perhaps that was him wanting her to be right. But he was a son fearing the worst and afraid to accept Georgie's conclusion in case that tempted the opposite result. Funny though how much he wanted to trust her verdict, even when she could only say she was ninety per cent sure his mother didn't have cancer. He shivered. He just had to get through the night and half the morning and there'd be some answers. Fingers crossed.

Georgie was stirring him in strange ways. Not that she'd said anything out of the ordinary to start him wondering about how he felt about her. The past hadn't been mentioned. Why would it be? Especially in the hospital when the focus was on his mother. But make no mistake, there was something between them. A hint of wonder, of belief, between them. Or had he felt it more because she'd been both professional and friendly without being too much of either, and therefore these emotions were running rampant? Because she was his mirror image when it came to the past and how they'd coped? He'd shut down on his heart, afraid to take any chance on being so badly hurt again. It made perfect sense Georgie might've done the same.

What was she doing right now? Relaxing before her surgery schedule tomorrow? Uptight about his mother's operation? Everyone seemed to be on the same page over that. His mother was stressing to bits while pretending all was fine and that she'd get through this like a piece of cake. Dad wasn't much better, saying little about what they were dealing with, preferring to chat about the case he was judging without actually telling him anything.

Georgie and Andrew may have said there was a remote chance that cancer was causing the swelling in the uterus wall, but he knew from personal experience with patients that once the C word was out there no one relaxed until the pathology came through saying negative. Pathology took days, if not weeks, to read samples and make a diagnosis.

Damn this. He was getting too despondent when there was nothing he could do but wait until tomorrow for any answers to the questions battering his mind. Getting off the bed, Blake crossed to the window to look down on the familiar street. The streetlights had come on as the sun made its last hurrah on the edge of the city. As a teen those lights used to annoy him when he was trying to sneak out the window to go join his mates at the park at the end of the road for an hour of talking nonsense and listening to hip-hop on someone's phone. They used to think that was the best in music. Nowadays he'd turn it off if it came on anywhere near his ears.

Georgie and her girlfriends would dance to it, shaking and bobbing around like they'd lost control of themselves on the lawn or the deck. Probably had, when he thought about the half-empty bottle of vodka he and Noah found behind her father's rosebushes one evening after the girls had gone to a nightclub in town.

Georgie didn't look like a woman who partied any more. Had she lost the zest for life that had been her trademark when she lost Noah? At first he'd gone the other way, taking up drinking and partying in a big way, stopped studying so hard as he tried to fill the gap Noah had left in an attempt to prove he was okay. But the feeling that a piece of him was missing and would never come back hadn't left him. He'd struggled to stifle the guilt for not being there to talk his mate out of taking a ride with a drunk that night. If not for Noah's father telling him to let it all go and stop ruining his own life who knew where he might've ended up? It didn't bear thinking about. A deep longing to talk to someone who knew him from the past filled him. It would be wonderful to talk without having to consider the other person wouldn't have a clue what he was on about. Someone who'd understand why he was so worried about his mother.

'What if Mum's got cancer?' he asked for the thousandth time. All very well saying they'd deal with it, that she'd be all right, but cancer had a mind of its own, and tough as his mum was, she might not win that particular battle. She'd certainly give it everything she had, and some, but cancer was a devil. He could not lose his mother. Neither could his sisters, or their children lose their grandmother. As for dad, he'd be decimated. He was already struggling with waiting for tomorrow to be over and them to have some idea where they were headed. Blake shuddered. If his dad was in a bad way, then so was he because he'd never let anyone come near him even to share a meal, let alone know his heart, if the worst happened. Losing Noah had been devastating, and call him naïve, or whatever word came to mind, but he didn't want to face that again. Yet life did throw curve balls. It was how it was. Just not tomorrow or his mum or his family.

Please.

Blake watched a young couple strolling along the footpath, holding hands as they chattered. His heart crunched for what might've been if life hadn't changed so abruptly the night Noah was in that accident. Love, laughter, children. Sure, his life wasn't exactly a desert. But love *was* missing. Someone to share his soul with. A woman to talk to, lie next to, make love with. Children were a dim dream. All because he couldn't let go of the past and look forward with hope and a smile.

Yet right this moment he wanted to share some of his fear and pain. Turning, he reached for his phone, picked it up and stared at the screen until the light went off. 'Nah, she'll think I'm crazy.' She might be right too. He didn't do reaching out to anybody, let alone Georgie.

'Enough.' His head was a mess which would keep him awake all night if he didn't do something about it. Going for a run usually did the trick. He dug in his bag for his gear.

Georgie ran along the riverbank, refusing to think about anything or anyone. Like that was working. Impossible. Blake kept coming to mind. How good he looked. How worried he was over Sarah. How his tired smile had hit her hard, and made her want to be there for him no matter what.

A man ran past, turned around and ran backwards slowly. 'Georgie.'

Could it be? 'Hello, Blake.' She slowed to a brisk walk. Hard to talk while running.

He stepped in beside her. 'Small world, eh?'

'Seems like it.' Of all the thousands of people in the city it was Blake who ran by.

'You do this regularly?'

'Most days in summer when it's not dark by the time I get home.' She'd been longing to talk to Blake all afternoon and here he was. So talk. 'It's my way of destressing from the day so I can sleep at night. You're the same?'

'Yes, I am. Of course today's different. I seem to have been sitting around one place or another most of the day, and figured some exercise might quieten the brain.' He glanced her way. 'Do you still stay up all hours and rush into work late?' There was light laughter in his voice that made her all warm and cosy.

'I try to be a bit more sensible these days.' She was so damned sensible it was boring even for her. She might be thirty-six but that didn't mean she had to start behaving like her grandmother. Actually, that was unfair on Gran. Gran was never at home, always out with her friends or walking in the hills around Diamond Harbour or helping at one of the community shops in town.

'Never thought I'd hear you say something like that.' Then his voice went flat. 'It's been a long time, hasn't it?'

Not going there. Seeing the worry in Blake's face earlier in the day had brought back her own past pain which she didn't need right now. 'Sarah's filled me in on some of the things you've been doing, including taking up a partnership in an orthopaedic clinic in central Auckland a couple of months ago. That's awesome.'

'You're a partner at Scott's Women's Health. Equally awesome. The pair of us have done all right. Career-wise any rate.'

'I used my training as an escape from joining in everything else going on around me.' A sigh escaped. Talking about this was unusual for her. Was it the same for Blake? But she wasn't ready to stop. There was something cathartic about it she hadn't known before. 'Why did you choose orthopaedics?'

'Hard to say, other than when a team mate in the

school rugby team broke his leg during a game I sort of pictured myself in Theatre helping him. I know, I'm weird, but it worked. These days I get immense satisfaction from getting people back on their feet, seeing their shock and relief when they realise they no longer have to put up with debilitating pain from an arthritic knee or hip, or can get back on their cycle once their shoulder is healed.' His voice resonated with enthusiasm and he walked easier. The conversation was on safe ground? 'What about you? Why gynaecology?'

'It was always my goal from the first day at med school. No idea why other than I've always been fascinated with the reproductive system and helping women with their problems gives me a sense of achievement I don't get with anything else.' She laughed. 'Like you, I love seeing patients realise they can move forward without pain or have the baby they'd once thought impossible.' Her laughter faded. 'Though I can't help everyone.'

'No one can, Georgie. No one.'

'How true.' Time to change the subject before she became maudlin. 'What else do you do with your time apart from work? Still hit a cricket ball around the paddock?'

'I've been known to on the rare occasions I go to watch one of my mates' sons play for his school. Have to say I'm useless nowadays. Don't seem to have the eye-hand-ball co-ordination I once had. I still run, go out fishing occasionally, and nowadays I take to the hills hiking a lot.'

'On your own?'

'Mostly.' Another pause, then, 'Because it's less demanding, if you know what I mean?'

No one to get close to or find himself actually talking with about personal subjects. 'I'm afraid I do. Letting go the past hasn't been easy, and talking about it even harder. I've still a way to go, if I'm truthful.' And why wouldn't she be? Blake made her feel as though a weight was being lifted off her shoulders. 'Does that mean you haven't got a partner at the moment?' There hadn't been anyone to support him today when he'd been with his mother. That he needed someone there had been obvious by the tension in his shoulders as he'd paced the room. Georgie knew she'd try her best to be there for him over the coming days despite this strange new awareness of Blake that she'd been trying hard to ignore because that was way better than letting her suddenly over-reactive body get out of hand.

'Nope. First I was too busy studying and working to have time for anyone else, then—I don't know. Too much time spent working, I guess.'

'Sounds familiar. Though I was married for a while. It didn't work out.'

'Did you marry that guy you met at university? If I remember rightly, you moved in with him in my second year.'

'Spenser. No, we didn't last long after Noah died. I was too wrapped up in my grief and he couldn't handle it. I wasn't a lot of fun any more.'

'You were better off without him if that's the way he treated you.'

He certainly knew how to make her feel all warm and soft. 'Thanks, but I wasn't easy to be around at the time.'

Blake looked her way. 'So? That's no excuse. He was your partner. He was supposed to support you.'

You would. Deep inside she believed that. He'd blamed himself for not being with Noah, who was so upset about being dumped by his girlfriend that he got drunk and then got in a car driven by a guy who was well over the limit. Blake had never let that happen again on his watch. 'Anyway, that's history. I'm flying solo these days. I have a couple of close friends I spend time with whenever possible, and it's enough.' Really? It had been. Why doubt it now? Her eyes slid sideways. Not because Blake Newman had turned up in her day and made her blood hum. That was not reason enough to change anything.

'I know what that's like. I don't spend a lot of time with my mates and their families.'

Sounded like he tried to stay away from them more often than not. But then he would, having lost his best friend. 'I understand. I meant it when I said I'm available if you want to talk about Sarah. Or anything else.'

'Thanks. I appreciate that. A lot.' He stared ahead for a moment. Then, 'You've stayed in Christchurch all along?'

Ever since she came back after Noah died? 'Yes.' A part of her wanted to talk to him as she once might have, lighthearted and free, but she was held back by the constraints she'd put in place nearly thirteen years ago. She'd already said more than normal. Seeing Blake's distress over Sarah had brought back the past with a bang, and her stomach churning with the need to share things with him, but how did one start saying stuff that had been kept under wraps for so long? Things that had probably hurt them both. Did he wonder what Noah might have been like nowadays? If he'd set up the architectural business he was passionate about? Married and had kids?

Let loose a bit, speak from your heart, not the left side of your brain.

Deep breath. Could she let Blake in where she allowed no one? But then Blake was a part of the past that had closed down her happy spirit and brought her back to Christchurch permanently. She understood all too well why he was so worried. 'At first I came back to be here for Mum and Dad. Then I realised it worked for me too. I wanted to be close to them for my own sake.' Her mouth dried. She hadn't put any of this into words in a long time, if at all. She'd tried not to dump her sadness on Tommy, and in hindsight, that was probably unfair since he did cop her mood swings, and because he'd wanted to know all of her, not only selective pieces of her past.

Blake was quiet, yet she didn't feel uncomfortable, more as though he was giving her time and space to carry on if she chose to.

So she did. 'In some ways it was hard. They kept checking up on me, like they were afraid I'd vanish off the planet one day. But then I pretty much did the same with them. It became our norm for a long time.' Over the years they'd all relaxed a little, but not completely.

'That's natural after what happened.'

'I guess. These days we're back to some semblance of what used to be our family normal, but I can't drop the fact that I should be here so that they're able to see me whenever they want. Not that I'm complaining. Christchurch is my hometown. I work in a private practice as well as at the public hospital. Most of my friends are still here. What more could I want?' Now she'd said it, she realised she was happy. Maybe in a quieter, less full-on way than she was when she was young, but happy none the less. Some of her dreams hadn't been fulfilled, but no one got everything they wanted. 'Honestly, I like living here. It's where I grew up, and I'm comfortable.'

See what talking from the heart did? It showed her she wasn't really deeply involved in anything other than work. A career she was very proud of. Her achievements made her feel good. In a lonely kind of way, really. Comfortable wasn't exactly exciting. So what about the biggest dream of them all? A man to love. Throw children in the mix and she'd be ecstatic. Except she'd lost a baby once, and didn't think she could face that if it were to happen again.

Drop it, Georgie. Talk with Blake while you've got the opportunity.

'What about you? Are you happy in Auckland? Got a good life going up there?'

Blake shrugged. 'I have my own home and the career I want. It's enough.'

Didn't sound like it by a long shot. They walked in silence for a few minutes.

Blake appeared to be miles away until he asked, 'Didn't your parents buy a campervan a little while ago?'

'You're not entirely out of touch then. Yes, they bought one of those big suckers and have managed to get away for short trips a few times lately when they're not bogged down with their jobs. In fact right now they're away for a couple of weeks on the West Coast. I know they want to do the North Island sometime. As in take months, stopping for long periods in places that interest them, moving on wherever the urge takes them.'

'I have called in to see them on a few of the occasions I've been back to see Mum and Dad. They were always good to me as a teenager. And later...' Blake's voice trailed off.

'I know they love hearing from you.'

And now she might be understanding a little better why, because deep inside there was a sensation of tension easing that she hadn't known she was carrying. Almost as if one small piece of her had clicked into place. The start of a zip closing, one tooth shut, many more to go. Something to look forward to? Yes, it might be. All because she'd caught up with Blake and was talking with him like there was nothing to feel uncomfortable about. As if she'd found the one thing that had been missing in her life for so long. Defining what that was might take a while, but one click showed it was possible. Whatever *it* was. Georgie stopped walking. 'That's my car. Do you want a lift home?'

'No, I'm good.' He was looking directly at her. 'It's been good catching up.'

'I agree.' Unexpected as it was, talking with Blake had reminded her of the past without the pain. Of course she still hurt, but Blake had been there, understood more than any of her friends what it was like to lose Noah. 'I'll see you tomorrow.'

'Will do.' He was gone. Hopefully only for a few hours, not years.

He'd be at the hospital with Sarah tomorrow, and

possibly the day after and maybe the next one too, so she would see him some more. Where had this need to get to know Blake come from? It was new, for sure. And worrying. No, make that intriguing. It made her body heat and her skin soften. And her fears loosen a teeny-weeny bit. Sensations she hadn't known in for ever. Bring them on.

Surely not? Surely yes. She headed for home, feeling more enthusiastic about everything than she had in a long, long time.

CHAPTER TWO

'YOU'LL BE FINE, Mum.' Blake kissed his mother's forehead gently. *You'd better be.* 'I'll be waiting for you
when you're taken back to your room.' *Hopefully your
surgeon will be right behind you.*

He needed to hear that his mother was in the clear
and only had the operation to recover from. Not that
it was a minor op, but way better than the alternative.

And hopefully Georgie would turn up at some stage.
He couldn't wait to see her again, which was kind of
bizarre considering they hadn't meant anything to
each other before. *We don't now.* Yeah, but he sensed
he wanted to. They had something in common—they'd
cut themselves off from normal lives because of the
past. Georgie hadn't come out and said as much but it
was there in her empathy and support yesterday. Also in
her voice when they'd talked last night. She made him
feel less alone. No one had made him feel that way in
so long an ache was beating in his head.

During the long, sleepless hours—running and walking hadn't helped—the idea of spending some time with
her had kept circling around his worry over his mother.
It was as though Georgie had thrown him a lifeline that

he couldn't quite catch. Let her in, or keep pushing her away as per normal? Sink or swim? For the first time in for ever the idea of letting go some of the fear holding him down was tempting. But not tempting enough to actually follow through. Though getting a little closer to Georgie was also tempting, with nothing to lose if it didn't work out. He'd be gone within a couple of weeks, back to reality.

Beside him his mother murmured, 'I know I will.' Except she wasn't looking so confident now that the pre-op room was just through the door and a nurse was taking her BP. 'I'm a doctor. I understand what's happening.'

Understanding was one thing. Being afraid was quite another. In this case one probably led to the other because of her medical knowledge as a GP. She knew all too well how badly this could end up. Blake held his breath, willing the sudden blockage in his throat to dissolve so he could talk properly without giving away his emotions and adding to her worries.

His dad held his mother's hand, squeezing gently. 'I imagine it's different when you're the patient, darling. Just remember you're a fighter.'

Blake looked from one parent to the other, saw the look of understanding passing between them. His parents had always been strong and fought for their children and raised them to be equally tough. What was always apparent was the love these two had for each other. After thirty-three years together—married in haste because he was on the way, unplanned for but looked forward to—and they still adored each other as though they'd just fallen in love. They'd added two daughters to the mix. Despite staying out of their lives, he loved his sisters, both of whom were married and lived in rural Canterbury. They'd said they'd be dropping in to see their mother after her operation. They were busy with their kids, and their families' businesses, and were thrilled when he said he'd come down to be around to help when Mum went home. Home. Families. Partners.

A shiver rocked him as a wave of longing rolled through his tense body. What he wouldn't give to have the same. Someone to love and trust implicitly, to share the good and not so good with, to raise children with, to age and climb into their rocking chairs side by side and cuddle grandchildren alongside each other. Except he was lying to himself. He was not prepared to chance his heart again. That he was already afraid of what was happening with his mother.

'Morning, Sarah.' The voice that had followed him into bed and finally a brief sleep cut through his wandering mind. Talking with her had started him relaxing a little and then he'd begun wondering if he should also try to get home to see his family more often. It was as if Georgie had made him aware of how he'd been missing out on being with them, if only to talk and laugh together.

'Hello, Georgie,' his mother said. 'It's lovely of you to drop by. I know you're busy.'

Georgie winked. 'You haven't seen me. I can't stay, but wanted to say hello to you all.' She turned and smiled at him. 'Morning.'

A smile Blake felt deep inside. 'You're looking

perky.' Like old times when she never seemed to stop smiling or laughing.

Then her smile slipped a little, suggesting it was a brave face for his parents, and maybe for him. Then it came back, bigger and brighter. Yeah, definitely a brave face. 'Of course I am. A good night's sleep is all it takes.'

Wish he could say the same. Talking to Georgie last night had added to the list of things to overthink and worry about. At the same time he'd come to realise he was glad he'd returned to be with his family through this distressing time. Catching up with this woman was a bonus he hadn't expected. 'I think you've cheered up Mum a little.' And him. There was definitely a lightness in his veins he hadn't expected. Could be he was being cheered up the most here.

Georgie kissed his mother on the forehead. 'Good luck. See you later.'

Oh, hell. Reality check.

Please be all right, Mum. Come through the surgery and not have cancer. Please.

Gulp. Hell, any minute now he was going to embarrass himself with tears spilling down his cheeks if he wasn't careful.

Georgie nodded at him with a gentle smile on her lovely mouth—as though she knew exactly what was going on inside his head.

Face it. She probably did, being a doctor and used to seeing pain in the faces of patients' loved ones. 'Bye,' was all he could manage.

'Right, Theatre waits for no one.' She was gone, a whirlwind of energy and focus. Surgeon on a mission. Friend supporting friends. Georgie of old in a new camouflage.

The pre-op nurse bustled in and went to the end of the bed to undo the wheel brakes with her foot. 'Let's do this, Sarah.'

Blake closed his eyes for a moment.

This is it. In a few hours we will have some answers, will know if Mum's safe, or if there's more stress and grief to come.

Hell, he'd believed he understood what his patients' loved ones went through when they were going into Theatre. He hadn't had a clue. There should be a paper about this that all doctors had to sit before they qualified to make them fully aware of the anguish people faced. It was a very lonely time, even with his dad here. But he did have Georgie onside. Even when she wasn't right here physically, she understood his torment.

Blake's father kissed his wife, locking his eyes with hers for a long moment, sending messages in their silent love language. Then he straightened, said, 'Be safe, sweetheart,' and turned away, surreptitiously brushing the back of his hand over his face.

Leaning over the bed, Blake gave his mum another peck on the cheek. 'See you soon.' Then he watched the nurse wheel her out of the room and down the hall towards Theatre, his heart heavy and his brain filled with worry. 'Come on, Dad. We'll go over the road and grab a coffee and some breakfast before you head to court.' He needed the distraction, and so did his dad.

'Yeah.' The older man's voice was clogged with tears. 'Yeah.' For the first time that Blake could recall he really did sound old. Or was that because he hadn't been around enough to notice his father aging? Something else to think about. There were a few hits coming his way at the moment. He straightened a little. He'd take them, and hopefully learn something along the way to improve his outlook on the future.

'She'll be fine.' Draping an arm over his dad's shoulders, Blake led him outside. 'She's got you, Dad. That's more important.'

'Georgie gives me confidence even when I know this operation isn't in her hands,' Dad said.

Blake agreed. 'There's something about her that makes me want to believe everything will be fine, that she won't countenance anything going wrong for Mum even when she won't be there. It's nothing new. She always exuded a confidence that was hard not to accept.' Only it used to come with laughter and jokes and fun. There'd been a seriousness behind all that, but she was great to be around. Not that he and Noah had spent a lot of time in her space because she hadn't wanted them hanging around, but he did remember how warm and happy she made him feel when sharing the same air. Could he feel that again?

'She's never faltered in her determination to be the best at what she does. And that's not only in her profession,' his dad added.

What else was going on in Georgie's life? Not a question to put to his father. If he wanted to know, he'd ask Georgie outright. Yes, he'd do just that. Even if it was only to get to know more about her. It might help him let go the past. Some of it anyway. Right then he decided that he was going to see some more of her, starting with inviting her out to dinner tonight. He only planned on spending a week in Christchurch so he needed to make good use of his time. Of course there was the following week when he'd intended doing some overdue work around his house, maybe even taking the boat for a jaunt on the Waitemata looking for fish. Hadn't he inadvertently said to Georgie he was here for two weeks? See? She'd got to him that early on, tossing common sense out the door like a piece of garbage. Though it wasn't hard when his focus had been almost entirely on his mother. Yet strange how spending a week in Auckland paled into insignificance when he considered the possibility of staying on to spend more time with his family and maybe get to know Georgie as he hadn't before. Because she did understand what he was going through at the moment? Or was there more to this new interest? Hopefully she'd join him for a meal or two, maybe take a day trip out to Akaroa. As long as his mother was doing well after her surgery. Going further than a few minutes' drive away wasn't happening otherwise.

Time to stop overthinking everything. 'Want to talk about the trial, Dad?' There wouldn't be a lot he could say but from past experience Blake knew he liked to vent when a trial went on for too long and there was a lot of repetition in the questions put to witnesses.

'It's doing my head in. You'd think by now I'd understand why people went off the rails, but I'm darned if I do.'

This was the man who'd told Noah's dad how afraid he was that Blake was wrecking his chances of a wonderful career and future. Even now Blake felt the relief at having listened to Lucas, who'd taken on board what his dad had said and immediately hopped on a plane to

Dunedin to talk to him. Lucas had turned him around before he made a complete mess of everything by making him understand how his waywardness wasn't solving anything, instead adding to everyone's stress. Blake had been grateful ever since. He owed Lucas, and his father. 'You do fine, Dad.'

In the café, with coffees and bacon and eggs before them, they continued talking about anything and everything except Blake's mother's operation and the trial his dad was ruling over. At eight on the dot, his father pushed his plate and mug aside, and stood up. 'I'll see you tonight. Keep me up to date on everything.' Then he was striding away, leaving Blake feeling bereft of his company.

Odd because he hardly ever spent time with him. But today there was a bubble of anticipation rising within him, and he wanted to share it, examine it with someone who'd not laugh at him. Georgie came to mind. Except he'd deliberately avoided mentioning her. Oh, yes, that would've worked a treat when his father had a soft spot for her and liked to bring her into conversations far too often.

Hey, Georgie, you're pressing all my buttons in ways I've never known and I want to talk to you about that.

For the record, she was the last person he'd talk to about these new sensations.

She'd laugh her beautiful head off. Tell him to get a life, as she used to often enough when he and Noah were trying to join her and her girlfriends for some fun. Actually, he'd enjoy hearing her laugh. She looked as if she needed to let off steam occasionally, as though the last few years had been all hard work and not a lot of fun. Which sounded a little too familiar.

'Can I get you anything else?'

He looked up at the waitress clearing the plates from the table. 'No, I'm good, thanks.' Yeah, and what was he going to do next? Wander along the bank of the Avon? That wasn't such a bad idea. He could do that—later. 'Actually, I'll have another long black, please.' It wasn't as though he didn't have plenty of time on hand.

Andrew had said the op would likely take up to two and a half hours, which meant if he'd started on time he wouldn't be finished until ten at the absolute earliest. Then his mother would be in recovery for a while so no visiting going on. Or any discussion about what the op had revealed. Coffee was a good choice right now, filling in a few minutes at least.

Blake took his time over the coffee, reading news headlines on his phone in-between watching people coming in for coffee or food on their way to work. Next he tried to stroll along the riverbank, but strolling wasn't really his style, so he changed direction and headed over the bridge and in the direction of his old school. As he approached he saw boys dressed smartly in uniform standing in huddles by the gate and further inside the fenced grounds where the imposing stone buildings dominated the landscape, talking and laughing as only teens could.

Memories stirred. He and Noah laughing uproariously over their mate's attempt to leap the fence when it was higher than he was tall. Complaining about the little time they had to play rugby. Plotting how to get girls to notice them. Yeah, those had been fun times.

They'd also worked hard and totally believed they could be whoever they wanted, and thought university would be a walk in the park. They took driving lessons at the same time, played in the same sports teams on those fields behind the impressive stone building facing the street and fought to get higher grades than the other. Competitive yet loyal, egging each other on into trouble while always having one another's back. That friendship had started at these very gates on the first day of term of year nine when he accidently slammed into Noah in his haste to get to the office. He'd never forget the cheeky grin that met him as Noah staggered back onto his feet, pointed at him and said, 'You'll pay for that, pal.'

'You think? Pal.' He'd smirked, like any hormonal just-becoming-a-teenager lad was prone to do.

'You any good at boxing?'

'I can go ten rounds,' he'd lied. Then laughed because he liked the look of the guy. 'Kidding. I'd be rubbish. But I know how to bowl a cricket ball.' He'd seen the red ball in a side pocket of the guy's backpack.

'Cool. Let's go toss a few pitches.' From then on they'd become inseparable. As easy as that.

Blake stood, hands in his pockets as a couple of cars pulled in and more boys leapt out and hurried through the gates. The best days of his life had been behind that fence. 'Damn it, Noah. We sure knew how to have a blast. Miss you, mate.' So much his life had stalled when Noah left them, and had never returned to full speed again. Some parts hadn't moved at all. Love being the biggest one. He swallowed hard. Looking around at the buildings, the immaculate grounds, the boys, some awkward, others overly confident as they strode across to the assembly hall, he felt something loosening inside him. They'd believed they held life in their hands, and that it'd only get better. Now he knew different. But had he wasted what he'd been given? Would Noah be proud of him for shutting down like he had? For walking away from everything and everyone he loved? Absolutely not, was the honest answer. And he owed Noah and himself that much at least.

A shiver lifted the skin on Blake's arms. What had he done? Thrown everything to the wind? Given up too easily? Yes, Noah would be furious with him for dropping the ball. For not being around for his family. For not letting them help him when he grieved so deeply. Georgie said returning home had been good for her. It would've been the same for him too. Was it too late to change so he could have love and affection, and share himself with his parents and sisters and their families? To have a woman to love, and maybe even children?

Damn it, Blake. Stop this.

Turning away, he strode purposefully toward the private hospital. He was in Christchurch to support his family, and not to up-end his own world. Not to start thinking there was more to Georgie than a friend from the past. Not to let Noah trip him up.

He arrived back at the hospital just after ten thirty to be told his mother wasn't out of surgery. Was that good or bad? Or routine? Due to a later start than scheduled?

'Now what?' he said without thinking.

'You're a friend of Georgie's, aren't you?' a nurse walking past asked.

'Yes.' How did the nurse know that? Friend was one word for whatever they had going. Try a shadow from

her past who'd like to get to know her way better than
as his best friend's sister. Though he'd decided that he
wasn't going there. But it was impossible to ignore the
need to get a little closer to her. Friend would be great,
really. A true, close friend he could talk to about anything, including the guilt he still carried about Noah
when knowing he didn't need to.

'Georgie mentioned Mrs Newman's son was here.
You're a doctor, aren't you?' the guy asked.

'Orthopaedic surgeon.' He tried to keep the pride
from spilling over but by the look of amusement on the
nurse's face he knew he hadn't got away with it. 'Just
another arrogant specialist who thinks the rest of you
owe me something for even putting my scrubs on,' he
muttered.

And got laughed at in return. 'I've dealt with my
share of those. But you are not talking about Georgie when you say that. She's mindful of everyone who
works here. She could be full of herself because she
is a brilliant doctor but she acts as one cog in a whole
wheel of them.'

'You're not telling me anything I don't know.' Or
hadn't guessed. 'Obviously I haven't worked with her
as our fields are very different, and I didn't start training until she had nearly finished, but that sounds like
the Georgie I knew.' He shouldn't be talking to this guy
about her, but he couldn't stop thinking about her and
wanting to hear her name on his tongue. But. Okay. Shut
up. 'I'd better go find something to do while I wait for
my mother to come out of Theatre.'

Heading into the city, he passed a florist, and back-
tracked to go inside.

'Can I help you?' the woman behind the counter tying a bundle of roses together with a bright red ribbon asked.

'Have you got any sweet peas?' His mum's favourite.

'There are some out the back. Would you like me to put a bunch together or make a bouquet with an assortment of other flowers?'

'A big bunch of only sweet peas would be perfect.' No-fuss Mum would prefer that over a fancy bouquet any day. 'I'll take those roses too, unless they're for an order.' Georgie came to mind for those. Bright, colourful and full of life. The old Georgie who had started to peek through the shutters on the two occasions he talked with her or watched her with his mother.

'They're yours.'

Pulling into the hospital carpark he drew a wobbly breath. What was he doing, buying flowers for Georgie? She'd think he'd lost his mind. It was less than twenty-four hours since he'd first seen her after so long and he'd bought her flowers. Anyone would think he was wooing her, and that so wasn't the case. He was interested in getting to know her as adults, but that's where it had to stop. He was settled in Auckland with the perfect job and ideal home for a single man. Georgie lived here, in the South Island, obviously happy with her work and having family and friends nearby. Damn it. He left the roses on the seat when he got out of the car, and slammed the door shut on his frustration. Should never have left Auckland.

Instantly remorse rose. 'Sorry, Mum.' As if he'd have stayed away while this was happening.

His phone beeped. Georgie.

'Heard anything?' she asked.

'Not a word.' He glanced at his watch. 'Should be any minute now.' He wasn't saying overdue, but the time it was taking to hear from the surgeon was winding him tighter than a ball of string.

'I'm between patients. Talk again soon.' She was gone.

Leaving Blake shaken. As though something was wrong and he didn't know what. But Georgie had nothing to do with his mother's surgery, and if she'd known something she'd have said, not asked if he'd heard from the surgeon. Wouldn't she? Glancing at his watch, his gut tightened. Over three hours since the nurse had wheeled his mother off to pre-op. What was going on? She should be out and awake and in her own room by now.

He raced to the hospital's main entrance. The automatic doors took their time opening, winding him tighter.

Calm down.

Yeah, right. As if. What if something had gone wrong? Room six was empty. Had her room been changed to another? Blake looked around for someone to ask, anyone. He needed to know what was going on.

Calm down.

Sure thing. As easy as that.

'Blake.' Georgie was walking towards him, calm as could be.

Damn but he was an idiot. So much for the cool, collected doctor he was known to be. He'd been acting like a crazed kid terrified something had happened to his mother. Drawing a lungful, he forced himself to relax. It didn't work. 'Thought you were heading back into Theatre.'

'Shortly.' She took his hand.

Immediately he knew. This was bad. 'What's happened?'

Georgie made to walk along the corridor, then stopped, obviously knowing he was desperate to hear what she had to tell him. 'Firstly, Sarah's going to be all right.' Steady eyes locked on him. 'She's haemorrhaging, badly. They're getting blood into her but they haven't been able to stop the bleeding yet. Andrew's doing everything possible.' Her hand tightened around his.

He opened his mouth but nothing came out. Mum was haemorrhaging and they couldn't stop it.

'Blake, Sarah will get through this. You've got to be strong.'

Sure thing. Just breathe in and plaster a smile on his face. Simple as. But Georgie was right. He'd come home to support his mother, his family, not to break down like a gutless wonder. Deep breath. 'Tell me what you know.'

'Only that the bleeding began after everything had been removed. I'm sorry but Andrew was too busy working on Sarah for me to interrupt with questions. I shouldn't've been in there but I saw a nurse taking a bag of blood into the theatre and as I'd just scrubbed up for my next procedure I changed direction and went in to see what was going on.' Her voice trembled on the last words. She wasn't as calm as he'd first thought.

Sweat broke out on his forehead. 'Georgie—' His voice cracked and he stopped.

'It's all right, Blake. I understand. Try to remain

calm. I have to go, but I'll be back as soon as possible. I don't want to leave you on your own but I have no choice. My patient's waiting.' She reached up and brushed her lips over his cheek. 'Be strong.'

It took all his strength not to haul her into his arms and hold her close. 'Thanks for coming out to tell me.' Now she'd have to start over with getting scrubbed up. 'See you later.'

'Better believe it.'

Leaning against the wall, he stared at his feet and hauled in deep breaths. Mum was in a serious condition. The surgery would knock her big-time, but adding bleeding to the mix meant she'd have a long road ahead getting back on her feet. If the worst happened and she did have cancer, then she was going to need every last drop of energy and strength to get through the treatments.

'Be strong,' Georgie had said.

She was right. He had to be. He would be. He *was* strong.

'Thank goodness that's over,' Georgie muttered as she pulled her gloves off and arched her aching back, rubbed hard with her knuckles to ease the kinks.

'I bet that's what your patient will be saying as soon as she wakes up,' one of the theatre nurses said.

'True,' Georgie agreed. She'd just completed a pelvic floor repair after a horrific bike crash caused tears in the muscles. Her patient was worried about her chances of conceiving being affected, but there'd be babies in the future for the woman and her husband.

Her hand touched her own abdomen lightly. What

would it be like to give birth to a baby? It wasn't something she'd thought about since the loss of her own baby. Not much anyway, because it hurt remembering those sharp pains as her body rejected the foetus. She'd probably never experience childbirth or being a parent now, unless she changed her mind about having a relationship.

'Anything you need before I head away?' the nurse interrupted her thoughts.

'No, you go. And thanks for your work.' Right, she was out of there. There were patients to see, then hopefully a quiet night with no babies deciding to come early.

'See you tomorrow.'

Tomorrow, another day with more patients needing her undivided attention. It was what she got so much satisfaction from. She couldn't imagine her life being any different, though what it would be like if she did have a baby was a mystery. Not something she'd stopped to think too much about because—because she didn't dare. That would open the floodgates on her emotions, and let the past pour in when she had managed to get it under control so she could lead a normal, if slightly dull, life.

But now uncalled-for longing gripped her. A baby. Small and soft, soaking up all the love she had to give. Totally reliant on her. Yeah, therein lay a concern. Would she be a good mum? She'd like to think so. She'd put everything into trying to be. *And* she had great role models in her parents. A baby, her baby, cuddled against her breast, nuzzling in for sustenance, crying or gurgling. Her heart lurched. This was plain silly. She was single and working all hours as a specialist. On the other side, she was financially set up, had wonderful parents who'd dote on a grandchild and she had a big heart to share. A heart that spent years locked down. But surely it would open up for a baby? It wouldn't be possible to remain remote with her own child. It just wouldn't. She did know how to love, just hadn't been prepared to risk it. Shaking her head to get rid of these dreams she usually denied having, a sigh escaped. Having a baby wasn't happening. Not any time in the foreseeable future. And that future was fast running out in terms of being able to conceive. Tick-tock.

Why, all of a sudden, was she thinking about babies and herself in the same sentence? Nothing to do with patients. It started after seeing Blake for the first time in for ever. Did she really think they might get along so well that she could think about a future with him? When they didn't really know each other very well? Certainly not after they'd grown up and got on with their lives in separate cities.

Blake. He'd be with Sarah by now. The despair in his face when she gave him the news about his mother's haemorrhage had cut to her heart. He'd been devastated and lost. But he'd begun to rally as she was leaving him. That'd been hard. If only she'd been able to stay and hold him while they waited for more news.

When she entered Sarah's room and saw Blake sitting all scrunched up in a narrow chair watching over his mother as she dozed, any idea of keeping him at arm's length fell away in a blink. She wanted to be there for him. Would he let her? Or, when Sarah was back up on her feet, would he walk away as he'd done from his family once before? 'Hi,' she spoke softly so as not to wake Sarah, who was lying so still the covers weren't moving at all. 'No more bleeding?'

'Not so far. Andrew doesn't think it'll start again, but—'

'But you're going to worry anyway. Fair enough. Want a coffee? I can bring it in here.'

He glanced away as though refocusing away from something that had been worrying him, then looked back to her. 'Spoil me, why don't you?' A slow, tired smile crept onto his face.

'That's a yes-please, thank-you-very-much then? How do you have it?'

'Black and strong.' The smile expanded a bit further. 'Though it's late to be downing coffee.'

'I'm a bit of a caffeine freak. It's my go-to whenever I'm exhausted.' Not good but she'd never claimed to be perfect. 'Be back in a few minutes.' See? She'd had no intention of staying away from Blake, no matter what she'd told herself.

When Georgie returned Sarah hadn't moved at all. She stroked the older woman's hand, and Sarah opened her eyes. 'Hey, hello.'

'Hello,' she croaked.

Reaching for the water, Georgie held the straw to Sarah's lips. 'Try a little.'

Sarah obliged, then turned her face away to look at Blake before her eyes closed again.

Blake was watching his mother like a hawk, worry and love filling his face.

'Has Andrew talked to you about anything else yet?' Georgie wondered if she should be asking, but then she was here as a friend who understood the situation.

Blake spoke slowly. 'He phoned Dad while he was in here with us. There's no sign of cancer. The fibroid came out without any difficulty and has been sent to the lab along with the organs he removed.'

Georgie gave Sarah's hand a gentle squeeze and laid it back on the bedcover. 'That's the best news.'

'It will be even better when the lab endorses Andrew's opinion,' Blake said flatly. Then he seemed to shake himself, and pulled out a wobbly smile. 'It's going to take longer than expected but we've got this.'

Pulling up the other chair, Georgie sat beside Blake and joined him in watching over his mother. He needed a diversion. 'You up for doing Sarah's gardens over the coming weeks?' The Newmans had a large property with stunning gardens. Tidying up the end of the summer debris would be something to keep him occupied when he wasn't in here.

'I'm a dab hand with a shovel these days. Even have some gardens of my own.' Blake looked her way. 'Are you into gardening at all?'

'Believe it or not, I am, but only if it's something I can eat. Growing vegetables is so rewarding that I usually plant enough to feed the whole street. While I like flowers, making gardens for them is a nightmare. I used to try, setting everything out neatly, in order of height and shape, and it would all look wonderful. Then the plants would start growing and there went my design for a pretty garden. Drove me crazy so I gave up and stuck to spuds and peas, and all things green, orange and red.'

'So what do you grow at the front of your house? I'm presuming you're living in a house, not an apartment, if you've got a veg patch.'

'Four-bed bungalow in Merivale. The main lawns and garden are dealt with by the energetic old man next door who loves being outside and needs extra money for his trips to Wellington to see his grandchildren.'

Blake was sussing her out with that deep look she now remembered from days gone by. He used to look at her and her girlfriends like that when he was trying to find a way to get them to invite him and Noah along for a party they were going to. 'That's a large house for one person.'

Hadn't he heard her say she was flying solo last night? Or was she reading him all wrong? That was more likely the case. 'A young girl has been living with me while attending uni, but a couple of weeks ago she moved out to live with her boyfriend.' Georgie smiled. She'd done much the same herself when she and Spenser had fallen for each other in her third year of study. He'd been her first love, but not her last.

'Going to take in another student?' Was that relief slipping across Blake's face? Couldn't be. He wouldn't be interested in her as anything but a family friend, if that. Anyway, she was getting ahead of herself. A man as good-looking and physically attractive as Blake would not be single. Or, if he was between women, it wouldn't be long before there was one hanging on his arm. The thought of which had her feeling flat all of a sudden.

'No idea.' There hadn't been time to do anything about it. Or much enthusiasm, to be honest. She was comfortable living alone, didn't need company just for the sake of it.

Blake glanced at his watch. 'Dad should be here soon. My sisters are coming in after they've fed their kids.'

Georgie stood up. 'I'll get out of the way, leave you to have time together.'

'Not so fast.' Blake stood up beside her. 'I was going to suggest that you and I go somewhere quiet for a meal. It'll get crowded in here when everyone arrives, and I've had hours with Mum to myself.'

'Blake? Are you sure you don't want to be here with them?' Was he doing a runner? Putting space between those he loved and himself because it hurt too much to get close?

'I'm having lunch with the girls tomorrow, and will spend time with Dad later tonight.' He hesitated, seemed to be gathering his thoughts. 'I'd like to spend time with you.'

Her eyes widened. What? Blake just said he wanted to be with her? Her stance softened. 'Sounds like a great idea.'

'There's a restaurant I spotted alongside the Avon that looks good.' There was a small lopsided smile stretching across those gorgeous lips, and a bit of a sparkle going on in his eyes.

'The River? It's excellent.' She went there often when she'd had a long day and couldn't face preparing something at home. 'I'll leave you with Sarah until your father gets here, and go take a shower and get into some half-decent clothes.' Clothes that she hadn't worn to work, but were hanging in her cupboard for those rare times she had something exciting to do after finishing up here for the day. There was probably a layer of dust on them. 'Back soon.' Had she put her makeup pouch in her handbag that morning?

CHAPTER THREE

'GOOD MOVE, SON.'

'I thought you were asleep,' Blake said through his surprise. Georgie had sidetracked him with her smiles and talk about gardening and he hadn't thought to check if his mother was awake when he suggested dinner. Though it wasn't a problem, he did like to keep different aspects of his life in separate compartments.

His mother's familiar chuckle was filled with exhaustion and not up to her usual vibrancy, but it gave him hope that she was halfway to waking up fully. 'You're both tiptoeing around each other like you're afraid there'll be a conflagration if you get too close. Let loose a bit.' She yawned, as though speaking took what little energy remained out of her.

But more awake than he'd realised. 'You're exaggerating, Mum.' He wanted to laugh at that but it didn't come. Instead he studied his mother, lying against the white bedding. She looked awful, so small and fragile against the white sheets. Nothing like the strong mentor she'd always been for him and his sisters growing up. His heart squeezed.

'I worry about you.' She obviously hadn't finished

speaking her mind, but there was nothing new there.
'I'm sure there are women in your life, but I never hear
you mention one in particular who tickles your fancy.'

'Old-fashioned term, that.' She wanted him to settle down? Well, guess what? He wasn't ready. Though
Georgie seemed to be winding him up some. Okay,
and tickling his fancy. So there, Mum. Not that he was
telling her.

'You should have children too.'

'Go to sleep, Mum.' He couldn't face that prepos-
terous idea. Adding to the grandchild pool? He wasn't
even close to considering parenthood. Too many doubts
about his ability to be there when he was needed. The
last thing he'd cope with was failing his child as he had
his friend. His hands clenched on his thighs. No way.
He'd let Noah down big-time, and who was to say he
wouldn't do that again with someone else? If it was his
child he failed next time, he didn't know if he'd ever be
able carry on. Which was why he never, ever contem-
plated the idea of having a family one day.

If he'd been able to put Noah's death behind him he
wouldn't be having this conversation with himself, or
with his mother. Other people managed to move on
when they lost someone close to them. Why hadn't he?
Had he not tried hard enough? Impossible when every
time he closed his eyes at night the first image he saw
was Noah. Over the years that had finally faded from
his head but the guilt still taunted him whenever he
thought about moving on.

An image of Georgie looking sad when Noah was
mentioned popped into his head. She hadn't moved on
either. He'd bet his late-model car on it. He felt the

things that were important to Georgie were similar to those he also thought vital.

A soft snore came from the bed. His mum had done as he'd told her, though she'd have been fighting the exhaustion to the last flicker of her eyelids.

So she wanted him to have kids? When his sisters already had five between them? Of course she did. Because that would mean he had come in from his self-imposed isolation and settled down with someone he adored. There'd be nothing more she'd like for him. So would he, if only it was possible. He'd thought about children on and off, wondered what it would be like being a dad, but he hadn't put that at the top of his bucket list. Hell, it wasn't even on the list.

'Relax, Blake. Enjoy an evening out with Georgie and stop thinking past midnight. Tomorrow's another day. Enjoy today while you've still got it.'

'So much for thinking you were asleep,' he muttered. 'Seriously, Mum, I don't need your help with Georgie.' What thirty-two-year-old man at the beginning of a wonderful career and living in his own house in a smart suburb needed someone—especially his mother—to start matchmaking for him?

Your success rate in that quarter hasn't been too flash so far.

True. But he hadn't been trying.

'Whatever you say.' Which meant she didn't believe a word he'd said.

He wasn't going to waste time arguing. For one, he never won against his mother, and more importantly, he wanted to enjoy the time here with his parents. He was looking forward to catching up with his sisters and their tribes too. They talked on the phone and had video calls but it wasn't enough. He would like real time with them all. Another first. Usually, on his fleeting visits, he avoided too much contact because it only rubbed in what he didn't have.

A new scent blew into the room. Light floral with a hint of sea breeze. Spinning around he looked at the beautiful apparition standing at the door. Georgie. His heart squeezed painfully. It would take little encouragement to move across and wrap her in his arms, hold her tight against him, breathe deep to absorb more of that scent. Damn it. What was he thinking? 'That was quick.' Her shower? Or his confusion over Georgie?

Tanned shoulders shrugged. 'You know how it is when taking a shower at work. No time for standing under the water absorbing the heat and daydreaming about whatever comes to mind.'

What was rushing to his mind was the vision she'd just painted. Her naked body under steaming water as she tipped her head back and closed her eyes. Her— Stop. Right. Now. That was not a vision he knew. Not of Georgie. One he'd like to see though. His fingers dug into his palms. Damn it, he shouldn't have asked her out for a meal. He wouldn't be able to swallow a single mouthful if those pictures started beating him up. Breathing slowly, he tried relaxing his hands. Think of the mess he'd cleared up on the street yesterday where a dog had gone through a rubbish sack out on the pavement outside his parents' house. Instead his gaze filled with the real vision in front of him with her long dark blond hair free of the knot she'd been wearing it in. 'You look lovely.'

Georgie had changed into a sleeveless white blouse with a pink floral pattern and navy trousers and her feet were ensconced in high-heeled sandals. Pink toe-nails highlighted the navy footwear. Definitely lovely. Good enough to…

'Thanks.' A faint blush coloured her cheeks to match that pink shade in her blouse. 'It's always a bit random when I get changed into whatever's in my locker.'

He knew what she meant. Though, 'It's not so bad for me. There're always trousers and a shirt, sometimes a jacket that matches.'

'Sometimes? Or always? I can't imagine you not having everything matching. Or have I made that up? I seem to remember you were always particular with your clothing.' There was a silly grin expanding over her mouth, sending spears of lust to his gut.

'You remember correctly.' Now what? Did they stand here, making idle chatter, keeping his mother company while waiting for his dad to arrive? Not that he begrudged his mother anything, but a sudden pulsing in his blood was making his feet restless and his head in need of fresh air.

'Get out of here.' His mother seemed to be reading his mind.

'There's no hurry,' Georgie said.

Meaning they had all night? Not likely, Blake thought. Too soon, if it was ever likely they'd spend that much time together. He also intended having time with his dad later. 'Let's go.' Sudden hunger pangs reminded him he hadn't eaten since breakfast. Nothing unusual when he was working, but there'd been loads of time for lunch, only he hadn't been enthused, the worry about his mother weighing too heavy on his mind. He kissed his mother's cheek.

'Have fun, you two. Don't do anything I wouldn't,' his mother whispered.

'Should be a quiet evening then,' he retorted through a strained laugh. His parents knew how to have a right old party when they wanted, so he knew she was teasing. Thank goodness. At the moment the last thing he wanted was a quiet night. At least not a dull, wish-he-wasn't-taking-Georgie-out-because-she-was-scaring-him kind of time. 'Let's get out of here before Mum comes up with any more crazy suggestions,' he said to Georgie and reached for her hand, only stopping from wrapping his fingers around hers as he felt her skin under his fingertips. 'Sorry.'

'No need to be.' Georgie gave him a quick smile.

So she wouldn't have run screaming from the building if he had taken her hand in his? So much for being sensible. Or was it cautious? Didn't matter which, the result was the same. His palm was tingling with anticipation and he was sorry he hadn't carried through on his whim. 'Do we walk or drive?' Those high heels could be uncomfortable for Georgie. But hell, she was beautiful. Always stunning in a happy-go-lucky, daredevil kind of way, now she'd matured into a woman that no man with a heart in his chest or blood pulsing through his body would be able to walk past without taking a deep breath and a longing racing throughout his body.

Not such a new feeling for him. He had felt the same years ago. But never in between. He hadn't really thought about Georgie, preferring to keep her buried along with everything else from that time, otherwise the guilt and despair would pour out of him. He'd promised her father to accept it wasn't his fault Noah had been in the car that crashed into a tree that night. Promised to stop feeling sorry for himself and get on with becoming the surgeon he'd wanted to be. Basically he'd promised not to waste another life. He owed her father big-time for bluntly pointing out how much he had to lose if he didn't pull his act together and stop brooding over Noah's death. And now here he was, thirteen years later, walking alongside Georgie on their way to dinner. Amazing.

'It's roughly three kilometres, and normally I'd say let's walk, but I'm feeling tired after such a long day in Theatre, so do you mind if we drive? We can take my car.'

'I've got Mum's and it's in the hospital carpark. I'm taking you out to dinner so I'll drive.' Hopefully she got it that meant he was paying for dinner too. Even if she'd invited him, he'd be putting his hand in his pocket. It was how he did things.

A gentle nudge from her shoulder on his upper arm, and another, longer smile. 'I'm looking forward to this. I want to catch up on what you've been up to over the years since I moved back up here from Dunedin.'

Blake relaxed. It seemed they were on the same page over wanting to learn more about each other. 'Bring it on. An edited version, of course.'

'You don't think I want to hear about the wild parties? Or the women you've dated?' That suck-him-in smile had become a wicked grin.

'I was thinking more along the lines of not mentioning what I like for breakfast or what day of the week I do my laundry,' he joked.

She flicked back her hair and laughed. 'This gets better by the minute.'

He held his hands firmly at his sides, avoiding the temptation to run them over those long dark blond waves falling down her back. Until tonight she'd been wearing her hair in a knot at the back of her head, so he hadn't realised how long and shiny it was. It brought memories of longing he'd felt as a teenager when she'd be dressed in a tight-fitting dress that showed off her legs and set his hormones on fire. He hadn't been the only guy who hung out with Noah to think that. She'd been every teenage male's fantasy. Eventually he had moved on, got on with reality in the form of other girls more his age, and had not expected to react to her this way at all.

But there it was. Georgie was making his blood fizz, and his head spin. Perhaps he should hand her the keys so she could drive them safely to the restaurant.

At the car, he opened the passenger door for Georgie, and wanted to slap his forehead.

'What beautiful flowers,' Georgie said and lifted the roses off the seat so she could sit down. 'Did you forget to take them into Sarah?'

'Actually, I bought them for you.'

Her head flipped back and she locked her eyes on him. 'Me?'

He nodded. He'd never bought a woman flowers before. Hell, it had been a long day. He was acting out of line, his usual take-me-or-leave-me attitude nowhere in sight.

A gut-clenching, heart-warming smile lit up her face. 'Thank you. This is starting to feel like a real date.'

He knew exactly what she meant. And it scared the pants off him.

I'm on a date. Georgie grinned around the fork she'd just slipped into her mouth. *With a really sexy guy.*

When was the last time this had happened? Her mind came up blank.

'The fish's that good?' Blake asked. 'You're grinning like the cat with the cream, a great bowl of the stuff.'

Oops. 'The best snapper I've had in years.'

'Except it's blue cod.'

Double oops. 'Whatever. I'm enjoying it, okay?' The company. The food in her mouth was all but tasteless now that he'd noticed her happiness. But it was fish of some sort, wasn't it? Why couldn't she keep a straight face? Pull on her surgeon's look? Because she didn't want to. She was happy being here with Blake, no longer the pain-in-the-butt teen but an interesting, exciting man she couldn't stop wondering about. What did he do outside of work hours? What was his idea of enjoyment? Were his kisses to die for? Of course they would be. Putting her fork aside she picked up the glass of champagne he'd ordered because they apparently deserved it for getting where they were in their careers. Not quite understanding, Georgie nevertheless took a sip, and smiled some more.

Blake was smiling. It suited him. 'Glad you're having fun.' Then the smile slipped.

Not changing his mind about dinner? That'd really kill the moment. 'What about you?'

He tapped his glass against hers and took a long sip. Then placing the glass back on the table, he reached for her hand, wound his fingers around it and squeezed gently. 'It's been a hell of a day, but being here with you is the best time I've had in ages.'

His smile had a seriousness that snagged at her, and brought a lump to her throat. He meant every word. Or she was hopeless at reading him, and she doubted that. Understanding what people weren't saying when they had lots on their mind was part of her job, and it carried over into everyday life. 'Me too,' she admitted—too easily. 'I feel as though we've always known each other far deeper than is actually true. Strange how that makes me comfortable talking about anything and everything.' Not that they had much, but she wouldn't hesitate once they got started.

'I know what you mean. We hung around in the same places, shared Noah, and yet the age difference, while not huge, was a barrier to talking about a lot of things back then. We were at different stages of our lives. We're grown-ups now and you being older than me means nothing.'

She pressed his hand in reply. 'So we can discuss anything?' There was no stopping the smiles now. 'I like that.' More than liked it. It had been so long since she'd had anyone she could tell whatever was on her mind. She'd become cautious since Noah died. Friends had been quick to support her, talk to her and tell her she'd get over his death soon and not to stop looking forward. After a while they'd become impatient, saying it was time to move on, to stop wishing for the impossible, to accept what had happened. What she had learned to do was stop sharing her heartfelt emotions. No one wanted to know about them. Except her ex-husband and by then she'd forgotten how to talk about the important things. Until now. Somehow it felt as though Blake might have knocked the barriers aside without even trying. Of course she still had to put this to the test. But she believed it wouldn't be hard.

'Even Noah.' There was a load of understanding in his eyes which had to mean he also still hurt over the past.

'I don't feel he's between us as a problem, but more as someone we both cared so much about and just want to be able to remember him without feeling angry or hurt or let down.' Now she was getting serious, and that had the potential to spoil the evening. 'Sorry.'

'Don't apologise,' Blake said softly, still with a smile on that gorgeous mouth that she'd wondered what would be like to kiss. 'Not to me. I get where you're coming from.' Another gentle squeeze and he let go of her hand to cut a piece of his steak and chew it slowly, still watching her.

Blimey, no one had ever got to her so easily, so quickly. What was it about this man? It wasn't in their history, so had to be something she'd not noticed before, or maybe it hadn't even been there. Had he become more understanding of others through learning how his life could be tossed about like a bouncy ball in the wind? Or had he always been this understanding of others? 'Mum and Dad are sorry they won't be catching up with you but they couldn't cancel their trip.'

'No problem.' He paused, then said, 'You know

your father came down to Dunedin to see me about six months after the funeral?'

'Never heard of that, but I'd returned to Christchurch by then, hadn't I?'

'You had. He flew down for the day, took me out to lunch and basically told me to pull my head in, stop acting like a misguided youth and get on with my studies because no one was going to wait for me to catch up. Said if I wanted to become a doctor I had to stop wasting the opportunity I had.'

'I can see Dad doing that. But why did he go down there in the first place? How did he know you were having problems? I mean, apart from the fact you were devastated by what happened.'

'Turned out my parents talked to yours one night about how I was missing lectures, drinking too much and generally falling off the rails. It was all true. I'd go out with my mates to the pub and instead of having one beer, I'd have one for me and one for Noah. Not so bad, except I never stopped at one each. I needed more, and since I was having one for Noah each round, I was downing a lot. But worse, if possible, I began lazing in bed instead of going to lectures, and didn't put any effort into studying.' He paused, fixing her with his keen gaze. 'Your father didn't have to say a lot. His words were true and concise, and he woke me up in a hell of a hurry. I got back on track and stayed there without any regrets.' He sighed. 'Other than not being able to have prevented Noah from going out with those idiots that night.'

'Blake, stop it.' Her heart ached for him. 'It was never your fault. Noah wasn't a child. He chose to get drunk, to hitch a ride with a guy who was so far over the limit that it's a wonder he could turn the ignition on, let alone drive.' She reached for his hand, liking the feel of him against her skin. 'You know he could get bolshy if he drank too much, and he had set out to get drunk that night because his girlfriend dumped him. No one has ever blamed you, or thought you should've been there for him.'

'I get that, but still feel bad. What if I *had* been with him? The outcome of that night might have been different.'

She wouldn't lie. He'd see through that and like her less for it. Which was the last thing she wanted. Blake was fast becoming really important to her and losing him already wasn't happening if she could help it. 'You don't know that, and that still doesn't make it your fault, Blake. It really doesn't. We're responsible for our own actions. Every one of us. Noah owned what happened because he chose to get in that car. End of.' Bad choice of words, but it was how it was. For once she wasn't getting uptight about her loss. For the first time she could talk about it without wanting to curl up in a ball to wait out the pain thinking about Noah brought on.

'To hell with this.' His knife and fork banged down on his plate. 'I need to get out of here, grab some fresh air.'

What? Where did that come from? 'Sure.' She was talking to his back as he strode through the restaurant, his hand pulling his wallet from his back pocket. 'Oh, Blake.' His mother's operation. Then here they were, talking about Noah. No wonder he was upset.

He returned, spoke softly this time. 'Come on. Let's walk a bit. Please?'

Yes, she'd do that. She wanted to be with him, to support him and share the pain and frustration he was going through. And to give a little of herself. Yes, she really wanted to give to Blake, to open up to him. Starting now.

Blake swallowed hard and stared up at the sky. What an idiot. Now Georgie would never want to spend time with him. 'Georgie, I'm sorry.' The day had caught up with him and he'd taken it out on her.

His hand was wrapped in hers. 'I get it, Blake. It's all right.' She began walking, leaving him no choice but to go with her or pull his hand free and turn away which was the last thing he wanted to do.

He kept his mouth shut, for fear of saying something irreparable, like 'I need you.' That'd go down a treat. He wanted her, all of her. To share the fear and pain, and even hopefully help her with moving past the devastation Noah left behind. But most of all, right now, he wanted to hold her close, to breathe her in, to meld with her.

The silence grew, tightened, became heavier. He couldn't stand it any longer. 'Where're you working tomorrow?'

'Public. I've got three surgeries first up, and then consultations in the afternoon.' There was tension in her voice which had nothing to do with what she was saying. 'It never slows down. No sooner do I finish with one patient and there are two more lining up.'

He kept trying for normalcy. It was the only way he

was going to get through the next hour. 'I wonder what it's like to have a nine-to-five, five-days-a-week job.'

'I can't begin to imagine it. I love what I do and wouldn't have it any other way. Except on those days when the stress and exhaustion catch up and all I want to do is curl up in the sun with a good book and strong coffee. Which isn't very often,' she added hastily.

A good book, not an exciting man, eh? Interesting. She had said she was on her own but was he missing something here? Like the point being that she needed to be alone on those kinds of days? For him, it was get out amongst it, be busy so his brain could move past what had kept him awake the night before. 'So no regrets with your career choice, even on a bad day?'

She blinked, like she was thinking 'Who is this guy?' 'None at all. Why? Do you have some?'

'Apart from wondering what it might be like to be a commercial fisherman and get to eat fish every single day, no, I'm more than pleased with what I do.'

Finally she laughed. 'Yeah, like I can picture you away at sea for weeks on end, being tossed up and down, smelling of fish, not dressing in your classy clothes.'

Exactly what he'd hoped for. Some of his tension backed off too. 'Put it like that, and you've got a point. Anyway, I'd probably get sick of fish after a while.'

'Do you still go skiing in winter?'

'I belong to a ski club at Ruapehu and try to get down there for a week at least twice a year.' Her question brought back memories of him and Noah skiing at Mount Hutt and Porters when they were teenagers. Georgie was sometimes there with her girlfriends. Watching Georgie swooping down the mountainside was like watching a ribbon on a light breeze, all soft movements that wound him up hard. 'You?'

She winced. 'I stopped for a few years.' Meaning after Noah died? 'Then when I finally decided to get back into it I couldn't believe I'd left it so long. But to be honest, I haven't done much in a while. There's never a lot of free time.'

All work and no play doesn't lead to an exciting life, Georgie.

Not that he was any better off. All the hiding his heart hadn't brought him any more pain, but neither had it brought happiness. 'Why did you give it up the first time round?'

She stopped walking and turned to look at him. 'I wanted to be safe. For Mum and Dad. And for me.'

There it was. Again. Noah, and how the accident changed them for ever. Blake reached for her hand, covered it with his. 'The ongoing ramifications.' He dipped his head once, then looked back at her, and sighed. 'You didn't want your parents worrying whenever you went to the mountains?'

'No. I didn't. They'd been hurt enough. I wanted to be the strong one for them.'

'And when you want something, you move sky and earth to get it. I knew that was your reason for returning to Christchurch to finish your training, but I guess I didn't think that you'd let it come into other things you undertook.'

'Whereas you didn't return here when you'd qualified as you'd once intended doing. Instead you headed north to establish your career. You needed to stay away from reminders of Noah and why he isn't here any more.'

They knew each other better than he'd realised. 'Two peas in a pod, though with different agendas.'

'Same cause.' Georgie removed her hand, started walking again. 'I believed I was helping my parents by being there for them.'

'And now?' Did she think she might've made a mistake? That she should've continued to study in Dunedin for those last couple of years before returning here? Or then head away to some other city to follow her dream of being a gynaecologist? 'Georgie?'

She was quiet for a long moment. Then she shook her head as though getting rid of whatever was in her mind, and answered him. 'Nothing. I'm good. I made the right choice, no regrets at all.'

'If that's true, then I'm glad for you. It would've been awful if you decided all the hard work had been for something you no longer wanted to do.' However, there was a 'but' behind what she'd said, and for the life of him, he couldn't see what it was. What he did understand was she didn't want to continue talking about it.

Georgie glanced at him. 'So, tell me about the practice you're a partner in.'

In other words, change the subject. He could do that. It might help him breathe easier too. 'You could say I got lucky. A colleague I was specialising with recommended me to her father who's an orthopaedic specialist and a senior partner in Remuera Road Orthopaedic Centre. The partners were looking for a junior partner to take over from John Harris, who'd developed leukaemia and wanted to retire early.'

'Straight from specialising to a partnership. That's pretty darned good.' She sighed. 'We've both done okay.' Wistfulness filtered through her voice.

'Is there something you feel you've missed out on so far?'

'So far? I like that. It puts those erratic dreams in perspective. Because, yes, there are things I want and don't look like I'm within reach of finding. Blimey, now I'm talking too much.' She stared ahead, as if there might be some answers on the path.

'Don't stop.' It was keeping him grounded. 'I want to hear more about who you are, and what you're dreaming of.'

'You want to rekindle our friendship?' Was that hope lightening her eyes?

'You bet.'

'Cool. Works for me. Though rekindle is probably a bit strong. We weren't exactly the greatest of pals back when we first knew each other.' Georgie's shoulder bumped gently against his and she didn't move away, stayed close and personal. Her scent was lightness on the evening summer air, and stirred him deeply. The little things seem to grow, feel big and important. As though he'd come home. Even that idea didn't make him stumble. He had no intentions of ever moving back to Christchurch. He was established in Auckland, comfortable with his lifestyle, engrossed in his career. But Georgie added another dimension to that contentment. He tensed. Breathed deep. Relaxed.

She slipped her arm through his and leaned in a little closer. 'You all right?'

'Absolutely.' Couldn't be better, despite all the questions popping up as they strolled along.

'Do you miss Christchurch at all?'

'Only my family. It would be nice to join in some of the Sunday barbecues at Sumner Beach with my sisters' kids, and drop in on Mum and Dad after work, but it's not as though I don't have anything to do with them. Kat and Dot bring the kids up to my place a couple of times over the year, and I try to get down for birthdays and Christmas.' His sisters made sure he didn't miss out on the important occasions, but it didn't always work out, as he often took on extra work to cover for his colleagues.

'I guess the birthdays are growing in number. Isn't Kat pregnant with her third?'

'Yes. This one was a surprise for her and Bart.' Did Georgie want to have children? Or was she so used to living on her own that the idea of littlies running around set her heart pumping in terror?

'It's kind of funny how some people still manage to get caught out, especially when they obviously don't take chances. I see it quite often with my obstetrics patients. Usually the couples who've planned everything from careers and who'll take time off to the house they buy and prepare for the family are the ones most caught out.' She sounded relaxed, not hyped up over missing out on anything. But then maybe Georgie had become good at hiding her real feelings.

He tested the waters by stretching the truth a little. 'I've never given much thought to the possibility of one day having a family. If I finally settle down with someone it might happen, I suppose.'

'You don't have a ticking clock inside that masculine body.' Her elbow poked him in the waist.

Maybe he did, since he seemed to be thinking about this a bit more since arriving in Christchurch. Since spending time with Georgie, if he was honest. 'Who knows what brings these thoughts on? Not me. I've been too focused on getting on with my career and making my house a home to consider that the years are going by at an alarming rate.'

'Now you're sounding like an old man,' she said with a laugh, and leaned closer as they walked past a low-hanging tree.

He tucked his arm tighter around hers, absorbing her warmth and softness. When he thought about that, it had been a long time since he'd felt quite so at ease with another person. 'Thank you for being here for me.'

Georgie's head flipped up and suddenly those beautiful eyes were locked on him as she placed both hands on his upper arms. 'I couldn't stay away.'

Thump. His heart slammed into his ribs. Her eyes were wide and dark, and filled with something he was afraid to believe. Longing. For him. He couldn't drag his gaze away from them. Nor could he step back from her body and her aura. He had to stand close, to breathe deep, to feel her heat, her kindness and sense of fun. 'Georgie.' He breathed her name out. 'Georgie.'

Heat seared his cheek where her knuckles caressed softly. 'Blake. I don't know what's happening but I want to kiss you,' she whispered. 'To be kissed *by* you.' Her fingertip traced his lips, seductive with the light touch.

He stood still, fighting the need to haul her into his arms and kiss them both senseless. Damn but he wanted her. So he had to turn away. Except he couldn't. Make that wouldn't. He always walked away. He'd gone away from family and friends to hide his guilt, to start over. He'd held back with women for fear he'd hurt them, or be hurt. Which he could do to Georgie. But not if he gave her everything he had.

Her hand fell away. 'I get the picture.'

Blake reached for her, pulled her up close, lowered his mouth to hers. 'No, you don't.' Kiss now, talk later. The moment he felt those soft lips under his, he knew there'd be no talking for a while to come. Kissing Georgie was like falling into a cushion of air that floated in one spot. Warm, hot, sensational, exhilarating. And most of all, Georgie was putting him back together again. All the doubts he'd carried for so long were evaporating so fast he couldn't keep up. 'Georgie,' he whispered between their mouths before plunging his tongue into her warmth to taste, to feel, to know her.

Then she pulled away.

His heart plummeted. 'Georgie?'

She squeezed his hand. 'Take me home.'

Georgie had the door open before the car stopped rolling up her drive, her house key in her hand. That kiss had woken a demon inside her. She'd been kissed before, even had some amazing kisses, but Blake's were a whole new level of wonder. They were filling her with hope and joy, and desire so strong she would've been in a heap at his feet if she wasn't clinging to him so tightly when they were kissing. And loving the feel of his firm muscles under her palms, against her breasts, around her waist. Every last bit of Blake was waking her up in ways she hadn't known before.

He was right on her heels as she shoved the door open. Stepping inside he pushed it shut and turned to take her in his arms. 'Hey.'

'Hey, yourself,' she whispered, watching him closely, looking for doubt or regret. He might not want this, might've decided on the way here to drop her off and head away. But he'd followed her inside.

'Georgie.'

Here we go. He's going say goodbye.

She waited for the crunch to come.

Blake reached for her, pulled her in against that long body and held her tight. 'I need you,' he whispered. 'I need you.'

No words could express the desire flooding her. Nothing but action could show him her need. Tipping her head back she stretched up and found his mouth with hers, began to kiss him with everything she had. This was what had been missing in her otherwise happy life. This was what could turn her world into amazing and thrilling and be the most important reason for waking up each morning. She needed this too.

Slow down, Georgie. You've only just caught up with Blake.

Which was exactly why she didn't want to go slow. Too many years had been lost. Years when she'd had no idea Blake was her match. She knew that now? Deep inside, yes, she believed she did. But of course it wasn't going to be that straightforward. Even if they went any further than this. Despite these feelings of wonder and desire filling her, she understood there were two of them in this picture to make decisions. She could also be totally wrong. Blake might kiss every woman like this, as if there were no tomorrow.

His mouth left hers, slowly, the absence excruciating even when she could still feel him on her mouth. 'I need you, Georgie.' The hope and longing and even pain in his gaze undid the last knots inside her.

'Touch me.'

He proceeded to do that. His hands were under her blouse, her bra, covering her breasts, teasing her nipples. His thighs against hers as he backed her up against the wall. And his tongue was circling her mouth, tasting, teasing, winding her tighter and tighter.

Heat poured throughout her body as she tore his shirt free of his trousers and ran her fingers over his hot skin, across his chest, down his back, undoing his belt and zip, back over his buttocks and around to his manhood. As she touched him, he was touching her, and her world came in to this—the heat and longing. Blake. And only Blake.

She froze as he pulled his mouth away, then smiled as he bent down for his trousers now around his ankles. 'Wait. Condom.' Stepping out of them he tugged his wallet out of the pocket and pulled a packet free. He had the condom on so fast she knew he was as ready as she was. And somewhere along the way she had removed her panties, and wound her legs around his waist to accept him. And Blake was pushing into her, and she was taking him and then—and then she was coming and crying out and exploding with desire and touching him and feeling him coming and hearing his roar before he shuddered his release inside her.

He held her tight, his chest rising and falling fast, his breath hot and sharp against her neck. Her head spun, her heart raced and warmth filled her, reaching to every corner, bringing her alive in ways she hadn't known in for ever.

Eventually Blake straightened, set her gently on her feet. 'Georgie,' he whispered. 'Where have you been?'

'Waiting for this, I think.' Talk about honesty. It might be too much for both of them, but she couldn't take the words back. Leaning back in his arms, she looked up at him. 'I don't know what's going on, Blake. I only know I don't want to bolt to my safe place just yet.'

His face was inscrutable as he looked down at her.

Her skin tightened. She'd gone too far, said too much. Being open and honest was new for her, yet the words had poured from her, riding on the wave of desire.

Blake took her face in his hands. 'Thank you for being honest.'

So he had heard her clearly. 'Just a little.' She wasn't about to forget those kisses or the desire that had ignited within her.

He placed the softest kiss ever on her swollen lips. 'Georgie, I don't know where I'd be without you these past two days.'

Her throat blocked with emotion. It hurt to see how vulnerable he was. This was Blake as he'd become the night Noah died.

Before she could speak, Blake's phone rang. As he apologised and retrieved his phone from his trouser pocket, she stepped sideways and reached down for her blouse. Too little too late, but suddenly she felt vulnerable. She had to remember that they hadn't made each other any promises. They'd made love, and now that was over.

Blake hung up. 'That was my dad. I think he needs to talk.'

Reality check, or an escape route? She finished dressing, trying not to let him see how his words stung. 'Sure, I understand.'

To cover her confusion, she directed him to the bathroom, then headed to the kitchen to make coffee.

Hip against the counter, arms folded under her breasts, she stared at the floor and wondered what was going on in her life. In little more than a day she'd become so much closer to Blake, and she didn't want to step away. There was a pull she couldn't deny. She had dropped all caution and followed through on the need and hope filling her, when maybe she did need to slow down. A little anyway. It wasn't like her to leap in without checking the bottom of the pool first. At least it hadn't been for a long time. So why start now?

Because she wanted to take a chance on Blake. Only Blake. She had no idea why he was waking her up so fast. He just did. As though his reappearance in her life was bringing the past and future together with a hell of a bang. She should be hauling on the brakes and aiming for slow and careful. But she couldn't. She'd done that for too long. The urge to get out there and really start living was grabbing her, shaking her roughly. Telling her it was time to get on with making her dreams come true before it was too late. Dreams she'd filed away when her brother died and she'd come home. Her parents had been getting on with living in the present for a while now. They didn't need her hanging around making certain everything was all right. They'd become her excuse for not risking her heart. Blake had started this. Had he always been lurking in the back of her head, her heart, waiting for an opportunity to step up into her life? Unlikely, but stranger things happened.

'Georgie, you all right?' Blake stood before her, his clothes back on straight, worry flowing out from those grey eyes. 'I don't want to hurt you.'

'I know.' She hoped she was right. 'Look, your dad needs you. You'd better get going'

He reached for her then, kissed her lightly. A kiss that didn't have the passion of a short while ago, but still held something special that made her step up to that wonderful body and hold him tight.

'I'll see you tomorrow.' There was relief in his voice. Had he been worrying she mightn't be patient with him?

'Goodnight, Blake. Take care and try to get some sleep.'

CHAPTER FOUR

'MORNING, SARAH. How did you sleep?' Georgie entered the room looking a damned sight better than Blake was feeling. But then he'd barely managed an hour's sleep throughout the long night. The moment the birds started their early morning tweeting ritual he had clambered out of bed and gone for a run around Fendalton, trying to find the answers to all the confusion in his head that hadn't been forthcoming during the night. Again he came up with nothing.

But he had found the familiar streets and houses soothing. The paintwork and gardens had changed since he'd lived here, some houses had been added onto, a couple had been torn down and replaced which was most likely due to damage in the earthquake years back. But mostly it was like fitting into an old, comfortable skin as he'd jogged along the sidewalks. To think he'd been in a hurry to get out of town when he headed to university, and now it was as though he was being beckoned to stop and look harder, to come back and slot into the place he'd left so fast. As if that'd be possible. No one could go back, only forward. The people he'd known back then had moved on, either to other places or with their careers and families.

His gaze shifted left to Georgie. Did his forward include the woman making his heart tap a little faster than usual? He watched her watching his mother.

'In between the nurses taking my BP and checking up on everything I slept like a log.' His mother's smile was tired, as was everything about her.

Now he looked closer, he could see shadows under Georgie's eyes and some tension at the corners of her mouth. Not relaxed as she had been in his arms kissing him senseless last night. Not like the hot woman who'd turned him on so fast he hadn't known if he was coming or going. No pun meant. There'd been tension in his muscles during those kisses and their lovemaking, but this morning a different tension was making him uneasy, preventing him from letting go of the fear gripping him.

'Pain level?' Georgie asked his mother.

She sighed. 'Honestly? Seven out of ten.'

'Honest is best.' Georgie brushed a kiss on his mum's cheek. 'Andrew asked me to drop by and check on you. He's coming along later, but he got called to an emergency during the night and is currently at home grabbing a couple of hours' sleep.'

'Seems everyone's missing out on that.' Blake pushed to his feet and crossed to give Georgie a quick hug. Roses wafted under his nose. He closed his eyes and breathed in some more. Red came to mind. Like the large, double blooms that had grown in his mother's garden for as long as he could remember. 'Good to see you, Georgina.'

A soft chuckle came to him. 'No one calls me that any more.'

'It's been a long time, I know.' As thirteen-year-olds he and Noah had used to chant 'Georgina… Georgina…' when they wanted to wind her up and get her attention. Definitely childish, but it worked a treat every time. 'But at least you haven't gone into a huff this time.'

'I can if you want me to.' Her smile was real, despite the strain in her eyes.

'Save it for another day.' He stepped back. 'Are you going to examine Mum? If so, I'll go and get us all some coffee.'

Georgie shook her head. 'No, that would be stepping outside the ethical boundaries. Andrew suggested that since I was coming in to see Sarah anyway I could make sure she's comfortable and there's no indication of further bleeding. He's ordered a coagulation screen to see if there's a deficiency of one of the clotting factors.' She gave him a smile that told him all was well between them. 'But feel free to get that coffee. I could do with another caffeine hit before I head off to Public. And a croissant with jam and chocolate if you're going to the cart outside the main entrance.'

'I am now. Back shortly.' There was a spring in his step as he left the room and headed down the corridor to the entrance and the coffee cart beyond. As hollowed out as he felt over his mother, Georgie seemed to light a spark within him. She'd been there for him last night in more ways than he could ever have imagined, and here she was again, checking in on Mum and letting him know she had his back.

'There you go, two cappuccinos and a long black.' The woman at the cart handed him a cardboard tray and a paper bag of croissants. 'Enjoy.'

He blinked. Where had his mind been? 'We will, thanks.' He was hungry this morning. Less than half a dinner and then the activity at Georgie's had caught up with him.

When he reached his mother's room he heard her saying, 'All my abdominal area hurts, especially when I roll over or sit up.'

'That's normal,' Georgie replied. 'Your muscles took a hit when Andrew operated, and don't forget he had to go back in a second time. The wound's approximately twelve centimetres long so he was able to remove the fibroid without damaging it and leaving behind a potential problem with cells floating around.'

'I expected pain, but not quite this level.' Just then his mother caught sight of him standing in the doorway. 'Come in, Blake. We're done with the medical talk.'

By the look on her face, Georgie didn't think so, but she shrugged. 'That coffee smells good. Just what I need.'

'Glad to be of use.' He handed her a cardboard cup with a smile. 'What time do you need to get to Public?'

'Five minutes ago.' She was smiling right back at him.

Sending his stomach into a riot. 'Then you'd better take that coffee and food with you.' He'd been hoping for a few minutes with her, but understood all too well how little time surgeons had first thing in the morning. That she'd dropped by at all meant a lot. And put to rest any concerns she mightn't want to see him after what went on between them last night.

'I'm about to.' She was watching him, still smiling, but there appeared to be a question she didn't know how to put into words hovering in the background. When she finally looked away, it was at his mother. 'You take care, Sarah, and do everything the staff tell you to. Make the most of being looked after.'

'You really think I'll be allowed to do a darned thing once I get home? There's not only Alistair to tell me what I can and cannot do, Blake will have more than his say when it comes to when I eat, breathe and move.'

'You're so right, and you'll love every moment of it.'

'True.'

His mother wasn't going home any time soon. Not when she looked like she'd been run over by a bus, and moved as though it had been a double decker that knocked her out. Not until there was colour in her cheeks, and the pain had diminished to almost nothing. Definitely not until Andrew and his team had found out what the hell was wrong with her. 'I'm extending my stay to include next week, Mum.' At least that long, and possibly longer, depending on how everything panned out with her.

'You don't have to do that, son.'

Yes, he did. Besides, 'I want to.' The look of pure love on his mother's face nearly did him in. He was only doing what any son would do, but then he hadn't been around for most things in the past so she was no doubt pinching herself under that bedcover. 'I mean it.'

Right then a nurse strolled in, a container of pills in

one hand and the pulse metre in the other. 'Morning, Sarah. I see you've had a restless night.'

Georgie stepped aside. 'I'll get going. See you later?' She looked to him.

Yes, please. 'How about we go out for a meal? Give the Ale House a go?'

'I'd like that. What about Alastair? He could join us, if you think he wants some company. I can share you.' She smiled.

'I'll ask him.' It would be good having his dad there too. They weren't used to spending a lot of time together though. Now was the time to fix that. 'He might want to come here, and catch up with me at home later though.'

'Play it by ear then. Shall I meet you at the pub?' She sounded eager to spend more time with him, which took away any doubts he'd felt when he'd had to leave her so quickly last night.

'There's good.' Bring it on. But first there were tests and scans and discussions with the specialist to be dealt with. And the answers to assimilate, good or bad. Blake gulped his coffee and sat down beside his mother to while away the hours until the day could really begin.

What to wear? Georgie did a mental flick through her wardrobe as she drove home from work. That new sky-blue top brought out the blue of her eyes and looked good when she let her hair down over her shoulders. What about the pretty blouse with a light blue and pink flower pattern that accentuated her slim face and throat? Or the red-and-white-striped dress?

She actually laughed. She felt so darn good after last night, despite Blake's abrupt departure. At first she'd been a bit miffed, but reality kicked in, reminding her that he had a lot on his mind and most of it had nothing to do with her and their lovemaking. But this new feeling of happiness was still Blake's fault. She didn't usually go around laughing over nothing. But this wasn't nothing. This was her letting her hair down and reaching out to have fun. Personal fun that involved a man. A spunky man who turned her on just thinking about him. Last night she'd been wearing a simple pink and white blouse and navy trousers, and they'd been going to a more upmarket restaurant. Those had been the clothes in her locker at the hospital, and not once had she felt uncomfortable. So why all this palaver about what to wear to the Ale House?

Because it had nothing to do with the destination and all to do with the company she'd be keeping. She wanted Blake to see her at her best. Hopefully looking sexy. She was letting someone in, undoing the knots holding her heart closed, taking a risk on caring about someone who might hurt her. Looking sexy had to help.

She'd hurt her ex more than he had her. All because of those knots and the fear of losing someone close to her again. Like her unborn baby. That's how she had lost Tommy and became even more determined to look out for herself. Until Blake turned up. And now all caution had floated out the window. She wanted more of Blake, of life, of everything.

The red and white dress for sure.

When she saw Blake's eyes widen and his mouth lift in a sexy smile as she pulled up outside the pub that night, she knew she'd made the right choice. Her toes tightened and her skin tickled, while inside her chest there was quite the pounding going on. Had she ever felt like this? Of course she had. Hadn't she? When she fell in love last time she'd been thrilled and excited, but there was something more to Blake. Sexy, drop-dead good-looking, serious and funny, focused yet able to step beyond being a surgeon. Whatever it was, Blake was different to any man she'd known and she wanted to grab him with both hands and never let go. Which was such an about-face from her usually reticent approach to men and relationships it should be scaring the pants off her. She wriggled her hips. Knickers were firmly in place. She might not know him well, but she understood what had driven him over the last thirteen years. 'Hi.' Leaning in close, she kissed his cheek.

He moved so their lips met. His kiss was light and short and thrilling. Pulling back, he gazed at her with something like relief. 'It's good to be with you. Dad's not joining us. He's sitting with Mum, and it'll take a bulldozer to shift him before lights out.'

'As long as he doesn't think I wouldn't want him with us. He must be so worried though.'

'Very.' As Blake sounded. 'And he said to say he'll join us on another occasion, when Mum's doing better.'

'Good. How was your day?' she asked.

'The sisters visited Mum and then dragged me out for lunch. Man, can they talk.'

'No wonder you look exhausted,' she teased.

He took her arm. 'I booked a table by the window. What would you like to drink?'

'A Pinot Gris would be lovely.' She sank onto the chair he held out. 'You enjoyed catching up with your sisters then?'

He sat beside her, not opposite. That had to be a good sign. 'You bet. They gave me a hard time about still being single and able to do whatever I like, but there's nothing unusual in that. I had to wade through hundreds of photos on their phones of the kids playing on the beach, bouncing on the trampoline, eating take-aways. You name it, they were doing it.'

'And you loved every photo.'

Blake was trying to be aloof but his mouth curved upwards and there was a sparkle in his eyes for the first time in a while. 'I think a new photo file's being sent through to me in the next few days.'

A waitress arrived with her wine and handed both of them menus. 'Today's special is pork belly. I'll give you a few minutes to decide.'

What was the rush? The place wasn't crowded. Georgie picked up the menu and opened it. 'I am indulging, eating out twice in one week.'

'I haven't left town yet. We could up the number quite a bit.' Blake's hand briefly touched her thigh. 'What are you doing tomorrow night?'

'You tell me.'

What about kissing you again?

Making love, this time slowly, getting to know each other's needs a little more. She reached for her glass, took a careful sip. How to stop the heat invading her cheeks?

'Yeah, well, who knows what tomorrow will bring.' He'd gone all serious in an instant.

'Want to talk about today's tests?' she asked quietly. She spied the waitress already heading in their direction and waved her away as they chatted about Sarah's condition.

'Blake, I know you're worried sick. Of course you are. We all are. But remember, Sarah's in good hands.'

He nodded. 'I know. And thank you for listening to me being so gloomy. I am sorry for being such a pain.'

'It's okay. Any time you want to talk, I'm here to listen, as long as you reciprocate if needed.' She meant it.

'No problem.'

'Want to decide on a meal?' She slid a menu across. 'We're getting evils from our waitress.'

'Tough.' He pushed the menu away. 'Tell me about your day.'

Georgie settled back in her chair and went with the flow. If he wanted to wind down, then she was all for it. It might bring them even closer.

'Dad'll be home by now, I guess. Probably wishing he could stay with Mum all night,' Blake said as he and Georgie walked towards her car after dinner.

'Have they always been so close?'

'Absolutely. They had a rushed wedding because I was on the way but always reckoned it was the best thing to happen.' Blake paused, smiled to himself. 'They've always been very loving with each other as far back as I can remember.' Hadn't they? His smile dimmed. When he'd been about ten there'd been some heated arguments behind the bedroom door, and frosty weeks when neither of his parents were very talkative. 'I suppose all relationships have their off times.'

'Mine certainly did.'

'How long were you married?' He'd felt sad when

he heard through his parents that she'd split up with her husband, thinking how she didn't need any more grief in her life.

'A little over three years.'

Mindful that he was setting himself up to have to answer some personal questions further on, Blake followed through on the need to know more about Georgie and why she was single when she'd always been so popular with the guys. 'Do you think Noah's passing had anything to do with it?'

'Yes. I wasn't as ready as I thought.' The words were clipped.

Blake felt the pain behind them. It was exactly why he avoided getting deeply involved with a woman. Except things were changing within him since he'd met up with Georgie again. Taking her hand in his as they continued along the pavement, he waited to see if she'd expand on what she'd said.

Her fingers squeezed his. 'When I fell for Tommy I believed I was open to love, could love him as much as he loved me.' She paused.

They'd reached her car and Blake stood with Georgie as she stared around.

'I tried. I really did. But it wasn't enough. I was afraid of losing someone I cared so much for again.' Looking up at him, she blinked softly. 'Instead I hurt Tommy.'

Without hesitation Blake wrapped his arms around Georgie and rested his chin on the top of her head. 'Which in turn hurt you.' He rocked back and forth on the balls of his feet, his hands splayed across her back, feeling the trembling in her body. 'It's okay, Georgie.'

Her head lifted enough so she could look at him. 'No, it's not. I inflicted the sort of pain I was trying to avoid for myself. That's selfish.'

'You didn't go into the relationship just for yourself though, did you?' He couldn't believe she was telling him this, and yet maybe it wasn't such a surprise given how well they'd been getting on right from the moment they'd met up at the clinic. It wasn't as though they hadn't talked quite a bit since then. Plus there was a definite empathy about the past resonating between them.

'Of course not.' Her head dropped to his chest, pressed against him. 'Not as far as I was aware anyway.'

He nodded, then leaned down and placed a light kiss on those beautiful lips that he hadn't been able to put out of his mind since he'd kissed them last night. 'We have known each other a long time, haven't we? Better than I'd realised, I think.'

She smiled and pressed her mouth to his, deepening the kiss to a full-blown, heat-him-up-fast connection.

'Georgie, Georgie.' He groaned and pulled her in closer, so close she felt as though she was a part of him. And then he began kissing her back, giving her everything he had. How had he lived without her? She made him come alive by being herself. A different woman to that fast, crazy one he'd been in lust with years ago, but equally enthralling and exciting. Although more grounded now, which wasn't a bad thing. Was he ready for wherever this might lead?

Didn't know, didn't care right now. His mouth fully claimed Georgie's, and his tongue slipped inside that warm moist place to taste and fill him with wonder.

'Get a room,' a male voice cut through the haze in his head.

In his arms Georgie stiffened, pulled back and looked around. 'Now there's a thought.'

Blake grinned down at her. 'You think?' After she'd been talking about her failed marriage only minutes ago? Despite making love last night, this *was* happening too fast. Last night had been about destressing and not fighting the heat between them. For him anyway, and Georgie had been as fast to react to him as he her, so that had to mean she had similar feelings about him. Didn't it? He hoped so. He'd show her more, give her more. Tonight would be more personal. Georgie needed to know what she was doing, where she was going, or she'd get hurt. So he knew what he was doing, did he? Nope. Not a clue. He only knew that holding Georgie close, kissing her and wanting more, was driving him on a one-way road and that he didn't want to turn back. Not yet. How about having a fling? It could be the best of both worlds for them, *if* Georgie felt the same. They'd definitely have fun if last night was anything to go by, and maybe along the way they could sort out what it was they were really looking for, could find out if this could go further and become something special and lasting.

'I'm thinking I haven't got a clue, but I'm letting go some of the hang-ups that have kept me uptight and on a very narrow path for so long it's embarrassing.' She stretched up on her toes and kissed him. 'Let's go back to my house for a coffee and see how things unfold.' Then she blinked, as though she'd just realised what she'd suggested. A light laugh crossed those gorgeous lips. 'I'm not good at this.'

'You are more than good. Try amazing.' He opened the car door. 'Come on, get in. I'll follow you home and then we'll see how we're feeling.' Ten minutes cooldown time wasn't a lot, but sometimes all it took to change a mind was sixty seconds of common sense filtering into an overheated head.

Her smile cut straight through to his heart, opening him up wide, and allowing too many emotions to rip free. Georgie really was beautiful, and exciting, and so many other wonderful things he had yet to learn about. Her laughter tightened his groin so hard he was never going to be able stand up straight again. Nor was there much likelihood of common sense finding him.

She'd put one foot in the car when bells sounded. A phone. Not his.

Georgie removed hers from her bag and stared at the screen, dismay removing the laughter from her face. 'I suspect this is just what the doctor didn't order.' Putting it to her ear, she said, 'Hello, Georgie Price speaking.' A pause. Then, 'How far apart are her contractions?'

Blake waited, the tension slowly ebbing from his groin when he'd believed nothing would fix it other than making love to Georgie. The chances of which were rapidly heading down the road as he listened to her end of the conversation.

'I'll be there shortly. Tell Anna not to panic.' *Yet*, she added after she'd hit the red button on the phone's screen. 'You heard that?' she asked.

'Who'd be an obstetrician, eh?'

She touched his arm softly. 'I'm sorry. More than I can tell you, actually.'

Her cheek was warm under his thumb. 'The timing stinks, but it could've been worse.'

'It's probably the first time I've regretted being a doctor.' Her smile was wobbly.

'Then you need to get out more.' He grinned. 'What are you doing this weekend? Babies and urgent surgeries not counted.'

'Spending time with you, I hope.'

Perfect answer. 'How about we go to Akaroa for the day?'

Go on. Put it out there. The idea's churning your stomach anyway. No matter what her reply, it can't get any worse.

'Or we could stay over for the night?' She might change her mind about being with him once she had time to think about where they'd been headed tonight. It could've been an impulsive reaction to suggest going home that she'd regret later. Whichever, he needed to say what was on his mind. 'You don't have to decide now. I'll talk to you tomorrow.'

'I'd like a night away with you.'

As quick as that. His breathing eased for the first time since he'd taken her in his arms. 'Leave everything to me.'

'Believe it or not, I was going to.' Her smile was almost shy. It *had* been a long time for her.

But then it had for him too. He wasn't counting the casual liaisons he'd experienced over the last few years. They meant nothing other than brief enjoyment with lovely women. Come to think of it, there hadn't been any serious relationship since he was nineteen. It was time to do something about that. Step one. Spend the weekend away with Georgie.

Then her smile slipped. 'Wait. What about Sarah? You won't want to be away overnight while she's still laid up.'

'It's a modern world. We have phones. Plus Dad wants to hog Mum all to himself when he's not at work.' He'd get in touch so often his parents would probably block his number. 'I wouldn't go if I didn't think they'd tell me if anything goes wrong. Besides we'll only be little more than an hour's drive away.' Not long ago he'd thought five minutes was too far away. He was changing. Georgie was changing him.

'If you're sure.'

'I am.' He could relax with Georgie like no one else. 'Keep in touch once you know how this delivery's going.'

'It could take for ever, but as Anna's only at thirty-four weeks, I don't think baby has any intentions of taking his time. Prems don't seem to like hanging around inside when they've made up their mind to meet mum.'

'Fingers crossed this one does.' Blake laughed. It didn't matter if he had to wait twenty-four hours, he'd be there when Georgie was finished with work and ready to relax. Then they'd go away for the weekend. 'Bet you've got a busy schedule tomorrow as well.'

Georgie smiled. 'Of course. While you'll be watching over Sarah all day.'

'True.' He couldn't be disappointed. If not for his mother needing surgery he mightn't have caught up with Georgie in the first place. It was the best thing to

SUE MacKAY 103

come out of the whole nightmare involving his mother. 'See you tomorrow. Take care.'

She brushed a light kiss over his mouth. 'You too.'

'You realise tomorrow's the anniversary of when Noah left us?' Georgie asked on the way to Akaroa on Saturday morning as Blake drove out of the cheese factory premises where they'd bought a selection of the famous cheeses to nibble later on.

'I do.' His reply was sharp.

Shouldn't she have mentioned it? But how could she not when it was such a part of who she was now? Bet it was the same for Blake, even if he didn't want to admit it. 'Thirteen years. A long time, yet sometimes it doesn't seem so.'

'Yes.' Softer tone this time.

'I don't know what you think, but I believe we're on the same page over Noah and how badly we were both hurt.'

Blake placed a hand on her thigh and gave her a rueful smile. 'Georgie, I'm sorry. I didn't mean to be so abrupt. Keep talking about him. Please.'

'Not if it upsets you.' But then that was back to hiding and she'd started moving away from those reactions. He needed to too. 'I don't know why but being with you has made it easier to talk about him for the first time ever.' Not that they'd actually spoken much regarding Noah, but she'd begun to feel she could if she wanted to. When she did she didn't want Blake making it difficult.

'It's been a taboo subject for so long I automatically pull down the shutters, even now when I'm feeling more relaxed than I ever have about him. This is good for me, and hopefully for you. In this together, so to speak.'

'Absolutely. I understand what you're saying. It's like me thinking my actions were to protect Mum and Dad when I now accept it was all about hiding my own pain. Plus my fear of being hurt so much again.' She glanced across to her friend. Yes, they were definitely friends, no matter what. 'Since you turned up in my life again it's as though a huge weight has lifted. I'm no longer feeling crushed.'

Blake pulled the car off the road and killed the motor before turning to take her hands in his. 'That would have to be the loveliest thing I've heard in for ever. Thank you. I'm starting to have similar feelings about everything.' He leaned close enough to kiss her, gentle yet exhilarating.

Georgie closed her eyes and accepted his kiss as though she'd never been kissed before. It gave her a sense of kindness, wonder and relief all rolled in together. It was as though she'd finally landed on her feet, had found what she'd been searching for over the last thirteen years without knowing what she was doing. 'Blake,' she whispered between them. 'I'm glad you came home.'

Blake kissed her lightly. 'I'm glad I came to town too. Otherwise I'd never have got this close to you. I am so thankful to you for being there for all of us, and more so for how we seem to be getting along so well.'

'It's been a bonus, for sure.' She touched his face. 'I want to move forward. I want to stop thinking about Noah and what I lost every time I get close to someone. I want to throw myself into this with you and just enjoy.'

'A fling with Georgie Price. Who'd have believed it?' He kissed her again. 'Bring it on.'

'Starting right now.' It was as much as they could have, given they lived in different parts of the country with career positions that neither would want to give up. A shadow crossed over her. Already she felt sad not to be able to look forward to a future together that involved more than getting together occasionally for fun and lovemaking. But better to be practical than unrealistic. And happy rather than sad.

Sitting back in his seat he reached for the ignition and tossed her a heart-melting grin.

'You're ready for some more fun then?'

'Bring it on.' They were on the road, heading to the beginning of something wonderful. That's how she'd look at this adventure. A fling was just what this doctor was prescribing, as of now.

'Good idea.' He was sounding relaxed again.

Georgie looked out at the passing scenery, glad to be moving again, heading in the direction of that fun he'd mentioned with a cheeky look in his eyes. They were getting closer, and neither of them knew where that might ultimately lead. At the moment they would make the most of what they had. Blake didn't live here and wouldn't be staying on any longer than necessary to see Sarah back on her feet, but that didn't mean they couldn't make the most of what time they did have and get to know each other on a new and deeper level. She would not waste time wondering where that might lead, because then she'd have to remind herself there could be heartache to come, and for the first time in years she did not want to consider that. It would put a dampener on letting go and making the most of time spent with Blake.

'How about we start with a walk along the wharf,' Blake said as he drove down the short main street lined with old French-style houses and shops.

'Fine with me.' She looked out at the fairly calm sea. 'There's no wind to toss my sunhat into the tide.' Yesterday when she'd stopped at the mall to pick up a new printer she'd ordered she'd gone past a clothing shop where there was a display of sunhats. A wide brimmed straw hat with a wide yellow bow had caught her eye and she'd had to have it. The yellow matched the cream and yellow top she was wearing with mid-blue three-quarter-length trousers.

'Don't ask me to dive in and retrieve it if that happens,' Blake laughed.

'I thought you were a gentleman,' Georgie laughed back.

When Blake parked, he was out of the car and opening her door before she'd gathered her hat and bag from the back seat. 'Allow me, madam.' He grinned.

'Cheeky so-and-so.' Georgie plopped a kiss on his cheek, except he turned enough that her mouth covered his, and the kiss went from light to intense. When Blake's arms wrapped around her, her body moulded to his in an instant, and she forgot everything but Blake. The feel of him, his scent, his mouth on hers.

Then he was pulling back just enough to look into her eyes. 'Georgie, you make me so happy.'

Her chest ached where her breath caught. 'Ditto.'

'Good.' He gave her another kiss, shorter, less intense this time, and took a step back, his hands sliding slowly from her back to her arms, to her wrists, before he took one hand in his and turned towards the wharf along the way.

His hand was strong and firm, making hers feel soft and feminine. His upper arm brushing her shoulder as they strolled along the jetty had her feeling small and cosy. Even protected. Most of all, it was happiness filling her throughout, bringing a smile to her mouth, a smoothness to her raw edges, putting a spring in her step. She knew there was a real possibility she'd get hurt. If she fell too hard and too deep.

Then don't.

She'd have fun, make the most of what was on offer, give as good as she got and then move on. At least she might be free of the fear that had held her locked in a solo state for so long. Free or tied down even tighter with more pain?

A deep sigh slid across her lips. She was not going back there. It was barely days since she'd started letting go of the past, but once the knots started loosening everything seemed to be rushing at her. She would be strong, and look forward, no matter what. She was over staying in the wings, watching life pass by. If they were only going to have a fling, then she'd grab every moment, no regrets allowed. Except already she was beginning to question whether she only wanted a fling. Sure there'd be obstacles to anything more, but surely they could overcome those if necessary?

Blake stopped walking and pointed out beyond the end of the wharf. 'Are those dolphins out in the middle of the harbour?'

Georgie focused on what was important and let the questions fall away. Staring past Blake's fingers, she nodded as she saw a large dark body leap through the air and splash down again. 'Quite a large pod if the area of churning water is an indicator.' It had been a while since she'd last seen dolphins and they gave her the warm fuzzies. 'I hope they come closer.'

Continuing to the end of the wharf, they watched the show being put on out in the harbour. Leaning against the rail, Georgie couldn't stop smiling. A perfect start to their weekend in a wonderful location.

The dolphins eventually left and Blake had a light smile on his beautiful mouth as he watched the mammals. 'I remember dolphins swimming around the boat once when we were heading out to go fishing beyond the harbour entrance. I stopped the motor and we bobbed around for about twenty minutes watching them until they swam away.'

She turned and leaned back against the rail to look directly at him. Blake was good-looking in an outdoor kind of way. Tanned with beguiling eyes that didn't miss a thing as far as she was aware. Firm muscles from top to toe, fit without being excessive. Long legs that had her pulse thudding as she thought about them wound around hers.

'What's putting that look of surprise on your face?' Blake asked. 'Have I got breakfast on my face?'

If only it was that simple. 'Yes,' she answered and laughed when he made to wipe his mouth. 'Easily fooled.'

Blake grabbed her and tipped her backwards so her upper body was leaning over the rail. Then he leaned over her and kissed her with a passion that made the thudding go crazy with need.

Georgie gripped his arms and kissed him back with all her longing pouring through to him.

'Wow.' Blake stepped back, pulling her upright. 'Talk about flicking a switch. Lights on in an instant.' His chest was rising and falling rapidly. He dropped his hands to his sides as he watched her. 'You're driving me to distraction, Georgie.'

'I know the feeling.' Was it wise to be this honest with him? For the first time ever she wanted to put out there how she felt, not to hide behind reasons for taking it slowly. They only had a week to go, and she didn't want to get to the end of it and not have given Blake some inkling to how she felt about getting closer.

'I believe you do.' He was still watching her, a serious glint in those grey eyes.

Blake took her hand. 'Come on. We're going on a picnic at the beach.' He began heading back down the wharf at a fast clip.

She hadn't been on a picnic since she was a kid. Hopefully this one would be a lot more fun. Maybe she would go swimming afterwards though. 'I can't wait.'

CHAPTER FIVE

EASY, MAN. TAKE this slowly.

There was a lot at stake; namely two hearts that could get battered beyond recognition if they weren't sensible. Blake accepted he and Georgie lived different lives in different parts of the country, lives he doubted either of them wanted to give up. They'd both worked so hard to get where they were; it wouldn't be easy to walk away and start over. But what if he fell hard for Georgie? Then what? Since catching up with this lovely woman who he was taking down to the beach for a prearranged picnic lunch, he had begun letting go some of the fear from the past. Just not quite enough to want to risk falling in love with her.

But he was getting ahead of himself. They were starting a fling. That's what they had agreed to.

'Cat got your tongue?' Georgie asked as they stepped onto the sand at French Bay.

'Something like that.' Not a cat in sight, but one look at Georgie and his tongue was in a knot and his throat blocked with longing.

'Got it bad, mate.' Noah's words tripped into his head. Blake stumbled, straightened, his hands tighten-

ing on the cooler he was carrying filled with their lunch. Noah had always teased him relentlessly whenever he caught him watching his sister. Had he suspected there was more to his adoration of Georgie than a typical horny young guy lusting after a hot girl? He was never going to know, and he was glad. Falling for his best friend's sister would come with some hard reminders of his role in her life. Not that he'd be any different without Noah here to keep an eye on him, but he felt more relaxed without him. There was a first. Not wanting Noah in on something going on in his life.

'The water looks so tempting,' Georgie said as she placed her bag and the sun umbrella he'd brought along on the grassy edge of the beach. 'I'm going in.' With that, she was pulling her shirt over her head and tossing it on top of her bag, revealing her bikini-clad upper body. Then she was shaking her sexy butt out of her three-quarter pants before tossing them aside too.

The cooler hit the ground with a quiet thud as his fingers lost their grip on the handle. Georgie was curvy and desirable, her backside making his hands itch to cup each side. Her skin was evenly tanned and looked so soft. And when she swept her hair up on top of her head and tied it in place, her breasts rose to point upward, stealing his breath.

'Coming?' she asked with a grin.

'In a minute. I'll spread out the blanket and put the umbrella up first.'

Get my breath back, and my hormones under control before making a complete idiot of myself.

Nothing much had changed since those teenage years after all.

'So you brought your swimmers?' She was eyeing him up and down, the tip of her tongue at the corner of her mouth.

Sending his heart rate into overdrive. No calming down going on at all. 'These shorts are my swimmers.'

A frown appeared as she once again looked him up and down. 'Have you put sunscreen on?'

'Yes, Mum.' Should've said no and let those slim fingers do a number on his skin as she rubbed cream over him.

Another grin and she was off, racing down to the water like a girl let free for the day.

Blake watched her stepping into the sea, not wasting time feeling how warm it might be but taking long strides until it came up to those smooth thighs, then she dived under.

'Damn it.' Stabbing the umbrella pole into the ground at a useless angle, Blake stripped off his shirt, kicked out of his sneakers and took off after her.

Georgie was already swimming out towards deeper water, her strokes regular and strong.

He could match her and some. Within minutes he'd reached her and continued on, only stopping to tread water once he felt he was far enough from the beach to be alone with her. He caught her to him as soon as she came up beside him, wrapping his arms around her. 'Hey, Sunshine.'

Georgie wound her arms and legs around him, leaving him to keep them upright. 'Hey, yourself.' She planted a salty kiss on his mouth.

They bobbed up and down, further down as their kiss got deeper. Pulling his mouth free, Blake dragged in a lungful of air and said, 'I think we'd better move inshore a little so we can at least touch the bottom with our toes.'

Taking his hand, Georgie began dog paddling back the way they'd come until her feet were on the bottom. Then she caught him to her again and returned to kissing him as though she needed his air more than hers.

Under his palms her skin was warm yet cool, smooth and wet, sending shivers throughout his body. Those perky breasts held in place by the skimpy yellow bikini were pressed into his chest, while her legs were locked around his hips. His reaction was pure and simple. He wanted her. Now. He was so hard he ached, and throbbed. 'Georgie,' he groaned against her neck as he sucked her skin.

And groaned some more as her fingers tracked down his back to his butt. A firm squeeze by those fingers had his heart pounding, and the need for her threatening to burst out of him.

Sliding a hand between them he reached inside the miniscule pants covering her core, and slipped a finger inside where she was hot, and moist from more than the sea.

'Oh, yes. Don't stop,' Georgie groaned and took him in her hand to squeeze and rub him.

He couldn't have stopped if the beach had suddenly filled up with a busload of sightseers. Thankfully he'd chosen an empty beach for their lunch, one not on the tourist track. At least he hoped he'd got that right because right now there was no halting this need pounding through him.

'Blake,' she gasped. 'Yes, again. And again.'

He obliged, feeling her heat and the tightening as she orgasmed.

They slumped into each other, gasping for air as they held on to one another to stay upright as the light waves bumped them around on their toes. He felt Georgie begin to laugh before he heard her, and looked down into her sparkling eyes. 'You are so beautiful.' Especially when she was relaxed and her hair was spilling out of the restraint she'd had it in. The splashes of water on her face and the sated look in her eyes added to her attraction.

Her mouth split into a wide grin. 'You say the nicest things.'

'I meant it.'

The grin slipped a little as she stared at him. 'Thank you.'

She wasn't used to receiving compliments? Or maybe she didn't believe them. He'd have to give her some more. It wouldn't be hard. She was stunning, and so sexy.

'You've gone serious on me.' Georgie pulled back, disappointment wiping away that grin.

Hardly. Reaching over the gap he caught her to him, tucked her against his chest. 'You have no idea what was going through my mind, but trust me, it wasn't bad.'

Pulling her head away from him so she could eyeball him, she said quietly, 'We just had the most amazing experience, didn't we?'

'It was sublime.' Leaning down, he kissed her. 'Next time will be even more so. Pulling back, he locked his eyes on her. Come on. Let's crack open the bottle of wine that's in the cooler.'

Her eyebrows rose. 'You really did prepare for this, didn't you?'

She didn't know the half of it yet. Once they'd agreed to come out to Akaroa he'd got busy looking up restaurants and accommodation, starting with the lunch in that cooler on the beach. 'Not for what we just did, but everything else, yes. A good start to the weekend.' He grinned, feeling so comfortable with Georgie it'd be scary if he thought about where they were headed. So he wouldn't. He'd make the most of every moment they shared and leave everything else until another day.

'*And* it was always going to be out of this world,' she added quietly.

So quietly he wondered if he'd heard correctly. It was what he was thinking so he might've been mistaken but he'd go with it. It made him feel great. Taking her hand, he pulled them both inshore and up the beach.

Georgie flicked the blanket out on the sand and flopped down. 'I haven't spent a day at the beach like this in for ever.'

'How many times have you done that in the water?' he said with a laugh.

'Relax, that was a first.' She grinned.

He felt absurdly pleased. Opening the cooler he took out the wine, poured them each a drink. 'To the weekend,' he said as they tapped their glasses together. She didn't say a word, merely sipped the Chardonnay and gazed out over the beach as he reached into the cooler for the plates. 'Hope you still like crayfish?'

'You certainly know how to spoil a woman.' She was laughing softly as she watched him open up the containers of salad, crayfish and fresh bread rolls.

'It's not something I do very often, but I couldn't resist doing something special for today. Careful,' he said as he saved his wineglass from spilling over when she leaned close.

Her kiss was like a warm caress on his chin, having missed his mouth because he'd moved so sharply.

He was quick to remedy that and shifted slightly so his lips covered hers. He could go on kissing her all afternoon and long into the night. She made his heart sing, and his body hot. With a long, deep breath, he pulled back, and tapped his finger lightly on her chin. 'Let's eat.'

Before I go crazy enough to take you right here on the beach.

Which would not be a good look when at any moment people could come walking around the corner. Some things were best kept between themselves.

Georgie stared down the beach to the glistening water and sipped her wine. If she was asked to get up and go for a walk or even a swim right now she'd have to refuse. Her muscles seemed to have lost their ability to function properly. Every part of her body felt soft and floppy, like wet tissue paper. Out in the water, when Blake touched her intimately, he'd woken her body up so that she'd been aware of every inch of it, while at the same time the sensations he created were off the scale.

Glancing sideways, she soaked up the sight of the long legs and flat abdomen and the wide chest sprawled beside her. He was gorgeous. More gorgeous than she'd imagined. His face was relaxed, his eyes hidden behind classy sunglasses, his hair all spikey curls now that it had dried with the salt stiffening it. Definitely gorgeous.

She shimmied down the blanket to stretch full length next to him. 'That was a superb lunch.' Crayfish was her absolute favourite seafood, something she only had occasionally, not wanting to lose the sense of pure indulgence she got when devouring it.

'You're welcome. Just hope you've got an appetite for dinner.' His hand covered her thigh, his fingers slowly caressing her skin.

'There's more?'

'Of everything,' he muttered.

Her heart filled, and she laughed. 'I can handle that.'

Blake rolled on to his side, put his head in the palm of his hand. 'You remember when you used to go out partying with your girlfriends on a Saturday night?'

'Sure can. We got up to all sorts of trouble.' They'd thought they were quite the thing back then, but in fact they hadn't been anything more than girls having fun without getting into any sort of trouble.

'Me and Noah, and some of our friends, used to watch you leaving for town and wish we could join you. You were hot, all of you, but for me, you in particular.'

'We always told you to go away.' Blake used to hang around trying to get her attention, but she hadn't realised he was quite that fired up about her. Probably just as well. She'd have thought that gross considering he was her little brother's mate. The four-year age gap was huge back then.

'You sure did.' He leaned in and kissed her. 'It's been a long wait, but worth it.'

Georgie snuggled into him and kissed him back. And

kissed him some more, and took his kisses and held them close and lost all track of time and where they were. It didn't matter. She was in a bubble with only Blake and their kisses while their bodies touched each other's, and life was a dream.

The dream continued all afternoon. When they became too hot and wound up with longing, Blake packed up their gear and took her hand to walk back to the car, and drove them a short distance to a luxurious cottage on another beach where they were booked to stay the night. Within minutes of opening the doors and windows to let the light offshore breeze through they were falling onto the super-king-sized bed, stripping each of their clothes and touching one another all over.

Later Georgie spied a spa pool out on the deck which she quickly climbed into.

Blake brought out glasses of wine before joining her to soak away the tightness in his body. 'More exercise than I'm used to.' He grinned.

Good. Hate to think he'd been making out lots with some other woman, Georgie thought as she sipped her wine and shuffled deeper into the hot water. Ahh, the warmth. Even on a summer day it felt wonderful, relaxing her sore, out of practice muscles. 'I could stay here for ever.'

'You'd look like a prune.'

'Thanks, pal.' She changed the subject. 'Do you think you should give Sarah a ring? See how she's doing?' She'd hate for anything to happen and Blake not know about it straight away. That'd put the biggest dampener possible on their fun.

'What? And interrupt her and Dad snoozing together

on that narrow hospital bed? Good idea.' He headed inside to get his phone. Ten minutes later he returned. 'All good. Andrew's even said Mum might be able to go home tomorrow. Her bloods are improving after the last transfusion. The white count has returned to normal so an infection's unlikely.'

'That is good news.'

'Yeah. It is.' Relief poured off him, then he tensed again. 'Now we only need a good outcome on the lab report.'

'You're looking for trouble.' She climbed out of the spa and wrapped a towel around herself before winding her arms around Blake, holding him tight. 'I know it's difficult, but Sarah is getting better. Hold on to that.'

He brushed a kiss across her forehead. 'I'm working on it.'

He needed a distraction, and she had the perfect idea. Slipping her hand down the front of his shorts she covered his manhood and began softly rubbing up and down.

A sharp intake of breath told her this was working.

'Slow down, Georgie. I'm not doing this alone. You're joining me.' He scooped her up in his arms and headed for the bedroom.

Dinner at a French restaurant on the main street of the town was delicious. Walking back to the cottage hand in hand with Blake, Georgie couldn't imagine life getting any better. 'This is magic,' she told him. 'I can't remember ever having such a wonderful time.'

'It makes me think about what I might've been missing out on by staying away from everyone.' He squeezed her hand. 'We might've got to spend time together a lot earlier.'

She thought about that. 'I don't know. I haven't been ready to have a relationship, even a fling, since my marriage folded.'

'More hurt on top of the rest?'

There was even more he didn't know about. She spoke in a low monotone, trying to quell the sudden ache in her heart. 'I lost a baby. Tommy and I had tried for a while and just when it seemed I might never get pregnant, it happened. Then I lost it.'

Blake instantly wrapped her in his arms and held her tight. 'Oh, Georgie, that's awful. How did you cope?'

'I just got on with things,' she replied against his chest. 'And decided I won't ever go through that again.' Except it could be time to move forward, along with everything else. Easy said.'

'I can't begin to imagine what you must've gone through. It's one of my nightmares to lose someone close again, and yet you've been there, and survived.' His hug intensified. 'You never cease to amaze me with your fortitude.' His hand was stroking her hair down her back. 'I am lost for words.'

'There's nothing to say.'

Just keep holding me.

'You are so strong. So damned tough, you amaze me.' His hug tightened some more.

Pressed against him, she felt safe and cared about. She smiled softly.

And in the morning when Blake woke her before the sun had risen to suggest they go to the top of a nearby hill to acknowledge Noah's anniversary, she kissed him.

'I'll take some of those flowers that are in the vase on the table and scatter the petals over the grass.' Noah had loved the outdoors, spent a lot of time hiking in the hills and skiing the snowfields. Being on a hill this morning, watching the sun come up, was the closest she could be to him.

'He was the best friend anyone could ever wish for,' Blake said as they sat on the hilltop watching the sun make its appearance. 'I've never stopped missing him.'

Dribbling some petals from her hand, Georgie agreed. 'Me either. I'd even be happy for him to be here acting like a pain in the butt.'

Blake was quiet for a while, then, 'These past few days with you have helped me start letting go the pain and begin looking forward, to accept I can pursue my dreams of being happy and not fearing what can go wrong.'

Tears filled her eyes at his admission. Thirteen years was too long for Blake to have suffered so much. Too long for her too. They'd wasted their younger years, when they could've both been happy with partners, families, the whole works, instead of following their careers so intensely while ignoring what was required for a balanced life. 'I have too. We can't go back and retrieve what we've lost, but we can make the most of every day that's ahead.'

'You think?'

'I know.' She did, deep inside. Looking around them at the hills and the sea beyond, the township below, the flower petals on the grass beside her, Georgie felt more knots falling away. She was free to move on, to love and be happy. She didn't have to feel guilty for living, or afraid of any hurt that might come her way. She'd survived and could now move on with an open mind. Look for love. A sideways glance told her she was close to finding it with Blake. Or was she looking for something that wasn't there? That could so easily be the case. All sorts of hope and excitement had begun rushing in, filling her up with wonder. She needed to slow down. Or take things one step at a time, starting with supporting this man who'd weaved a spell around her and made her start looking at the world differently.

'I like your confidence. I'll go with one day at a time for now.'

'No problem.' She understood, and one day was better than none at all. Turning, she reached for him, slid her arms around the body she'd come to know very well in the past twenty-four hours. 'Blake, you are wonderful.'

A stunned look appeared in those grey eyes, and when he opened his mouth, she covered it with hers, not wanting to hear him say he wasn't interested in her other than as a friend who'd become a lover. They were having a fling, probably a very short one since he was returning to Auckland in a week, but she'd deal with that when he'd left town if she had to, not now out here in the fresh air with the hills around them and her heart playing a merry tune in her chest.

Blake returned her kiss with a fervour she had not known before. It was as though he'd decided, like her, to make the most of now and not waste time thinking about anything else.

That suited her perfectly. Falling backwards, she sprawled across the grass, taking Blake with her.

* * *

Eventually they had to return to reality and life on the other side of Little River, and the time came round far too quickly. Georgie sighed as she reluctantly buckled her seatbelt for the return trip. 'I've had a fantastic time, thank you, Blake.'

Blake smiled. 'Thanks, Georgie. It was good up on the hill. That was the first time I've remembered Noah on the anniversary without getting angry at the injustice of life. Instead I recalled how much zest he had for the outdoors and the way he went about making sure he was always doing something to keep fit for the hikes he did. I owe that to you.'

'To us. Getting together has been good on so many levels. Noah's only one of them.' She almost giggled. Almost, before managing to act her age. 'I haven't had so much sex in for ever. I'm going to ache from head to toes for days.'

Blake threw her a wicked grin. 'That'll look good on my résumé should I rewrite it.'

Yeah. He was happy again. Which made her even happier. 'Now what sort of job would you be applying for with those credentials?'

'Wouldn't you like to know?' He laughed, then frowned as he stared at the van in front of them. 'Whoa. Watch out.'

'What's going on? Did I miss something?'

'That van swerved halfway over the white line. The driver must've been distracted for a moment. He seems to have it under control now.'

'That's dangerous around here.' They were on a windy road heading up the side of a hill now, and there wasn't a lot of margin for error. She tried to see into the van. 'Looks like there's a few people inside. Guess they're all talking, and it would be easy to lose focus briefly.'

'Not the way to drive—' Blake swore and braked sharply. 'What the—?'

Georgie stared in horror as the van veered towards the edge. It didn't stop, went over the side. 'Stop, Blake. Pull over.'

He was already parking on the verge a few metres beyond where the van had disappeared, flicking the hazard lights on as he scrambled out of the car.

Georgie leapt out, phone in hand, ready to press 111 for the emergency services if needed. At the edge of the road she stared down at carnage, her heart sinking. The van had rolled at least once before slamming into a tree which appeared to be the only thing saving it from going all the way to the bottom some hundred metres or more below. 'I'll call this in.'

'I'm going down.' Blake was already on his way.

After talking to the ambulance service, Georgie pocketed her phone and followed him, slipping and sliding on the steep slope.

Above them she heard other vehicles stopping. 'Hey, want a hand down there?' someone yelled out.

'Don't know what to expect yet,' Blake called back.

'I've called the emergency services,' Georgie said. 'But someone might want to get onto them. They'll want updates as we have them. Tell them there are two doctors here, and we'll likely need the rescue helicopter.' The hospital was more than an hour away by road.

'Female thrown out of the van.' Blake was peering

in through a hole in the shattered windscreen. 'I can see three people inside. No, make that four. Hello? Can anyone hear me?'

'Don't you dare get inside before you've checked that the van can't move and roll down the hill,' Georgie said through gritted teeth. There was enough of a disaster here without adding to it. And the thought of Blake getting hurt was tying her stomach in knots.

'On to it.'

Georgie checked he was making sure the van was firmly wedged as she crossed to the woman lying in an awkward bundle like a rag doll on the grass. 'Hello? I'm Georgie, a doctor. Can you hear me?'

No response. Blood oozed from the woman's head, and her legs were at odd angles to the rest of her body. Georgie felt for a pulse. Throb, throb, throb. Phew. The woman wasn't out of trouble, but at least she was alive. No other major external bleeding apparent, and no sign of swelling in the abdomen area. The ribs didn't appear to have been pushed inwards. She wouldn't move the woman without fitting a neck brace in case of a spinal injury.

There was nothing on hand to use for a temporary swab for the bleeding head wound. There were tissues in the car but she wasn't about to climb back up there when this woman needed her attention. Hopefully someone else would turn up any minute who might have a supply.

Georgie couldn't do much else until help arrived, and Blake might need assistance with the people inside the mangled vehicle. Reluctant to step away from this woman, she looked around to see if anyone else had come down the hillside but no one was about. She'd pop back every few minutes to check on the woman.

At the van, she drew a breath. Blake was squeezed inside the cramped space between two women, working on one as though nothing was out of order. Her heart softened for this man she already adored. 'Need a hand? I don't want to leave the first patient for long spells. She's got a GCS of four. Stat two.' Time was critical to get her to hospital where emergency doctors with all the equipment required could save her life.

'No one quite serious in here that I can see. But I could do with a hand to triage these people to make sure, then you can get back to her.' He didn't look up. 'The woman in front of you is twelve on the scale. She's in shock but seems physically unscathed. I haven't got to the men in the back yet.'

'I wonder if the driver had a medical event,' Georgie said aloud as she pulled her shoulders together to make herself small as possible to push through the narrow gap into the interior. 'Nothing to indicate cardiac failure.'

'Stroke? Aneurism?'

'Again, nothing to suggest so, but if it was a mild stroke, it's possible. Except she's unconscious, though that could be due to impact rather than whatever caused her to drive off the road.' The doorframe was firm against her shoulders and she tried swivelling a little to get through. 'How did you get through here?'

'With difficulty.'

Looking beyond the two women, Georgie saw two men sprawled over the back seats. 'Hello, can either of you hear me?'

'I can,' one muttered. 'I'm stuck, can't get my foot out from under the seat in front of me.'

'Any other injuries?'

'Not that I can tell.'

'Right, we'll get to you shortly. What about your friend?'

'He's not saying anything, even when I shake him. There's a lot of blood.'

'Maybe lay off the shaking. We don't know what injuries he's got.' Georgie shuddered at the thought of fractures being shaken. 'I'll go back there,' she told Blake.

'No, I'll do that. You stay with these two where you can get out to go to the driver.'

He didn't want her taking a chance on being caught in the back if something went wrong and the van moved? Well, she didn't like the idea of Blake stuck back there either. But arguing only wasted precious time. These people needed their attention. 'Fine.'

Waiting while he awkwardly moved and slid through a gap by the seats and over into the back section, she focused on the woman by the door. 'I'm Georgie, a doctor. What's your name?'

'Evelyn.'

'Evelyn, can you move your legs?'

'I think so. It's going to hurt getting out through that narrow space though.'

'Hurt where?' Georgie asked.

'I don't know. My hip hurts and my neck.'

Blake looked over his shoulder. 'Whiplash is a possibility. I've checked her over and didn't find anything serious.'

Georgie focused on Evelyn. 'When they arrive we'll get the ambulance paramedics to put a neck brace on you, Evelyn. Now which hip hurts?'

'This one.' The woman tapped her right hip.

'Have you ever had problems with it before? A hip replacement? Arthritis?' The leg didn't look as though the hip had dislocated, but once Evelyn shifted that could change.

'Nothing.'

'When the van rolled do you remember any impact in that area?'

'Yes, I slammed into the side of the seat where the bar is.'

'Can you lift your leg for me?'

Evelyn did that, wincing with pain.

It probably wasn't fractured for her to be able to do that, but Georgie wasn't taking any chances. 'Right, you'll stay here until the fire service arrives.'

'No. I want out of here. It's creeping me out. What if the van moves, rolls further down the hill?'

Then we're all in trouble.

'It's firmly wrapped around the tree trunk. I don't think it's going anywhere.' Georgie mentally crossed her fingers. It had better not.

'What about Glenda? Is she going to be all right? She had a headache before we crashed.'

'She'll be the first to be taken to hospital when help arrives.'

'Want some help?' A man spoke from close by. 'I'm not a medic of any description but might be of some use.'

'Can you keep this woman company, talk to her,

hold her hand if necessary? Her name's Evelyn. She wants to get out but that's not wise until we've got the paramedics and their gear to assist. She'll be bruised and possibly has hurt her neck,' Georgie answered as she turned around with difficulty to look at the other woman lying half on, half off her seat with the safety belt digging into her chest and stomach.

'No problem. Hi, my name's Murray and we're going to get you out of this mess.' He was already reaching for the woman's hand.

'Thank you.'

The second woman groaned, and lifted an arm before dropping it again, crying out as though struck by pain.

'Hey, I'm Georgie, a doctor. You've been in an accident. Can you hear me?'

The woman's eyes blinked open, shut.

'Good, now I'm going to touch your arms and legs looking for fractures. Can you blink if it hurts anywhere?'

Again the woman managed to open her eyes briefly, and this time she gave a slight nod. 'Arms.'

'Both arms?'

Blink.

'Right. I won't touch them.' Georgie ran her hands over the woman's thighs and knees but could go no further as her seat had been shoved close to the one in front. They'd need cutting equipment to free her. 'Now, try a deep breath.'

A short gasp was all the woman could manage.

Georgie ran her hands over her chest and ribs as far as she could reach. There was a severe indent on the ribs at the left side. The woman's breathing was short but regular, suggesting her lung hadn't been punctured by a fractured rib. Stat two. Make it three with that rib issue.

A woman appeared at the door. 'I hear sirens. Can I do anything to help you? I have done first aid courses for work.'

It was hard deciding who to give her attention to, but she really needed to go check on the driver. 'I'd like you to take my place to keep an eye on this woman. She's aware of us, and answers questions by blinking. She's in lots of pain, and mustn't move at all. If anything at all changes get someone to tell me or Blake, the guy in the back. He's another doctor.'

'No problem.'

Georgie squeezed her way back out of the van and crossed to her first patient to kneel down and take her pulse. 'Hello, can you hear me?' Still no response. She lifted an eyelid, got a blank stare. The pulse rate hadn't changed.

'What can we do?' More people were making their way down the slope.

'Apart from other medical people, keep everyone up on the road. There's not a lot of flat space and we don't need it taken up by hangers-on.' Georgie was torn between remaining with this woman and getting back to the seriously injured one in the van. She looked over the woman's body, felt around her ribs and over her abdomen again and found no changes. Her breathing had become erratic, short gasps in between stillness. An aneurism was looking more and more likely. The bleeding from the head wound had slowed to a trickle. They needed splints for those legs but she'd have to be patient.

'Excuse me, when you've got a moment the other doctor wants you in the van,' someone told her.

'On my way. Can you stay with this woman, and let me know instantly if she opens her eyes or tries to move?'

Back at the van, the man who was with the woman nearest the door said, 'Evelyn says the woman on the grass is called Annie and she had a sudden massive headache just before the crash.'

'That ties in with what I'm thinking. Thanks for that.' Georgie again squeezed inside and found Blake still with the men in the back. 'What have we got there?'

'Internal bleeding caused by that seat arm that must've come free in the impact.'

'Is he still unconscious?'

'Yes, seems he hit the head rest on the seat in front as well.' Blake glanced back at her. 'I don't know how we're going to get these people out.'

'The fire brigade will have the jaws of life. Makes everything so much easier. I'm going to check this woman and get back to the driver.'

'How's she doing?'

'Looking more like an aneurism. Need that chopper here ASAP.'

'I think I can hear one,' said the man sitting with Evelyn. 'And paramedics are coming down the hill from the road.'

Relief filtered through Georgie. While she and Blake knew what they were doing, the paramedics were highly trained and did this every day. 'I'll talk to them.'

Within fifteen minutes the driver of the van had been carried on a stretcher up the hill to be loaded onto the rescue helicopter while firemen were cutting the van open so the other men and women could be retrieved. The second seriously injured woman was also put on board the chopper and then the air was flattening everything around them as the rotors began spinning.

As the helicopter lifted off the road, Blake joined Georgie. 'Let's leave the paramedics to finish up. They've got the gear and the ambulances to take everyone back to hospital. It's all under control.'

Georgie briefly leaned against Blake and drew a deep breath. 'What a mess that van ended up in. It must've been terrifying for everyone sitting inside completely helpless as it plunged off the road.'

He hugged her to him. 'Very scary. I'm glad we saw it happen or who knows how long it might've been before someone found them.'

She hadn't thought of that. A shiver tripped down her spine. 'We were joined quite quickly so someone else must've seen it. But the consequences could've been terrible for the driver. Not that she's in the clear by a long way.'

Blake hugged her tighter. 'Once a doctor, always a doctor, eh?'

'Yeah,' she sighed. 'There's no such thing as taking time out, is there?'

'You wouldn't change a thing.' Blake took her hand. 'And what's more, we did it together.'

A warm feeling spread through her. 'Yes, we did.' It was kind of lovely to think they'd done that without thought or conflict, just go on with what had to be done and accepted each other's role.

'Come on. We've got a hill to clamber up.'

Now that the victims of the accident were on their way to hospital Georgie had relaxed and her legs were like jelly. The slope in front of them seemed to grow as she stared at it. 'One step at a time.'

A bit like how she was facing her new relationship with Blake. One step—or kiss—at a time. And it couldn't be better. She hadn't felt this excited about anything in a long time. No matter how things unfolded in the future, she was making the most of today.

CHAPTER SIX

Blake sat on the back deck of his parents' home, enjoying the sun while he ate breakfast, listening to the sound of tuis and bellbirds as they flew from tree to tree and fought for their patches. As soon as he'd finished up here he'd head into the hospital to spend time with his mother. Hopefully she was feeling better today. The infection that set in on Sunday and quickly gone rampant had at last been brought under control, and leaving her even more exhausted, but it was her lethargy that had them all worrying. She seemed to have lost the fight in her. It had been a long week.

The shrill tone of his phone broke into his thoughts. 'Morning, Mum.'

'Blake,' she was almost squealing. 'I haven't got cancer. It's true. Andrew's been in and he talked to Alastair while he was here. I'm in the clear.'

'Really and truly?' Blake slumped in the chair. 'Thank goodness for that.' He rubbed his face but the tears kept spilling down his cheeks. The biggest hurdle was over. Mum was going to be all right.

'I am in the clear,' she repeated as though she didn't believe it. But then, it was a lot to absorb suddenly, after the weeks of waiting and fearing the result. 'I'm okay,' she reiterated.

Okay didn't begin to describe the rush of relief pouring through him. Everything was going to be great. 'I'll be in soon.' He leapt up and stepped off the deck, looking around the back garden where he'd done some work over the days, trying to still the many worries tumbling around his head. His mother and her health. The latest problems with the infection that had taken hold. Georgie and their fling. Georgie's ability to ground him and make him want to look forward, not back. Georgie and that hot body that had him hard in a blink. Georgie had got under his skin and he didn't know how to move on. Or if he even wanted to. How was he going to leave Christchurch after this emotional roller-coaster ride? Easy, he had to. There was a job he had to return to. A position he'd worked hard for and wouldn't give up easily.

He had to tell Georgie his mother's news. Now. She was at work, helping another woman, another family, through a medical crisis so no doubt his call would go to voice mail. Didn't matter. He had to try. Hearing her voice always set him up for the rest of the day. 'Hey, Blake. You caught me at a good time. Much needed coffee in hand. What's up?'

He didn't need coffee to set his heart rate going fast, just Georgie. 'Mum hasn't got cancer.'

'Fantastic. Wow, what a relief. You've made my day. That's brilliant. Give her a hug from me, will you?' Georgie laughed. 'I know, I'm babbling, but it's been a bit of a strain waiting. Wish I could hug *you* right now.'

Blake felt his heart give way a little more. 'Cyber hugs coming your way. Want to do dinner tonight?'

'I've got a better idea. Why don't we spend the weekend together at my house?'

'What time will you be home? I'll be waiting on the deck.'

'Thank goodness you said yes. I suddenly wondered if I was being a bit too rash.' She was laughing softly. 'This is crazy, and I'm loving it. There's a key to the back door in the garden shed, under the seedling packets.'

He laughed too. It was so easy to do with this woman. 'I'm not good enough for the front door?'

'Next week, maybe. Oh, got to go. I'm needed in ED.' She hesitated. 'Take care.' Had she been going to say something else? Something more intense? Special?

Not likely. Too soon, if at all. They'd spent every spare moment together throughout the week since Akaroa, dining, making love, talking about the past, the present and not at all about the future, and that was fine. They were having a fling, and what a fling it was. But crunch time was coming. When the infection broke out and everyone saw how debilitating it was for his mother, he knew she wouldn't be getting back on her feet for quite a while so he'd organised almost another fortnight off work to support his family and help out around the house.

He had to be back in Auckland for a board meeting by Friday week. Not attending would not be tolerated by the senior partners. By then he'll have been away nearly four weeks. He was still getting his head around that, since he didn't do staying so long with those that mattered for fear of getting so involved he couldn't walk away. At least with having his own house and the job he'd worked so hard to obtain, he knew he had to go home. He couldn't stay here any longer. Especially not so he could continue having a fling. He'd laugh if that didn't hurt. What had he done? Georgie was so special, and she'd got through his barriers so damned easily it had him wondering if he'd been trying to keep her out at all.

Slipping the phone into his back pocket, he began pulling the dead sweetcorn plants out of the ground. The plants came out easily and he put them in the compost bin before getting the fork from the garden shed to turn the soil over, picking out the weeds as he went. The rhythm of pushing the fork in, lifting it laden with soil, turning it and dropping the soil back to poke and break apart the clods quietened him. Soon memories of playing on the lawn with his sisters, kicking a football with his dad, hearing stories from his mother as she planted bulbs, came flooding back. He'd had a great childhood. Secure, loved and shown how to work for what he wanted. From things they'd said, his sisters and their husbands did the same with their kids. What was that like? By staying away, he'd missed out on many celebrations and fun times together with them all.

Glancing around the yard, he could picture himself playing with a toddler. Hell, he could see himself pushing a child on the swing that now stood in the corner. Not anyone's child but his. Laughter and shrieks of excitement would fill the air. Or a baby crying, waiting to be fed. His heart would beat hard. His heart *was* beating hard.

He stabbed the ground with the fork. There wasn't a baby or any children to interfere with any decisions he and Georgie made. Nor was there likely to be. He'd used protection every time. It was an unbreakable rule. He had never had unprotected sex. Chances were Georgie wouldn't want to risk getting pregnant either. She would not want to go through the pain of losing another baby. Or even just the worry of that happening throughout a pregnancy. The beating in his heart slowed. Damn. He should be saying thank goodness, because he'd sworn he'd never be a parent.

Stab, stab, went the fork. He had never had this conversation with himself before. There'd been no reason because he understood exactly where he stood on the subject of parenthood. It would not happen. But he had been thinking about the future and Georgie in the same sentence. It had to be because their relationship had taken off in such a hurry and he was still getting his head around it. They were happy together. It was nothing like when they'd been young and annoying the hell out of each other. This was different. Comfortable. Understanding. Caring. And he loved it. That didn't mean he loved Georgie. No, he didn't. So why this feeling that he mightn't be able to live without her? Wasn't that love? Slow down. He was getting ahead of himself. Too many emotions were ramping through him since his mother's call. Too fast, too soon.

He would be heading home to Auckland soon. That was a solid fact. No changing it.

Tonight he was going to stay with Georgie, in her space, and relax. Everything was looking up for his mum, and now he and Georgie could have some fun without having to pause and take a breath as they waited for the results that would banish the pall hanging over his family.

Georgie looked at her watch for the umpteenth time in the last hour. Four thirty-five. What was making the time drag so slowly? Apart from the fact her last patient for the day was late for her consultation, and she was sitting here twiddling her thumbs when she could be using the time to look for any incoming results on yesterday's patients' lab tests? Blake, of course. She wanted to get home and sit down with him, to chat about their days, and Sarah's wonderful news, to share some wine and make dinner.

Patients at the private and public hospitals were awaiting her visit once she'd finished here at Scott's Women's Health. It would be hours before she got home and could spend time with Blake. Hours and hours. Georgie laughed at herself. About two, maybe two and a half. Not exactly a lot. Would she be this harebrained when he returned to Auckland and she wasn't seeing him at all? Daily phone calls weren't going to cut it. They'd remind her of what she was missing out on. Making love, sharing a meal, walking along the Avon. A hundred little things that were her and Blake together. This was more than a fling. For her anyway. She'd fallen for him hard and fast, and suddenly couldn't imagine life without Blake in it every single day.

'Georgie, Sonia Davis is here to see you.' Jane, the receptionist, led a young woman into the room.

'Hello, Sonia.' Georgie held her hand out. 'I'm Georgie Price. Please, take a seat.'

'Hello, Doctor. I'm sorry I'm late but I got a flat tyre on the way.' The woman did look a little dishevelled.

'That's fine.' She closed the door behind Jane and returned to her desk. 'You've been referred by your GP as you've got endometriosis. Correct?'

'That's right. I'm ready to have a hysterectomy now that I've had my second baby.'

Where was the husband? Or partner? Georgie knew this was hard enough for any woman to be going through without having to do it on her own. 'You've had counselling for what's ahead? You and your partner?'

'We have. Dave would like to be here but he's in Dunedin for work and couldn't change his roster. Mum's looking after the kids.' Sonia looked crestfallen.

'That is a shame. However, let me examine you and then we'll go through the procedure. I'll send in a booking for Theatre and we'll have an answer by tomorrow and hopefully your family will be able to arrange things to suit so you have support at the time of your surgery.'

Relief blinked out from Sonia's face. 'Thank you so much. Dave is planning on taking leave and has warned his bosses that it could be any time in the next few weeks. I really wanted him here today to be able to ask you questions, but he couldn't avoid going south.'

'It's always better if you can bring someone with you. Two sets of ears are more reliable than one. If you have any worries after today's appointment please call the office and they'll get a message to me and I'll get back to you.' Georgie stood up. 'Right, can you sit in the gynae chair and I'll take a look?'

When Sonia left fifteen minutes later, Georgie headed out to her car to drive to the public hospital to do a round of her patients there. By the time she reached home it was nearly seven and she was humming inside and out. Blake was staying with her for the weekend. Woo hoo.

Disappointment rose fast when she realised Blake wasn't waiting on the deck for her to arrive. Nor was he inside.

Relax. He'll turn up.

He was reliable.

At least she had time to take a shower and change into something casual. Pouring a wine, she took a sip. It was a bit sour. The bottle was one she'd opened earlier in the week and it had been oaky then. She took another sip and it was fine. What was that about?

When she came out of the bathroom the smell of something delicious reached her. She grinned. Blake was here. Sauntering into the kitchen, she said, 'I hope that's dinner I can smell.'

'It'll go cold if you don't put on something more than that towel.' He reached for her. 'Though you do look wonderful.' His mouth covered hers and for a few minutes she was aware of nothing but Blake.

When they broke apart both were breathing heavily. She locked eyes on him.

And he laughed. 'To hell with dinner.'

Taking his hand, she led him down to her bedroom, letting the towel fall to the floor on the way. This was going to be the weekend of her life.

The weekend became a week, followed by the next weekend. They spent hours making love in bed, on the couch and in other places she'd never tried before. 'I'm surprised I can walk at all,' Georgie said one night as they snuck back inside from the deck. 'I think every bone in my body, every muscle, has been having a workout.' She grinned.

'Here, this'll help.' Blake handed her a frosted glass of wine.

She sipped the wine, and shuddered. 'That tastes a bit off.' Like the night Blake moved in temporarily. Since then she hadn't noticed anything different about the wine she liked but now that slightly sour taste was back. 'Maybe I'll have a sparkling water instead.'

Blake took her glass and tasted it. 'Seems all right to me.' He shrugged and headed out to the deck, her glass in his hand. 'I'll put some steaks on the barbecue.'

The deck was used for so many things these days the rest of the house apart from the bedroom and bathroom were almost obsolete. Until Blake headed back to Auckland.

She tried not to think about him leaving, but as the days sped past, it was getting harder to deny their fling was running fast towards the finish line.

Her heart slowed. Blake was going back to Auckland. Only a few days left to make the most of him. She was going to miss him so much it was hard to comprehend. Impossible to think about not seeing him regularly, to have him close by and be able to unwind with after a difficult day at work. What were they going to do? Go their separate ways with Blake visiting when he came home on those rare occasions he did come to see his parents? Or would she spend her weekends flying up to Auckland to be with him? 'Blake—' She paused.

'Yes?'

She wanted to know so much. Not now. They still

had days ahead to make love, laugh and talk, share space and time. 'Want a salad with that steak?'

'It's in the fridge.'

I love him.

The bottle of water slid from her fingers. Picking it up, she filled a glass with the bubbly water. Somehow, without any effort, she'd fallen in love with Blake Newman. Funny how she'd never thought she'd fall in love so quickly. After her first relationship fiasco, she'd always believed she'd go slowly and make sure she got everything right next time. It didn't work, hence her failed marriage. Went to show how wrong she could be. There'd been nothing slow about falling for Blake, no checking out where he stood in this. Chances were that he'd be telling her *'thanks for everything but nothing's changed, see you next time I come to town'* and then he'd walk out the door, closing it behind him.

She had to work out what to do about it. First find out where she stood with him, if he felt anything more than friendship with benefits for her, or if she was wasting her time and giving her heart a battering it certainly didn't need. But not tonight. Tonight was for enjoying. So was the weekend. Maybe on Monday she'd talk to him. Possibly on Tuesday. When had she become so gutless? That happened the moment she realised Blake meant a lot more than a friend to her, meant more than a short-term lover. Like right about now.

Not the way to go, Georgie-girl. You've got this far in life by being strong.

Strong meant hiding behind her parents, using them as her excuse to stay in Christchurch? Using Noah's death as the reason not to get close to anybody?

'You okay?' Blake's voice sounded full of concern as he stood on the other side of the counter watching her.

Wouldn't he love to know what was tearing through her mind? 'All good.'

'Really?'

'Really.' She was, if she closed down her brain and went with the flow. Opening drawers she got plates and cutlery, then salad servers to take out to the table on the deck. The table where they'd made love. How her life had changed in the past couple of weeks. For the better. 'Here, take these. I'll get the salad and dressings.'

He was still watching her far too carefully for comfort.

Brushing her lips over his chin and shivering at the hot sensations that light stubble gave her, she smiled from deep inside. 'Just daydreaming about what we've been getting up to.' Despite all the worries about what lay ahead, she was happy. They were great together in so many ways.

Instead of taking the plates and cutlery, Blake caught her chin in his palm. His forefinger caressed her mouth. 'Why daydream when we've got the real thing right here?'

'Because I'm greedy and want it all.'

His eyes widened at that. He took a step back, not breaking the eye contact.

Georgie went very still, which only underlined what she'd said, even when she hadn't meant to put it out there. Not like that. Certainly not now. 'We're getting on so well I can't imagine it coming to an end. When you're not right beside me, I bring up the images of being with you in all ways possible.'

Reaching for the plates, Blake gave her a wry smile. 'I'd better get back to the steak.'

'Blake, I'm not trying to put pressure on you. Or me for that matter. Being with you, having this fling, is so wonderful I have to pinch myself at times to make sure it's real.' She would not think how she was going to cope once Blake left. Going back to normal, spending time with friends, her parents, at home with a good book, taking walks in Hagley Park seemed dull as dull could get. Yet she'd been happy with that until Blake turned up in her life, and now the idea of returning to that was as exciting as eating porridge without cream and brown sugar.

'It's real all right.' His grin backed his words, before he headed back out to the deck where the sound of meat sizzling on the hot plate tempted her to follow.

She smiled to herself. There were still plenty of days for a lot more lovemaking.

A whole weekend with no babies due, no rostered duties, lay ahead. A weekend to spend with Blake. She was going to grab it with both hands and make the most of everything that came her way. Blake was the best thing to ever happen to her.

Friday night floated into Saturday morning and shopping at Riccarton Mall.

'Something else we have in common,' Blake grunted as he stacked bags of clothes in the back of Georgie's car.

'Come on. I only shop once a season.' There'd been a definite nip in the air when they'd managed to climb out of bed that morning. 'Autumn's just around the corner and I don't want to get caught out.'

'You mean in those two full wardrobes you've got, there aren't any clothes suitable for the next season?' Blake was laughing as he closed the door.

'We are two peas in a pod, aren't we?'

'Nothing to do with peas. But yes, I own up. I have suits from here to Africa but they're my uniform for work.'

'You wear a different one every day of the month? And change your shirts at lunch and dinnertime?' He'd just bought six shirts.

'I give away a lot to the charity shops.'

She laughed. 'That makes it all right then.' Something she could do as well. Her wardrobes were so full it was a struggle to go through and find what she wanted to wear. Clothes were her thing, though she tended to keep to understated outfits for work so didn't have a lot of fancy dresses and blouses because there weren't lots of occasions for getting dressed up. Or hadn't been until Blake turned up. And now that she'd started wearing more up-to-date clothes she wasn't going to stop when he left. Another notch in the zip had closed. She was getting her old self back, and enjoying it.

'What's next? Coffee? Lunch?'

'How about we drive over to Lyttleton for lunch. I hear there's a great bar-cum-café overlooking the harbour.'

'Can I drive?'

'Thought you didn't like having your knees up around your ears.' She tossed him the keys. It wasn't often she got to be the passenger and she liked it. As though she was being pampered somehow.

As he set the seat further back, Blake said, 'I don't understand why you've got a small car. Stylish, sure, got some power, yes, but there's no space.'

'It's economic, gets into most parking spaces and goes like a racing car when I want it to.' Fast driving wasn't her thing, but sometimes it felt good to go as fast as was legal on the motorway.

'I'm just about sitting on the back seat,' he said with a laugh.

'Get a move on or the bar will be closed by the time we arrive.'

'Yes, ma'am.'

Saturday ended with lovemaking in the shower and mugs of tea in bed afterwards. 'Like two oldies,' Blake joked as he drank from his mug.

'Nice and snug,' Georgie agreed.

Sunday was more of the same, and then Georgie went back to work on Monday feeling like a teen on a high. Or what she thought that might feel like. Blake was wonderful, everything she'd dreamed of a man being, back in the days when she used to dream about those things. Yes, when she'd been young and carefree.

Slamming her car door shut, she did a little dance on the spot, then looked around to make sure no one had seen her. Carefree. That was the word for how she felt. Not a worry in the world. Except that wasn't true. She was playing the avoidance game very well, if she believed that. Blake was leaving. Soon he'd be gone. Not out of her life for ever. That wasn't possible after this fling. They were making memories as vivid and sharp as any she'd known. But memories weren't going to be enough. She wanted the real deal—for ever.

They needed to talk. To let each other know what they were really feeling and thinking, regardless of how scary it might be to open up. Most of all, Georgie sighed, they needed time and it was running out.

Time was something she'd had a lot of over the years since her marriage failed. She'd filled it hiding from the past, and denying the future could be exciting and loving and, well, full of all the things she'd like to be happy. Now the need to get cracking with living at the top of the rainbow, enjoying everything that came her way, making the most of opportunities that presented, of loving with her whole heart, was taking over. All of that had to include Blake. So she had to talk to him. Before he left tomorrow. He'd had to bring his flight forward because of a board meeting he was obliged to attend. Which underlined the problems that lay ahead.

She strode inside Scott's Women's Health clinic and picked up the pile of notes in her file basket. 'Morning, everyone.'

'Hi, Georgie. You look like you've had a great weekend,' Jane said.

'I did. A fantastic one.'

'New blouse and skirt?'

'Yes. You like?'

'I do. Andrew wants to see you.'

She wondered what he wanted. 'On my way.'

Her phone vibrated. Blake.

Have a great day. xxx

You too. xxxx

I'm cooking tonight. xxxxx

Smiling, Georgie headed for the office next to hers. 'Morning, Andrew.'

'You're looking perky this morning,' Andrew said as he got up and went to close the door.

This had to be serious then. He was one of the senior partners in the practice so he had her full attention. She sat in the chair he indicated, and waited.

As he crossed to sit down on the nearest chair, he smoothed his trousers and pulled his shoulders back. Definitely a serious meeting. A bolt of concern hit her. Had she made an error with a patient? But surely she'd be the first to know? She thought back over the past weeks. But nothing raised any flags. So what else? It had to be important if that board-meeting look on Andrew's face was anything to go by. Her palms moistened, while her mouth dried.

'What's up?' The question came out too sharp, but she couldn't take it back.

'Relax, Georgie. Everything's fine.' Then why did he sound as though he was about to deliver a grenade with the pin already pulled?

'I hope so.' Ouch. That sounded weak, something she wasn't around here. Or never showed anyway, not even to this man, who'd been behind her all the way since she'd first started training to become a gynaecologist and obstetrician under his tutelage. But he'd known her weaknesses, especially how she had to succeed no matter what. He'd even tried to tell her to take time out, become more rounded as a person, not so focused on her career, or she might burn out one day. So far he'd got that wrong.

'Right, let me put this out there. Tom has decided to start his retirement next month.' Andrew paused. 'And you are top of the list to replace him as a senior partner.'

What? 'Really?' This was a dream come true. From the moment she'd started working here she'd been dreaming of a senior partnership. The first step as a junior had been wonderful, but this was over the top exciting.

'Yes, really.' Andrew smiled. 'We had a breakfast meeting earlier this morning and everyone's in agreement. You are ideal for the position.'

Deep breath. Give the man an answer. She didn't have to waste time thinking about it. 'Thank you so much. It's unbelievable, really.'

Andrew came around his desk and held out his hand to shake hers. 'Congratulations. You deserve it.'

Shaking his hand, she knew she was grinning stupidly, but hey, she'd been aiming for this for so long. 'Thank you so much.' How exciting. Blake. She couldn't wait to tell him. He'd be thrilled for her. Wouldn't he?

I want this. More than anything.

A knot formed in her stomach. Now that she'd had a glimpse of what she could have with Blake if only she could let go of the stranglehold on her emotions, was it still the most important thing in her life right now? Hell, yes.

She went back to her office in a daze, her feet almost skipping. Senior partner. Woo hoo. How cool was that?

She wrapped her arms around herself, grinning. Senior partnership. She had to tell someone. Blake. She picked up the phone.

'Hey, have I got some news. I've been offered a senior partnership.'

'That's awesome. Georgie, I'm so proud of you,' he said. 'Seriously proud. You must be stoked.'

'I keep pinching myself. It's still sinking in. Definitely have to celebrate tonight.'

'I reckon. I'm buying the champagne.'

There was a knock, and the receptionist put her head around the door.

'I've got to go. Talk later.' And share some delicious kisses.

CHAPTER SEVEN

LATE THAT AFTERNOON Blake stood on the back porch of his parents' nineteen-twenties house and watched his nieces and nephews running around like crazed monkeys.

So Georgie had been offered a senior partnership. Good for her. She deserved it. And did she sound thrilled, or what? Something he understood. The day he'd been offered his position at the orthopaedic practice he'd been ecstatic. He'd be even more so if, no, when, he was offered a senior partnership. It was the penultimate position in their careers. Georgie had now achieved it. This definitely called for a celebration tonight.

'Aren't those rascals cute?' his mother said from her seat beside him. She still looked tired but since coming home she'd begun to get some colour back in her complexion and be able to move around comfortably.

'They won't be when they finally crash. Bedlam will rule.' There was a smile in his heart for the little guys. Something about them got to him without any thought or care. He loved them, end of. It had been great catching up with his sisters and their families. Every hour was indelibly etched in his heart, ready to be taken back to Auckland when he headed away tomorrow. 'I don't get to see them often enough.' The moment the words left his mouth he knew he'd made a mistake.

Sure enough, his mother picked up on it straight away. 'You can always move back here.'

But was he ready to up stakes and shift his whole life back here? Tomorrow he'd go back to his real life: sterile, quiet and work filled. Yet Georgie was squeezing his heart. Her smiles, her understanding, her love-making. Damn it, everything about her had touched him beyond measure. What had started out as a fling which was meant to help put the past well and truly behind both of them had become something far more serious and brought the future into focus.

He had to face up to the fact he might be falling for Georgie whether he wanted to or not, in a way he hadn't done before with any woman. Other women had been easy to keep at the friends with benefits level. Georgie was not.

Then there was today's news. She'd been given an offer she wouldn't hesitate to accept. He couldn't blame her for that. So relinquishing the partnership she was so proud of was not going to happen. He couldn't ask that of her. That'd be beyond selfish. So back to square one. He lived in Auckland, she was staying in Christchurch. If anyone made the move, it had to be him, and he wasn't sure he could manage that. What if he came down here and they couldn't make it work? Whichever way, one of them would have to make huge sacrifices if they were to get together.

Blake swore under his breath. New Zealand wasn't exactly a big country. It took less than an hour and a half to fly between the two cities. They could be in either place for any party, dinner or family get-together with little trouble. It wasn't as though they'd be living on the opposite side of the world from the people who mattered the most to either of them. They could see how it went before making those changes required if they lived together. Except that was hardly a full-on commitment, and he'd want that if he was going to step up. So would Georgie. What's more, she deserved no less.

What did Georgie think about this? Would she say, *'Hey, it's been a great few days, but it's over and now we get back to normal'*? Remind him he hadn't been in a hurry for more than a fling? Somehow he doubted it. She'd said how being together had made her feel so happy and at ease over a relationship for the first time in years. He wanted to share that with her, help dispel any fear she had going forward. Commitment meant opening up to anything and everything.

Something he understood all too well, and had been avoiding for too long. Now, with Georgie, he felt he could put all that out there and not have to feel exposed. She wouldn't take advantage of his pain. Pain which was getting smaller the more time he spent with Georgie. They understood each other, knew what the other had been through. He was ready to move on for the first time since the night Noah died. Almost ready. All because she got him.

But did that mean they were together about everything? Nothing got any easier. Of course he could be looking for trouble when the answers might be straight-forward.

He sent her a message. Another new habit, this keeping touch over trivia.

What time do you think you'll get away? Was looking forward to an evening together?

Blake smiled to himself. Of course not, but down-playing it was his way of dealing with emotions.

Any time soon.

Blake popped the cork and poured two glasses of cham-pagne. Handing one to Georgie, he leaned in to kiss her. 'To you, you amazing woman. Congratulations on your promotion.'

She tapped their glasses together, her eyes shining with glee. 'It's pretty exciting.' She took a small sip, and leaned her hip against the counter, one foot tap-ping nonstop on the tiles. 'Actually, it's so unbelievable I have to keep pinching myself.'

'You're looking more like the Georgie I used to know. Can't keep your feet still or the smile from your face.' Next she'd be dancing around the room.

She moved and a big kiss landed on his cheek. 'Since you came to town my life has been changing in all di-rections.' Laughter burst from her as she locked those sparkling blue eyes on him. 'The most wonderful fling with a man I can't believe understands me better than

I do myself sometimes. And he's so sexy as well. Then today's bombshell.' She grinned and swallowed some of her wine. 'Cheers to us.'

Tapping his glass against hers again, he took a mouthful. 'Cheers.' To them. To them and whatever lay ahead.

She drew a breath, and said in a quieter voice, 'Blake, these weeks have been the best of my life. The very best.'

'Culminating in this news,' he said quietly. It was epic, and yet it had raised questions about what they were going to do after he left Christchurch. He didn't want to finish what they had going, but even he understood it couldn't continue. It was the line between two futures and he wasn't sure he could give up everything to take a risk on his heart, and Georgie's.

'You go home tomorrow, back to your career. I've stepped up a rung with mine. I can't see how we can continue a fling and be happy about it. Tripping up and down the country for a night or two together?' She shook her head. 'I don't think I can do that. I'm an all or nothing kind of woman. Mostly nothing.'

Did she mutter, 'Until now'? His heart sank. He couldn't imagine not being a part of her life. So he was prepared to drop everything and move back here? His throat closed. Just like that? Give up everything he'd worked so hard for? Why not? Because he was afraid. Because he didn't trust himself to be able to let go the past completely. Clearing his throat, he said, 'Georgie, I worry that if we were to take this further the past might get in the way and ruin everything.'

'So am I,' she whispered. 'I want to think I can handle whatever happens between us, can take the knocks. I want more, yet I can't ask you to give up what's important to you.'

'Georgie—' He needed time to think this through. She was everything to him—if he had the guts to step up and put his hand out. But could he do that and not look back in a few months' time and think he'd made a mistake? He was in love with Georgie, but did he *love* her? As in every way possible? Risk his heart? She'd look after it. But caution was such a habit. He didn't know what he wanted. Or wasn't ready to accept. Be honest. It was the only way to go. Placing a hand on her cheek, he said softly, 'I don't think either of us is ready for more than what we've had. We need time to be certain about the next step.'

The colour leeched out of her cheeks, and she straightened up. 'Sure you're not running away again?' When she wanted to hurt, seemed she went for the jugular.

Pain struck him in the chest hard. He was in love with this woman. Probably did *love* her. Yes, he was ready to admit that much.

So tell her and get down on your damned knees and beg her forgiveness, tell her how you feel and what you hope will unfold between you.

She sank onto a stool and took a big mouthful of wine. 'I'm sorry. I was out of order, saying that. You're right, we'd both have some major decisions to make.'

'We do.' Could be he *was* running away *again*. He was afraid to step up and take whatever hit him on the chin. Afraid to take a chance on not being hurt, of losing one of the people he gave his heart to. Suddenly

Auckland seemed safe. A lot safer than remaining here and committing to Georgie. Better to let her down now than hurt her badly further down the track if their relationship didn't work out. A resounding 'no' slammed through his mind. No. He was not running away. He had to put Georgie before his own needs. But how when his heart was involved?

'I don't want to continue with our fling, only to have it dwindle away to nothing. I say it's over.' Georgie's fingers were rubbing her thighs hard. Her smile was wobbly, but her eyes were full of what looked like love to him.

His ribs were aching from the thumping they were getting. This was really it? He didn't want that, nor was he ready to leap in and say he loved her, only to realise he'd got it wrong and hurt her. 'Catching up with you hasn't been what I'd ever have imagined, but I've no regrets whatsoever.' Another squeeze to his heart. Really? When she was his moon and his sun? How was he going to leave her behind tomorrow? He had to. He could not hurt her any more. Going home would give him the space to really take a long hard look at himself, and what he was going to do.

'Honest to the core. But I wouldn't like it any other way.' She straightened. 'It's been one heck of a day, and I'm shattered. Think I'll make a mug of tea and curl up in bed.'

The other night they'd sat up together in her bed, drinking tea and laughing over how they were like a couple of oldies. Now they were on a knife edge, their futures hanging in the balance.

He itched to reach for her, to haul her into his arms

for one last time, but that would add to the pain bubbling up through his chest, spreading throughout his soul. 'I'm going to miss you when I go home tomorrow.' He couldn't begin to imagine not being beside her, shoulder to shoulder, thigh to thigh, as he went to sleep, or hand in hand as they walked along the riverbank, or— Stop. This wasn't doing any good for either of them.

She pulled away. 'Goodnight, Blake.' She turned and walked out of the room.

Out of his life for ever? No. He couldn't handle that. He loved her. 'Georgie,' he called.

She didn't hesitate, or look back, just continued down the hall to her bedroom.

And with every step she took, his heart cracked a little bit more. He loved her.

So go after her, pledge your heart to her and say you'll do whatever is necessary to keep her happy.

Was he absolutely certain of that? To love Georgie meant everything about him was committed to her. To do whatever it took to keep her happy and safe. And if they got it wrong? She'd said she hadn't loved her husband enough. What if the same happened with him? Or he found he couldn't let go the past enough to be able to be at her side throughout the journey of their lives? His heart dropped to his feet. So much to lose. For both of them.

'Goodnight, Georgie,' he whispered as he let himself out of the house.

His heart was heavy, his head aching. What if something bad happened? Not Georgie falling out of love with him—if she ever fell in love with him—but an accident or illness taking her away from him? What if it happened to him and she was on her own again? Could he live with that? He'd let so many people down when Noah died. By letting the guilt and fear wreck his life he'd hurt his family. He could not do that to Georgie.

He needed time out. Time on his own to do some serious thinking. That's how he operated best. Alone with nobody to intrude upon his thoughts. It was when he was most honest with himself. He'd just spent nearly four weeks surrounded by Georgie and his family. He hadn't been that amongst people for a long time. He needed space. Alone time.

But first he had a board meeting tomorrow that he'd given his word he'd attend.

Then he'd work out what he was going to do. Though he was already halfway there. Leaving Georgie, hearing her front door click shut behind him, had hit him in the heart. There were major things to sort out before he could lay his heart on the line because, when he did, it had to be without any problems hanging over him.

The week was endless. Every night after work, Georgie mowed lawns, weeded the garden, cleaned the house and thought about Blake nonstop. Most mornings she arrived at the hospital far too early and filled in an hour before her first patient arrived for surgery drinking copious quantities of tea and wondering how she was going to get through the coming weeks.

Blake either loved her or he didn't. Seemed to her, he didn't. He hadn't got in contact, but neither had she called him, hoping that by giving him space that would work in her favour. He'd said he'd miss her. Big deal. She was missing him as she would an amputated leg.

So the fling was over. Finished. As flings tended to do. But she'd fallen in love with him. So much for avoiding getting hurt again. This time seemed worse than the others. Far worse. Blake felt like her other half, the man to go through the rest of life with. To raise children with. To just be plain old happy with. It wasn't happening.

On Thursday morning Jane put her head around her office door. 'Megan Roper's at the desk. She had some bleeding overnight and is a bit frantic.'

Megan had had her third artificial insemination eight weeks ago, and had been on tenterhooks ever since. 'I'll see her straight away. And can you get me a mug of tea? I ran out of time this morning.'

'No problem. You sure you don't mean coffee though?'

Georgie shuddered at the thought. Which was bizarre. She loved coffee. 'Tea for a change.'

'Want a sandwich too? I'm presuming you didn't have time for anything to eat either.'

'Sounds good, thanks.' Blake had made toast for them both, but she'd left hers on the plate. She'd better not be coming down with a stomach bug. Not while Blake was still here. That time was for him, not lying in bed feeling unwell.

'Dr Price, I'm sorry to barge in without an appointment, but I can't lose another baby.' Megan stood in the doorway, pale and trembling. 'I can't.'

'You know I'm here whenever you need me. Come in and close the door, then tell me what's been going on.'

Georgie sat in her office and stared at her phone. Her hand rubbed her stomach lightly. As it had been doing often since Megan Roper left here that morning. The younger woman had been panicking over losing her baby, a fear Georgie recalled all too clearly. The sheer panic that disabled clear thinking, followed by the anguish and sense of failure, and then the grief. Hard, fast and debilitating, the grief was the worst.

Thankfully she'd been able to reassure Megan she wasn't miscarrying. The spotting was normal, but as the woman had already lost two babies through miscarriage she wasn't entirely convinced. Georgie could only offer time on that.

Time mightn't be on Georgie's side though. Not if her suspicions were right. How could they be when they had used condoms every single time they made love? Her stomach was tight, as were her chest and neck. She was making this up because it fit nicely into the picture of her and Blake and family. A picture he did not want. He'd been adamant about not being a father. He might've got close to her but children were still not on his radar. He hadn't said so after that one time, but he didn't need to. She had got the message loud and clear. She'd also felt he didn't love her. But hell, she loved him, and she would love their baby as she'd never loved before. She'd be devoted to him or her. Completely and utterly.

Now she was waiting for another message—from the lab this time. It had been a lightning bolt moment. Megan was leaving the office and the receptionist was walking towards Georgie with the sandwiches she'd offered to get for her, and she'd thought, 'That's why I couldn't face breakfast most mornings. I'm pregnant.'

It would also explain why the wine had suddenly tasted sour the other night.

If she was pregnant it was very early for this to be happening, but she knew from her patients that what the books on pregnancy symptoms and timing spouted all went out the door more often than not. Last time she fell pregnant she hadn't been aware of it until she'd missed a second period, and even then she'd been dubious, thinking it couldn't happen when she and Tommy hadn't decided on being parents quite so soon. But the moment she'd seen the thin blue line on the stick she'd been in raptures, thinking that at last her life was getting back on its feet. Not a good idea to be remembering that. Take this one moment at a time. A result first.

She stared at the phone. It was silent. Far too silent.

She should call Blake. He'd support her as she waited. Her hand shook as she reached for her personal phone. Stop. That was the last thing she should be doing. If Blake knew, he'd be hoping for a negative result. While she— Did she want a baby? She'd always hoped that one day she'd have moved on and be able to try again, but that meant being in a relationship with someone. That someone now had a name, a loving face, a mind she adored. Blake. Now it was too late to be wondering if she wanted a baby. She either was or wasn't, and if she was, then yes, it would be wonderful and she'd love him or her to bits. To hell with everything else. She was over holding back on loving.

Leaning back in her chair, she stared out the window at the newly weeded gardens. Until she heard from the lab she wasn't going anywhere.

The phone vibrated.

Snatching it up, she stared at the screen.

The message read: Georgina Price HCG 45mIU/ml.

She was pregnant. She and Blake were going to be parents. It was too much. She needed to talk to somebody, and the only person she wanted was Blake. Nor could it be anyone else. It wasn't as though she could mention the pregnancy to someone before he knew. How was he going to take the news when it was the last thing he ever wanted?

He needed to know.

She had to tell him. But this wasn't something to do over the phone. She had to be there, see his reactions, know what he was thinking. That meant flying to Auckland and knocking on his door to tip his world upside down. At least she could hold his hand while she did that.

She stared at the result on the screen. A storm of emotion poured through her. She was pregnant. A baby to love. Someone to give her heart to without any restrictions. Tears streamed down her cheeks. This had to be one of the best days of her life. If only Blake was here to share in the news, to enjoy it as much as she was.

She had to share the news, no matter how he took it. No matter that she wasn't in front of him. She knew his voice, his nuances, she'd know how he felt. Her thumb banged the phone, brought up Blake's number, pushed Dial.

His voice mail answered. He must be having a busy day at work.

She hit Stop. No way was she giving Blake this news in a message. This had to be dealt with face to face. She'd fly up on Saturday after her rounds in the morning.

Once at home, Georgie made a ham sandwich, pulled out her laptop and typed in 'gynaecologist positions in Auckland,' then held her breath as the screen filled up with headings leading to advertisements for jobs. It looked promising until she began going through them and found there were very few opportunities in the big city.

Relief had her clicking out of the screen. She really didn't want to go there. It would be hard to start at the bottom of the ladder again. But if Blake didn't want to move back here, then she'd consider it for their child's sake, at least.

If she carried it to full term. A chill settled over her, as it did at least once a day as memories of her miscarriage rose. They rattled her like nothing else could. She wanted this baby. Loved it already. If she lost it, she had no idea how she'd get beyond that.

Blake, I love you. All of you. The best bits, and the not so great ones, like when you hog all the sheets or leave your dirty coffee mug on the table when you leave the house.

If only she'd told him that before she walked away, leaving him standing in her kitchen looking bewildered that last night. He'd have laughed.

Now Georgie laughed for the first time in days. He did that to her when she wasn't being all uptight about what they were going to do.

Blake, I'm coming up to see you on Saturday, and you'd better be prepared for life-changing news.

On Friday afternoon, Georgie helped deliver twins, but they didn't lift her spirits as they normally would've.

All she felt was sadness at what she and Blake were missing out on. Especially Blake. She was pregnant and he wasn't here. Not that she looked any different yet. And it was too early for baby to kick. But she was carrying his child, and she was certain he'd want to be a part of its life, even when he'd sworn he'd never be a father. Hopefully he'd want to be a part of hers too. She headed outside to go home and pack her overnight bag.

Outside in the carpark, her phone rang.

Blake.

Her heart jerked. 'Hi.' Where had all the things she wanted to tell him gone? Her mouth was dry as a desert and her tongue too big for her mouth. 'Blake?' she squeaked.

'Georgie, sorry I haven't called earlier. It's been hectic up here and I've had little time to spare.'

'I did wonder if you'd gone silent on me. But it's all right. I don't want to lose touch.'

That's everything.

She could try begging him to give their relationship a chance, but she didn't do begging. Never had and wasn't about to start.

'We're not going to.' He sounded fierce, like it was the most important thing for him.

'Good.' Because she was going up to see him tomorrow. 'Are you busy over the weekend?' Should she share her news now? Then when she got to Auckland he'd have had time to absorb all the implications?

'Yes, I am. Oh, damn, sorry, Georgie. I've got to go. Take care. Talk again soon.'

The call ended.

'What? Hello, Blake. Don't call me only to hang up

suddenly. Talk again soon. Not if I see you coming.' Her patience evaporated in an instant, if it had been there in the first place. Punching Blake's number again, she got the bland voice saying to leave a message. She snapped, 'Don't shut me out, Blake. I deserve better than that. So do you.' Her hand holding the phone lifted above her shoulder, aimed at the furthest wall. Two deep breaths and she lowered it. 'Damn you. Blake Newman. I love you, and that has to be good for both of us.'

Moving to Auckland might not be an option after all if Blake wasn't going to be available some of the time. She'd be alone, new job, new house, new baby. She shook her head. He said he was busy. On a late Friday afternoon? Well, it did happen. She knew that, but why phone when there was every chance he'd be called away? Was she being fair? He didn't know she was pregnant. Not yet. Tomorrow he might have a different opinion about everything.

She'd become entrenched in Christchurch. Most of her history was here. There'd been a time when she planned on moving away, and then she'd used her family as an excuse to cancel that dream, and had continued to do so whenever anything risky came into her life. A picture came to mind of her mother's excitement about the enormous campervan they bought a few months ago. She'd been thrilled to think they'd be able to go on holidays up and down the country without having to plan ahead. They hadn't gone far afield yet, and only for a couple of nights as they both had to go to work. But retirement loomed for both of them once summer was out, and they were adamant they'd hit the road then. Go north for a warm winter, take in the sights and enjoy the various golf courses on the way. No, they didn't need her hanging around, being at their beck and call. They had moved on, and were enjoying everything that came their way.

Not like her. She loved her work, and had believed she wouldn't change it for anything. But now there was a hollow inside her that was waiting to be filled with love and laughter, with a partner and children. She had moved beyond the fear of being crushed again by losing someone she loved, and had immediately fallen in love with the man who'd helped do that. So shouldn't she be helping Blake move beyond his demons too? Here, or in Auckland, it didn't really matter where as long as they were together. If he wanted to be with her, that was. And wanted to be a father to their baby.

Blake dropped into his allocated seat, buckled his seat-belt and stared out at the runway. Georgie had left a message on his phone. She was spitting mad and he didn't blame her, but he'd thought he'd have a few minutes to talk to her before the taxi reached the terminal. Now he'd have to placate her when he arrived at her house. Hopefully she'd give him a few minutes of her time so he could explain what he'd been doing since he'd left her last week.

Work had been hectic which usually made him grateful for keeping the gremlins at bay, but there'd been so many other things needing his attention he'd been frustrated all week. Odd how he hadn't felt comfortable in his house since he'd returned from Christchurch and left Georgie behind. It felt large and gloomy, lonely with no laughter to tighten his groin and soften his heart.

These past days the stream of patients and surgeries had only frustrated him further and had him realising he didn't really want to stay in Auckland following his dream career if it meant not being a part of Georgie's life. He was still afraid of what could go wrong and the pain that would inflict on both of them, but especially he didn't want her hurt. He was ready to step up and take the chance with Georgie. Otherwise what was he doing with his life? Why bother with his career if he couldn't share the highs and low with her? Why get the house looking wonderful and all comfortable if he only used the kitchen, bathroom, lounge and one bedroom? It sounded hollow after the nights he'd spent in Georgie's.

Hell, nothing had been the same since the moment Georgie walked into the clinic where his mother was seeing her specialist. From that moment on he'd been fighting a losing battle to keep his heart safe. Not that he'd tried too hard, had given in to the need she cranked up in him with little more than a glance. And when that glance came with a gut-clenching smile, then he was a goner in all ways imaginable.

He loved her. He wasn't in love with her. He loved her outright. No ifs, buts or maybes.

So what was he going to do about it?

First, he was walking away from his partnership.

He was going to be happy for the first time in years. Make that, continue to be happy as he had been with Georgie.

Become a regular part of his family again.

Add to that family by marrying Georgie, if she'd have him.

Then there was the big one that still made him suck a

breath whenever he thought about it. He wanted to have a child with her. Maybe not quite yet. Too soon. They could enjoy getting to know each other even better.

Georgie or Auckland? He'd made the decision. Simple as that. He would not ask her to move up here when she was settled where she was. Far more settled than he was, really.

The fact was he struggled to get through every day without her. The decision had been made weeks ago without him realising, and not seeing her, or holding her, was driving him crazy. Love was a damned thing. It grabbed your heart and sure as hell had no intention of letting go.

He leaned back and closed his eyes and waited for the plane to depart Auckland.

A little over an hour later Blake stared down through the small window as Christchurch City came into view. Home. The place he'd been born and raised, had gone to school and met the best mate any guy could ever hope for. The city had expanded and altered in the years he'd been away and it felt a bit like how he was feeling about himself really. Old but new. Strong but desperate to make a change. To start over. The hang-ups from the past had gone, and he could move forward with a lightness in his heart he hadn't known for a long time, if ever.

All because of Georgie. Who'd have believed it? He would've, if he'd ever stopped to think about it. About her. It was as easy as downing a glass of water to recall how his blood used to heat at the sight of her when he was a teen. Back then he had known instinctively he didn't have a chance of getting close to her. She was his best mate's sister. She was also a few years older and wouldn't have seen him as anything but the teenager he was. He'd known to keep his thoughts to himself. As he'd got on with living and studying and becoming an adult he'd somehow managed to put those feelings aside to the point he believed he had forgotten about Georgie as anyone more than Noah's sister, someone to ask for information about aspects of campus once he'd started his university degree.

Had he ever really got over those feelings for her? Or had he buried them along with all the other emotions that took over when Noah died? More than likely that was the truth of it. Otherwise why had he reacted so positively to Georgie so fast? It had been as though his body had been waiting for her to reappear in his life. Come on. Body? It was his heart mostly affected here. His heart had never been so involved with another person.

Which had nothing to do with Georgie and how he felt about her. Or did it? His heart was so tied to her he couldn't imagine life without her at his side, pushing him to be the best he could at anything he attempted. She wouldn't let him down, wouldn't say he wasn't good enough for her—because he'd make damned sure he was.

You left her behind in Christchurch. Walked away as if there could be no future with her.

Yes, he had, because he had to be absolutely certain he was doing the right thing by both of them. It hadn't taken long to know he couldn't live without Georgie. Now he was heading back, hoping to convince her he loved her and wanted to spend the rest of his life with her. Now he understood that life did crush people, hurt them beyond measure sometimes, and when that happened he'd be there for Georgie no matter what. She was special, deserved love and kindness and caring, and not being let down. And she'd made him whole again. Hopefully he could do the same for her.

She was his heart.

Blake checked his safety belt was buckled, and leaned back in the upright seat, closing his eyes to breathe deep as he waited for the plane to touch down.

Damn, how he'd missed Georgie's smile. Her beautiful face. That long, silky hair that slipped through his fingers. He missed the softening in his heart whenever she was near, or right up close, pressing that divine body into his. But most of all, he'd missed that smile. It got to him every single time she wore it.

Less than four weeks was all it had taken to tip his world upside down. Nearly four weeks of sun-kissed days and nights. Georgie-kissed hours of pleasure and excitement. Days of talking, sharing points of view on politics and medicine, disagreeing on car models and fishing. Ordinary days that were filled with love, and amazement that he could have so much fun with one person.

Ka-thump. The plane was on the ground.

He'd come home. Now all he had to do was convince Georgie to give him a chance. He loved her. Did she love him? There'd been something like love in her eyes when they'd been calling it quits on their fling. She wanted all or nothing. Well, he was about to offer her everything.

* * *

A car door slammed, making Georgie sit back in her seat on the deck and look towards the drive. Who'd come to visit? Her parents were still away, and her girlfriend was on duty in the ER.

The hairs on her arms began to rise. Could it be? No, it couldn't. He hadn't returned her calls, apart from that one abrupt time. Settle down, heart. He wasn't coming back.

Blake came around the corner of the house and into her befuddled view.

Blake. What was he doing here? Her mouth dried as the blood in her veins drained into a pool somewhere low in her body. Her hand spread across her still flat stomach. 'Blake.' He was stunning. So good-looking her skin heated. But then she was biased. Her dream come true stood before her, holding out his hands to her, while she was kneeling down here like a stuffed toy, unable to move for fear she'd wake from the dream to find nothing but chilly autumn air in front of her.

'Hello, Georgie.' He stepped closer and reached for her hands, tugged her gently to her feet. 'Thought I'd pay you a visit. Without warning,' he added around a hopeful smile. 'I didn't want to be turned away.'

Just as well he was holding her or she'd be in a heap in the vegetable patch. 'I'd never turn you away. You have no idea how I feel seeing you standing there. Oh, my message on your phone. Sorry, I was peeved you couldn't talk for longer. Now, I'm over that. You're not getting away for at least the next hour.' Her smile felt crooked and there might be a smattering of tears in her eyes, but her back was ramrod straight, and her chin had a determined angle to it. He had come back. Why? For how long?

'I've missed you.' He stepped up to her and put his arms around her, and rubbed his chin over the top of her head. 'I've missed you so much it hurts.'

She pulled away. 'Slow down, Blake. I want to know what this is about.'

Tipping his head back so he could lock that steady grey gaze on her, he said clearly, 'I've come home, Georgie. To you. And yes, to my family also. But most of all to you. I know I've been aloof at times, but it has been hard to accept I can change, can move on, and I owe you for that.'

Her mouth fell open. It was what she'd been hoping for, but not expecting to happen. Not for a long while anyway. 'You're serious?' she whispered.

He dipped his head. 'I couldn't be more so. I haven't come for a one-night party. I've come for the whole deal. I love you. To the moon and back. Everything about you. I love you, Georgie.'

Her heart soared. Blake was serious about this. About him and them. As serious as she was. 'Blake, I love you too. I nearly told you the other night, but I got cold feet, thinking you'd run.'

'Which I sort of did.' His arms tightened around her. 'When I said I'd been busy, it wasn't only work keeping me on my feet. I've given up my partnership and have put the house on the market. I mean it when I say I'm coming home. Even more serious about loving you.' His mouth found hers. His kiss sent a thrill down her back, and into her heart, touched her toes and a lot of places in between.

Blake had come back for her, to be with her. Georgie pulled back. There was more news to share. It could be a deal-breaker, but from that genuine look of love in his eyes she was starting to doubt that. He looked so happy, as happy as she felt.

'I'd crawl to the other side of the world and back if it'd make you happy.' He was smiling. He meant what he said.

'You don't have to go that far.' Warmth stole through her, around their baby he knew nothing about. 'Come inside.'

He followed her in and closed the door behind them. 'I've missed this place, being here with you. I have finally found what I didn't know I was looking for.'

She pinched herself, then him. 'When do you finish at the practice?' she asked to give herself a moment to get her thoughts together. This news could be a deal-breaker.

'I've got to work for another two months and then I start down here at Orthopaedics United. The two months give the partners time to find a suitable replacement. And me time to pack up, and make plans down here, hopefully with you.'

Okay, here we go.

'Blake, before we go any further, there's something you need to know.' Deep inhale. 'I'm pregnant.'

He looked as though someone was shining a headlight into his face. Good? Or bad? 'You're what?'

'Having our baby.' She picked up her phone and

scrolled through the messages until the lab report popped up. 'I had the test done last week.'

His eyes dropped to the screen, but he didn't take the phone from her. He blinked, stared some more, a smile creeping across his face, lightening his eyes. 'You *are* pregnant.'

This had to be good. Surprisingly good.

'Wow. I mean, who'd have thought when we were so careful. Blimey.' He was still staring at the screen. 'We're having a baby,' he shouted. Then he picked her up in his arms and swung her around. 'This is getting better and better by the minute. This is the best news after hearing you love me. I thought we might try, just not so soon.'

'No trying needed.' Laughter fought with relief bubbling throughout her body as the last drop of tension left her. Blake was okay with the pregnancy, more than okay. He was as thrilled as she was. 'I can't wait to meet him or her.'

He was grinning at her. 'I'm stunned, but I'm also excited. I can't believe how happy your news makes me. I came here to tell you I love you, and to ask you to marry me, and now this. I did say I couldn't cope with the idea of children, but neither would I have believed a few weeks ago that I'd fall in love with you and want the whole picture.' He was pulling her up against him, placing kisses on her cheeks, her throat, her mouth.

This was what she'd missed so much. She kissed back with all the love in her heart.

His mouth lifted from hers just enough for him to say, 'I love you, Georgie.' Then he went back to kissing her. He was serious about being with her. Really serious. She threw her arms around his neck and held him tight. Made her kisses longer, deeper, and felt as though she was the one who'd finally come home.

Suddenly he pulled back, still holding her but looking into her eyes. 'I meant what I said. Will you marry me, Georgie Price?'

'You bet.' Her whole body had gone so soft with love it was hard to stand upright. 'I love you too, and want more than anything to be Mrs Newman.'

His smile went right to her toes. 'Thank goodness. I love you, Georgie. I always have and I always will.'

It couldn't get any better than that. She leapt into his arms. 'Yes, yes, yes. I love you, Blake, so yes.' Her lips found his and she kissed him as though her life depended upon it. Which it did.

When they finally came up for air, she grinned. 'So you're returning home at last. Think you'd like to move in with me?'

'I'd love to move in with you, starting right now. I'll be a commuter for a while, but as of now this is officially my home address along with my fiancée.'

Georgie rubbed her tummy lightly. 'You hear that, baby? Daddy's coming home.'

Blake looked away, wiped his eyes, turned back. 'I love you beyond measure. Why did it take so long to figure it all out?'

'Guess that's how it was meant to be.' And now the zip was closed right to the last click. The past hadn't gone away, but it was done with ruining the future. She was so happy her chest ached. So damned happy she had to pinch herself.

Blake's smile was so wide it had to ache. 'Let's not

take too long to tie the knot. You seemed ready to commit before I was, and now I don't want to waste any more time.'

'I had reached the point where I couldn't go on with the fling, but I didn't want to lose you either. It was the hardest thing hearing you leave that night, but I couldn't run after you and demand you stay. You had to be ready.'

'I am. Totally.'

Seven months later, message on Georgie and Blake Newman's web page

To all our family and friends—Jacob Noah Newman arrived four hours ago, checking in at six and a half pounds. He's healthy and already has a cheeky grin. Wonder where he gets that from? Georgie's looking great, but then, when doesn't she? Me? I'm ecstatic beyond description. Never knew I could be so happy.

Blake. X

Oh, and yes, I love these two so much it hurts, and I can cope with that.

* * * * *

SAVING THE SINGLE MUM'S HEART

ALLIE KINCHELOE

MILLS & BOON

For my family.
Like the characters in this book,
things haven't been easy for us.
But we've made it through.
I love you.

CHAPTER ONE

"You know what would be great? If I had a dad to pick me up from school."

Jess Daniels glanced up at her son in the rearview mirror and tried not to sigh at the familiar topic of conversation. Mason was relentless with his idea that she needed a man in her life, if only to be his dad. "Miss Freya says no one should be alone as much as you are. Miss Freya says that she works all the time and she still goes to see her friends more than you do. Do you have any friends besides Miss Freya?"

"I have friends, Mason." She just didn't see them as much as any of her friends would have liked. But that came with the whole single mom situation, didn't it? Getting a sitter was hard and expensive.

"Do you know how to get a boyfriend? Miss Freya says if I want a dad, then we gotta find you a boyfriend first. But I've never seen you have a boyfriend, so you might have to take lessons or something. Like when I go to karate lessons."

"Boyfriend lessons?" Jess snorted.

That boy was determined he needed a dad, and soon. And as long as the man knew how to play video games and throw a ball, then her son wasn't too choosy. From the time he was old enough to realize that most kids had a dad somewhere in their lives, Mason had been asking questions about his own father. Questions that were proving harder to answer now that he was no longer content with the explanation that his father had passed away before he was born. But she sure wasn't ready for him to learn the truth about his paternity.

She'd have to have another talk with Freya about encouraging Mason like this. Why couldn't anyone understand that Jess wanted to be alone? She *might* have let Freya believe that her lingering love for Mason's dad kept her from dating since it gave her a reprieve from being set up. Some things were harder to get over than grief though, like broken trust. It had been almost eight years since she'd lost Clint, and it might be another eight before she could bring herself to trust another man. She got so tired of hearing about how she really needed to just be brave and put herself out there. One heartbreak didn't mean all men were all bad. Take a chance on love. Have faith.

Meh.

The potential positives didn't outweigh the probable negatives. She was fine being single. *Mostly.*

"There's a Doughnuts with Dad thing at school next week," Mason informed her. "And I can't go because I don't have a dad."

"Tone down the dramatics. You know I'm allowed to go with you instead." She'd gone to the Muffins with Mom and the Fruit Cups and Family events with him already—why not a doughnut day? She hated the designated days for each parent. It was unfair to the kids who didn't have an intact traditional family.

"It's not the same," Mason huffed. "I need a dad."

"If we ever see a dad store, I'll be sure to pick one up."

"Ha-ha." The kid didn't appreciate Jess's sarcasm. "I'm not going to fall for that. I'm not five anymore. Hey, what do all those lights mean?"

Jess swallowed hard as she took in all the icons illuminated on the gauge cluster of her aging sedan. A lot of money for repairs she just didn't have at the moment, that's what they meant. Her chest tightened as she glanced into the rearview mirror and changed lanes before pulling the car off onto the shoulder.

"The car seems to be having some trouble."

"What about my ice cream?"

"Mason, honey, we will get your ice cream as soon as we can." The upbeat tone she spoke with only partially masked her worries—hopefully enough that Mason wouldn't catch on. She thanked her lucky stars she was able to get the car out of traffic and that her son's biggest worry was that he might not get ice cream.

After easing the car to a stop, she put it in Park. The faintest whisp of smoke curled up from under the corner of the hood. That could not be a good sign. Would this finally be the repair that crossed over the value of her little car? Jess rubbed a hand over the steering wheel and sent up a little prayer that the car would be fixable. A new one was so not in the budget right now.

"Stay here while I see how bad this is." She looked over her shoulder to her seven-year-old. "Do not get out of this car until I tell you it's okay."

He nodded, but she'd have to keep a close eye on him. Mason could get into trouble faster than she could blink. She dug her cell phone out of her purse and handed it to him. That should keep him occupied and safe for a few moments, at least.

"Call Freya and ask her to come get us. Tell her we're on the interstate coming home from baseball. Okay?"

At his nod, she popped the hood and, after checking for traffic, stepped out of the car. She lifted the hood and stared at the smoking engine. She knew nothing about cars, but still, she had to look. What was she going to do?

Whatever it was, it wouldn't be fixing this car by herself; that was for sure.

Rather than step back into traffic, she moved to the passenger side of the car. She opened the front door and tried to reassure Mason that everything was fine. "It's going to be okay. Is Freya coming?"

"She said she's got a meeting with the hospital mister tater, and she can't come till after." Mason handed the phone back to Jess with very little concern for what Freya's words meant.

"The hospital administrator?"

"Yeah, that." Mason shrugged. "Whatever."

Jess wanted to laugh at how completely unbothered Mason was about his vocabulary mix-up. She envied the confidence her son showed sometimes, how he could make a mistake and just brush it off and move on. He didn't dwell on it like she would. Her mind liked to remember embarrassments from her childhood like they were current events. And the mistakes she'd made as an adult? Those were practically on a reel in her mind, circling through anytime she found herself in similar scenarios.

"Well, let's see if we can get the tow truck out here soon." She looked up the number for the repair garage, although she should have it memorized or saved in her phone given how frequently she used it. She gave them the location and the mechanic confirmed they'd send the truck out but it might be a while. She thanked the man and hung up the phone.

"Gonna be here a while?" Mason groaned.

"That obvious?" She reached back and brushed a lock of hair away from his eyes.

"It's always a while when we gotta wait for the tow truck." He shrugged. "Wanna play a game?"

CHAPTER TWO

BECKETT WILDER PULLED UP behind the black sedan with the hood raised. He'd driven by the first time and then his EMT instincts had kicked in. Leaving someone stranded on the side of the road went against the fiber of his being, so he'd looped around at the next opportunity. He flicked his emergency flashers on to warn passing drivers to be cautious. When there was a gap in traffic, he climbed from the cab and approached on the passenger side.

A woman climbed out of the car. She looked to be a few years older than him, maybe. Her blond hair was in a ponytail, and she wore a Woodvale Woodchucks baseball T-shirt. "Thanks for stopping but I've already called for a tow."

"How long until they get here?" Unless things had changed since he'd left home, Woodvale had a single tow truck and the owner tended to take his slow, sweet time about getting his job done.

She hesitated before answering. "A couple hours."

That wouldn't do. He couldn't leave her out here for hours. As an EMT, he'd seen more than his share of roadside accidents. A stalled car or a flat tire led to someone getting hit more than it really should. The caution those experiences instilled in him, combined with the knowledge that his own sister had died not three miles down this very same road, made him anxious to get her out of here.

"You alone?" A glimmer of fear sparked in her green eyes, and he wanted to kick himself for not introducing himself or doing something to put her at ease. A lone woman on the side of the highway being approached by a strange man? Of course she'd be concerned. "I'm Beckett, by the way. When I'm not being a bonehead and scaring the people that I'm trying to help, I work as an EMT."

His attempt at humor during his introduction fell flat. She didn't even crack a smile. Her eyes narrowed as she said, "I know all of the EMTs here and you aren't one of them."

"You're right. I don't work here in Woodvale." He pulled his wallet out of his pocket and flipped it open to his driver's license. "I did grow up here though. You may know my parents, Richard and Elaine Wilder?"

Tension left her shoulders and she visibly relaxed as she read his name on his identification. One pro of being the son of the richest couple in town was name recognition. At least, it was a pro in this instance. That same recognition had forced him to leave town to get enough anonymity to grow his career as an EMT on his own terms.

"You look like your dad," she finally acknowledged.

"I hear that a lot. So, now that you've verified that I'm not a serial killer or something, can I give you a ride home?" His eyes flickered to the small cross set back away from the highway. His sister had a similar cross marking the spot where she had breathed her final moments. "This isn't the safest spot to be sitting."

She glanced over to the little white marker placed near the tree line. "The tow truck said it would be a while and to leave the keys under the front mat if we left."

"Then let's get you somewhere safe."

Her teeth worried her lower lip as she considered his offer. The wind picked up and blew her hair around her face. She shoved it back with an impatient hand. "I really appreciate you doing this. Did I introduce myself? I don't think I did. I'm Jess Daniels."

"It's nice to meet you, Jess. But I wish it were under better conditions."

She shrugged before she opened the back door. A little blond boy climbed out of the back wearing a Woodchucks baseball uniform. The little boy waved happily, and Jess kept a firm grip on him as she steered him toward the truck. "Come on, sweetie. Mason, this is Mr. Wilder. He is going to give us a ride."

"Hi, Mason." Beckett opened the back door. "He needs a booster seat, right?"

"Yeah, I just wanted to make sure he was inside a vehicle before I turned my back long enough to unclip it."

"I got it." He hurried over to the car and made quick work of disconnecting the child seat. It had been the glimpse of that seat in the back of the broken-down sedan that had really driven home the need for him to stop and offer his assistance. He carried it over and had it installed in his own vehicle before she could offer to try to do it herself.

When her son climbed up into the seat, she had him buckled in quickly. "Thank you," she said softly as she closed the back door. "I really do appreciate you stopping. I'm sure you had better things to do."

"Nothing is more important than making sure the two of you are safe. Got it?" Beckett's words were sincere. He never wanted another family to go through the pain of losing a loved one on the side of this highway like he had. Impulsively, he reached out and touched her hand. Their fingers tangled for a moment, and his heartrate quickened when she didn't instantly pull away. The shy smile she gave him made him want to pull her in close, but then the shutters in her eyes slammed closed and she yanked her hand away like he'd burned her. The action made him curious, but he didn't push. He opened the passenger door and gestured for her to get in. "In you get."

He waited for a break in traffic before walking around. She avoided eye contact when he climbed into the cab. She gave off a very independent vibe. He liked that in a woman, but Jess had walls built up around her the size of Fort Knox.

If circumstances were different, he might try to flirt, to see if they could have some fun together. Jess was exactly his type in every way except for one key factor: she was a mom. Long-term relationships weren't in his wheelhouse. He dated, frequently, but never for more than a few months at a time. Once things started getting serious, he was out. Kids in the mix were a major nope from him.

As he pulled back onto the road, he asked, "Do you

see those clouds coming in? They're saying we're in for some rough storms, maybe even some flash flooding."

Weather was neutral, unoffensive. Merely a small-talk topic that would hopefully distract him. He picked a subject that had nothing to do with either of them. The woman had so much tension after his simple touch that he thought better of flirting with her. He was only in town for six months, and she might need that much time to thaw the ice around her heart. Too much work for a short-term thing.

"I'd heard that. Mason was really glad that it didn't come in before his game."

Baseball was another solidly neutral topic, one that they could include her kid in. "I bet. Nothing worse than being excited to play and then have it called for lightning. Is this your first year playing?"

"I played last year too." Mason squirmed in the backseat, catching Beckett's eye. A pained expression crossed his face. "I like baseball."

"You okay, buddy?"

"I need to go to the bathroom really bad!" Mason cried in response.

Beckett stepped a little harder on the gas. The last thing he wanted was for that kid to have an accident in the backseat of his truck. He took the Woodvale exit, sighing when he passed the pair of crosses there. Passing that spot still sent an ache through his chest.

"Someone you knew?" Her voice was soft, cautious even, like she knew she might be treading on sensitive ground.

"My sister."

"I'm sorry for your loss. It's hard to lose a loved one." Experience tinged her voice.

"I miss her every day." Beckett turned at the light at the end of the ramp. Memories of his sister flooded into his mind. "Sloane was…spoiled. She was materialistic and thought she was better than most everyone. But she got me in ways that my dad never could. She could translate for us into language that we could each understand. Some days I still can't fathom that I'll never see her again."

"I feel the same way about my parents. It's been four years since I lost my mom, and I still pick up my phone to call sometimes before I remember that I can't."

"It's supposed to get better with time, or so they say." He pulled the truck to a stop in front of the gas station. "I'll wait here if you want to run him in to the bathroom."

"Thanks," Jess murmured. She got out and took Mason inside.

Beckett leaned his head on the steering wheel and tried to quiet the riot of emotions that talking about his sister always stirred up. Eight years and it still hadn't gotten any easier to be in this town. To be so close to where his sister lay dying on the side of the interstate while the town's sole ambulance took the other driver in because his wounds were more visible. Visible, but not as serious as the internal bleeding that Sloane and her fiancé had suffered.

He let out a ragged breath. He'd get this town the services they needed and then he'd be gone. Away from all the painful memories that surrounded him on every corner. He'd be counting down the days until he could get back to Lexington and the career he had waiting for him there.

Jess and her son came back out to the car, and he could tell by the way her expression shifted that she was misreading his mood. He tried to clear the frustration from his face, but it was too late. She'd already gotten the wrong opinion.

"I'm sorry we bothered you. If you could just drop us off, we live just a few blocks away."

"But, Mommy, what about my ice cream?" There was a tone of urgency, sort of a "how dare you forget?" in Mason's question.

She made sure Mason was buckled in properly before climbing back into the front seat. She didn't once make eye contact with Beckett. "Mommy will have to get you ice cream another day. We can't keep Mr. Wilder any longer than we already have."

Mason huffed. "But you promised!"

"I'm sorry. I didn't know when I promised that the car was going to die. I'll make it up to you once the car gets fixed." Her expression held no trace of emotion. "I think we have some popsicles at home."

"It's not the same."

Beckett looked up in the rearview mirror. Mason had his arms crossed over his chest, lips poked out in a classic pout. Poor kid. He'd had a morning and just wanted to have his promised treat. Beckett remembered all too well the feeling of having a reward snatched away after the fact. In his case, usually because his dad found something more urgent to do.

"We live just up on Sycamore," Jess directed him, ignoring the sulking child in the backseat.

When he glanced Jess's way, he caught the resignation on her face. Having to accept help from a stranger had probably been a hit to her pride, and that was something she needed. Asking for something like ice cream—not a necessity—seemed out of character, at least as much as he could judge after such a short acquaintance. She was simply trying to make it through the day with a few shreds of dignity left.

Instead of turning right on Sycamore, he drove past and turned into the lot of the ice-cream parlor. He could make this day a little better for them by helping her keep her word to her son.

She put up a token protest. "You don't have to do this."

"A promise is a promise." He shrugged. "It's maybe an hour out of my day. And ice cream sounds good."

The smile she flashed him made it worth it. "Mason, you need to say thank you to Mr. Wilder. I wasn't going to ask him for yet another favor, but he seems to be as determined as you to get that ice cream."

"Hey, us ballplayers gotta stick together," he said, tugging on the brim of Mason's hat as they walked toward the door.

"You play baseball?" A look of awe crossed Mason's face. "My coach this year is Colby's dad and he never played baseball. We do coach pitch, and he's awful."

"Mason," Jess warned, "be nice."

Mason rolled his eyes and continued, "He tries, but he throws like a girl."

"Mason!"

"I know, I know, I shouldn't say throws like a girl because sometimes girls can actually throw." Mason gave Beckett a look that said, *Moms just don't understand.*

"Totally get that." Beckett tried really hard not to laugh. He hadn't been around kids much, but this one was cracking him up. Between the boy's actual comments, and the full range of expressions that the kid was bringing out on Jess's face, Beckett was having a hard time keeping the laughter in. He hadn't been this amused in a long time.

Mason gave him a calculating look. "We could really use a coach that knows how to play."

"Mason!" Jess hissed the boy's name out, her cheeks pinkening up.

Mason shrugged before running up to the counter to check out all the flavors, leaving Beckett and Jess alone for the moment. Silence stretched between them while Beckett scrambled for a neutral topic of conversation that might pull some of the embarrassed color out of Jess's face.

"I would never…" She paused to take a deep breath. "I swear I did *not* put him up to recruiting you—or anyone else—to coach."

Beckett brushed it off. Kids were known for having no filter, right? And he could tell that she hadn't put Mason up to asking. "No need to apologize. Let him enjoy his ice cream."

"Thank you for this, and for coming to our rescue." She reached out and touched his wrist. A prickle of awareness raced up his arm from the point of contact. "But don't let him talk you into anything. I really appreciate all this, but I don't want you to spend any more time than necessary with him."

"What?" Beckett snorted. He pulled his hand away from her touch, stuffing it in his pocket. He'd tried to make a nice gesture, and all it got him was accusations. The desire to defend himself rose up, but he had no idea what he'd done to give her the impression that he might do something to her kid. "You can't think I'm a bad influence on him."

"I never said that." She sighed. "I'm making this worse. Bear with me for a second. You don't live here, right?"

He shook his head slowly. What did that have to do with anything?

"Are you planning to move here?"

"No way." This town would be in his rearview the moment it was feasible. Once his dad's cancer treatments and this urgent project his dad had called him home for were finished, he had every intention of going back to his job.

"Then it's not fair to let him get attached to you and leave. He doesn't need that." She flashed him a sad smile. "He's…more fragile than he seems."

"Got it." He might be mistaken, but he thought maybe she was warning him that her own heart was fragile too.

CHAPTER THREE

JESS BIT HER LIP. Had she hurt Beckett's feelings? Getting attached to a man and then losing him could only hurt Mason. Men lost interest fast. She'd learned that the hard way. It was better for all of them if they kept their distance and then she could protect Mason from the same hardships that she'd faced.

Beckett moved away from her, his expression grim. He stood next to Mason at the ice cream counter. When he bent down to talk to Mason, his face softened into genuine interest at whatever Mason was jabbering about.

Jess took several deep, slow breaths. It was one day. It would be okay. Mason couldn't get too attached over a single order of ice cream, right? Even as the thought crossed her mind, she could see the hero worship in her son's eyes as he stared up at Beckett. And she could see why—not only had Beckett literally rescued them from the side of the road, but he'd brought them to get ice cream and he knew about baseball. The only way he could get more awesome would be if he wanted to go to the arcade too—at least according to Mason.

She'd have to be extra vigilant at keeping them apart.

Really though, there was no reason for the two of them to be together after today. That realization went a long way toward calming her nerves.

One hour.

Maybe even less.

She just needed to keep them from bonding too much over the next hour. Then she could get back to her lonely life. No, her *normal* life. She wasn't lonely. She had Mason and Freya. She had a few other friends. And work, of course.

Pathetic.

She sighed.

"Don't have your flavor?" Beckett asked, his eyebrow arched. The way he looked at her made the question feel like it wasn't about ice cream at all. Heat crept up into her face as they made eye contact. If she were looking for a man, Beckett would definitely be her "flavor." Tall, dark hair and strong. Oh, he would be any woman's flavor…

Jess looked away quickly, angry at herself for reacting to Beckett's gaze. This was not who she was. Men were not on her menu, especially not men who didn't even live in her town. She ordered a scoop of chocolate without looking at the other options.

She kept a running commentary in her head of all the reasons why she needed to keep her distance from Beckett.

He's the enemy, Jess. He'll love you and leave you, just like Clint did. His time in Woodvale has a clear expiration date. Don't forget that.

Beckett insisted on paying for the ice cream, swiping his card before she could even pull her wallet out of her purse. "Come on, it's less than ten bucks. Don't worry about it."

She would though. Worry about it, that was.

Because one day, he might want to even the score. And she was currently down by two. She murmured a thanks and they headed out to one of the covered tables on the patio to eat their treats. The sunlight peeked through the clouds for the moment and the warmth of the spring day contrasted nicely with the cold ice cream. In another situation, Jess would enjoy soaking up a little sun after the chill of winter had passed, but that was proving hard for her with Beckett nearby. Beckett was the first man since Clint that she'd been this attracted to, and it wasn't sitting well with her.

Thankfully, Mason's chatter kept an awkward silence from developing. That child never ran out of things to say, and the sugar rush from the ice cream kept that running commentary coming at a fast clip for a while. For once, Jess was glad that her little boy could happily chat with anyone about anything.

Even so, there was a tension at the table. When Beckett stretched his leg out and it brushed hers, it pulled the air from her chest. She gasped for breath and tucked her legs back up under her seat tightly. The contact should have felt casual—*should* being the operative word. It was anything but casual.

"Sorry." He voiced the apology, but based on the look in his eyes, he didn't mean it. His gaze held a playful mischief that belied his words. He was flirting with her!

She gave him a little shake of her head.

His eyes twinkled, but he turned his attention back to Mason's recap of that morning's game. Every play was described in excruciating detail, complete with actions and sound effects.

Jess swirled the chocolate ice cream around in the dish with her spoon. The look on Mason's face sent all kinds of red flags up. The warnings were lighting up like all the icons on her gauge cluster had a short while ago. She wanted to snatch the melting ice cream away from Mason and insist that Beckett drive them home immediately. She wanted to put some much-needed space between them. And then she could get back to the way she liked things—where she was alone. If she didn't let anyone close, then her heart—and more importantly Mason's heart—couldn't be in danger.

People always said she shouldn't be alone—Mason, her mom before she'd passed away, Freya. They loved to point out how long it had been since she dated. She usually shut that down hard, but occasionally, the longings for someone to share her life with rose up from somewhere deep. The long, hazy summer nights were the hardest. That's when she remembered walking along the lake at sunset with a man she loved at her side. When she missed the feel of a strong pair of arms around her, holding her until the sun rose.

Then a swift recap of the past would put that silly notion back in the locked box at the bottom of her heart where it belonged. No, while being a single mom was tough, dating was not something she could do. Trust enough to let someone in? Nope. That wasn't gonna happen again. Not after the third-degree burns Clint had given her.

But she hadn't seen Mason this happy in a long time. He was reveling in the masculine attention Beckett was providing. Just having a man listen to his chatter and share in his conversation had put a light in her son's eyes. So, despite her reservations, she sat back and let the conversation play out while the ice cream in front of her melted.

She hated that giving her son what he needed meant allowing someone else to help. Since the day the child was born, it had been the two of them against the world. With Clint gone, Mason had only been hers. Sharing him was not something she was good at. It chafed to know that what he needed most right now was a man.

If she'd had a motto these last seven years, it would have been that "love was nice while it lasted, but the pain it causes is not worth the risk." She'd thought she'd found the type of love her parents had when she met Clint. She'd given herself over to him—mind, body and soul. After having her heart ripped out and stomped on, she'd kept anyone of the male persuasion as far away as possible. Had keeping her heart wrapped up tight behind layers of emotional bubble wrap been the right thing? For herself, absolutely. For Mason? Now she was starting to wonder.

Some days, finding Mason a dad sounded like a good idea. Usually on the days when she'd been on her feet for twelve hours straight, when a protein bar served as the closest thing she'd had to lunch or the space between paydays got a bit too stretched out for comfort...

They did all right though. The bills were paid. They had plenty of food and a solid roof over their heads. It was hard, yes, but she held her head high with pride at all that she had done on her own. Mason had everything he needed and a few things he wanted.

Except a dad. Had she underestimated how important that was to a little boy's well-being?

"Are you ready?" Beckett's deep voice interrupted her thoughts.

"Yes, sorry. I think I zoned out." She'd gone so far into her thoughts that she was questioning years of decisions. That wasn't good. "Thanks again," she said, shooting him a grateful smile.

"No problem." He grabbed a napkin and wiped at Mason's face. "Little dude, I think you're wearing as much of this ice cream as you consumed."

"Do you have kids?" Mason asked.

"Mason…" Jess winced at the bald question, sure she knew where this was going. She hoped to cut it off before Mason took it all the way. "I'm sorry, Beckett. Someone has forgotten his manners."

Beckett chuckled. "It's fine. And no, I don't have kids. My mom really wants me to though. She's been on my case for a while now."

"I think you'd be a good dad," Mason said softly, flinging himself into Beckett's chest. "I wish I had a dad like you."

Oh, way to lay it on thick, kid. Mason usually didn't take to people that quickly, but in such a short time he'd effortlessly bonded with Beckett. Her fears were coming to life, right before her eyes. Attachments could only end in pain when they were severed. Was there any way this situation could get worse?

CHAPTER FOUR

ON MONDAY MORNING, the special committee members slowly trickled past Beckett and into the conference room to join Freya. He'd been happy to see at least one friendly face in his old buddy from high school. Tugging at the tie around his neck, Beckett only managed to tighten it and make it feel more like a torture device. It had never been his dream to wear designer suits or represent his family foundation, but here he stood. He had to take several deep breaths before his nerves were calm enough for him to walk through the door himself.

Returning to Woodvale hadn't even been his idea. This town held a lot of hurt and a lot of sad memories for him, but he was a dutiful son. When the call came that his father needed his help, what else could he do but move home and step up to the plate? He just wished it didn't feel like that plate sat on unstable ground.

When Beckett entered the space, he noted with surprise that the woman he'd picked up on Saturday was now seated across the conference room table from the empty seat his father had reserved for him. So she worked at the hospital? Well, that would explain why she'd known he wasn't an EMT here. He stole a glance at her while his father was quietly conversing with someone.

She flicked her long braid over her shoulder and returned his gaze boldly. When he didn't look away, she raised a single brow at him and gave her head a bit of a shake. So far, she was the one challenge this town held that he'd willingly take on—if she didn't have a kid. He had a feeling that any relationship Jess got involved in would need to have that promise of happily-ever-after and that wasn't what he was about. Still, he couldn't deny that seeing her here had unsettled him.

And anyway, dating in Woodvale came with its own complications. The burden to carry on the family name was building, added to by his mother's not so subtle jabs. He was their only hope now that Sloane was gone, after all. She didn't stop the guilt trip there though. No, over breakfast this morning, she'd tossed in the suggestion that if he didn't start a family soon his father might not be around to meet any potential grandkids.

So, no pressure. No pressure at all.

Did he even see himself as the white picket fence type? As a dad?

That was something he wasn't so sure about. He liked kids well enough, when they weren't his and he didn't have to handle the discipline and misbehaviors. Maybe, someday, he might decide to take that plunge, but when—if—he got married, it would be on his terms.

"Are we ready to begin then?" his dad asked.

Beckett sat up straighter. His heart raced even though he knew what his father was about to say. Still, the idea had been abstract before—announcing it to a room full of people would make it far more real. And harder to ignore.

"I'm not sure I need to introduce myself, but on the off chance I haven't met some of you, I'm Richard Wilder. You may have heard rumors to this effect, but the Wilder Foundation has decided to make a rather large donation to Woodvale Memorial."

The room broke into an excited murmur. The people around the table perked up. Gone were the resigned expressions. They'd been replaced by ones of hope. Tentative in a few cases, but still far more optimistic than before the announcement. Jess's entire countenance had brightened and the change in her was striking. For once, Beckett felt like his family's money might do something that truly helped people.

His dad held up a hand, asking for silence. When the room quieted, he continued, "Now, before you get too excited, much of the money has been earmarked for a cancer center. I have had the misfortune of finding out the hard way that Woodvale has no resources for someone with cancer. None. It's unacceptable for residents of our growing community to have to travel two hours each way for chemotherapy or radiation treatments."

Several people at the table nodded. How many of them had experienced firsthand, through themselves or a family member, exactly how lacking the health care in Woodvale was? Beckett rubbed his thumb against the face of his watch—the last gift his sister had ever given him. Woodvale's lack of proper ambulances had taken Sloane from them, and he wasn't sure he'd ever forgive this town for that.

And now this small town's medical limitations were

causing his dad problems as well. Cancer didn't discriminate based on how close someone was to a treatment facility. His dad was lucky enough to have the resources to make those drives to get the care needed. Many of the poorer residents might not.

"With that said, I had them set up this special committee so that we can look at what other areas of our healthcare system are lacking. Through this group and individual meetings with the representatives of each department, the Wilder Foundation will look at funding requests and see how many we can grant."

The excited chatter picked up in volume.

His dad cleared his throat. "My son, Beckett, will be heading this project for the Wilder Foundation. He's the contact for all proposals and requests. He's the one you need to woo to your side."

Beckett stood, though he couldn't help but notice Jess's reaction to that news. She did not look happy in the least. He gave the little spiel he'd prepared about how they should ask for big-ticket items, not little things. "In the next two weeks, I'd like to meet with each of you individually prior to the submission of your proposals. The final decisions on funding will be made shortly after I've had time to review each request. I'm only in Woodvale for the next six months, so everything will be completed within that time frame."

"What are the individual appointments for?"

Beckett turned his attention to the older man who'd asked the question. "Those meetings will be for you to show me around your departments. Explain your needs. Let me see firsthand what your department means to this community and help me understand how the Wilder

Foundation can help you help others. As you write your proposals, put the emphasis on how the project benefits the community as a whole, rather than only a select few."

"Can't you just divide the money up equally among the remaining departments and let us decide how the money should be spent?" Jess leaned forward, elbows on the table. "It would be faster and give us more flexibility in how it is used. And it wouldn't take time out of our already busy days to meet with you."

"We could, yes. But we prefer to make directed donations with specific purposes that can make the biggest impact, and dividing the money between departments doesn't address that." He leaned forward too, hands on the surface of the table. "If you prefer to put in a general request for money, you can certainly skip the individual meetings and send in an unspecified proposal. However, I will prioritize the proposals from departments that have proven to me that they have the greatest needs for funding and shown me how they will make the best and most efficient use of the funds."

He could hear Jess's teeth grinding as she struggled to bite back her initial retort. Was her desire to minimize this process simply to avoid him after the way her son had taken to him on Saturday? Or because she was as attracted to him as he was to her? Either way, he had no plans to act on that attraction, so she had no reason to worry about spending time with him.

"What department are you with?" he asked.

"Emergency."

Beckett tapped his fingers on the table. That figures,

he thought ruefully. "Ambulance services and EMTs fall under your department here, correct?"

"Beckett," his father warned from beside him. Though his voice was low, his dad censored him with only a name. His position had long been clear when it came to Beckett's involvement in anything ambulance related. In fact, it was Beckett's decision to become an EMT in the face of his father's disapproval that had put an additional strain on their already struggling relationship.

Despite how the lack of ambulances and qualified EMTs had taken his favorite child, Beckett's father had never seen a reason to support an expansion of the ambulance program in Woodvale. If anything, Richard Wilder blamed the EMTs for not saving his only daughter.

For Beckett, it had been Sloane's death that steered him toward becoming an EMT. Initially, he had wanted to make sure that no other family suffered such a devastating loss simply because there wasn't a qualified EMT around. But it hadn't taken long before he realized that emergency medicine was his true calling. He'd only accepted the responsibility of these directed donations so that he could finally do what he'd wanted since the night his sister died: get more ambulances and the personnel to staff them up and running in Woodvale. The current service level was the reason his sister was gone. Why was Jess putting up so many objections? They were trying to donate money to improve the medical services available to the town!

As the memories of his sister and the frustration he felt at his father's refusal to accept his chosen career

path clouded his brain, he felt emotion well up inside
him, and before he could check himself, he snapped,
"The emergency department provides a woefully inadequate ambulance service for the town so I would
suggest that a one-on-one to secure additional funding
would be in your best interests."

CHAPTER FIVE

JESS SHOT TO her feet. Was he accusing her of misman-
aging her department? Of…stealing department funds?
No way would she take that without argument. And in
front of all her peers and colleagues as well. He may
have rescued her and Mason from the highway, but
calling her work woefully inadequate was more than
she could stand.

She slapped her hands down on the table so hard they
stung. Who did this egotistical piece of work think he
was to come in here and tell them all how to do their
jobs?

The youngest son of Richard Wilder, that's who.

She'd learned the hard way that anyone from *that*
sort of family couldn't be trusted. And she'd fight tooth
and nail to stop another rich man from messing with
her head and her life. She wouldn't bow down easily
simply because this man's family name hung on one or
more walls in this building.

He would not mess with her career. Years of her life
had been dedicated to this hospital and building a solid
reputation here. Years ago, she'd lost her dignity, her
pride and her ability to trust any man in a suit. She'd

had to start over when she moved home to Woodvale, but she'd made a name for herself here. She would not lose her hard-earned professional credibility because some jumped-up rich boy thought he knew better than she did how to run her department.

"What exactly are you implying, Mr. Wilder?" The little muscle at the corner of her eye twitched in her fury. Hopefully, it didn't make her appear to be winking neurotically at him. He may look like a Greek god come to life, clad in that custom-tailored suit, but she wouldn't lower herself to flirt with him. If she'd known he was like this she would never have... Never have what? Accepted his help? Let him take her and Mason for ice cream? Reacted to the lightning bolts he set off in her stomach?

Beckett crossed his arms over his chest, and she had to swallow hard at the spark of desire that flared up as the fabric stretched tight over his muscular frame. Not desire, Jess told herself. That's anger, pure and simple. A fact that would be much simpler to remember if he didn't look like God's gift to women. Why couldn't he be homely? Or married? No, he had to be single and drop-dead gorgeous. And Mason hadn't shut up about him since Beckett had dropped them off on Saturday.

He raised one dark eyebrow, and his eyes issued a dare for her to contradict him. "I'm not implying anything, Jess. I just want the best for this hospital and for the town, same as you."

Jess refused to let his arrogant, know-it-all tone make her behave in a way she would regret in front of her colleagues, but she could feel her fury rise up inside her all the same. Before she could do or say something rash, Freya put a calming hand on Jess's arm.

"Okay, you two. I think that's enough for today." Freya flashed them both an icy look.

The chair squeaked and rolled a few inches backward when Jess sat down with an audible harrumph. Having been best friends for five years, Freya had to know how much Beckett's words bothered her. Was she speaking in her role as the assistant hospital administrator or as her friend though? Either way, Jess grudgingly admitted to herself that Freya was right to separate them, and was grateful for the interruption. After all, her department *did* need additional funding and she couldn't afford to risk that by antagonizing the man who would decide how much she got and what she could spend it on. But she didn't have to be happy about it.

Jess kept her gaze focused on Beckett who stared right back at her from across the table. He laced his fingers together on his flat abdomen and leaned back. His pose suggested he was relaxed, but his entire frame held a visible tension. Beckett had an air of dangerousness about him. Like a panther waiting for a moment to strike.

He'd thrown her off-balance from the moment they'd made eye contact. The elder Mr. Wilder had grated on her nerves during the one meeting at which they'd both been in attendance, but Beckett did something far worse—he made her feel things she'd shoved away for years.

Her professionalism served as a shield she wrapped around herself when she entered Woodvale Memorial Hospital. Nothing upset her at work. Personal feelings had no business in the workplace, but today, Beckett had made her forget that. The kindness he'd shown over the weekend and her complicated feelings about that had made it harder for her to remain impartial with him. As a result, his presence had put her on edge and nearly made her lose her temper in a way it would have been hard to come back from with any dignity.

"I think that's the meeting adjourned for today," Mr. Wilder said forcefully. "Make sure you take the information sheet. It has Beckett's contact info on it, and you can set up those individual meetings with him."

Around them, Jess heard and felt the other special committee members filing out of the room. Beckett made no move to leave, so neither did she. The stare-down between them continued. If the only win she could take today was being the last one to blink, so be it.

"Really, guys, you two are ultimately fighting the same war." Freya's voice held a level of exasperation she normally saved for conversations about her on-again, off-again boyfriend. Hearing that tone at work and directed at her made Jess want to wince. "You see that, right? You both want a better-funded emergency department."

"Woodvale needs more staffed ambulances," Beckett said bluntly. "They should be budgeted for."

"I don't disagree with that," Jess allowed. "I just can't fund them out of the current budget from the main hospital emergency department. We're already on a rail-thin margin. You seem to be suggesting that money has been misspent or squandered inefficiently, but every single penny under my control has been accounted for with receipts to prove it and a comprehensive annually reviewed strategy. It's not that I don't want to fund more ambulances—it's that I *do not* have the money to do so without pulling that money away from the nursing staff or the medical supplies."

Beckett closed his eyes. Briefly, resignation crossed his face before he smoothed his features into a more neutral expression. "This is why I want to meet with each department separately. So we can see where the greatest needs are. We want the money to go where it can do the most good."

"And you think the answer is simply to provide another staffed ambulance?" Jess snorted. "We can cart the whole town in here, but if we can't treat them once they get here, how have we done anything good?"

"The two of you need to negotiate a truce." Freya put a hand up to stall any protests. Her face held the serious, no-nonsense expression of a frustrated assistant administrator, but when she walked out of the room, she muttered something under her breath that sounded suspiciously like, "worse than teenagers with a crush."

"Did she just say—? You know what? Never mind." Beckett rolled his shoulders, looking as tense and uncomfortable as Jess felt. "We need to work this out though. She is right about that."

"My responsibility is to make sure that the Emergency Department of this hospital is staffed and stocked with functional equipment. I'm sorry if this frustrates you, but adding more ambulances isn't a high priority for me. It takes funding away from the lifesaving personnel and equipment my department needs to function on a day-to-day basis."

"Ambulances, paramedics and EMTs are the first

line of defense when it comes to saving lives," Beckett argued.

Jess could kick herself for walking right into that one. He wasn't wrong. She had all sorts of respect for the first responders who brought the patients in to them each day, and if the budget had any wiggle room at all, she'd gladly agree to the funding increase. The funding just wasn't there. "I know, and I agree, but—"

"There is no but. Ambulances and EMTs are every bit as necessary to your department as X-ray machines and nurses." Beckett's tone was far calmer than earlier, but his impatience still came through loud and clear.

"That may be true, but the budget is still stretched to the point of breaking. Are you going to purchase those ambulances and pay for staff to cover them…forever? What about the supplies to keep them stocked?"

Jess flinched when Beckett suddenly reached a hand toward her face. She brushed him away before he could touch her. Her fingers grazed his, and even that briefest touch sent her heart rate on a brisk upward climb. "What are you doing?"

"I wasn't going to hurt you, Jess." He hesitated before gesturing at the twitching muscle next to her eye. "Does that happen often?"

"Only when you're around and making wild accusations in front of my colleagues."

Beckett looked like he wanted to say something else, but when he spoke, his tone was neutral. "Would it be possible for me to look at the budget? Maybe I can see ways to finagle it that you haven't. A fresh perspective can often see things overlooked by someone who's been immersed in it, day after day. If that doesn't work, at least we'll have an idea of what direction you should go with your proposal."

Had he phrased it like that earlier, they might not have had such an argument. Her quick temper had flared when he'd called her out like that in a room of her peers. And if he'd hadn't insulted her ability to do her job, then her stupid eye wouldn't be twitching.

Jess couldn't stop the gentle rebuke that formed on her lips. "Asking, rather than accusing...works better every time, you know. I'll need to clear it with Freya for confidentiality reasons but given the current situation I don't see why that would be an issue."

"Can I have your number?"

Heat rushed up over Jess's face. Was he really about to ask her out? After the argument they'd just had? Surely, not.

"That way I can find a good time to look at the data and to follow up regarding the individual meeting."

Of course...

She swallowed hard. As much as she didn't want to date, she wasn't completely immune to the charms of a handsome man. Hopefully, he hadn't caught her moment of girlish stupidity at thinking that he might be flirting with her. Beckett grinned widely when she glanced up at him though.

Great.

The blush would have been bright on her pale face. He wouldn't have missed it. Now he would think she was interested in him. She rattled off her number, stumbling twice over the numerals because she was still so darn shaken.

That's what happens when you barely speak to men,

she thought. *You get so out of practice that you don't know what flirting even is!*

When her phone buzzed in her pocket, she nearly jumped out of her skin.

"Now you have mine as well. I promise to only contact you if it's budget related." Beckett leaned in close, the heat of his breath teasing across her cheek and sending her pulse racing up into an eager pace. The smile he flashed her was nothing short of pure male satisfaction at knowing that a woman was interested in him. "At least until you open the lines of communication to more."

"That will never happen."

"If that's what you want." He shrugged. "You've got my number if you change your mind."

CHAPTER SIX

HE'D THOUGHT HE'D SMOOTHED her ruffled feathers after the initial committee meeting last week, but when he showed up for their scheduled one-on-one discussion, she'd been frostily professional. No, more than that, because most of the time she had looked at him like she might stare at a malfunctioning printer.

But then there had been the rarer moments, when the sparks in Jess's eyes as she looked at him had left Beckett with so many questions. Even though she clearly felt some physical attraction toward him, she remained as prickly as a cactus. She intrigued him. It wasn't just that she didn't fawn over him like most women did. No, this was something more.

Rather than pushing him away though, her stand-offish nature made him want to find a chink in her armor. And there were times when he'd catch something fascinating in her expression. She may not like him as a person, yet, but she certainly found something about him impossible to ignore. Occasionally, her eyes glowed with pure female interest and even a hint of longing. And he hadn't missed her reaction when he'd "accidentally" brushed his leg against hers outside the ice cream parlor.

The desire to flirt with her was one he was struggling to squash. He didn't want forever or long-term or any of the things that Jess would be needing. But the drive to win one of her soft smiles was powerful, and when he got one he felt the same rush that he'd experienced in his early days on an ambulance, and he missed that feeling.

"I've seen enough here today, but I'd love to take you to lunch. We could discuss any ideas you have. They don't have to be hospital related." The words came out with the hint of a meaning he hadn't intended, but he figured that a bit of harmless flirtation wouldn't hurt. They both knew the boundaries, after all, and Jess was on the same page as he was. Even if there was an attraction there, she clearly didn't want to give in to it and neither did he. The distance between them was too much to bridge.

Jess shook her head no, just as he'd known she would. "I don't think that would be a good idea."

"No?" He took a step closer. When her hair dipped down into her face, he gave in to the urge and swept it back before tucking it behind her ear. That wasn't an outright no, and something about the shy look that the normally confident woman was giving him tempted him. "How about dinner then?"

"You wish, Captain Trust Fund." Pink tinted her cheeks, the blush coloring her soft skin and making her even more beautiful, but the defenses in her eyes backed up her words. Jess didn't just have walls—she had a moat filled with alligators.

He'd picked up that stupid nickname around the hospital once it came out that he'd been an EMT captain before he came back to Woodvale and was from *the* Wilder family. He didn't love the assumptions behind the label, but it had never really bothered him much until he heard it roll off Jess's lips. She'd probably be surprised to learn that while he did technically have a trust fund, he couldn't access it for a few more years. After the way his sister had blown through money—including well into the six figures for a sports car that she let her fiancé drive far too fast and which had ultimately led to their deaths—Richard Wilder had locked Beckett's own trust fund up tight.

Beckett had worked for a living, something Sloane had never had to do. In fact, he missed being just plain old Captain Beckett Wilder, EMT. He'd hung up the uniform and traded it for custom tailored suits when his dad's cancer diagnosis had come in, reluctantly accepting the mantle of being Richard Wilder's heir and next in command on an official level. He hadn't realized the toll not being on an action-filled ambulance would take on his soul though. Man, he missed the adrenaline rush that came when that bell went off. Thankfully, it was just temporary. He couldn't wait to get back to his real career.

Leaning a little closer, Beckett dropped his voice and teased Jess a bit. "What if I up the ante to dinner and breakfast the next morning? Could you get a sitter for Mason for Saturday night?"

"You are incorrigible. I've got to get to work," she muttered and walked away without a backward glance.

"That wasn't a no," he called after her.

The tiniest hint of a laugh just reached his ears. His lips twitched at the sound. One day soon he'd get a full laugh from her. He'd make sure of it.

"Beckett," Freya said, pulling his attention away from Jess's retreating form.

"Hmm…?" When Jess scanned her ID badge and went through the doors that led back into the emergency department, Beckett turned to Freya who stared at him with this stern teacher face. "What?"

"Don't toy with her." She crossed her arms and rose up on tiptoe so that she could properly look him in the eye. "Don't start anything that you aren't serious about."

"Wasn't planning on it," Beckett reassured her. Freya was a good friend, and she was only looking out for Jess's best interests. "Jess and I are on the same page. She's completely safe with me, so don't worry."

Freya gave him a skeptical look but let the subject drop. "Don't you have a meeting to get to?"

"I met with Jess this morning. I was supposed to meet with General Surgery, but they had an emergency surgery pop up so had to reschedule."

He and Jess had gone over the numbers, but he'd had to admit that she was right. The budget as it was just wouldn't allow for more ambulances. It wouldn't even cover the empty EMT position that had been sitting open for months. Hammering on about ambulances wasn't going to get it done though. No, this issue would have to come from higher up the food chain because more funding would have to be allocated from above. He'd asked Jess to submit the proposal to include ambulances, salaries and supplies on top of the things she'd pointed out this morning, like a replacement for their ancient X-ray machine, though this was more than the scope of what could be covered by a one-time donation.

"Ah, well, I take it things didn't go your way?"

Frowning, he asked, "What makes you say that?"

She pointed at his face. "Those crinkles of frustration around your eyes. They make you look like your father."

Taking a deep breath, Beckett tried to relax his face. One day he would look like his father, but he wasn't quite ready for that yet. "I'm trying to get more ambulances and EMTs so that what happened with Sloane doesn't happen again. Jess and I spent all morning looking at the numbers though and she's right. There is no wiggle room. The hospital needs to do a better job funding that department."

"You know how those bean counters are. If it doesn't affect their bottom line, they're gonna kick that can down the road as far as they can." Freya shrugged; she'd been fighting against the system for years and knew there was no easy fix. She started walking away, but tossed over her shoulder, "If you want to beat the rain, you might want to hurry."

Beckett wanted to hit the gym and work off some of the frustrations seeing that budget had brought up. *And the tension from being so close to Jess in that tiny closet-sized office.* Exercise usually helped give him clarity and he needed it to find a way to get the services he wanted funded. *And put the soft scent of Jess's light perfume out of his mind.* The pitch-black sky made him second-guess that choice. The cars in the lot were nearly impossible to see through the furious rain. A large piece of something yellow flew past the window and stuck to one of the columns marking the pedestrian crossing, flapping like a canary's wings against its constraint. Staying at the hospital a while longer seemed like a better plan.

His phone buzzed, and when he pulled it out of his pocket, an emergency notice flashed across the screen. The weather alert he read on the screen sent a shiver down his spine. This was not good.

"Everyone move to an interior hallway!" He jumped into action and shepherded people away from the wall of glass at the front of the hospital, urging them farther into the building. "There's a tornado just outside Woodvale and it's heading our way."

CHAPTER SEVEN

THE ENTIRE EMERGENCY DEPARTMENT fell into chaos. Panicking patients shoved stressed employees as they tried to get deeper into the building. Doctors and nurses steered others through the hallways to a safer part of the hospital. Jess got caught up ensuring patient safety. Thankfully, her meeting with Beckett had ended, so she could devote her time to helping the overwhelmed emergency room staff.

Jess groaned when, instead of moving with the others to safety, one of their medical receptionists crawled under her desk. Apparently, Sasha's flight-or-fight mode had triggered the third option of freeze. Jess would worry about getting her out once she'd gotten everyone else sorted. She had to focus on the people she could help right now.

"You'd think they'd never lived through a storm before," Jess muttered to herself. With a disbelieving shake of her head, Jess helped a patient into a wheelchair. After pushing her to the designated hallway, Jess left her with one of the nurse's assistants.

The squeak, squeak, squeak of Jess's shoes kept her company as she hurried back to the ED. The few stragglers were heading in the right direction. One man limped along holding on to a friend, slowly trekking up the hallway.

After grabbing another wheelchair, Jess jogged their direction with it. "Here, this will make the trip go a lot faster."

She took one last look around the department. All clear. With a glance up to the ceiling, Jess sent up a quick prayer that the damage to the hospital would be minimal, and the elementary school wouldn't be in the tornado's path. *And above all else, please keep Mason safe.* As soon as she got herself to safety, she was going to pull up that weather app and see if there was a projected path. She'd taken three steps toward that interior hallway when the sound of crying hit her ears and she remembered.

Sasha…

Only the terrified medical receptionist remained, still sobbing beneath her desk. The poor girl was frozen with fright, but with the large bank of windows right above the desk it would not be safe for her to stay. How could Jess get Sasha to go with her though?

"Sasha, we need to get to the hallway, come on." Keeping her voice low and steady, Jess tried to reason with the woman even though her own heart raced like a Thoroughbred at Keeneland racetrack. "I don't think this is a good place to stay. We need to move away from these windows."

Outside those windows, the sky held nearly no light. A roar grew louder and louder. Jess swallowed hard. This was so not good. Why did there have to be a tornado on her watch? She didn't have time for this today.

"Please, Sasha, let's go!" Jess crouched down and held out a hand. Calm and collected wasn't working with the medical receptionist. Maybe authoritative? It might work if the panicked woman didn't notice how bad Jess's hand was shaking. "Sasha, get out of there now!"

Sasha rocked back and forth, eyes wild with fear. She ignored Jess's outstretched hand. The orders Jess had issued fell on effectively deaf ears. Between sobs, Sasha muttered a prayer.

"The good Lord helps those who help themselves." Jess sighed. "And Sasha, you really gotta help yourself right now."

"She's not coming out," a man's voice called from right above Jess's head. "Leave her."

Jess jerked, slamming her head into the edge of Sasha's desk. Pain rocketed through her skull, radiating out from the point of impact. No good deed goes unpunished. Hadn't life taught her that by now?

"Sorry to startle you." Beckett held out a hand. "You aren't safe here. Come on."

Jess put her hand in his and let him pull her to her feet. As she rose to her full unimpressive height, she got a good look outside the window. No longer inky black, the sky now held an odd tint. Through the murky green glow, she could just make out the funnel cloud.

"Oh!"

Beckett must have seen it just as Jess did. He shoved her under another desk, blocking the opening with his body. His voice lowered to a growl. "Get down."

Something large and heavy crashed through the glass and hit the floor nearby. Jess's view, however, consisted solely of Beckett's broad chest. The wind blew his tie, whipping the silk up around her face. She brushed it down and held it to his chest. Tension locked his frame into a protective barrier. He took the brunt of the wind and rain, sheltering her, protecting her from the onslaught.

Metallic pings rang out sharply and contrasted with the roar of the wind. Objects hitting the tile floors created an erratic tempo. Beckett grunted as his back was pelted, the muffled thumps adding to the din surrounding them.

"Is that hail?" They were inches apart, but the deafening roar of the wind nearly drowned out Jess's words.

"Not sure if it's hail or what," he yelled back. "Stings though."

The desk Beckett had shoved Jess under started sliding back as the floor grew wet. Beckett crept along, keeping as much of the protection of the desk as he could. Still, the wind continued.

Water puddled up under her, and her scrubs soaked up the icy liquid like a wick.

The wind stopped, suddenly, as if someone had flipped a switch and the room grew quiet. "Is it over?"

Beckett groaned and eased back from the desk. "I think it might be."

"Oh, man." Jess crawled out and stumbled to her feet. "That was terrifying."

Jess couldn't identify the impulse that overtook her logic. Relief at being alive? Gratitude for his protection? It could have been any number of reasons, but before she could second-guess it, she flung herself against Beckett's chest. Instinct drove her. Wrapping her arms around his neck, she tugged his face down. Her lips were nearly to his before the dots connected in her brain that she was standing on her tiptoes, about to kiss Beckett Wilder.

Stress. It had to be stress. Or maybe pure appreciation that she was alive and safe thanks to him. There could be no other rationale for why she'd have nearly made a mistake that monumental. Releasing him as quickly as she grabbed him, Jess stuttered over an apology.

"It's okay," he said slowly, but there was a hint of something in his eyes. Something vibrant, eager and far too intriguing.

"I'm sorry," she murmured. "Adrenaline got me."

New subject required. Right now, before she stupidly threw herself at him again. She needed to do a status check. Physically, she was in great shape. Wet, but uninjured. Mentally, she was shaken.

This area of the hospital hadn't fared quite so well. The emergency department looked like a war zone. Spinning in a slow circle, she tried to take it all in. Broken glass was scattered across the floor, glittering in the odd light. Dripping-wet sections of insulation hung from the ceiling like sad party streamers. Papers and brochures littered the floor and flat surfaces. Computer monitors were upended. The emergency lights flickered as if the generator couldn't decide if it was needed or not. Everything around them was either broken, soaked or both.

"Are you okay?" Beckett's color looked a little off. But, then again, they had just survived a tornado.

"I am thanks to you." Jess probably didn't look her

best either, even though he'd protected her from the worst of it. "Do you know what the expected path was for the tornado? Was it heading for the elementary school?"

"I have no idea," he said, leaning against one of the supports. Blood appeared at his shoulder and trickled down the white column. "My back doesn't feel so great."

She strode over to him. "Take off that jacket."

"I kinda like it when you're bossy." He winced as the suit coat slid from his shoulders.

She took the jacket from him. There were dozens of holes in it. "Okay, shirt off too. Let me see your back."

"If you wanted to see me without a shirt, all you had to do was ask." He tried for a grin, but it was weak. Once crisp, the white button-down was now ragged. He tugged it gently from his torso. A grimace marred his handsome face when the shirt stuck to a cut on his shoulder. "This went on a lot easier than it's coming off."

Blood speckled the back of the shirt. He turned his back to her, and Jess had to bite her lip to avoid a gasp. Dozens of little shards of metal were embedded into his skin.

"I need to find some supplies. Don't lean against anything else until I get all that shrapnel out." If Beckett hadn't pushed her under that desk, those metal slivers could have been lodged in her face. She let out a long sigh. She didn't like the wave of concern that washed over her. It's gratitude, she told herself. Just gratitude. Taking a deep breath to regain her focus, Jess began looking for the supplies she'd need to remove the debris from his back.

"Do you think you could try to find out what else got hit in town?" she asked as she searched through a tipped-over supply cart for an undamaged package of gauze. "Start with the elementary school, please. I need to see if Mason is okay."

"I'll see what I can find out," Beckett called as she rifled through the remains of a storage cart. "Look out for that ceiling though. It looks like it could fall at any time."

Jess gave a quick glance up. One ceiling tile hung precariously above her head. Why wasn't this place constructed of sturdier materials? Probably so that rich men like Beckett and Clint could have more money to spend on asinine things like fancy cars and golf tee times. She stopped herself; that was a mean thought about the man who had probably just saved her life. What was wrong with her?

Where were the dang tweezers? Finally, she found a pair.

"Watch out!" Beckett's strong arms pulled her into his bare chest and away from the sudden crash of falling debris. Jess's heart raced. Was it because a giant chunk of ceiling had nearly flattened her into a scrub-covered pancake or because she was being pressed into the deliciously muscled chest of a good-looking man who'd saved her life twice now in the span of an hour?

The ceiling, Jess. It has to be the ceiling because you cannot start liking any part of Beckett. Not even a chest so perfectly sculpted as his. Didn't you learn your lesson about messing with a rich guy?

"Thank you," she muttered as she pushed away from his chest. Images flashed through her mind of having her hands on his body during a more intimate encounter. Swallowing hard, Jess pulled herself together. She was a professional, not some lovelorn woman who couldn't control herself around a handsome man. "You're going to make your back worse if you don't stay still."

"Are you really gonna stand there and chastise me? Woman, I just saved you. Where's my gratitude?" He shook his head.

"Once everything is clear, I'll set up a parade. We can start right here at the hospital and parade down Main Street."

Main Street... Oh, my goodness, what else has been hit? My house? The elementary school? Mason!

Where was her phone? Jess patted her pockets, searching for the missing device. Nothing. Quickly, she scanned the room. She'd clad her phone in a hot-pink case. How hard could it be to find? She grabbed one of the desk phones. No dial tone.

Of course.

"Do you have a phone?" She held her hand out impatiently.

He reached for his discarded suit coat. From the inner pocket, he pulled a cell phone. "Who do you need to call?"

"I want to check on the elementary school."

"Of course. I was about to do that when I realized that ceiling was going to drop on your head." He held out his phone, and Jess took it from his outstretched hand.

What was the number? Her hands shook so badly

that she nearly dropped the phone. Why couldn't she remember the number for the elementary school? This was the downfall of programming numbers into phones and no longer having to dial them. No one, including Jess, memorized numbers anymore.

"Can't remember the number?"

She clutched the phone close in case he had ideas of taking it back. "I just need a moment."

Typing in the area code, she hoped that the familiarity of those numbers on the screen would help trigger the memory of the rest. Thankfully, it worked. She typed in the rest and hit Dial.

Instead of an answer, or even the sound of the call ringing through, she was met with an automated voice saying that the call could not be completed at this time and to please try again later.

"Won't go through." The lump clogging her throat made her sound like a croaking frog.

"Probably too many people trying to make calls, either for help or to check on their loved ones."

"You think?"

"Lines and towers may be down. Or are simply overloaded." He gently took the phone back. "Let me see if I can make a call." He tapped on his screen and then held the phone up to his ear. "It won't even call one of my preprogrammed contacts. I think cells are just down."

"Landlines too." Jess nodded toward the dead phone on the desk. "At least that one is, anyway. If the tornado hit the school, there could be a lot of injured kids. We need to make contact and see if they need help."

He nodded. "Okay. Get this shrapnel out of my back and I'll find a way to make contact. Even if I have to drive over there myself."

CHAPTER EIGHT

"Beckett—"

"I'll see if I can get a text or call out while you get this mess out of me." When Jess didn't move, Beckett gave a little more encouragement that he hoped would appeal to her nursing background. "You don't want to be responsible for my back getting infected after I saved your life, do you?"

Crossing her arms over her chest, Jess snapped, "You're never going to let me forget that, are you?"

"Nope." Turning, he grinned at her over his shoulder, happy that his tactics seemed to be working. He was learning how her mind worked and guessed correctly when he'd narrowed in on her professional sensibilities. She'd never leave someone to get an infection she could help prevent, especially not someone who had helped her. He did feel the slightest smidgen of guilt himself that he had to use that against her, but he needed her to focus. And he needed the metal slivers out of his back, for sure. "But think of how much you'll enjoy the pain of pulling these bits out. You can really enjoy torturing me."

Jess grew quiet, but she gathered the rest of the supplies needed to pick his back clean. He knew she was worried about her son. He had to admit, he was worried about the little guy too. There was something about that kid that Beckett found hard to forget.

Kinda like his mama.

Unlike Mason, Jess didn't want to talk. She was probably only speaking to him in that moment because he'd forced the issue. By being in the right place at the right time to save her life, or at least her pretty face, from the shrapnel she was about to extract from his back with tweezers, he'd earned at least a scrap of respect from her. Maybe that would push them over the line from enemies to friends on which they'd teetered recently. A few times, he'd noticed a softening in her demeanor, so quick he nearly missed it, but if he opened his mouth, she slammed those defenses into place so fast it nearly gave him whiplash.

Occasionally, her hands on his back softened into more of a caress than a strictly professional touch though. Her spur-of-the-moment almost-kiss sat front and center in Beckett's mind. Had it been a by-product of adrenaline or something more? The look in her eyes had been far more than gratitude. He'd adamantly refused to consider anything more than a friendly professional relationship with her, albeit one with a little good-natured flirting, but the way it felt to have her pressed against his chest tempted him to reconsider.

Teeth grinding together, Beckett bit back a curse. She'd dug way in to get that piece out. He'd teased her about torture, but maybe she'd taken that as an order. Geez, that hurt. He puffed out a breath, trying to breathe through the pain. The only good thing about it was that it distracted him from his increasingly intimate thoughts of Jess. He needed to remember that he wasn't interested in long-term, and Jess practically had the word *forever* stamped across her pretty face.

"I think that's the last of it. That piece was in the deepest." She moved around him to make eye contact, but she seemed to have trouble meeting his eyes, with her gaze focusing more on his chest than his face. "I still need to bandage you up. I hate to put a dozen small bandages on your back, so what do you think of one larger piece of gauze?"

"Both sound annoying. Do what you think is best." He trusted her medical judgment.

When she'd finished with the bandage and removed her gloves, tossing them into a trash can that she'd righted, air whooshed from Beckett's lungs and he breathed a deep sigh of relief. He had needed her ever-so-enticing hands off his bare skin. The more Jess touched him, the more his thoughts drifted to places they shouldn't.

Picking up his discarded dress shirt, Beckett's nose wrinkled. The blood stains would never come out, not to mention the multiple poke holes. Easing one arm through the sleeve, his lip curled up in disgust when the crusty, dried blood scraped against his skin. How inappropriate would it be for him to be roaming the halls of the hospital half-dressed?

"Don't put that nasty thing back on." Jess tossed something blue his direction. "That scrub top will look silly with those fancy pants of yours, but at least it's clean."

"My pants aren't fancy." Looking down, Beckett

frowned. They were tailored, yes, but they were a classic-cut suit pant. Hardly fancy.

"That suit probably cost more than my car," she said dryly.

He didn't let the retort fly that her car wasn't worth much. His gut feeling said it wouldn't go over well. The car might be a broken-down hunk of junk, but it was hers, and he'd learned already that she was protective of what was hers.

"And now it's trash." Beckett shrugged, refusing to wince at the pain that little gesture caused. "There are… certain expectations that come with being a Wilder. Expensive suits are one of them."

Expensive suits, five-star restaurants, and oversize houses on the lake. None of it was really who Beckett was, though it came part and parcel of carrying the Wilder name. They hadn't managed to pry the keys to his truck from his hands just yet, but he worried the day was coming when his dad forced a luxury car on him with the admonishment of "What will people think if they see you stepping out of a pickup truck? Beckett, you are a Wilder, but we are not wild."

Jess tossed a reply over her shoulder as she walked away. "Imagine the ambulances you could fund without all the posh trappings that you seem to hate anyways."

Beckett gingerly slipped the blue scrub top over his head. It really seemed to irk her that his family had money. What he didn't know was why. If she'd take even a minute to get to know him, she'd see he wasn't the guy she imagined him to be.

When he caught up, she was trying to clear some debris blocking the hallway into the main hospital; that explained why none of the other hospital staff or patients had appeared yet. He took a chunk of busted ceiling tile from her hands and threw it down the hallway. It shattered against the wall. Side by side, they silently dislodged debris so they could access the hospital. Every movement made him aware of all the small cuts on his back, but it had to be done. Was there more devastation on the other side or had the emergency department sustained the brunt of it?

Soon, they cleared the doorway. As soon as they opened it, Freya appeared. She looked frazzled, but nearly as immaculate as when they'd spoken earlier. Peeking beyond her into the hospital, Beckett could see some broken glass and overturned chairs, but nothing too bad.

"Jess!" Freya cried as she ran into Jess's outstretched arms. "Oh, thank goodness. I couldn't find you and I thought…"

Beckett watched the two women embrace with no small amount of envy.

"I'm good. I don't have a scratch on me." Jess looked Beckett's way and her lips tipped up in the briefest hint of a smile. "Someone took the brunt for me. How are you?"

Freya took Jess's hands in hers and the expression on her face gave Beckett pause. She seemed to be steeling her nerves before she could share her news. Dread dropped in the pit of his stomach. It sat heavy and solid, stirring up his adrenaline again. Nothing she was about to say could be good.

"Jess, we got a radio call. Woodvale Elementary was

directly in the tornado's path. There's no word on how bad it is yet, but part of the building has collapsed."

"Freya…" Jess breathed more than she said.

Her knees gave way, and she would have hit the ground if Beckett hadn't moved to catch her. She shook against him. Mason was her everything, if something had happened to him, Beckett wasn't sure how she'd handle that.

The sudden action sent little stabs of pain across the entirety of his back as the cuts were pulled and scrunched, but he seemed to be programmed to protect Jess. Even at his own peril.

"I have to go there." Jess's voice cracked, sounding nothing like her normally smooth tones.

"You have to pull yourself together and be strong." Freya pulled Jess in for another hug. She held on for a moment, holding so tight that it looked like she was trying to lend Jess her strength. "Okay, so, listen to me. The plan is for us to send someone over to set up a first-aid tent. I'm getting some supplies together and need to find someone who we can spare to go when we are already going to be strapped here."

"I'll go," Jess volunteered.

"Honey, I don't think it's a good idea. You're not in the right mindset to treat patients." Freya looked apologetic, but Beckett could see that denying Jess was costing his old friend. "We are trying to rouse one of the off-duty EMTs, but phones are down everywhere."

"I'll go." They didn't need to get in touch with another EMT. He was standing right there and more than willing to help. "I'm available and I have the experience. You don't need to short the hospital when I'm happy to step up."

Freya nodded. "Yes. This is good. Thank you, Beckett."

"I need to go to that school," Jess argued, crossing her arms over her chest. The defiant look on her face said she was going with or without permission. "I'm okay. I can handle this."

She did seem steadier on her feet than a moment ago, but a certain fragility surrounded her. Maybe because he'd already protected her several times that day, or maybe because of the way his heart had skipped a beat when she'd nearly kissed him, he didn't want to see her upset any more. "I am qualified to do this. Just because I've spent more time recently in suits than in the back of an ambo doesn't mean I've forgotten my training. And no one here is counting on my presence. We don't know how many kids are injured. Do you honestly believe that you can maintain enough emotional detachment to treat the others if Mason is injured?"

Terror flashed in her eyes, stronger now than when they were under that desk. Her eyes closed for a moment, lashes fanning across her cheeks, and when they opened, determination replaced the fear. "I'm going to find my son, with or without you. Now, if you will excuse me, I don't have time to argue with you."

CHAPTER NINE

THOUGHTS OF WHAT could be happening at the school rushed through Jess's head, like scenes from the most traumatic movie ever made. Her brain quite vividly showed her images of injured children, maimed teachers, and worst of all, the numerous ways that her own son could have been harmed.

My sweet boy...

She pictured him with glass in his little body, like she'd just pulled from Beckett's back, with broken bones, and—she swallowed hard—worse... She blinked away the tears that final image brought forth. Breathing grew hard. *Don't panic yet, Jess.* He could be fine. Mason could be perfectly fine. But the growing lump in the pit of her stomach wasn't going away until she could verify with her own eyes that her little boy was healthy and whole.

"Do you really think this is the best course of action?" Beckett asked from behind her.

Jess spun to face him. Why was he still here? His presence at the moment served as a distraction she didn't want or need, and he should have been heading over to the school since he had volunteered to do so. "I really will be okay."

She had no choice. Panicking was a luxury that she didn't have. Most people might not think of being able to panic as a luxury, but when you were a single mom, there was no one else to lean on. She'd had her moment of freak-out, but now she had to focus. With her job, she compartmentalized things every day, removing emotions from the equation. It was harder to do with her own son potentially in danger, but now she had to.

"I know you are worried about Mason, but it's that fear that might make you make a mistake today. You need to trust me."

"Trust you..."

Once upon a time, she'd been an eternal optimist who would put her faith in anyone and everyone. When she was a young, idealistic nursing student, she still thought men could be trusted and naively believed in all the other romantic jazz—love at first sight, soul mates and even the idea that she could find the man of her dreams. When she'd met Clint, she thought she'd found her forever. He'd swept her off her feet so hard that she doubted her feet touched the ground that entire summer.

It had been perfect.

Until she found out it was all a lie.

It was crushing to find out that her entire world was based on falsehoods and secrets, but she got through it. And if it made her more wary of men like Beckett, she was better for it. Men couldn't be trusted, particularly ones with more zeros at the end of their bank balances than limbs on their body.

One amazing thing did come from that relationship with Clint—Mason.

Right now, Mason might be in trouble. And she wasn't going to let anyone keep her from her son any longer. But she wasn't about to lower her guard and trust Beckett or any other man.

"Fine, let's go." She headed for the main supply closet. She wanted to get those supplies and get to the school. She left Beckett to trail behind her. She made it ten feet before she stopped cold in her tracks, realizing that she'd left someone else behind—Sasha.

Sprinting back through the ED, she looked for the other woman. "Sasha? Are you here, honey? Call out if you can hear me."

"Is that the woman under the desk?" Beckett asked. He was tenacious; she'd give him that.

"Yeah, she's one of our medical receptionists." Jess looked under each desk as she passed it. So far, she could see no sign of the frightened young woman. Where could she be?

"There," Beckett said, pointing to where a single white sneaker and scrub-clad leg poked out of a pile of debris. "Help me uncover her."

Working swiftly, but carefully, they started to uncover Sasha. "Do you think there's enough weight on her that we need to worry about crush syndrome?" Jess asked. While she was confident in her nursing abilities, she had never worked Search and Rescue or as an EMT. She saw the injuries after the patient had reached the hospital and at the very least some lifesaving measures had already been applied.

Beckett moved more debris. "I think if we move quickly, she won't have been under the weight for long enough for that to be a factor. It hasn't been fifteen minutes yet, so we should be okay to completely uncover her. We could be dealing with some crush injuries though, for sure."

Jess checked Sasha's foot. "No pulse."

Beckett moved enough to find Sasha's other foot where he too sought for a pulse. With a negative shake of his head, he said, "Nothing here either."

Quickly, they cleared the rest of the debris from Sasha's body. Her chest and head had been partially protected, thankfully, by an overturned office chair. Once they had her fully uncovered, Jess started checking vitals.

"Pulse is weak. Not seeing any respirations." She scrubbed her fingers against Sasha's sternum. "Sasha, honey, can you hear me?"

The medical receptionist didn't respond to the stimuli that Jess provided. *Dang it.* Jess pressed her palm against Sasha's forehead and lifted her chin to make sure her airway was open. She leaned forward, hoping to feel the woman's breath against her face. Nothing. "She's not breathing."

"Starting CPR." Beckett moved into position next to Sasha's shoulders and placed the heel of his palm on the center of Sasha's chest. He counted out the chest compressions.

When that was done, she gave the required breaths. She looked around for a mask or Ambu Bag, but none were visible.

Beckett continued chest compressions until Sasha started to cough and pushed him away.

"Wh-what happened?" she asked, trying to lift her head.

"Hey, take it easy. Lie back down for me." Beckett put a gentle hand on her shoulder. "A tornado hit the hospital and you were knocked unconscious. Don't try to move just yet. It would be best if we could get you checked out properly before you move too much."

Sasha blinked rapidly, her eyes struggling to focus. "My head hurts."

Jess was certain that the younger woman had a concussion. The worry was that she had far more than a concussion—internal injuries or something. A lot of very hard materials, some with fairly substantial weight, had fallen on Sasha.

"Yeah, I'd imagine it does. Hold still." Beckett kept his hand on her shoulder, preventing her from moving much. "Jess, you think you could go find some help? I'll stay with Sasha and make sure that she doesn't move much until we get her good and checked out."

Jess hesitated to go, preferring to stay with Sasha herself, but Beckett had the woman calm and Sasha was responding well to his relaxed demeanor. So she rose to her feet. "I'll be back as quickly as I can."

She hurried to the main lobby where Freya had said they were setting up a temporary ED. "We have an injured medical receptionist back in the ED. I need a doctor and a gurney. I'm not sure if it's safe to move her. We did have to perform CPR, but she's conscious now and talking."

Within a minute, Jess had a doctor and a nurse following her back to where Sasha and Beckett were. Beckett still sat on his knees next to Sasha making sure she stayed as still and calm as possible.

"Hey, Jess," Freya called. "Tina has all those supplies together. If Beckett is ready, you can hand off your patient to Dr. Newton and get on over to the school now. Be careful and check in when you can, okay?"

CHAPTER TEN

"I'LL GET MY CAR." Jess took off out the door, leaving Beckett no choice but to follow her. Now that they'd handed Sasha off to the care of one of the emergency department doctors, she was gung ho about getting to the school. He went out the door a few paces behind her, but he had to pause because he couldn't see. He blinked several times at the sudden difference in light. Man, it was bright out there.

When his eyes adjusted, he saw Jess standing a few feet away, staring, hand up over her mouth. He figured she'd be halfway to her car by now. Maybe the change in light had gotten to her too.

"What's wrong…?" But then he took in all the devastation outside, and words failed him. Even after seeing the havoc inside the emergency department, the scene outside managed to shock him.

Trees and power poles were down all around the hospital. In the parking lot, several cars were completely flipped upside down. Several more had been tipped onto their sides. Many of the vehicles had no glass left in them.

They walked carefully through the debris-laden lot.

Not a single vehicle seemed to have been spared. Even the ones that remained on all four tires were covered in tree branches, or pieces of trash.

"Well, I guess we aren't taking my car." Jess stopped in front of her aged black sedan and let out a shaky breath. "I just picked it up from the shop too!"

The car had another vehicle tipped into the side of it, and the little black sedan was partially crushed under the load that the much larger SUV put on it. There was no way they were getting that car out alone. Even if they could have freed it, the car's road worthiness remained questionable.

"Okay, well, let's take my truck then," Beckett said, steering Jess toward the parking garage with a gentle hand on her elbow. It had only been a few hours since he'd made the drive to the hospital, but it seemed like it had been days. Time had a way of becoming uncertain when traumatic things happened. He knew that, but the reminder still slapped him in the face hard.

They hadn't made it one hundred yards before they saw the live power line down across the exit of the parking garage. The wind blew a branch in and out of contact with it. Blue sparks of electricity shot up at every contact. He let out a low curse.

"So, it looks like yours isn't an option either. What now?" Jess closed her eyes and looked up to the sky. Was she praying? Beckett realized that he had no idea if she was religious or spiritual in any way.

"The school is only about eight blocks that way." She opened her eyes and pointed north. "We could walk. We'd have to take even fewer supplies though. You might be as strong as an ox, but I don't think you could cart all that for long, especially with your back the way it is."

"At least it looks like the rain is gone." Beckett tried to recognize the one positive he'd found since they'd walked outside. He wasn't looking forward to walking eight blocks in wet dress shoes though. The blisters he'd get from that would be the size of dinner plates. He had his gym bag in the truck, and if he was lucky, his sneakers were with it.

He took a deep breath and stared at the parking garage. Woodvale Memorial's parking structure was multilevel, but the drive lanes were far too narrow to have two vehicles pass and not hit the parked cars. Very much a one-way only. An idea sparked, but the only way it would work was if Jess didn't let anyone else come in. "I can possibly get my truck out if I drive down the entrance. If you can block any other cars from driving into the garage, I'll give it a try."

She nodded. Once again, she took off walking without a word, leaving Beckett to scramble to keep pace. For someone so tiny, she sure could move when she wanted to.

"Have you always lived in Woodvale?" he asked as he caught up with her.

She shot him a look. "What?"

He hoped his random attempts at conversation would help keep her mind off the situation at the elementary school and her terror of not knowing what was happening with her son. He shrugged in response to her question. "It looks like we're going to be spending a lot of time together today. Maybe we could talk a little— unless you'd rather spend it in awkward silence, that is."

"Yes."   .

"Yes, you've always lived in Woodvale, or yes, you'd rather go all day without speaking?"

"Both, really."

Becket chuckled. "I'm not great at silence. Never have been. So, you might as well accept that I'm just going to talk even if you don't participate much in the conversation."

"Oh, joy."

"I grew up here too. Not sure how I didn't know you before?"

"I don't get out much."

Her deadpan delivery made him snort. "For your entire life?"

They walked around the parking garage to the entrance and Beckett noticed that the streetlights on the corner weren't functioning.

"Go get your truck, or I'll hoof it with all the supplies I can carry alone."

"Got it." He left her standing in the entrance of the garage and hurried to where he'd parked his truck.

The parking garage seemed to have withstood the storm without much damage. He saw a few busted windows, likely from the debris thrown by that wicked wind, but most of the vehicles in the garage appeared to be in drivable condition. Thankfully, his truck was intact.

He drove carefully back down the entrance ramp. To get out, you normally had to circle through all the levels to the top, then circle back down the other side. He really hoped that Jess was blocking anyone else from coming into the garage, because it was too tight for even a small car to pass by his truck.

When he could finally see daylight again, he could also see Jess. She stood in front of the entrance, squaring off with a guy in an SUV trying to turn into the garage. He backed down when he saw Beckett's truck.

Jess ran over and hopped into the passenger seat. "Took you long enough," she muttered. "I nearly got murdered while you were in here caressing your leather seats."

Snorting, Beckett didn't give her any further reply. Fear already had her in a snit, and he wasn't going to push her into taking more of that frustration out on him. He pulled around the front of the hospital, getting as close as he could to the emergency department given the downed trees and flipped vehicles.

"Let's get the supplies and go." She jumped out before he'd even put the truck in Park.

"That was the plan," he muttered under his breath. This was going to be a long day if she insisted on flying solo for everything yet being angry with him for not keeping up.

He followed her inside where a pile of supplies had been set aside for them to take. "Anything else you think we will need?" he asked as he sorted through some of it. It would be easier to grab anything else they needed while they were still here, rather than having to come back because they had overlooked something necessary.

"It's not a fully loaded trauma room or even a stocked ambulance, but hopefully it will be enough for first aid for the elementary school. There's a huge stock of bandages, gauze, antiseptic, a portable defibrillator that

I'm praying we don't need, plus KT tape and wrap for any sprains."

"Instant cold packs? Gloves?"

"Yup." Jess stood, hefting up one of the large bins. She nodded her head toward the two remaining bins of supplies. "Can you get those?"

Freya motioned to Beckett to join her for a moment. When he walked over, she lowered her voice. "I need you to look out for her today. Especially if…" Her words trailed off but Beckett knew exactly what the rest of that sentence would have contained.

Especially if something had happened to Mason…

"I promise you I'll not let her out of my sight."

"Thank you." Freya reached out and put a hand on his arm. "But you'd better go, because she's leaving without you."

He turned to see Jess walking out the doors with her arms loaded down. Beckett hoisted the rest of the supplies and followed her once more. She was waiting next to the truck. Pressing his load against the side of the truck, Beckett fished his keys out of his pocket and unlocked the back doors. Soon, all the supplies were in the backseat. He dug quickly through his gym bag and changed his dress shoes for dry socks and sneakers.

Jess huffed a protest, but thankfully didn't say anything. This was a fight he wasn't going to engage in though. He needed dry shoes, or he'd have blisters and need medical treatment himself. Simple as that. Tossing the wet shoes in the back, he slid behind the wheel.

He turned north out of the parking lot. With all the debris on the roads, he had to creep along, well below the speed limit. From the impatient noises coming from the passenger seat, he sensed the pace was killing Jess. Couldn't be helped though since he had to weave and dodge around downed trees and wrecked cars. It wasn't safe to drive anywhere close to the posted speed limit. They'd be of no use to anyone if they crashed before they made it to the school.

When he made the turn off Main onto Wood Street, the most direct route to the school, that's when things got really jammed up. There were several large tree branches in the street, blocking both drive lanes. Beckett hit the brakes and brought the truck to a quick stop.

"Can we move them?" Jess asked.

"We can look and see." He put the truck in Park and stepped out. As he moved up to get a better look, he could see that the road was completely impassable. Even in a truck, trying to go over limbs that size would be dangerous, and they'd take too much time to move.

"This is going to be a no-go. We're better off going back to Main."

"Shh…" Jess held up one finger—*wait*.

"What are you—?" The rest of his words were muffled by her hand covering his mouth.

"I said, shh. Could you please be quiet?" She whispered her words as she stood against his chest, her palm pressed to his lips. "I heard something."

Blood raced through his veins, and he couldn't have heard anything over the pounding of his pulse. His body was all too aware of how close she was and how much closer they could get. His hands came up to rest on her waist.

His grip tightened at her sudden intake of breath. He

kissed the palm of her hand and she snatched it away like the kiss had scorched her skin.

"Stop that," she hissed. "Please, listen."

Closing his eyes, Beckett tried to do what she asked, tried to ignore the heat thrumming through him still. He wanted to ignore her commands, to pull her tight against his chest and kiss her with everything he had.

"There, do you hear that?" She took a few steps down the street. Beckett followed her and soon he heard it too. A faint cry for help.

The street was lined with older houses in various states of disarray. Some looked unaffected by the storm but ravaged by the passage of time. One lot held a foundation with a single wall. Most were damaged, but still standing.

The farther they walked down the street, the louder the pleas for help grew. It sounded like an elderly woman. "Is anyone out there?"

"I think that's Mrs. Glass," Jess said, picking up her speed. She ran to a blue house three doors down from where they'd been. The house seemed mostly okay, if you looked at it only from the left. The walls on the right side had been ripped away, as if it had been built that way for a movie set or something.

"You think it's safe to go inside?" She paused at the stairs.

Nothing was safe about going into a house missing a side wall. If they called 911, would they even be able to send anyone, given the widespread destruction? Brushing that idea away as doubtful, Beckett steeled his nerves for what he knew he had to do.

"Help!" the shaky voice called from somewhere inside the structure.

"Do we have a choice?" Beckett asked. "Look around. Do you see anyone else on this street? It's us or nothing."

CHAPTER ELEVEN

JESS TROD CAREFULLY as she entered Mrs. Glass's damaged house. The floor creaked and with every step she took, the house gave off a shiver. The wind whipped around the open wall that was screaming its wounds into the breeze.

Beckett bumped into her from behind and the house gave a deep groan. His hands slipped around her waist. His touch remained gentle, steadfast. "Maybe you should wait outside. I'll find her and bring her out."

"She doesn't know you." Jess turned to face him, arguing the point. She'd known Mrs. Glass since she was five years old. "She might be hurt and afraid. A familiar face might make her calmer."

"She was my teacher too, Jess." Beckett waved his hand at the gaping hole where the exterior wall had once stood. "And even if she hadn't been, if this place collapses down around our heads, then it won't matter if she saw a familiar face or not, because we will all be in need of rescue!"

"Is someone there? I need help," Mrs. Glass called from the back part of the house.

"Beckett—"

"Will you go out there in the yard, *please*? If she can't walk, I can carry her out easier than you. I'll bring her out." He stuck his hand out, keys resting on his outstretched palm. The look in his eyes was what finally convinced her to let him be the one to go in. "Run back to the truck and get some basic supplies. If it collapses, I need you on the outside to go get help. Let me be the one to do this."

When she took the keys, he squeezed her shoulder and then disappeared behind the stairs. Jess didn't want to admit it, but he was right. It didn't make sense for both of them to be at risk in that trembling wreck of a once beautiful home. Being inside that damaged house was a dangerous choice.

Besides, there was Mason to think of.

She ran as fast as she could back to Beckett's truck. By the time she reached it, her calves burned from the exertion and her lungs reminded her that cardio was more necessary than she gave it credit for. Rather than empty one of the supply bins, Jess picked up Beckett's gym bag. She dumped the remaining contents on the floor and stuffed it with a variety of supplies. She left the AED. Mrs. Glass had been shouting, so Jess made a calculated decision that they wouldn't need it.

Swallowing hard, she tried to shake the guilt that stopping to help Mrs. Glass filled her with. She should be going straight to her son. But how could she have ever lived with herself if she'd continued and left that sweet elderly woman trapped, possibly injured and at risk of the house falling down on her? Stopping was the right thing, even if it was hard to convince herself of that at the moment.

As she ran back into the yard, Mrs. Glass's house gave out an ear-piercing screech and listed slightly toward the damaged side. A few loose shingles crashed to the ground. Oh, this was not good at all!

Jess stopped at the bottom of the steps. She peered into the interior of the house but couldn't see him or Mrs. Glass. "Beckett, it's not going to stay up much longer!"

Biting her lip, Jess agonized over what to do. Should she go in? Then they could all end up flattened like pancakes. With one foot hovering over the bottom step, she wavered on whether to risk going in to see if she could help somehow. Her desire to help warred with her self-preservation instincts.

"Beckett!"

"What's all the shouting about?" He appeared in the open doorway with Mrs. Glass held safely in his arms. The elderly woman was grinning from ear to ear. Shaking his head, he smiled down at Mrs. Glass. "You'd think she thought we were in danger or something."

Backing out of his way, Jess clung to the stone birdbath for support. In the emergency room, she was rock-solid. But when it came to the people she knew, the people she loved, those nerves of hers were less steady. Right now, she was on a tightrope looking down on her life. The only way to safety was a narrow path with danger on all sides.

And as much as it shamed her to admit it, that safety today was about six-foot-two and broad shouldered. She'd leaned on Beckett that day, even as she pushed him out to arm's length. She wasn't the lean-on-a-man type. Men were a luxury, not a necessity in her life. So, what was making this one so indispensable?

The fact that he'd saved her life? Because he had.

Even though she'd depended on his steady presence, she still wasn't sure that she could trust him. Could she ever really trust him, given her past? Maybe not. Depending on Clint hadn't gone well for her in the past. Although, she was already seeing that Beckett was nothing like her ex.

Beckett was kind, where Clint had been selfish. He was thoughtful, where Clint had been oblivious. Yes, they shared a similarity in terms of their financial situations in life, but every passing moment she spent with Beckett made her think that she'd misjudged him. Clint would never have risked his life for a complete stranger, but Beckett had not only done so, he'd done so after being given an out.

Still, it was only when he came out of that house, safe and sound, that she could truly breathe again. And she didn't want to evaluate that *why* any further. Chalk it up to an adrenaline-fueled connection, but for the first time in years, Jess could almost see a future with someone.

Beckett moved to the middle of the front lawn, easing Mrs. Glass to the ground. Before he could rise back up, the house gave out an eerie howl before imploding. A cloud of mothball-scented dust whooshed from the collapsing structure.

"Oh, my!" Mrs. Glass let out a sob. How much must it hurt to watch your home of fifty years reduced to nothing more than a pile of rubble? Jess knew that her former teacher had lost her husband a few years back, and now her home as well? What did she have left?

Jess's throat was thick with emotion thinking of all the elderly woman had lost. While she couldn't change the destruction around them, she could make sure that Mrs. Glass was physically okay. Jess sank down next to her. "Are you injured? Let me take a look at you."

Pulling her stethoscope out, Jess listened to Mrs. Glass's heart and lungs. Nothing sounded unusual. Her heart rate was up, and probably her blood pressure as well, but she was in her late seventies and had just been through something life-threatening and traumatic. Elevated heart rates were going to be the norm for a while. Jess was certain that if someone were to check her own vitals at the moment, hers would be high as well.

"I got trapped in the bedroom. I went back in there to get my sweater just as the storm hit. Something got wedged in the door. And then a chunk of the back wall fell into my shoulder." Her age-spotted hands shook, as did her voice. "This shoulder does hurt something fierce, but I'll survive. Be doing better if you help get me off this cold, damp ground before I catch my death though."

"We will look at your shoulder in a minute." Jess shielded Mrs. Glass's eyes from the light, trying to check pupillary response. "Did you bump your head?"

"Jessamine Daniels, I taught you how to write your name. If my head hurt, I would have said. I think I can tell when I'm injured or not. I may be getting old, but I'm not senile yet."

"It's a valid question!" Jess huffed. "And it may have been a long time since I was in your classroom, but I'll never forget how much you helped me after I lost each of my parents. Let me look after you, please."

Mrs. Glass wobbled a bit at Jess's plea, but she finally gave a nod. "Okay, but I didn't hit my head."

"Mmm-hmm." Jess moved around behind her former teacher. "Let's get this sweater off though because it looks like you might have a cut under there that's bleeding."

Mrs. Glass simply nodded.

Beckett gently helped her pull the sweater off the injured shoulder. The thin blouse beneath it had a large spot, bright red with blood. "Looks like the damage happened through the fabric, but the fabric seems intact at least. Should make for a cleaner cut."

"Hmm…" Jess murmured. "Mrs. Glass, we're going to need to slip your shirt aside so I can get a better look at that cut."

"Not out in this yard you're not!" the elderly woman protested. "I can't have the whole neighborhood seeing these expired goodies."

Beckett chuckled. "How about in your car? Don't suppose you have the keys on you? It looks like it made it through the storm okay."

"I have them in my pocket," Mrs. Glass said, grinning up at Beckett like he'd just given her the world. "At least the car will give me a hint of privacy."

Beckett helped her to her feet and let her lean on him as he guided her over to the car. Jess swallowed hard. A man who was that sweet to the elderly and so good with kids couldn't be as dishonest as Clint, could he?

She let out a shaky breath and picked up the supply bag. Treat Mrs. Glass and then get to the school, she told herself. No time to think about what kind of man Beckett Wilder truly was. Priorities sorted, she climbed into the backseat with Mrs. Glass, asking Beckett to turn around and block the view from the opposite side. She eased the blouse off and the cut started bleeding afresh. She quickly stuck a clean gauze pad against the gash and applied pressure to slow the bleeding. "Cover yourself from the front with your sweater," she suggested.

Once Mrs. Glass had done so, she called out to Beckett that he was safe to turn around. He leaned into the car and asked, "How's it look?"

"Decent-sized gash. Started bleeding again when I pulled the fabric from the shirt away." She lifted the gauze and saw the blood well up in the wound again. "Still bleeding."

Beckett reached out. "I can apply pressure if you want to try some Steri-Strips?"

"Thanks." She dug through the bag and found some of the sterile strips to close wounds. "If you want to get another piece of gauze ready, I'll pour some of the antiseptic in and see if anything washes out. I don't want to try to close it up until I'm sure none of the fabric made it into the wound."

"Already on it," Beckett said, managing to rip the clean gauze wrapper open single-handedly.

"Ready?" she asked, holding the antiseptic up. "This might be cold. I'm sorry."

The elderly woman tensed but nodded. "Let's get it over with."

Beckett pulled the used gauze away as Jess began. Antiseptic poured into the wound and Jess caught the excess with another piece of gauze to keep it from running down Mrs. Glass's back. Thankfully, the bleeding had significantly slowed.

"It's looking better already!"

"Gonna need stitches though," Beckett said as he put the clean gauze over the freshly cleaned wound. "I'd also recommend a more thorough cleaning than we can give here in the backseat of a car."

"Agreed." Jess nodded at him. "Let me see if I can get a couple of these Steri-Strips on it to help slow the bleeding though."

Beckett watched her carefully, moving just as she needed him to and without requiring verbal instructions. Once they'd done as much as they could with their limited supplies, Beckett stepped away from the car and closed the door to allow Mrs. Glass privacy to get dressed.

"I like him," Mrs. Glass said as Jess helped her put the soiled blouse back on. Jess hated the idea, but the elderly woman didn't have anything else, and she was already complaining of the cold. "How's that sweet Mason doing?"

Jess had to fight back a sob. It would only upset Mrs. Glass to know that by stopping to help her, they were delaying reaching the children, including Mason. "He was smiling like crazy when I dropped him off this morning."

She stepped out of the car and swiped at her eyes before Mrs. Glass could see her tears. "Beckett, can you radio Mrs. Glass a lift to the hospital?"

"Already have. Can't get an ambulance, but they are having other city employees transport noncritical patients. They said it would be about ten minutes. I let them know that the end of the street by Main was blocked, so they'll be coming from the other direction."

"You think we can safely leave her?" she asked Beckett quietly.

"I don't see any signs of concussion. The bleeding isn't bad enough to worry about her bleeding out. Seems safe for us to continue on to the school."

Jess quickly told Mrs. Glass that someone was on the way for her and to watch out because it might not be an ambulance. She stuffed the unused supplies back into the gym bag. Now that she wasn't occupied with caring for Mrs. Glass, the fear and panic that Mason was hurt slammed into her chest like a wrecking ball.

If something had happened to Mason... If it was exacerbated because she had stopped to help someone else...could she ever forgive herself?

CHAPTER TWELVE

JESS HEADED DOWN the street toward where they'd left the truck. She didn't look back and Beckett found himself staring after her, admiring the sway of her hips. The woman made scrubs look sexy, and that was a feat.

No "See ya later." No "Thanks for the help today." Not even an "Adios." A thousand potential ways she could have said goodbye flashed through his mind, before it dawned on him that he needed to pick up his feet and go after her or find himself stranded. She still had his truck keys.

Was this woman going to make him chase her for the rest of their lives?

The thought gave him pause. The rest of their lives? When had he started thinking about Jess in the terms of having a future? Jess had made clear that her heart was surrounded by razor wire, and she wasn't interested in taking it down for him or any other man. And he wasn't staying in Woodvale, while she had a career here. Plus, there was Mason to consider.

All these things needed more thought than he had time to give. Something had shifted somewhere leaving him off-balance. He didn't like it.

"Hey, Jess, wait up." He hurried after her.

When he got close, he could see that she'd left so quickly in order to try to get her emotions together. The proof of her momentary lapse of control trekked down her face.

"Tell me about Mason." First grade, that was what, six? Seven? Most parents he'd met couldn't wait to tell anyone who'd listen about the amazing feats that their offspring had accomplished. His best friend had a new story every time they spoke, about what his daughter had said or done.

"Mason is my world. And if I were to lose him, I couldn't go on." She sighed and wrapped her arms around herself. "That's why I need to get to the school. I need to make sure he's okay."

There was a hefty weight in her words that resonated deep within Beckett's soul. He'd lost loved ones and it was a position he never wanted anyone else to be in.

The fear from the night Sloane died came back to him. The family had been told Sloane and her fiancé had been in a bad car accident, but they didn't have details. It had been one of the most terrifying moments of his life, as an eighteen-year-old on the cusp of adulthood. He had no idea how much those fears would be amplified if they were about your own child though.

"Come here," he said, pulling her into his arms. The need to comfort her overrode the self-preservation instinct that said touching her would only make his confusion worse when it came to Jess. "I'll get you to your son. That's a promise."

He just hoped the kid was okay when they got there.

CHAPTER THIRTEEN

ALLOWING HERSELF JUST one single moment of weakness, Jess let Beckett hold her. Being a strong, independent woman was her hallmark, but today was one of those days when she wanted a set of broad shoulders to lean against, some muscular arms around her and a deep voice murmuring reassurances in her ear.

God, why did Beckett affect her like that?

Restless butterflies fluttered around in her stomach at his touch though. Seeking comfort from Beckett Wilder, of all people, was such a dangerous proposition. She needed to be reinforcing the walls around her heart. Bubble-wrapping herself to cushion her heart from all the ways he could break it. Not snuggling into his chest and letting him murmur sweet reassurances in her ear.

Logic intervened and she sucked down a deep breath. She pushed Beckett away and fought down the rush of anger that surged up. Anger at herself, and the situation as a whole, since Beckett had done nothing but be supportive. She just needed to survive the next few hours in his presence without falling into his arms again. And she had to find a way to keep him and Mason apart. She couldn't get involved with Beckett and keep them separate forever, so she had to put the distance back between them. For Mason's sake, she couldn't let them bond any further...

"I need to get to my son," she said as she climbed back into his truck.

He looked pained at her brusque tone, but she had to focus. She couldn't let herself be swept up in a whirlwind romance. There'd been enough wind already, and like the devastation that the tornado had caused, Beckett had the power to devastate her heart. A stronger person would have never let him get this close.

Jess was ashamed of how much she'd started to rely on him today. This wasn't her. She didn't lean on others to get through the day. She faced problems head-on and without hesitation. People looked to her for an example of what to do. Jess had a reputation for being calm and collected during an emergency, and very few people knew her well enough to know that she did her falling apart after everything was over. Being around Beckett was making her soft, and it couldn't continue.

After Clint, she'd vowed not to get involved with another man who held any sort of power over her. Wealth alone put Beckett in a vastly different league, and she didn't like the imbalance. There was something about Beckett's touch though that seemed to skip past all those red flags and strip her bare.

He reached over and picked up her hand. When he brushed his lips across the back of her wrist, she swore the temperature in that truck cab shot up a solid ten degrees. Man, it was hot in here. The way he looked at her, his eyes locked on hers, with his firm steady grip

on her hand, holding her close, sent her internal ther-
mometer sprinting up.

"I don't want to fall in love with you," Jess finally
blurted out when she regained the ability to form words.

"Ah, Jess, I don't want to fall in love with you either."
He looked right through her just then, it seemed like.
Like he could see her every insecurity and wanted to
put them to rest. "I don't know what happened to you
in the past to make you so skittish around me, but I can
see it in your eyes. My mind says stay far, far away. I
can't seem to keep my distance though."

He had to be toying with her. Maybe he was looking
for a hookup, because men like Beckett Wilder didn't
get serious with single moms like herself. And her life
definitely didn't have room for casual. "Are you considering coming home to Woodvale permanently?"

"No."

She pulled away from his touch. Breaking eye contact, she looked out the window. "Can we just get to the
school, please? I don't have the right energy or mindset
to deal with whatever this is right now."

Beckett turned back on Main Street. They drove two
blocks down before either of them spoke again. "And if
I was considering a move home? Why do I get the impression that it still wouldn't change anything?"

Shaking her head, Jess started to argue. Words failed
her when she realized that Beckett had just turned onto
her street and what might be waiting a quarter of a mile
down the road filled her soul with dread. She hadn't
given much thought to the state her own home might
be in after the tornado.

"What's wrong?" He reached for her hand again,

before giving it a reassuring squeeze. "You look like you've seen a ghost."

The level of attention he paid astounded Jess. Women searched for that, but rarely found it. To be noticed was one thing, but to have a man so attuned to your expressions that he caught a mood shift in a split second... So very rare. Especially when they'd just been arguing, and he dropped it in an instant to be so supportive.

Stop thinking of him as a possible boyfriend, Jess admonished herself. Get through today, and he won't look so delectable. *Hopefully.* Waving her free hand up the street, she said, "My house is just up the way."

She'd already lost her car. Her place of work was severely damaged and might take months to repair. Mason's status was still unknown. And now she had to worry about their home.

"Can you see it from here?"

"No, it's just out of sight. Third on the right, just over that hill."

His thumb rubbed slow circles over the back of her hand. "And it just hit you that you don't know what we're going to find?"

Jess nodded. Fear clenched around her gut like a fist. Everyone had a limit. Where was her breaking point? Would she find it today?

"Yes." She swallowed hard. What if...? No, she couldn't keep dwelling on the negatives. It was growing harder and harder to focus on the positives though. She tended to be positive overall, but she couldn't bring herself to be that person right then.

"We're nearly there. Let's hope your home has been spared."

CHAPTER FOURTEEN

KEEPING THE TRUCK barely above a crawl, Beckett eased down the street. Debris blocked the lane in places, so it kept their speed greatly reduced. As they drove by, Jess commented on a few of her neighbors' houses, showing sympathy for the ones that had damage and expressing her relief for the ones that had escaped unscathed.

As they neared the top of the hill, she murmured. "I don't know if I can do this."

After stopping the truck, Beckett reached over and took her hand. He offered her as much comfort as he thought she'd accept. "You can. And I'll be right here beside you."

"What if the house is...?" She bit her lower lip and stared up at him, unable to verbalize the rest of that worry.

"Where's your bravery?" He teased a bit, trying to lighten the mood. Today had been a lot. Facing the potential loss of a child would be a drain on the strongest of people. Now her house as well? Jess was bearing up with a lot of grace.

"It blew away in the wind." She winced, and he could see that she hadn't meant to say that out loud. "That was far meaner than I meant it to be. I'm really not so weak as today might show. I'm sorry."

"I know." Beckett pressed his lips to Jess's forehead. He hadn't known her long, but he could already tell that she was one of the strongest women he'd ever met. It had to be rubbing her all kinds of wrong to feel weak in front of him. "It's fine. You're doing fine."

She took a deep breath, gathering strength. "Okay, let's do this."

He put the truck back in motion and they crested the top of the hill. She gasped when she got a good view of her house. It was still upright, but the entire roof was gone. The trusses and rafters, gone. Not a shingle in sight.

Shaky breaths that verged on crying but didn't quite cross over came from the woman at his side. "My house," she whispered. The single word carried a wealth of emotion—pain, fear and a hint of hope.

While Jess was giving her house a once-over, Beckett pulled out his phone and tried to call his parents. The call connected this time, but there was still no answer. He got their machine instead. *You've reached the Wilder residence. Please leave a message and we will return your call at the earliest possible convenience.*

"Mom, it's me. Call me back." He hung up and tried her cell. Straight to voice mail. Same with his dad's. He left a message for both that he was fine, asking for them to call him back and check in so he knew how they had weathered the storm. The lack of communication began to worry him. He fired off a text to each of them just in case they weren't getting the calls through on their end.

With that done, he turned back to Jess's house. The

structure here seemed to be solid, thankfully. Badly damaged, but in no real danger of falling. At least to his untrained eye. The extent of his construction knowledge was limited to weekends spent working on a Habitat for Humanity house though, so he could hardly claim any expertise. The heavy rain would have drenched the exposed top floor, given that it was entirely open to the elements. If they were lucky, the downstairs would be salvageable, but even that was iffy. The house was in bad shape and wouldn't be inhabitable for a while.

He couldn't help her with the house, but he'd made her a promise to get her to her son. "Anything you need to grab before we go on to the school?"

CHAPTER FIFTEEN

BECKETT STOOD NEARBY, ready to take her on to the school. Thankfully, he was giving her a little distance. She'd already let him get far too close. Maybe when she got home tonight, she could put him out of her mind.

That was when reality hit her like a sledgehammer right in the heart. Her home was destroyed. Yeah, the main structure remained upright, but the roof was completely gone. She sucked in a deep, ragged breath. There was no way they could live in that house.

"Oh, I…" Words failed. They were effectively homeless.

"We'll worry about where you're going to stay after we make sure your son is okay. He's the first priority." Beckett anticipated the topic dominating her thoughts.

"I know."

"Maybe your son can stay with his dad while you get the house fixed? Or at least until you find some temporary housing."

"Not an option," Jess snapped.

"Okay then," Beckett stepped back, and Jess could see the hurt in his eyes. He'd had no way of knowing that his suggestion was completely unacceptable. After all that he'd done for her, he deserved better than her ripping his throat out over something so innocuous.

A few hours ago, she'd been dead certain that she was too good for the likes of Beckett Wilder, but maybe he was too good for the likes of her. She'd been a complete mess today, while he'd been a solid foundation, willing to let her lean on his strength. He needed a woman who was open and kind. She'd been none of those things, and yet he still stood by her side.

When she spoke again, the bite was gone from her voice. "My emotions are all over the place today and you seem to be my favorite target. It's just me and Mason now. My sister is a couple hours away. There's no one else he can stay with."

"You are under a lot of stress today, and I'm the safe target." Beckett gave a weak shrug, like it didn't bother him. But he stuffed his hands in his pockets, clearly still smarting from her biting his head off once again. "You ready to get moving then?"

Ten minutes later, they were pulling into the school parking lot. There were so many cars that Beckett had to park in the grass. As she took in the damage to the school, once again, the devastation was hard to bear.

Clutching at Beckett's arm, Jess let out a pain-filled gasp. "That's where Mason's classroom is…was." Seeing that large pile of rubble that should have been classrooms stabbed a shard of emotional glass down deep in her soul.

The notion that her little boy could be under all those broken bricks and shattered glass left a hollow hole in her gut. She swallowed hard, but the lump in her throat wouldn't budge. They should have been there already. She shouldn't have stopped to help others or to see whether her home was still standing. What if their delay had cost Mason his life or caused permanent damage?

"Let's find out who's in charge. Maybe we can get a status update on Mason and find out where we can set up to do any first aid that's needed." Beckett squeezed her hand.

Jess nodded. The only thing keeping her from a full-blown panic attack right now was Beckett's calm voice and the grounding his touch brought her. She didn't deserve his compassion, but she was thankful to have it. Her gaze jumped around, scanning the faces of all the crying children lined up along the sidewalk. They walked past class after class of children, none of which was the one she was looking for.

"His class isn't here." Her grip tightened on Beckett's hand. "Where is he?"

"We'll find him, Jess." Beckett's voice tried for reassuring, but he could no more promise that Mason would be healthy and safe than he could change who he was. One of the first lessons she'd learned working in the emergency room was to never make promises to a victim's family. Despite best efforts, things didn't always go the right way. And in a natural disaster situation with possible crush injuries, the risks were even higher that things wouldn't be okay.

"There's the principal." Jess headed over to a small woman in a wrinkled and dirty suit. "Mrs. Caruthers, I don't see my son, Mason. He's in Shannon Couch's first-grade class."

The principal visibly shrank, tears filling her eyes.

"They're still in there. Rescue crews are still trying to get the kids out. We made contact with Shannon a bit ago. She said they were in a small void, but all the children are with her and there are no serious injuries. The problem is that the situation is volatile, and status could change in an instant."

Dread plopped down hard in Jess's stomach and sent up a wave of nausea that took some effort to swallow back. If she'd had more in her stomach, it might have ended up on Mrs. Caruthers's shoes. The fear she'd carried all morning, the worry that she'd been able to shove back as a mere possibility, was now a confirmed reality. Mason was missing. He was buried alive.

She sucked in a ragged breath. Mason was buried alive. Her baby was under a pile of rubble. The tightness in her chest nearly took her to her knees. She had to keep a grip, somehow. For Mason's sake, if not her own.

"How can we help?" Beckett asked. He kept his grip tight on Jess's hand, whether through an awareness that he was the only thing keeping her from spinning out entirely or as an attempt to keep her from rushing full steam ahead into the rubble she wasn't sure. "Jess and I want to help. She's a nurse and I'm an EMT. We have limited supplies, but what we do have is knowledge. We were sent over by Woodvale Memorial. Do you have a triage area set up yet?"

"There's been an ambulance in and out over there. A few of the teachers are doing their best." Mrs. Caruthers gestured to a corner of the playground. A lone swing squeaked ominously in the breeze. "The fire department ordered us not to touch anything on the building. Said we could make things worse if we went in wrong." She rubbed a shaking hand over her face. "We have thirty-three kids, two teachers and an aide still in there."

"Including Mason," Jess whispered. She didn't trust her voice at normal volume. If she tried to speak, and her voice cracked, that would set off the tears. She had to keep it together and stay strong.

Beckett led her away from the principal toward the place she'd pointed out as the designated triage area. He wanted to triage and bandage injured children? She just wanted to find her son.

"I don't know how to do this. How do I care for someone else's child when mine is buried alive over there?"

"You're a nurse, aren't you?" His low voice soothed her nerves the tiniest bit. "This is just another day in the ED. One patient at a time. Treat those babies like you'd want someone treating Mason if he was hurt."

They were heading toward a group of crying kids crowded around a couple teachers. The teachers looked overwhelmed, with hair sticking up in all directions and marks of dust and grime on their faces. Every one of them looked like they needed a savior. He was right that they did need to help the other kids. She could do nothing for Mason except wait, but she couldn't seem to wrap her mind around that. Around not being able to help her son.

"Start triaging these kids while I go grab our bins of supplies."

Jess nodded and let Beckett give her orders. She had enough mental clarity to know that she wasn't in the right mindset to lead. She introduced herself to the frazzled teachers and explained that she and Beckett were there to take over for them on triage. Their relief was palpable. One even cried.

She spent the next hour treating Mason's schoolmates. She put bandages on cuts, and even splinted a few potentially broken arms. She glanced frequently over at the front of the school, hoping for news, waiting impatiently for the rescue crew to dig Mason and his classmates out of the pile of ruin that was the first-grade hallway.

Beckett hovered close by, keeping a watchful eye over her. His nearness and concern made her feel protected. For the first time in her life, a man was watching out for her. It was nicer than she'd imagined. Somehow, she'd pictured anything with this level of power imbalance being, well, unbalanced. Experience had taught her that a man like Beckett should be overbearing, controlling her every move, right?

He wasn't like that at all.

Her relationships had been few, and even the most serious had never felt quite like this. Never had a man made her feel cherished just by the look in his eyes, or the way he put his hand on the small of her back when she needed a little extra support. What did it say about her past boyfriends if a man she'd never been on a single date with was more supportive than the lot of them combined?

Focusing on Beckett was the only way she could feel any emotion other than total fear. It helped keep her mind off the fact that her son was still buried, hopefully alive, only a few yards away. The distraction of providing first aid and the soft, gentle touches from the man at her side were the only things keeping her from curling up in a ball and sobbing until there were no tears left.

CHAPTER SIXTEEN

"WHY HAVEN'T WE heard anything?" Jess had asked at least once every ten minutes since they'd started delivering first aid to the students and teachers. Her lower lip was dark from how she was worrying it between her teeth.

"There's nothing yet to report," Beckett told her patiently. He wasn't a parent, but he could still find empathy for her situation. The knowledge that her son was still buried under the remains of the school had to be torture for her. "I know you want answers, but right now the best thing we can do is stay out of Search and Rescue's way and patch up as many kids as we can."

He was anxious and he'd only just met Mason. Low-level nausea roiled in his stomach every time he thought of how the bricks and stone that were currently giving Mason and his class a sheltered area could come down at any moment. Jess was bearing up fantastically, given how that thought had to be in the forefront of her mind as well.

Luckily, none of the children had presented with serious injuries that would have required full concentration. About half of the students had been picked up by worried parents, but they still had a few more to check out.

A little girl limped up to them.

"Hi, sweetie." The smile on Jess's face didn't reach her eyes. She was really trying—no one could fault her effort—but she wasn't quite succeeding. "What's hurting you today?"

They'd briefly tried a swap where Beckett treated the kids and she gave him the supplies, but her distraction had been far too great, and he'd ended up working alone. She'd told him that she needed to be working directly with the kids, to help keep her mind focused as best she could, so that was what they'd done. It was working fairly well. He didn't miss the constant glances over to the school though.

"Hurt my foot." The little one pointed down to a pink sneaker-clad foot. "Tripped over a rock."

"Okay, can you sit down here and let us take a look?" Beckett patted the dusty lid of a cooler that someone had dragged out of the back of their vehicle. They weren't using it for its intended purpose, but as a makeshift exam table.

The girl sank down onto the cooler and dutifully propped her foot up. She winced, but bravely held back her whimper when Jess eased the sneaker from her foot. A tear trekked down her cheek, leaving a muddy trail in the grime the day had left on everything.

"Light swelling." Jess manipulated the ankle slightly. "Does this hurt?"

"Yes," the child said with a hiss.

"Did it feel like anything cracked or did you hear a pop?"

"No."

"Okay. I think it's just sprained."

Beckett nodded when she looked up at him. He agreed it was likely a sprain from the looks of things, and it didn't change how they'd treat her today if it was broken. Without an X-ray or scans, the best they could do was immobilize it. He dug out the PT tape and some wrap.

"Mr. Wilder here is going to put some gauze and tape on that for you. It might still hurt, but this will keep you from hurting it more until your grown-ups can get you to see a doctor and maybe have a special picture of your bones called an X-ray done on it."

He'd been confused the first time Jess had referred to a kid's grown-ups. The look on her face when she'd explained to him that she never knew what a child's home life might entail had really dug deep into his mind. He'd had the ideal family, in a lot of ways, with both biological parents in the home and involved with his life. Overbearing, yes, but never abusive or cruel. He had an older sibling to follow behind. The idea that some kids had only one parent, some lived with other family or with virtual strangers, had never really been in his thoughts. He knew it happened, of course—he wasn't *that* naive—but it had never touched his life personally. Talk about feeling shallow and entitled.

His ignorance on that had probably reinforced Jess's opinions of him. He'd gotten the impression that Mason's dad had come from a wealthy family and wouldn't have concerned himself at all with the feelings of others. And if he was honest, his sister Sloane probably wouldn't have cared about hurting a kid's feelings if she asked about their mom or dad only to find out that parent was dead. For all her good qualities, his sister had been pretty self-centered. If Jess thought he was like that, that was probably why she kept him at such a distance. Hopefully, one day she'd be able to look at him and see him for himself. And stop comparing him to a man long gone.

"Let me see that ankle." He crouched down and turned his focus toward taping up the little girl's ankle. He'd just ripped the final piece of tape when Jess stood up and left.

"Make sure your grown-ups have a doctor look at that, okay?"

She nodded.

He waved to the teacher standing nearby and got her attention. "Can you keep an eye out? I need to see where Jess went."

As he walked in the direction she'd gone, he could see the SAR guys filing out of the school. He didn't see more kids though. A bitter taste filled his mouth. This wasn't good.

Jess stood in front of the school arguing with the principal and a member of the SAR team. To say that she wasn't taking whatever they'd told her well was a vast understatement. Her hands were planted firmly on her hips and the tension in her frame was visible from a distance.

"You can't just stop!"

He got within range to hear that last exclamation and caught the gist of the conversation. The SAR team was taking a break or stopping for some reason, and she wasn't having any of it. Beckett sucked in a deep breath. He wasn't sure he could find a way to smooth this over with her. It looked like she was far too fired up to be simmered down now.

Beckett stepped up next to them and tried to put a hand on the small of Jess's back. Her anger was too strong for her to allow the touch and she moved just out of his reach. The vibe around her was outrage, pure and simple.

"Ma'am, we aren't stopping. We need to get some more equipment brought in and my men need to get a meal and take a short break. If we had a second team, I'd send them in, but these guys are worn out. Most of them were out last night doing swift water rescues and haven't slept since night before last. If I don't give them a break, I'll need someone to rescue them."

Jess pressed her point hard. "My son is only seven years old. You have grown men who can't suck it up for an hour or two more?"

The SAR team leader scrubbed a hand over his eyes. Exhaustion deepened the lines of his weathered face. "You have to be worried half out of your mind. I would be. Trust me, we will do everything we can to get your boy and the others out safely and as quickly as we can without getting anyone else injured. You can stand here and yell at me 'til we both fall over, but those men are my responsibility, and they need to eat. They need to hydrate. Simple as that."

"Jess, they're doing the best they can," the principal argued. "This isn't easy for any of us. We're all worried, but the best thing we can do is to remain calm."

"Easy for you to say! He didn't stop looking for your child!" Jess jabbed a finger at the SAR leader.

"He hasn't stopped looking, Jess," Beckett tried to

calm her down. It wouldn't do to make an enemy of the man leading the search team, and if she were thinking at all clearly, she'd see that too. "He's just making sure that his men are safe. They can't work if they're weak from hunger. Maybe you should think about going over and getting a sandwich yourself."

A local business had come out with sandwiches, bottled waters and some protein bars. They were handing them out to the kids still awaiting pickup and the adults there helping in various capacities. The SAR team that had come out of the school were currently all lined up getting themselves some food and much needed water.

"I'm not hangry," she growled out, her eyes flashing dangerously with anger as she turned her attention to Beckett. "I'm worried about my son."

"As are we all," Beckett soothed. It might have been a mistake to tear her attention from the SAR leader, but he had a better chance of getting her calmed down than the man she thought wasn't doing enough to save her son. "But it doesn't do Mason any good if his mom falls down from low blood sugar, now, does it?"

Her jaw tightened, and he thought she might continue to argue, but instead she stomped away over to the sandwich table. Her muscles were so tense that she'd be sore tomorrow, from the looks of things.

"I'm sorry." Beckett apologized for her. "She's normally much calmer."

"Worried mamas come with the job." The man shrugged and let out a little chuckle. "I don't let it get to me anymore."

"Good." Beckett shook the man's hand. "I appreciate the work you do."

Giving the principal a nod, Beckett went to get himself a sandwich. He had just walked up to the table when Jess moved away, sandwich in hand. His eyes followed her for a moment, content when she sank down in the shade of a tree to eat.

"Ham or turkey?"

"Turkey," Beckett said. "And can I have a few of those protein bars for later? I'm going to be here until all the kids are out."

The lady held two protein bars out. "Sure thing. Terrible thing, this, isn't it?"

"Beyond terrible." He took the proffered protein bars and stuffed them into his pocket. "Thanks."

After going over to Jess, he sat next to her. She glared at him for a moment. When she didn't say anything, he started eating.

"You okay?" he asked between bites. She seemed even quieter than usual, and that worried him. Too much thinking might not be a good thing for her. There was far too much negativity today and he didn't want her to get too deep into a depressive mood.

"No."

The unshed tears in her eyes nearly broke him. "They will find him."

"What if it's too late?"

"Jess, you gotta have faith." Even as he said it, he knew it was easier said than done. "How 'bout we focus on something positive? Tell me something funny that Mason does."

"He has this obsessive desire for a dad." Her lip quivered. "At the ice-cream parlor the day we met, I was sure that he was going to propose to you for me."

"Propose?" Beckett laughed.

"Oh, yeah. He's done it before. Once, he went up to a complete stranger in the grocery store and asked him if he'd marry me so that he could have a dad."

Beckett snorted. "Well, since you aren't wearing a ring, I guess that didn't work out."

"The man was in his sixties!"

The question of why Mason didn't have a dad burned hot on the tip of Beckett's tongue. Earlier, she'd said Mason couldn't stay with his father, but she hadn't elaborated as to why. He wanted to dig into that, get a deeper explanation. It seemed to be a touchy subject though and he didn't want to poke that bear again since she'd only just started to settle down.

"He's obsessed with baseball," she continued. "You might have noticed."

"I played baseball all the way through high school. Still play rec league when I can." It had been one of his greatest joys for a lot of his childhood, the one moment where he and his dad had found a connection. Baseball was high on the list of things Beckett hoped to share with his future children. He leaned back and tried to consider just when the idea of having kids had shifted from a maybe to a definite want.

"You know you've got superhero status with him." The smile she flashed him was bittersweet. She was dwelling on the what-ifs again.

He wanted to push those thoughts from her head—knowing they'd only build and grow to Jess's detriment—but he couldn't seem to find a way. The only thing he knew to try was to focus on happy things with Mason. To treat the future as a given.

"I'll happily play catch with him anytime he wants. Maybe show him a few pointers." Beckett put his hand over hers. He wanted to give her something to look forward to, something optimistic. "The three of us could even go to see a game?"

"We'll see."

Whenever his mom had said that growing up, it meant no. It was only second to *Let's see what your father thinks* in terms of ways she could say no without directly saying no.

"Is that universal mom code for no?"

"No."

Beckett let out a slight chuckle. "Why don't I believe you?"

"I'm going to throw away my trash." Jess stood and left.

Beckett finished the rest of his sandwich. When a cold feeling of dread dropped low in his belly, his eyes automatically searched for Jess.

CHAPTER SEVENTEEN

JESS RUSHED INTO the school, hopefully before anyone saw her. They'd said to stay out, but if the rescue crew wasn't going to find her son, she'd do it herself. She was a strong, independent woman. She could do this.

Some decisions she could agonize over for days, taking an exorbitant amount of time to make her choice. Others, like this, were made almost without any deliberation at all. This was pure instinct.

Physically, she couldn't wait any longer. Mentally, she knew it might not be the best choice, but that part had been overridden by the emotional part of her crying out that now wasn't the time to be logical. Now was the time for action.

"Jess," Beckett's voice called behind her. "What are you doing?"

Busted. She kept walking though. He could come with her or leave her be. She wasn't at his beck and command. Even if she'd accepted him taking the lead earlier, he wasn't her boss and he couldn't order her back like a wayward subordinate. Or sweet-talk her back either. She thought he was more likely to try the latter of those options. And she wasn't falling for either. She needed to find her son.

The inside of the school looked a lot like the emergency department had that morning. Glass shards littered the floor and insulation hung from the ceiling. At least in the spots that still had a ceiling. Some of the hallway was open to the blue sky.

"Jess, wait!" He caught up with her, grabbing her hand and tugging her to a stop. "This isn't a good idea."

"You're not going to stop me." She yanked her hand away and crossed her arms over her chest. Righteous determination filled her, and she rose up as tall as her petite frame would allow. "The only way you're getting me out of here is to carry me, and I'll be fighting you the whole way."

Beckett raised a brow at her. "You think I'm not capable of doing just that?"

Jess couldn't stop her eyes from traveling the length of his frame, taking in his broad shoulders and clearly toned chest. He absolutely could cart her out of here over his shoulder like a fireman. She swallowed hard at the images that carved into her mind. In another place, another time, she might not be opposed to the man going alpha on her and carrying her off to somewhere private. He was one-hundred-percent capable of taking her away from this wreck of a building.

A rush of panic that he might do just that rose up and she swallowed it back. Surely, he wouldn't take her away from her son when she was this close. "Maybe you can. I'm hoping that you won't though," she finally admitted.

He shook his head but didn't move to touch her. Even

after spending the day with him, she had no idea what his thought process was like. The only thing she was sure of was that she'd been so far off on her estimation of him that it was like she knew nothing.

He'd been her rock today. And that had been entirely unexpected. Maybe, in a different time, a different life, they could have explored the attraction between them. But right now, she needed to get to Mason. She didn't have time for the push-pull of a potential new romance. And she certainly didn't have the patience for anyone getting in her way.

She'd used up every scrap of patience she had today. After a two-hour meeting with Beckett in which she'd felt like she had to justify every dime spent by her department, the hospital had been destroyed by a tornado during which she could have died. She couldn't dwell on how it had been Beckett who had saved her life. Then she had found out her son was in danger, and she'd had to convince Beckett to bring her along—okay, she might not have given him much choice, but it had tested her patience that she had to waste time arguing with him. She'd waited outside for hours, despite her intense need for action, while others tried to rescue her son and yet Mason remained trapped. The time for patient waiting was done.

Now she wasn't going to let Beckett or any other man stop her. She'd find Mason, if it was the last thing she did. "You can carry me out, but I'll just come right back in. I won't stop until my son is found."

Years ago, when she'd been dating Clint, she'd never had the courage to stand up to him for what she wanted or needed. He'd called the shots, decided who knew they were dating and where they went for dinner, even how they spent their time. She'd grown a backbone since then and when her son's life was at risk, the world had better believe she was going to use it.

"That I believe." A large sigh escaped him. "Okay, fine. We'll do this. But I'm coming with you."

"Just go home, Beckett."

"Not happening." He shook his head. "Even if I were inclined to leave you to your own stubborn fate, which I'm not, I gave Freya my word that I'd take care of you. You may not know this about me, but I don't break promises."

She wanted to argue, but what would be the point? She could see the determination on his face and knew any efforts to talk him out of it would be futile. If he had one trait that she was certain of, it was his stubbornness. She had yet to decide if it was a pro or a con.

With a glance at her watch, she said, "Mason has been trapped for going on four hours now. We don't have a solid idea of where, or how much space they have, and worst of all, if they have enough air. I just can't wait anymore."

"That's why I said I'm coming with you."

"It could be dangerous." She squashed down an uncomfortable amount of guilt. Endangering Beckett seemed unfair. She absolutely could go on this journey alone. Should go it alone, even.

"And you think it's safer if you go by yourself?" Beckett tugged her up against his chest. He pressed a brief kiss to her forehead. "Woman, what am I gonna do with you?"

Why'd he have to be so sweet? She'd built Beckett up

in her head to be a bad guy. He'd personified her own personal boogeyman who would come and break her heart. Mason's heart too. His actions had proven that she'd been entirely wrong in her assumptions about him though. Still, getting involved with him was a risk she wasn't sure she was brave enough to take.

"Let's go then," she said, pulling away from his embrace.

He wouldn't let her go entirely though, keeping his grip on her hand. Beckett had been generously sharing his strength and she was just selfish enough to keep accepting it for now. Soon though, she'd have to take that step back and stand without him again. It might be nice to have someone share the burden, but she couldn't put Mason through losing someone else he loved. Beckett was leaving, and she couldn't let herself get into the habit of depending on him.

"Left, I assume?" Beckett asked when they came to a T in the hallway.

Left led them toward the collapsed section. They turned the corner and at the very end, they could see the pile of rubble. There was a narrow pile leading up to it, where the SAR guys had been removing debris to pile it up out of the way. They hadn't managed to clear the hallway though.

"Mason's classroom is just past that blockage," Jess choked out. Visions of her son buried under those giant concrete blocks and chunks of ceiling and roof flashed through her mind.

Beckett's hand tightened on hers. "Positive thoughts only," he encouraged, but his voice sorely lacked enthusiasm. "Looks like we have our work cut out for us."

They proceeded quickly down the hall, intent on clearing the debris and finding Mason. After moving several big stones, a small landslide of debris slid down the blockage and knocked Jess off her feet. An ache sliced though her right ankle and she cried out in pain.

"Jess, are you okay?" Beckett placed the block he'd hoisted onto the excavated rubble and jogged to her side. "What hurts?"

"My stupid ankle," she groaned, clutching at the offending appendix. "I wasn't fast enough to get away. One of the bigger chunks rolled into it."

Beckett gently touched the ankle she indicated. "You think it's broken?"

"I don't know." She bit back a curse as he manipulated the joint and the pain intensified. "That really hurts though."

"Can you stand on it?"

"I'll have to try," she said with a whimper, allowing him to pull her to her feet. When she put her weight down on it though, she crumbled forward into his chest. "Nope. Don't think it will hold my weight."

Pressing her face against his chest, she fought back tears. Mason needed her and she needed to be able to get to him. How on earth was she going to do that if she couldn't even stand up right?

"Hold on to the doorway here. Let me see if I can find something to make a makeshift splint or wrap with." Beckett helped her hobble into the closest still upright doorway. "I may have to run out and get a splint from the triage area though."

She'd only just told herself that she couldn't depend on Beckett, yet once again was leaning on his strength.

It shocked her how much she'd already come to rely on him. And that was just foolish… The man had made it crystal clear that he was leaving town in only a few short months.

From the doorway, she could see that this was one of the second-grade classrooms. The interior of the room looked windswept, but significantly intact. Most of the posters still clung to the wall, although one corner of the one declaring that Second Grade Rocks was flapping in the light breeze. The only other sign that a tornado had hit this room was the far corner where a sliver of light came through via the missing roof and ceiling. Only about a one-square-foot space, sunshine beamed through it, highlighting that corner of the room like a spotlight, and providing the opening for the air moving the poster.

Beckett searched through the teacher's desk and the cabinet behind it. He moved on to the closet, carrying a roll of tape that he'd found in the desk. He pulled a sweater out and tossed it over his shoulder, still looking for something. When he turned, he had two rulers in his hands as well.

He held out his finds with a sort of grimace. "Not ideal, but I'm going to splint your ankle with this. Unless you want me to carry you outta here or go out and get a real splint?"

"No. They may not let you come back in." Or worse, they'd make her go out. Now that she was in here, closer to Mason, they'd have to carry her out under protest. Being near her son was something she desperately needed, even if she couldn't see or touch him.

"Didn't think so." He helped her over to the teacher's desk and lifted her up on it to sit. "Foot out."

Within a couple minutes, Beckett had used his scavenged sweater and rulers to tape her ankle. The snugness and extra support didn't take away all the pain, but the stability improved, and it did take the sharp edge off.

"I need to get that x-rayed," she admitted.

"Yeah, you do."

"Mason—"

"Comes first." Beckett tossed the remaining tape onto the desk beside her. "But you have to take care of yourself too."

"Yeah," she said, brushing off his concern. She'd take care of herself once her son was found. Until then, she'd keep fighting to locate him until she physically couldn't.

Easing off the desk, Jess tested her weight on the ankle. She could stand to bear weight on it after Beckett's rudimentary splint, but only just. She hobbled back toward the hallway. A few times she had to pause because the pain washing over her was too much. The only things keeping her from curling up into a ball of defeat and bawling her eyes out were pure stubbornness and maternal instinct.

Before she made it to the doorway though, concrete blocks started to fall and the wall crumbled before her eyes. It happened almost in slow motion, like when a special effects crew played with the speed on a video to give a moment in a movie more impact. She'd never had that phenomenon play out in her own mind like that before, but it was unnerving.

"Jess, watch out." Beckett snatched her back and she landed on the injured foot. Pain shot through her like a lance.

When the dust cleared, Jess let out a curse.

CHAPTER EIGHTEEN

BECKETT PULLED UP the flashlight app on his cell phone and aimed it at Jess. The doorway she'd been headed toward was gone, filled with concrete blocks, ceiling tiles, wet insulation and a chunk of roof—at least from what he could tell now that the only light came from that busted ceiling corner opposite the door. That wall had come down fast and far too close to Jess for his liking. He shone the light up and down her limbs, searching her for injuries. "Are you hurt?"

The dust swirling through the air glittered under the artificial light from his phone. She coughed roughly as she inhaled some of those particulates. "It didn't hit me."

"Good. Try not to breathe too much of that junk in."

Once he verified with his own eyes that she was at least as whole as she had been prior to the wall's collapse, he angled the phone so that the light was aimed at their new impediments. Once, there had been an opening in the white-painted concrete block wall, and now there was a tightly packed cluster of rubble. He was no contractor, but he could hazard a guess that the roof over that section of hallway had completely collapsed. Everything he could see looked like bad news.

"This is really bad, isn't it?"

He didn't answer yet. Moving closer, he used the flashlight to get a better look at the blockage. He pushed at the top, cautiously at first, then as hard as he could single-handed, but it didn't shift at all. Not even a pebble moved under his efforts. They were well and truly stuck. The question was for how long.

Stepping back, he rubbed at the nape of his neck. How could he tell Jess the only way they were getting out of here was by being rescued? And that their fate might be in the hands of the SAR team leader that she had shouted at less than an hour ago?

"Don't suppose you have a signal on that thing and can call us some help?" she asked, waving a hand toward the cell phone he held, its light still on.

He glanced at the screen. Zero bars and No Signal in bold print. "Afraid not."

Another potential complication was that his battery was down to less than 20 percent and he had no way to charge it. He would have to conserve what power he had left on the off chance he could get a signal later or in case they needed the flashlight again. He shone the light around the room once more, trying to get a feel for where things were and any resources that they might be able to scrounge up.

An idea sparked.

"If I can slide this desk over to that open corner, maybe I can break enough of that ceiling over there loose and see if there's a way out over there."

If it wasn't too dangerous...

"Oh, that would be great!"

"Honey, it's a risky plan that we can't bank our hopes on yet." Dismay rose in him. Was he giving her false hope by mentioning a potential escape plan? The chances that he could get out of that hole and have a stable space to drop down to safely were slim to none. But it was the only plan he had at the moment.

Afraid that he might see disappointment on her face, disappointment that he had put there, he shut the flashlight off without looking at her again. With a big shove, he got the desk moving and pushed it as far into the corner as it would go. After hoisting himself up quickly, he tapped at the wall as high as he could reach. It seemed solid enough, but the only way to find out if it could bear his weight was to jump up and grab the top.

The top he couldn't see.

There could be rusty nails, sharp slivers of glass or any number of things that could slice his hands right open. His back was still aching from the glass earlier and every movement exacerbated it. He had to try though, for Jess's sake. To be able to look her in the eye when the world stopped spinning and the smoke cleared, Beckett had to do everything he possibly could to get her to Mason.

Including the colossally stupid idea of trying to heave himself through a square opening roughly the size of his head. If he could at least get up there enough to get a good look, maybe he could come up with a better plan.

He'd always been good under pressure. It had been one of the things that made him a good EMT. He thrived under chaos, taking charge when others were losing control. He never cracked. All he needed was something to work with. What he was not great at was being patient and waiting for assistance.

Jumping up, he grabbed the edge of the exposed wall, leaving his body weight low and close to the desk. If it crumbled, that way he wouldn't have as far to fall. It didn't collapse. So far, so good. He pulled himself up. He could only just squeeze his head through the opening. If only Jess weren't injured, he could have boosted her up, but knowing her stubbornness, she'd vault right over into the unknown and injure herself worse—or leave him behind.

He could just squeeze his head through but couldn't get enough height to truly see anything. Dropping back down, he shook out his arms. It was a lucky thing he hadn't given up his conditioning routine after moving back to Woodvale.

"See anything?"

"Not yet. I'm going to have to try to peel back some of the roof and make the opening larger so that I can fit." He jumped back up, holding himself with one hand, and started to enlarge the opening. "Stand back. I have to toss this stuff down somewhere and I don't want to toss it out when I can't see what's out there."

He heard her shuffle backward. Once she was clear, he dropped a small piece of roof down on the floor next to the desk. He propelled back down and gave that arm a good shake. The next time he sprang up, he put his weight on the other arm. He alternated arms and bit by bit expanded the opening until he could fit his shoulders through. When he'd gotten up that morning, his biggest worry had been what tie to wear and how he could avoid the lecture from his mom about how it was

time to settle down. Now he was trying to fit his not so
small frame through a hole in a ceiling while the dozens of cuts on his back protested as sweat trickled into
them and burned. He would never have guessed how
this day would turn out.

He paused for a moment, moving his arms in and
effort to stop the trembling from all the pull-ups he'd
just done. If he could have varied his grip, it might not
have been so bad, but as it was, all the muscles in his
arms twitched from the hardcore workout.

With one big jump, he was up again. This time, he
hoisted himself up to waist level and looked down over
the wall. He had to wait a moment for his eyes to adjust
to the sudden brightness. Once they had, and he got a
good look at what they were dealing with, he couldn't
hold back the curse that slipped past his lips.

"What?" Panic laced Jess's voice.

He eased himself back down, not trusting the soles of
his shoes on the slick top of the desk. Not the way sweat
had been dripping off him. He sank down to sit on the
desk. He couldn't see Jess as his eyes had yet to read-
just to the difference in lighting inside the classroom.

"Can you come over here?" He wanted to be able
to see her face more, so that he could better judge her
emotions. So that he could ease her through this news
if she took it badly—although he briefly wondered who
was going to ease him through it. There'd been very few
times in Beckett's life that a feeling of helplessness had
overwhelmed him, and this was one of them.

The light pouring in from the opening above him
highlighted her features. Even with a layer of dust
on her cheeks, she was breathtaking. Holding out his

hands, he wasn't disappointed when she stepped up and put her hands in his.

"Just tell me, Beckett. I have so many scenarios running through my head right now that it can't be worse than I'm imagining." Worry etched fine lines on her face.

"Behind me is just rubble. There's no way that we could jump down and not break an ankle." He frowned when he remembered that her ankle may already be broken. "Poor choice of words. You get what I mean though. It's a definite no-go."

"And the other side?" She still held a note of hope in her voice.

Hope that he was about to squash like a bug. "You know how the school has the walk-out basement?"

She nodded.

"This room is on the second story if you look at it from that side. With dropping from the roof, it would be a good thirty feet. It's not safe to try to jump."

"What do we do now?"

"Wait to be rescued, I'm afraid." Beckett rested his head on the top of hers. He wasn't a wait-to-be-rescued kind of guy, and he doubted that Jess was used to being slotted into the damsel in distress role, but the hole in the ceiling provided no viable escape route. The only doorway was blocked, and he'd been unable to get even a pebble to shift. Plus, they could make the collapse worse if they continued to dig at the blockage.

Jess stiffened in his arms. "Excuse me? Can you run that by me again?"

"You heard me." He rubbed his hands up and down her arms to try to soften the news. He couldn't keep the tension out of his voice though. "Do you have another idea? Any at all?"

His sharp questions seemed to throw her. His borrowed scrub top tightened as she clutched the material tight in her fist. Gently, he kissed her brow. So much for keeping calm. Good job, idiot, he rebuked himself. She was hanging on by a thread, so what was he doing letting his tone get so frustrated with her.

"Jess, it will be okay." *Somehow...*

The sun was beginning to set. Light that had once poured in and brightened the classroom took on an orange tint and the room grew dimmer with each passing minute.

"Mason has to be starving by now."

"I know." Even if the boy had eaten a huge breakfast, it was long past lunch. Beckett spared a moment of battery life to check the time. Six forty-five. They'd been trapped themselves for a few hours now.

"I'm getting hungry myself. Wishing I'd had two of those sandwiches now." Jess's stomach punctuated the comment with an audible roar. "Hopefully, they don't actually make us wait till tomorrow to get rescued."

Beckett pulled the protein bars from his pocket. He couldn't feed Mason, but at least he could make sure Jess had something to keep her going. "I had a feeling we might want something more than a sandwich. If I'd known how prophetic that feeling was, I'd have asked for more than two."

She took one and let out a shaky breath. Tears leaked out of her eyes, but she didn't sob. Her breathing was far more rapid than he would have liked, though, and she had a look in her eyes that sent a chill down his spine.

Before he could react though, a whirring noise from the vicinity of the collapsed wall distracted him. He turned the flashlight on again and watched as a large drill bit came through the still solid section of the wall. It backed out and a ray of light came through the small opening it left.

"Hello?"

"We're here!" Beckett and Jess chorused.

"You two safe in there?" the SAR team leader asked through the hole.

"Yeah," Beckett answered for them. "We're okay. Plenty of room, no worries about air."

"Okay, good. Well, I've got some good news, and I've got some bad news." He paused, and Beckett wasn't sure if it was for dramatic effect or just because he didn't know which to share first. "The good news is that this collapse that the two of you caused kicked out another wall which freed Ms. Couch and the kids. They're all fine, just some bumps and bruises. Getting fed right now. The bad news is that it's gonna take us all night to dig through this crap. Any chance you can see another way out?"

"There's a hole in the roof along the outside wall. Big enough we could squeeze out, but too high to jump off."

"Lemme see if I can get a crane out here then. Maybe we can hoist you out of there. Sit tight. And don't cause any more collapses." The light disappeared.

CHAPTER NINETEEN

"DID YOU HEAR what he said?" Jess sniffed. Relief coursed through her. "The kids are okay. Mason's okay."

She could finally breathe for the first time in hours. Truly breathe, as the weight that had been pressing on her chest lifted. Her greatest fear was to lose her son. Knowing that he was safe, that meant everything.

"That's the best news I've ever gotten in my life." Beckett's arms slipped around her waist and pulled her up to his chest. "Is parenting always so hardcore? I haven't even known the kid a week and I've been half sick to my stomach all day worrying about him."

"Worse," Jess confirmed. "Were you really worried about Mason? You barely know him."

"I was. I know it doesn't make sense, but I really feel a connection to that little boy. The thought of losing him...it just tore me up inside."

She tiptoed and brushed her lips against his. "That's just the sweetest thing."

He returned her kiss, lightly at first, then deepening when she shivered and moved closer. "You want me to stop?" he whispered against her lips.

"Mmm," she murmured, wrapping her arms around

his neck. Anything else he might have said was cut off by her lips pressing against his.

Tracing his thumb lightly along her jawline, he kissed her gently. Sparks flew between them, kindled by mutual physical attraction, until it was a raging inferno. After easing back on the kiss, he brushed his lips over the hollow of her temple.

"When we continue this, I want it to be somewhere safe, somewhere private and somewhere respectable. Not on a dirty desk in a disaster-damaged school." Beckett buried his face in the crook of her neck. "But don't doubt that I want this. I just want more for you than this."

She sighed and leaned into his embrace.

Hands skimming up and down her back, Beckett held her close. Even just this mostly innocent touch kept her fired up. She wanted to take this further, but he was right that it wasn't the right moment. Even though she wanted it, she knew it could never be anything more than a few stolen kisses in the dark.

Guys like Beckett didn't go for single moms like her. Why would he give up his freedom and his career for her? He wouldn't…

"So, now what?" Jess asked.

"Well, we might as well get comfortable. We may be here for a while." Beckett sighed. "Along the far wall is probably the safest spot. We should probably settle in before we lose all the light."

"I hate this."

"It's not exactly my favorite place either." Beckett gave her a little squeeze. "The company is growing on me though."

Her heart raced at his words. Several times that day,

he'd said something along those lines, and she'd brushed it off as flirtatious attempts to relieve some tension. Now she wasn't so sure. Maybe it was wishful thinking on her part, but she thought he actually meant it. She desperately wanted to believe this was more than an itch to scratch for him.

"At a loss for words?" he asked, nuzzling his face into her throat.

"Today has been a lot to process." So much to process. Even now, she was trapped and couldn't see her son. She had to take the SAR leader's word that Mason was safe and sound. That nagging little worry in her gut wouldn't ease until she could see him for herself, but at least the crushing weight was off her chest.

With the worst of the worry about Mason gone, now she could focus on the man currently holding her so tenderly. Beckett had been a real surprise. She'd expected him to be like Clint, but other than their backgrounds, she couldn't find many similarities.

His breath was hot against her throat as he murmured, "Mason's safe now. We are all going home safe."

"But I'm pretty well homeless." She closed her eyes, her throat tightening as the thought rushed in. That house was all that she had left of her mom. And it was wrecked. The water damage alone was probably astronomical. Her insurance was up to date, at least, so the financial burden wasn't her biggest worry.

She needed to figure out where they were going to stay in the immediate future. And the sentimental loss of all her mother's things. All Mason's things...

"We'll figure it out."

There he went with the "we" again. She sighed. "There

is no 'we' though. You keep saying 'we,' and the more I hear it, the more you make me want to believe that you mean that."

"I do."

"You know, following me in here and spending the night alone with me is going to make the town paper." The locals would have a field day with this. There was nothing a small town liked more than some juicy gossip about what man was sneaking into what woman's bedroom at night. Or, in their case, who got trapped together alone overnight. No matter how much she proclaimed that there was nothing between Beckett and herself, the black-and-white evidence would be hard to refute. "The article in the paper…" She trailed off without finishing her thought.

"Might as well serve as an engagement announcement?" Beckett chuckled. "I remember all too well how the gossip train works around here. Let them think what they want."

"Easy for you to say when you're leaving town in a few months." Jess feared her response sounded a bit strangled. When Beckett didn't seem to notice, she pulled away from his warmth. She wrapped her arms around herself, trying to recapture the heat but fearing that the chill wasn't physical. "You won't be the one getting all the side-eye glances and hearing the whispers stop when you walk in a room. I've been there and really don't want to go back. You'll be back to your normal life while Mason and I try to pick up the pieces and remember how to live life alone again."

"Is that what you're really worried about? Me leaving?" His fingertips grazed her arm as he reached for her in the dark. "What if I stayed? Would that change your mind about there being an us?"

"You've made it clear that your time in Woodvale has an expiration date."

"This place is home to you, right?"

"Yes," she said softly.

"I don't feel like I have a home. After I lost my sister, things here deteriorated rapidly. My father and I... well, we've never had the best relationship. But Sloane, she had a magic touch with my dad. She could charm him into anything she wanted—even cutting me a little slack." The sound of Beckett grinding his teeth reached her ears. Pain laced his voice when he spoke. "Without her, his expectations for me grew exponentially. No human could meet that man's criteria for what it means to be a Wilder. I couldn't wait to get as far away from that as I could."

"I'm sorry," she whispered.

"I know you see a spoiled rich guy when you look at me, but that's not who I am. Maybe I've never had to go hungry or worry about how I'll pay for a car repair, but that doesn't mean my life is free of hurt and struggles."

"I'm starting to see that." She'd hurt him with her prejudice, something she'd never meant to do. When his fingers grazed her hand again, this time she entwined her fingers with his. They stood, close but barely touching; only the fingers of a single hand kept them connected.

Outside, the noises dwindled off and Jess wondered if everyone had gone home to get some sleep. The only noise for a while was the sound of their own breathing and the ribbiting call of a nearby frog.

"So, what if I stayed?"

CHAPTER TWENTY

JESS'S FINGERS TENSED in his. While he couldn't read her expression, he could feel the anxious energy radiating off her. She tried to be casual, to pretend that she wasn't interested in dating at all, but he could see through that thin armor. She had been hurt, badly. And he had a good idea that Mason's dad was the culprit simply based on her responses to him and his background.

But he wasn't that guy.

"Woodvale isn't what you want though," Jess finally replied.

A few weeks ago, she'd have been one-hundred-percent correct. Then he'd met her and Mason. He wasn't going to claim love at first sight or anything that cheesy, but there was a connection. A longing to be with them that almost made him want to throw aside his previous beliefs about Woodvale and give his hometown a second try.

Or better yet, maybe he could convince Jess to follow him when he went back to work. She'd said herself that she had no one here really. Maybe he could persuade her to relocate. Now, there was an idea he could really work with. With her house destroyed, what did she have to keep her here?

The idea would be one he'd have to ease her into though. No use bringing that up at the moment. He rubbed his thumb slowly over the back of her hand. "Maybe the people in Woodvale are growing on me."

"The people?"

He could almost hear how she'd raised a brow at him in amusement. "Okay, so there's this kid…" Mindful of her injured ankle, he moved closer to her. Slipping his arms around her waist, he turned her toward him. "He's pretty amazing and actually thinks I'm great. He and I…we're gonna be BFFs by next week."

She snorted. "Oh, yeah? Is that so?"

"Yeah." He sought her lips, tempting her, teasing her with a ghost of a kiss. "And I shouldn't even tell you how crazy his mom makes me."

"You are an incorrigible flirt." Her soft laughter filled the space.

"Maybe, but you're starting to like it."

"I will neither confirm nor deny that statement."

Beckett cradled her face in the palms of his hands and captured her lips with his own. Her reply was confirmation enough for him that she was getting over whatever obstacles she'd put between them. Each stroke of his lips over hers made him ache for more. Every caress of her hands across his shoulders reached deep into his soul and soothed the ragged edges that years of being afraid to love had created. Never before had he considered a long-term future with a woman. It was as if he'd been waiting his entire life for the right woman— this woman.

He'd been with his share of them, but never had he felt like this before. And Jess was unlike the partners he normally chose. If anyone had asked him if he'd ever get involved with a single mom, the answer would have been an emphatic *No way!* Yet here he was. Not only was he getting involved, but he was also the one doing the pursuing. Attracted or not, Jess would have let him walk on by, never engaging, never exploring the chemistry raging between them.

The vibe between them had him second-guessing his long-held opinions about this town and that had to mean something. The urgency he felt around her scared him a little. Something about her drew him in like gravity though, and he was powerless against the pull.

He was a person who valued control, who needed to have choices and options. But the thought that he didn't have a choice when it came to Jess fled his mind as fast as it landed when she shifted closer. Her soft curves pressed into the firmness of his muscles, and the fit was perfection. He could get used to this.

"Mmm…" She tore her lips away from his with a gasp. Her hands applied firm pressure to his chest as she put a little space between them. "This is amazing, but we are moving a bit fast for me. I haven't done this in a long time and it's overwhelming."

Beckett groaned but allowed her to pull away. Things weren't moving fast enough for him. He knew what he wanted, and that was Jess. Fumbling for his cell phone, he murmured that he was going to turn on the light. They needed to find a spot where they could relax some and maybe get some semblance of rest.

"That corner right there looks like our best bet," he

said, pointing at the farthest corner away from the collapsing wall and open ceiling. He scanned the room quickly, but there was nothing they could use to soften the tile floor or use to stay warm. The spring days had been warming up nicely, but the nights still got quite chill. "We will have to rely on each other's body heat to stay warm tonight. Hopefully it doesn't get too cold."

If it did, they'd be in real trouble. They'd survive without more food, and without water, until morning. But if it got below freezing, they'd have bigger concerns than being hungry or thirsty. He sat down in the corner and patted the floor next to him. "Might as well get comfortable. My phone's almost dead, so I think this is the last of the light."

She hobbled over to him, and he helped her ease down. She snuggled up against him and released a contented sigh when he anchored her to his chest with his arm. Jess acted like she was a loner, that she didn't need anyone else, but the way she reacted to him and leaned on him told a different story.

"Can I ask you something?"

"We're stuck together for the night. I don't think you need to ask permission to ask me questions." One of her hands trailed across his chest in a slow, deliberate pattern. "Ask away."

"What happened between you and Mason's dad?"

She sucked in a breath and didn't exhale for a very long time. He thought she wasn't going to answer and was ready to apologize for overstepping when she finally let that breath out. Tense in his arms, she hesitated before answering.

"Mason thinks he died."

"Did he?"

She sighed. "No. I… I told him that because it was less painful than telling him that his father had no interest in parenting him. I thought I'd found the man I'd spend my future with, and it turned out that I was simply a summer fling for him."

"Ouch…"

"Yeah. I excitedly told him that I was pregnant, and he told me that I had two weeks to clear out of our shared apartment. When he blocked my calls, I didn't know what to do next. So, I tried to tell his mom, thinking maybe she'd be able to talk some sense into her son."

"And that was a no-go?"

"She accused me of being a gold digger out to ruin her son's name. Like your parents, they were big boosters at the hospital where I worked at the time. She made me a deal—leave quietly with a good reference or she'd destroy my reputation both professionally and privately. I tried to stand my ground, but it was less than a week later that I was called into the HR office and let go. I moved home to Woodvale and never tried to contact Clint again. Mason's better off without that in his life."

Beckett ruminated on her words. No wonder she had built such walls. He embodied everything that had hurt her in the past. Even if he stayed in Woodvale, would he be able to convince her to take a chance on him?

CHAPTER TWENTY-ONE

"HELLO, IN THERE?" a voice called.

Jess stirred from an uneasy slumber, rubbing the sleep from her eyes. She tried to ease away from Beckett, but he had a solid grip on her in his sleep. She'd snuggled into his chest last night like he was her security blanket and they'd happily shared body heat and more than a few kisses and intimate confessions.

She still couldn't believe she'd told him everything that had happened with Clint.

"Beckett," she said, prodding his chest with her palm. "I think we're about to be rescued."

"Hmm," he muttered, his arms tightening around her.

"Hello?"

"We're here!" Jess shouted, her body still pressed to Beckett's since he had refused to release her.

His eyes blinked open since she'd just yelled practically in his ear. The fog of sleep still clouded his eyes. "You're loud," he said in a sleepy murmur.

"Someone's out there." Jess waved vaguely behind her. "I heard them."

"Try up here, lovebugs," the voice called again. The

search-and-rescue leader peeked in from the hole Beckett had enlarged. The morning light created a halo around him. His flashlight passed over them.

"You two look nice and cozy. Maybe I should give you a little privacy and come back in a while?"

"Go ahead and tease," Beckett said with only the slightest of grumbles. "But if you're coming back later, could you at least bring us some food and water first?"

"I'll have you out in a jiffy, assuming you two don't mind scaling down the side of the building over here."

"We don't mind that at all, if there's safety gear. But I think Jess's ankle might be broken."

Jess let Beckett speak for them both. She'd found herself tongue-tied at the first tease that crossed the SAR leader's lips. Lovebugs? Was that what they looked like? Her lips turned up at the thought. Given that they had been asleep in each other's arms and hadn't separated even after awakening, she supposed that was a logical conclusion.

"I'll be right back with the gear."

"Wait!" Jess found her voice. "Any news on the first graders? I know you said you rescued them, but do you know anything about my son, Mason?"

"I only know that we were able to get them all out with only minor injuries. Not sure which one is your boy, so can't say for sure." Jess didn't miss the silent scold in the man's words. Her rash actions had caused more work for the SAR team, and she'd put Beckett in danger too. Still, she couldn't say she wouldn't risk it again. A mother's love was a mother's love. She'd do almost anything for that boy.

Mason was safe though. Even if she couldn't see

him yet, he was safe. This whole ordeal was finally almost over. Soon, she'd be able to hold her sweet baby boy in her arms and she might never let him go again. Tears trekked down her face at the relief that realization brought.

"I told you to have faith." Beckett rubbed her back gently, murmuring those sweet reassurances. His steady voice and presence gave her exactly what she needed to pull herself together.

"I don't need any 'I told you so' from you." She nudged him and pulled away from his embrace.

He reached up and smoothed her hair. "You might need to use the bottom of my shirt to wipe the mud smears off your face though. Currently, you look like a cross between a raccoon and the chick who gets chased through the woods in a horror film."

Forty-eight hours ago, she wouldn't have cared what Beckett thought of her looks, but she hoped maybe after all they'd been though that he'd cut her a little slack. She knew she wasn't a supermodel, but she had been happy with how she looked. Her self-esteem hadn't been fragile. "Gee, thanks," she said dryly to cover the hurt his words had caused.

"I don't think that came across how I meant it to." Beckett tipped her face up to look at him in the dim morning light. "I think you're stunning, even when you have dirt on your nose and rivers of tears in the dust on your cheeks. But you might want to wipe some of that off before Mason sees that you've been crying. That's all."

"You are too perceptive. I'll never be able to keep anything from you, will I?" She struggled to her feet, trying to put a bit of distance between them. Beckett saw through her, like straight down to her soul. It was a bit unnerving.

"A spot clean should be enough to get some of this muck off you." He stood next to her and whipped the scrub top over his head. He flipped the shirt inside out and used it to wipe her face.

His gentle, firm touch reminded her of her father. Once, many years ago, her dad had taken her to the county fair. She'd tripped and fallen face-first into a puddle. He'd used the inside of his shirt to clean her face just like Beckett was doing now.

"You'd be a great dad." The words slipped out before she could think about filtering them. She wanted to recall them the moment they crossed her lips, but the sentiment was true. He would be a great dad, just like her dad had been.

The hand holding his shirt fell down to his side. "You think so?"

She nodded.

"Good." He brushed his lips across hers. "In case you forgot, I kinda have a thing for this hot single mom. Think that earns me some bonus points?"

"Hmm…" She moved closer to his bare chest. "I think just taking off your shirt might earn you all the bonus points you need."

"I really can come back," the SAR leader said with a laugh from above them.

Jess choked back a laugh and pressed her face against Beckett's chest. This was getting ridiculous. Were they back in high school getting busted kissing in the stairwell?

"Nah, man, I think we can postpone this until after you get us out of here." Beckett answered for them. He stepped back from Jess and slipped the dirty shirt back over his head. "To be continued?" he asked in a low voice that only Jess could hear.

She swallowed hard. A fear settled over her that once Beckett laid eyes on Mason again his relationship with her and with Mason would be tainted by his newfound knowledge of Mason's paternity. Would the sweet connection they'd found within the broken walls, of this damaged classroom carry over into the light of day?

"Jess?" he prompted softly.

She could only nod.

"Okay, which one of you two lovebugs wants to go first?" The SAR team leader lowered a harness and it dangled over the desk.

"She's going first." Beckett guided Jess over to the desk and lifted her up onto the surface with ease. "Watch her right ankle. I splinted it as best I could with the limited resources I could scrounge up."

"Can you harness her up or do you need me to drop down?"

"I got it." Beckett fastened the buckles on the harness around her. He tightened them carefully, checking each one before he nodded. "She's ready."

"Beckett," Jess said softly.

"I'll see you on the outside."

"We weren't in prison." She snorted.

"Go see your boy. I'll catch up in a few."

The SAR team pulled her up slowly, and she watched Beckett's face as she ascended away from him until she was up in the open air above the school and the contrast in light made it too hard to see him. When she looked around after clearing the opening to the classroom, her heart started racing as it dawned on her that the ropes they were on were attached to a crane. He'd actually been serious about getting a crane! Somehow, she'd imagined that the SAR guy had just scaled the side of the building or something.

"Don't worry—there's not enough rope for you to hit the ground." He grinned at her. "Although, I think maybe we'll lower you down and then go for a break before we unstrap you."

"Ha-ha." Jess faked a laugh. He might be teasing her because of her attitude yesterday, but she wasn't sure of anything at the moment. "If I apologize for running my mouth yesterday, will you let me all the way down and point me in the direction of my son?"

"I was only messing with you a little." They reached the ground and he moved quickly to release her from the harness. "I'll be going back for your boyfriend now. But if you want to go around the side of the building there—" he pointed at the still upright section of the school "—you should see a small red tent there. I believe your boy is waiting there. If not, they will know where he's gone."

"He's not my… Thank you." Denying that Beckett was her boyfriend had been on the tip of her tongue but, given that the man had caught them kissing and cuddling, there was no way he'd believe her anyway. She hobbled toward the end of the building. At this point, she was functioning purely on stubbornness and the desperate need to lay eyes on Mason. Every step she took was agony as pain radiated through her injured ankle.

The uneven ground stretched before her like a never-ending obstacle course. Still, she kept going, because Mason was just around the corner of that building and she wasn't going to stop until her boy was back in her arms where he belonged. Adrenaline must have given her energy, because her last two meals had been skimpy at best.

"Need a lift?" Beckett's voice startled her as he swept her off her feet.

"They got you out faster than they got me." She wrapped her arms around his neck. Maybe she wasn't quite done relying on him yet.

"Nah, you just walk slow." He shifted her position in his arms. "Where we headed, limping beauty?"

"Red tent," she said, waving a hand toward the temporary structure in question. "You don't have to carry me. I can walk."

"Sorta," he said with a laugh. "I hardly think that shuffle you were doing counts as walking. And what if I wasn't ready to let you out of my arms just yet?"

"Fair enough." She put her head down on his shoulder and let him carry her the remaining distance to the tent without protest. There was time enough later to get used to life alone again.

"What?" he asked.

"How do you do that?"

"Do what?"

She sighed. "Catch on to my thoughts almost as fast as I have them."

"You were relaxing in my arms and suddenly tensed

up." When they reached the tent, he carefully set her back on her feet. "Even an idiot could notice the shift in your mood."

Before she could formulate a reply, she heard the sweetest voice in all the world call out a tentative, "Mommy?"

"Mason!" She spun so fast that she nearly lost her balance. Beckett steadied her while she embraced her son for the first time in over twenty-four long hours.

First, she squeezed her baby tight, only releasing him when he said he couldn't breathe. Then, she scanned every visible inch of him for injury. He was a filthy little thing, but other than a small cut on his forehead and a scrape on one arm, she couldn't see a thing wrong with him.

"You're really okay?" she asked, trying not to cry.

"Yeah." He looked down at her ankle. When he made eye contact with her, she could see the questions and a hint of exasperation in his blue eyes. "But you aren't. Mommy, how did you get hurt when my school fell down and I didn't?"

Beckett chuckled behind her. She elbowed him and smiled in satisfaction when his laugh became a grunt.

"Do you know how she got hurt, Mr. Wilder?" Mason decided to bypass her entirely and take his questions to someone else. "And why were you carrying my mommy? Are you going to get married now?"

"Mason," Jess hissed. "What have I told you? You can't just go around asking men to marry me."

Mason rolled his eyes and turned his attention back to Beckett. "You see what I have to work with? I'll never get a dad at this rate!"

Jess kind of wished that she could just go back to that isolated dark classroom for a minute. At least in there, no one could see the visible signs of her embarrassment. She had warned Beckett about this at least, but it didn't make it any less mortifying.

Beckett laughed and ruffled Mason's hair. "I was carrying her because of her hurt ankle, which she got while trying to dig you out. Now that we know you're okay, what do you say to taking your mom to the hospital and getting this ankle looked at? I think she'd better have an X-ray on it and get a real splint or maybe even a cast, don't you?"

Mason nodded like he and Beckett were actually making plans. She kept waiting for the moment when Beckett decided that being involved with a single mom was too complicated. It was coming; she knew it was. And each of these moments where Beckett grew closer to Mason would only make that break harder.

"When the two of you have finished making plans for me, I'd like to get out of here," Jess grumbled. Her stomach let out an audible growl. "Have you eaten, baby? Mommy is starving!"

Mason pointed across the grass. "That lady over there has muffins. I think she likes me. She gave me two chocolate muffins and said I could have a blueberry one if I wanted after I finished those, but I got all full from that."

"Mom!" Beckett shouted happily, leaving their side to rush over to Mrs. Wilder who was standing with a huge basket of muffins in her arms.

CHAPTER TWENTY-TWO

"BECKETT!" HIS MOM TURNED at the sound of his voice. "What are you doing here? I've been trying to reach you since yesterday. Your father's gone to the hospital, thinking you were there. But when I heard there were still rescue efforts here, I felt I was needed more here."

He embraced her tightly.

"Darling, as much as I'm happy to see you whole, what are you wearing? I presume that you are aware of your need for a shower." She hugged him back briefly, but then pushed against him. "Don't share your stench, please."

Beckett laughed and tapped a finger to his mother's wrinkled nose. "This stench was the result of being trapped all night in that school and trying to dig my way free."

"Why were you in the school?" Confusion filled her eyes, along with a touch of concern. "If you hadn't left those messages that you were okay, I'd have really been concerned. You are all we have left now."

"I know, Mom." Guilt over worrying his mother rose up in him. After all that she'd been through, he hated to add to her pain. How could he explain that he was trying to spare another mother the trauma she'd gone through without reopening the wound of losing a child? It had taken his mother a long time to seem okay after Sloane's death. He didn't want her to backslide and get tangled in that web of grief again.

He turned to look for Jess, wanting to introduce her to his mother. She was still over by the red tent with Mason. She kept glancing his way. When they made eye contact though, she let her gaze drop quickly to the ground. That seemed unlike the bold Jess that he knew.

"Come on. There's someone I want you to meet."

"Oh, really?" His mom perked up. He could see the wedding plans in her eyes already. "That beautiful young woman talking to little Mason?"

"Yes, but please keep your cool. I haven't even taken her on a date yet."

"I'm going to take that as a hopeful sign that you want to though. That Mason is such a sweet child." And he was starting to regret that he'd offered to introduce her to Jess. She'd been angling for grandchildren for ages now.

"Jess," he said softly as they walked up. "I'd like you to meet my mother."

"It's nice to meet you, Mrs. Wilder. Your son has been a big help to me over the last twenty-four hours." She smiled softly at him, looking a bit shy. "I don't know what I'd have done without him."

"You'd have managed." He reached out and tucked a bit of hair behind her ear. "You're strong. I'm glad I could help though. Now, we need to get that ankle x-rayed."

Jess gave him a look. "I'll get it looked at. I promise. You can go now. You don't have to worry about me anymore." She hugged Mason tight. "I have everything I need now."

Beckett took a couple muffins from his mom's basket and held one out to Jess. "Except you haven't eaten since yesterday and you're only standing because of a sweater and a couple rulers."

"Rulers?" Mason squatted down to look at his mom's ankle. His little forehead wrinkled up as he stared at the makeshift brace. "How are rulers helping her stand up?"

Beckett sank down to the ground next to the boy. He was too tired to squat like the child was doing. He'd passed the age where a few hours of sleep on a tile floor was an acceptable night's rest. He explained how he'd made a brace to help stabilize Jess's ankle as he ate a muffin. His mom could chastise him for talking while eating another time.

"He reminds me of you as a child," his mom said quietly. "Always curious about everything. You had so many questions. Those questions would spawn more questions. You couldn't accept *I don't know* as an answer either. And it wasn't as if I could simply google it then. You drove me batty some days."

"That's definitely Mason." Jess smoothed the boy's blond locks and sighed. "Curious from dawn to dusk."

Beckett looked up at her. She had a grim set to her jaw, but he could see she was trying to put a smile on. Probably for Mason's benefit. She needed to get off that ankle and get a proper brace on it, most likely a cast.

"Mom, did you drive here?"

His mom looked confused at the sudden change of topic. "No, dear, your father dropped me off. Why?"

"Because we're heading to the hospital now and I don't want to leave you if you need a ride."

"Beckett—"

"Jessamine," he replied back evenly. "You need an X-ray. You have no car. Unless you want to get in the back of one of these understaffed ambulances, you are going to let me take you to the hospital."

They had a bit of a stare off, but finally she sighed. "Bring your truck over here. I don't think I can walk around that building again."

"You didn't walk around it the first time," Mason said with the bluntness of a child.

Beckett tried to keep his lips from curling up into a smile. He really did. But then Jess gave Mason a look of pure frustration and the chuckle he'd tried to choke back escaped. "He's not wrong," Beckett finally managed to get out around his peals of laughter.

"Hush, you." She wagged a finger at him. But he could see that she wasn't offended by their teasing. "Both of you. I don't see either one of you walking around with rulers and a stranger's sweater tied to your leg."

Moving swiftly, Beckett swooped her into his arms again. "You two ready to go?"

If his mother was surprised by his actions, she didn't show it. Jess gave a token protest, but then settled into his arms. He was a little surprised when she didn't fight him. He'd expected her to insist that he just bring the truck around, but she didn't. She must be in more pain than she was willing to let on.

Leaning in close, he whispered, "On a scale of one to ten, how bad is the pain?"

She murmured, "About a fifteen."

"That's what I thought." He didn't slow his pace until they reached his truck. He set her gently down on her uninjured ankle so that he could fish the keys out of his pocket. He unlocked the doors and had her installed in the front seat before she could issue a complaint.

"You should let your mother sit up front," she said as he slid behind the wheel.

"She'll be okay back there for the short trip to the hospital," he said. "Won't you, Mom?"

"Of course, dear." His mother's reply was swift and confident. She wouldn't take offense to Jess being up front, especially given her injuries, and if she had been offended, she was polite enough to address the slight in private later. "I'm content back here with this sweet child."

Jess tensed up.

"You okay?"

"Just a sharp pain," she said. But he wasn't quite sure he believed that was the cause of her tension. Still, he let the subject drop for the moment.

Mason was all too happy to keep the truck cab from lapsing into silence. He regaled them with a play-by-play. Surviving a tornado and being nearly buried alive was for certain an adventure to a small boy—one that he'd be proud to tell for the rest of his life, if Beckett was any judge. The child was quite animated as he told his story sitting next to Beckett's mother in the backseat. He soaked up her attention like a sponge, beaming at her whenever she made the appropriately awed sounds.

When he looked in the rearview mirror, Beckett could see the longing in his mother's eyes when she gazed at the little boy. He hadn't realized just how much she wanted to be a grandmother until that moment. She'd pushed for years, introducing him to women, suggesting how he might meet others, but it had never really occurred to him how much it truly meant to her.

He reached over and took Jess's hand. Stepkids had never been something he'd really considered one way or another until extremely recently. Seeing his mom with Mason though made him think that she wouldn't mind so much if her first grandkid wasn't a biological one. His dad might have other ideas, but he'd get over it.

Beckett rubbed his thumb against the back of Jess's hand. Would she even consider him as a potential stepdad for Mason? The idea was growing on him. Being with Jess meant that one of them had to move though. Woodvale's job market was hardly booming, and he'd established himself in Lexington. They'd been through a lot this past day together, and they'd certainly gotten a lot closer. But was that just from the stress they'd shared? Had she leaned on him for support because of her fear? And now that Mason was safe, would she push him away again?

CHAPTER TWENTY-THREE

GLANCING INTO THE BACKSEAT, Jess had to fight off a wince. Mason was engaged and clearly bonding with Mrs. Wilder, and she appeared enthralled with him. Great. Now there was a second person who had the power to break her little boy's heart. That was exactly what she'd feared might happen if she got involved with Beckett. She should have pushed him away. Sent him back when he had followed her into the school yesterday.

The best thing she could do would be to shut off all contact with Beckett. Keep her son far, far away from the Wilder family and anyone else who could hurt her son. The older woman ran her hand over Mason's hair and Jess had to blink back tears. How could she believe that someone so gentle might hurt her son? But it wasn't a physical hurt that she worried about now, was it? No, it was something far worse. Emotional pain could linger for years. She wanted to protect her son from that.

Beckett's thumb rubbed a tantalizing pattern against the top of her hand. Every brush of his skin against hers made her second-guess putting distance between them. Distance would mean no more of these loving, supportive touches. No more firm chest to rest her weary head on. No more strong arms to hold her when she felt weak.

Biting her lip, she stared down at their entwined hands. How had she let it get this far? There was no way to end this now without getting hurt. Even if she ended this as soon as she got to the hospital, she was already too attached. And so was Mason.

Tears filled her eyes and she fought valiantly to blink them away before anyone could see. Even if her heart was breaking at the thought of never being in Beckett's arms again, she had to do what was best for her little boy. She sniffled once. Oh, how she'd love to be selfish, to give herself over to Beckett's attention and let him love her. Mason's safety came first.

She shifted and pain shot up her ankle. Her grip on Beckett's hand tightened. Even while she was convincing herself to walk away from him and all that he had to offer, she was seeking his comfort. What had happened to her? She'd been a strong, independent single mom two days ago.

I fell in love.

She looked over at him when that thought sank in. She'd done the stupid thing and gone and fallen for him. She really had. Closing her eyes, she let her mind consider all the paths forward. There was no way out of this where she didn't get hurt now. The best thing she could do was reject Beckett before he became attached to her. At least that way she could protect him from the heartbreak of losing a loved one.

Beckett pulled the truck to a stop in front of the main lobby of the hospital where there were crews putting up giant sheets of glass to replace the ones that had been shattered in the storm. "I'll need to go park the truck. But I figured you didn't want to walk from the parking garage or have me carry you that far."

He came around and helped her to the ground. "You good? I can take you inside and find a wheelchair or something."

She glared at him. Just because she had a bum leg didn't mean she was ready to accept a wheelchair. Determined to retain some measure of her independence, and to prove to herself that she could do without Beckett's assistance for a moment, she stood up as straight as she could. Her tone was firm, assertive, when she said, "I'll make it."

"I'm sure you will." Beckett just smiled at her, like he knew what she was thinking. Annoying man probably did. He'd known the whole time they were together, so it shouldn't surprise her that he did now.

"Go park your truck," she growled out at him.

"Yes, ma'am." He ruffled Mason's hair and told him, "Take care of your mother while I'm gone."

"You're going to the parking garage, not to war," Jess grumbled.

He laughed as he walked around the truck. "Falling in love is the biggest war there is."

And with that, he got in the cab and drove away.

"He… I… Ugh!" Jess shook her head. How infuriating! And to think just minutes ago she'd fancied herself in love with him!

"Mommy, I like him. Can we keep him?"

Jess opened her mouth and closed it again without speaking. She wasn't quite sure how to answer Mason's innocent query without shattering his hopes.

"While your mama does her goldfish impression, I'll tell you what you want to know." Jess bit the inside of her lip, hoping that Mrs. Wilder wasn't going to be rude. "You cannot simply keep people like they are stray puppies, but if you're lucky, they decide to stay of their own accord."

"Okay." Mason's lower lip popped out and he looked for a second like he might cry. But he quickly rallied. "He said he likes baseball. You think he would play with me?"

Mrs. Wilder answered with a smile that crinkled up her eyes just like Beckett's smile did his. "He more than likes baseball. He loves it. He was quite good when he used to play too. I'm sure if you ask nicely, and your mommy says it's okay, Beckett would love to take you to a game or maybe play catch."

"Yay!"

Great. Now Mason would for sure be heartbroken when she broke things off with Beckett. She took a step toward the hospital entrance too quickly, and in her haste, the injured ankle nearly gave way.

Mrs. Wilder caught her arm, helping her find her balance. She met Jess's eyes with a kind, steady look. They didn't share the same eye color, but there was something about her gaze that reminded Jess of Beckett. "Let's get you off that foot before you do further damage. Do you need to lean on me as we go in?"

Jess shook her head, reluctant to take help. As she slowly made her way inside, Mrs. Wilder hovered at her elbow, ready to steady her again if she were to wobble. She swallowed down the notion that she'd misjudged Mrs. Wilder just as she had Beckett.

"Thank you," she murmured when they reached the temporary check-in desk.

"Hey, Jess," Becky at the desk said. "Whatever have you done to yourself?"

"Broken or badly sprained this ankle. I could use an X-ray to be sure."

"Sure, sure." Becky tapped a few keys. "Are you up to date in the system?"

Jess nodded. She'd had to update all their info when Mason had needed stitches a couple months back. "Yeah, nothing has changed."

"Okay, I'll get you called back as soon as we can. It's a madhouse around here." She waved a hand at the cluster of chairs along the side wall. Most of them looked to be filled with people suffering various degrees of injury. "Take a seat…if you can find one."

She hobbled over to the seating area. Mrs. Wilder had found two seats together and there happened to be two across from them that were also unoccupied. Mason sat next to Mrs. Wilder, jabbering on happily to the older woman. Jess sank into one of the open seats, in too much pain to put an end to the obvious bonding her son and Beckett's mother were doing. "Dare I ask how y'all managed to find us seats together in this craziness?"

"If I know my mother, she gave someone a look until they decided they didn't need to be at the hospital any longer," Beckett joked as he sat next to her. "You get checked in?"

She nodded at him.

"Okay, good." He slipped an arm around her. "These chairs always seemed so uncomfortable before. It's amazing how spending a night on cold tile can change your perspective, huh?"

He'd changed his shirt while he was parking. Gone was the dirty, sweaty scrub top. He'd replaced it with a T-shirt advertising a local gym. And he had freshened up a little and now smelled like deodorant, rather than sweat and wet insulation.

"That shirt looks silly with those fancy pants," she teased.

"You know you like my fancy pants." He leaned over and brushed his lips across her forehead.

Jess tried to look at his mom and Mason, hoping they hadn't noticed Beckett's display of affection. That was too much to hope for. Mason and Mrs. Wilder were both grinning from ear to ear. Jess looked down. This was all too much. The longer she let this go on, the more people were at risk of getting hurt. She just didn't know how to put an end to it without seeming like a rude, un-grateful cow.

They all sat quietly until Jess was called. Mrs. Wilder offered to watch Mason while she saw the doctor, and Jess reluctantly agreed. Beckett stood and moved to go with her.

"I don't need a chaperone," she said softly.

"Maybe not." He followed along at her side, sharing her weight so that she could put less pressure on the foot. "But right now, you do need someone to lean on."

She didn't have the willpower to turn him back. If he wanted to offer his support, she'd accept it. At least for a little while longer. But soon, she'd have to step up and tell him that they could never be more than friends.

But she knew, deep in her heart, that she could never

just be Beckett's friend. It would have to be all or nothing. If the day had taught her anything, it was that she couldn't resist Beckett—not his touch, or his words or the silent support his mere presence provided. One day in the very near future, she'd have to find a way to make that break. Before she got so attached to his presence that she couldn't.

She wasn't able to accept that maybe she was already too far gone to ever send him away. There was far too much at stake.

"This way, Jess," one of the newer nurses said, leading her down the hall to Radiology.

With Beckett's makeshift splint removed, Jess could see the swelling and the purple color tinging her skin. Even before the X-ray was snapped, she knew it was broken. Each time she'd shifted during the night, the jabs of pain had told her that she'd fractured the bone, but there'd been the tiniest sliver of hope that it wasn't. That hope vanished faster than candy with Mason's baseball team.

They put her in a curtained-off area to wait for the doctor.

Beckett sat next to her. "What color cast do you want?"

"You think it's broken too, don't you?"

"Afraid so."

She leaned her head back against the wall and stared up at the ceiling. "This is not the best time for this."

He pulled her hand into his lap and threaded their fingers together. "Honey, I don't think there's ever a good time for a broken ankle."

"Do you realize that I'm effectively homeless? My

job is sorta rocky, considering the state of the emergency room. And I have a very active son to keep up with. Crutches just ain't gonna cut it."

"Your accent gets thicker when you're upset."

Jess let out a deep sigh. She worked hard to minimize her slow Southern drawl, but in times of stress, those old speech patterns came back to haunt her. "I'd tell you to hush up, but I'm too tired."

Dr. Newton came up just then. "So, it's definitely broken. The good news is that it's not surgical."

"And the bad news?"

"You're going to be rocking a cast for about six weeks. Longer if you don't stay off it and let your body recuperate." Dr. Newton paused and then gave Jess a knowing look. "Let's just go ahead and say you'll have the cast for eight weeks."

Beckett shook next to her with the effort of suppressing a laugh. "Sounds like she knows you, Jess."

"Now, no husbands or boyfriends are allowed where we're going, so I'm afraid I'll need to ask you to wait in the lobby." Dr. Newton flashed Beckett an apologetic smile. "We need to set the break and get her casted. Give us about two hours, give or take."

Beckett leaned over and brushed the softest of kisses against her lips. "I'll make sure Mason gets some food that's not sugary muffins, and maybe a nap. Call me when you're done?"

Once he'd walked away, Dr. Newton helped Jess into a wheelchair and pushed her up to the orthopedics unit. "I've seen him around the hospital. You are one lucky lady to go home to him every night."

Jess ignored that comment. Or tried to, anyway. "Do

you think there's any chance at all that I could get a quick shower and a clean pair of scrubs before I get this cast on? I'm filthy."

Dr. Newton grunted. "I'll see what we can do."

It was a big ask, but if she didn't get a shower soon, she might lose her mind. And she did not want her sweaty, dirty leg casted where it would itch for weeks from the start.

Dr. Newton put her in a room. "We'll have to see if we can find someone to help you shower, unless you want to call your boyfriend back up?"

Jess shook her head quickly. "Could we call Freya Anderson? She's my best friend. Maybe if she's not too busy, she wouldn't mind helping me."

Freya, of course, came when she was called and had a clean set of scrubs in her hands. Shaking her head, she looked down at Jess with worry filling her eyes. "Tell me how badly I need to hurt him?"

"Who?"

"Beckett!" she exclaimed. "He was supposed to watch out for you, not let you break a leg. I suppose I should be glad that you didn't break your frickin' neck!"

"This is all on me." Jess shrugged. "I did that impulsive thing where I think I know better than the person in charge and rushed in without a plan. This is where it got me."

"He still promised me that he'd stay with you."

"Oh, so you're the reason he's been babysitting me?" Jess winced as Freya helped her to her feet and into the shower. Freya helped her undress and stood outside the curtain while Jess quickly washed the muck and grime from her skin.

As the water poured over her, she tried to wash away the hurt feelings that Freya's words manifested. How much of Beckett's attentiveness had been because he wanted to be with her and how much of it came from a promise made to Freya?

"I know what you're thinking," Freya said loudly enough to be heard over the water. "Jess, if you think for one second that man didn't stay with you of his own accord, you are blind. I just wanted to make sure he didn't let you run off alone. You needed someone with you, in case—"

"In case Mason had been hurt, or worse," Jess finished for her.

"But since you're here alone, the jerk did leave you. He promised me he wouldn't."

Jess pulled the curtain back so that she could see Freya's face. "He's down in the lobby with his mom and Mason."

"Oh, is he now?" Freya's mood brightened considerably. "Is that why you were so anxious for a shower that you paged me away from the chaos I've been dealing to help you clean up?"

"Maybe I was tired of smelling myself." Jess tugged the curtain closed and dried herself off as best she could without putting any weight on her foot.

Freya had to help her get the clean scrub pants on. "Oh, come on. That man is hot. Girl, I saw you noticing him. You can't lie to me." Freya raised a brow and stared Jess down.

"Yes, I noticed that he's attractive. I'm celibate, not dead." Jess didn't like the calculating look Freya gave her. It didn't bode well.

"Jess…"

"Freya, just leave it alone. Please? I'm single and happy that way." And she could nurse her achy heart in peace without her best friend's fussing if she didn't tell Freya about how close she was to changing her opinion on being single.

"Are you sure?" Freya's eyes sparkled. "Oh, wait, I forgot who I was talking to for a minute. You know there is more to life than this job and your son, right? Let your hair down on occasion. Have a little fun. Spending some, shall we say, adult time, with a man might do you a world of good. Especially with a guy who looks like Beckett Wilder. Just think about it."

Freya left her with that and went back to work. Just think about it. As if Jess hadn't been doing just that… She could think of nothing else. Her work was a mess, her house was unlivable and she had a broken bone. Did any of those things jump to the forefront of her mind? Nope. All she could think about was Beckett Wilder and the way her heart sped up when he smiled at her.

Jess toughed her way through the bone reset with only minimal pain medication. She didn't want her head to get too foggy when she had Mason with her to think about. But she also knew better than to try to do it with zero medication.

Once the bone was set, they slipped a stockinette over her foot gently and started wrapping it with thick padding. Once they had the padding spread so that there was even pressure around her foot and ankle, they showed her the fiberglass casting options. She really didn't care what color her cast was, but she settled on the purple since it was her favorite color.

The technician worked quickly, wrapping the damp material around her foot and ankle, over the padding. The fiberglass casting was lighter weight than the traditional plaster and allowed better airflow.

"Am I getting fiberglass because Dr. Newton wants more X-rays soon?"

"Yes, ma'am." The technician stood and washed her hands. "This will take at least thirty minutes to harden enough for us to let you out of here. But it should be completely dry in about two hours. When I come back in to check that it's dry, I'll bring your care instructions. Don't touch it while I'm gone."

CHAPTER TWENTY-FOUR

WHEN BECKETT GOT BACK to the lobby, his dad stood in front of his mom's chair. His shoulders drooped with visible exhaustion. How long had he been on his feet?

Mason had fallen asleep. His head rested in Beckett's mom's lap. His mouth gaped open in sleep, and he was the picture of pure innocence.

They all looked worn out.

"Beckett," his mom said with a warm smile when he walked up. "How's she doing?"

"Broken ankle, as I expected. She's getting a cast now. They said it would be a couple hours before she was ready to go." He smoothed a stray lock of hair out of Mason's face, taking care not to wake him. "Forgive me for saying this, but you all look exhausted. Mason is clearly worn out. Would you consider taking Mason home with you and getting some rest?"

"Is Jess okay with that?" his mom questioned.

"I think she'll be upset, but I'll take the blame." He didn't just *think* she'd be upset. He knew it for a fact. But Mason was exhausted, and he couldn't sleep in these chairs. Not to mention, they had nowhere else to go really. He'd take whatever Jess had to say with the knowledge that he'd done what he thought was best at the time.

"We'll take him home with us, but you be sure you tell her that he's okay. She'll worry."

"Got it." He bent and lifted Mason easily into his arms. The boy shifted, and murmured something, but thankfully didn't wake. "I'll help get him to the car."

When his dad cleared his throat, Beckett paused. Maybe he should have cleared this plan with his parents first since he was commandeering their house, but it wasn't like there was another real option. "If that's okay with you?"

His dad nodded slowly. "Of course."

With that settled, he helped them out to his father's car, settling Mason in the backseat. Hopefully, they could get the boy in the house without too much trouble. His father didn't need to be lifting Mason's weight with his chemo port.

His dad waited until his mom had gotten in the car too before he spoke. "The boy's mother, she means something to you?"

Beckett nodded. It was a little early to be professing his love, but he definitely had caught feelings for Jess. Strong ones. And he found himself already feeling protective of Mason. It was a lot to communicate in a nod, but his dad interpreted the message without issue.

"I'll make sure he's safe then. We'll see you soon."

Beckett breathed a sigh of relief when his dad drove away with Mason. He and the man had certainly had their issues over the years, mostly in regard to Beckett's career, but his father was a man of his word. Beckett knew without a doubt that his dad would take them straight home where his mother would then fuss over Mason like he was royalty. And with them all safe, he could devote his full attention to Jess.

He went back into the hospital lobby to wait. After managing to snag a chair in the corner, Beckett closed his eyes to rest a moment while he waited for Jess. He needed sleep, a shower and a sandwich and he wasn't even picky about the order he got them in. He must have drifted off, because the next thing he knew, Jess was in front of him in a wheelchair poking his knee.

"Where's my son?"

Beckett sat up straight and blinked at her for a moment while he tried to clear his sleep-addled mind. "He's at my parents' house."

"Excuse me?"

"He was exhausted. My parents were both dead on their feet. I thought they'd all be more comfortable at my parents' house." He hoped that would take away some of the ire he read in her expression. His mom had been right about Jess's reaction. But this icy anger was a little scarier than the fiery temper she'd shown before.

"I'd really like to get my son and go home."

"I'll get my truck." He stood and moved around her without touching her. The ice queen was back, and he wanted to give her a moment to thaw before he reminded her that her home had been destroyed by the tornado.

Soon he had her in the cab of the truck and headed away from the hospital. They'd gone about three blocks when she said, "Did your parents move? I thought you grew up on the lake."

"No."

He pulled into the drive of her damaged home. "I'm not trying to hurt you here but look at your house. Honey, you can't stay here. You can't go home. You're pissed at me, aren't you? But your son was asleep in one of those miserable waiting room chairs. Which he almost fell out of, by the way. So, I made a judgment call. I chose to send him home with my parents where he would be safe, looked after and could rest in a proper bed."

"You should have asked me first," she said quietly.

"Where you'd have protested that you'd rather go to a hotel. Look around. With the widespread devastation in Woodvale and the surrounding communities, there won't be a hotel room for miles. My parents have the space."

"You still should have asked me."

"I did what I thought was right. I won't apologize for it."

Beckett backed out of the drive, and they drove the rest of the way to his parents' house in silence. He'd done nothing wrong. How could she be mad at him for taking care of her son when she wasn't able to?

They were still not speaking when he parked his truck by the front steps. "I'll have to carry you in, but we have a set of crutches in the attic. I'll get them down for you so that you can have some freedom back."

"Thank you."

He expected her to hold herself stiffly in his arms, reluctant to accept his touch, but she wrapped her arms around his neck and leaned into his shoulder. "You are driving me crazy, woman," he told her as he carried her over the threshold.

"Ditto."

"The guest rooms are just over here," he told her as they passed the open living room and kitchen. He didn't see his parents or Mason. They must all be resting. "There are two guest rooms on the left that share a bath, and my room is on the right."

"I just want to see Mason," she said.

He eased her down at the doorway to the first guest room. It wasn't shut completely. Peering through the crack, Beckett saw Mason curled up asleep wearing one of his T-shirts. He looked as though he'd had a bath.

"Mommy?" Mason said sleepily.

"Hey, baby," she said, holding on to the door frame for balance. "I didn't mean to wake you up."

"If you're good here, I'll go find those crutches for you," Beckett offered.

"Thanks."

It took him a few minutes to find the crutches. His mom tended to be a pack rat and she wanted to keep everything because she might use it someday. When he came back down, he paused when he heard a snippet of conversation that set his mind churning.

"Mommy, I like it here."

"You do?" Jess responded. "I'm happy that you like it, but…" Beckett heard her sigh.

"It kinda made me miss Nana though. I wish I still had a nana or a grandma or grandpa." Beckett dared to peek around the doorway. "Since you kissed Mr. Wilder, does that mean he's going to be my dad now?"

"Honey, it's not that simple."

"Grown-ups make everything hard."

He didn't want to be accused of eavesdropping, and

he sure didn't want to tell her what he'd just overheard, so he backed up quietly and then made more noise than usual when he walked up to the bedroom again. Mason wanted him to be his dad? The first time Mason had said it Beckett had been amused, but it was different this time, because now Beckett had feelings for Mason's mom and becoming his dad was a real possibility. A shard of fear lodged itself in Beckett's heart.

He tapped on the open door. "I found those crutches. I'll be across the hall if you need anything."

After going into his room, he closed the door and leaned against the cool wood. Thoughts spun through his brain, powered by a tornado of emotions. The last day and a half had given him a lot to process. Most importantly, was he really dad material?

CHAPTER TWENTY-FIVE

AFTER BECKETT HAD said goodnight, Mason had settled back down relatively quickly and dozed off, leaving Jess with far too much time to think. Physically, she was exhausted, but her mind kept going over the conversation with Mason she was sure Beckett had overheard. He had a look in his eyes, sort of a panicked confusion. If she wasn't mistaken, that was the moment it had really hit him that she came as a package deal with a son.

Twice, she got the crutches and went to the door, but she chickened out before she could go talk to him. They had no future, and she knew that, but she needed one more night with the illusion that things were different. She had finally calmed enough that she was dozing lightly when she heard Beckett and his dad talking.

Hearing her name brought her back to being fully awake.

"If your plans haven't changed, then why would you get involved with her, son?" His dad didn't make much effort to keep his voice down. "Her life is here, and yours is in Lexington."

"She could come with me."

"Have you talked to her about that?"

Beckett's silence was answer enough. The conversation trailed off, leaving Jess with even more to think about. Beckett had told her that he would think about staying in Woodvale, hadn't he? She wracked her brain trying to remember the exact words he'd used, but she was too tired to clearly recall.

Still, sleep was a long time coming. When she did finally nod off, her slumber was restless and filled with dreams of Beckett leaving them and breaking Mason's heart.

When she woke at five, she gave in to the impulse to talk to Beckett. She had to find out how he felt, and what he planned to do, so that she could figure out how to move forward. Tapping lightly on his door, she waited for him to answer.

"Is something wrong?" Beckett opened the door wearing nothing but a pair of low-slung athletic shorts. He rubbed the sleep from his eyes, the movements causing the muscles in his arms to ripple intriguingly.

"We need to talk."

"Talk?" Beckett pulled her into his arms. "I'm all for a private conversation."

His mouth scorched hot against hers. Her arms came up around his neck and she leaned into his embrace. Her crutches fell to the carpeted floor with a muffled clatter.

Not what she came for, but she enjoyed his attentions for a moment before reluctantly pushing him away. "I meant really talk," she said as she tried to catch her breath.

"Okay, we can talk." He pushed the door closed behind her.

"I overheard part of your conversation with your

dad." She waited for him to say something, to deny that he was still planning to leave. There was still the tiniest sliver of hope in her heart, but his silence squashed that. She swallowed hard and put a hand on his chest to push him back, to put some distance between them so that she could think. "You are still planning to leave, after all that you said."

"I have a career in Lexington." He tried to move closer. "You and Mason could come with me."

"No," she whispered. "My life is here. Mason's life is here."

"We can make a new life, together," he argued, his hands clutching at her waist. "Won't you at least consider it?"

She shook her head, as angry with herself as she was at him. She'd let her guard down with him, and that part was entirely on her. Still, he'd told her that he would consider staying in Woodvale. And that simple fact had been part of why she'd let him get so close. "I knew I shouldn't get involved with you. I knew that letting you near Mason was a bad idea. The day we met, I warned you to keep your distance. And this is why."

"You were afraid I'd want to have a future with you?" he scoffed.

She choked back a sob. "I was afraid that you'd walk away and leave me just like Clint did. But now it's not just my heart on the line. It's Mason's too."

"I'm not Clint," he growled out through clenched teeth. "It doesn't have to be that way."

"I know that." She wrapped her arms around herself, trying to give herself the strength to get through this conversation. "But I totally called this one, didn't I?"

"You assume that I'd, what? Knock you up and bail? Hurt your son?" He shook his head. "Is that really what you think of me?"

"I didn't think Clint would hurt me either." She snorted. "Then I found out that the man I was in love with wasn't who he said he was. He was my everything, and to him I was just a sidepiece. I lost my boyfriend, my pride and my reputation in a single blow. Now I have Mason to think of."

"You think I'd hurt Mason." Pain layered over his words, and she clenched her hands against his chest.

"Maybe not intentionally," she had to admit. "But when you go back to Lexington, he's going to be hurt. Even if this morning is the last time that you see him, he will still be hurt that he doesn't get to hang out with you again. He's crazy about you already."

"So you're pushing me away because me leaving will hurt Mason?" He huffed. "You know that doesn't make sense."

"You are the one leaving town! I'm not pushing you away—you're doing that all on your own." Tears welled up in her eyes and she swiped roughly at them. "This is why I didn't want to get involved with you!" Fat tears ran down her cheeks. "I knew it could only end in tears. But you had to be so…you."

"So me?" he said with a hint of a smile. "Is that an insult or a compliment?"

"Why did you have to be so caring? So supportive? If you'd been even half the jerk that Clint was, I could have walked away without giving you a second glance. But no, you had to be this perfect package. All good-looking and kind and taking charge without being a jerk about it. You had to go and make me…".

"Make you what, Jess?" Beckett moved closer, slowly like a predator easing up on his prey. "Make you like me?" With the barest of touches, he let his fingertips trail along her jawline. "Make you want me?" Barely a breath separated them when he whispered, "Make you love me?"

"I can't."

"But you already do, don't you?" His lips traced the curve of her throat. "What I'm feeling isn't one-sided here."

She couldn't stop her reactions to him any more than she could stop the sun from rising or rain from falling from the sky. "I can't," she argued, even as she clutched his shoulders in her hands and wished that things were different.

"You just have to let me in. You and Mason could move with me to Lexington when I go back." He held her so tenderly that she almost thought they could make something work. "I've got a job waiting for me there. You know there's no job market here for an EMT. But I'm sure you could find a job in Lexington easily, as a nurse or another management-type position."

He wanted her to give up everything for him. Put herself in a place of being totally dependent upon a man again. A position she'd sworn she'd never be in again.

"Woodvale is my home."

"What's keeping you here?" Tension tightened his frame. "Memories and a falling-down house? I'll buy us a house in Lexington."

"My dad grew up in that falling-down house, and

so did I. If I have any say, Mason will grow up there too." That damaged house held so many memories. And memories were all that remained now of her mom and dad.

Frustration showed on his face. "So you're choosing a town that's done nothing but keep you down and a damaged house over me, because of what?"

"That damaged house is all I have left of my parents. I may not have much here, but I have Freya who is the closest thing I have to a sibling. And I have my job that I happen to like." Her heart was breaking even as the words slipped past her lips. "I can't go with you to Lexington."

"Won't."

"What?"

"You *can* go, you just won't."

"That's not fair. Woodvale is my home, and my son's safety and well-being has to be my top priority."

Beckett suddenly took a step back. He bent and picked up her crutches. Ice laced his voice. "If you don't trust me with Mason, and you don't want a future with me, then I suppose there's nothing left to say. You're welcome to stay here until you can make alternate arrangements. I'll do my best not to burden you with my unwanted presence."

Jess shivered at the sudden coldness between them. She'd gotten what she wanted, hadn't she? She'd just been asking him to let her go, but she hadn't expected it to feel so wrong. "Beckett…"

"Do I need to leave, or can I have my room back?" He opened the door and kept his eyes trained on the floor.

"I'll go." She tucked the crutches under her arms.

When she cleared the doorway, Beckett closed the door behind her. He didn't slam it, but the audible click of the closure carried a finality to it.

The moment she got back into her room, she used the landline on the table and called Freya. "It's early, but can you come get us?"

"Tell me where. Why do you sound like you've been crying?"

She gave Freya the address and a promise to explain later. She couldn't rehash the conversation with Beckett without bursting into tears, and she would be doing so with a heavy heart. The best thing for Mason was for them to make a clean break from Beckett and the Wilders, wasn't it? So why did it feel like the worst thing for her?

CHAPTER TWENTY-SIX

THE HARDEST THING he'd ever had to do was put the woman he loved in a car and let her drive away. He rubbed at his chest, trying to ease the pain around his heart. Sinking down on the porch steps, Beckett tried to remember how to breathe.

He'd told her that he was falling for her, that he wanted a future with her, and she'd walked away. He'd been sure that she'd returned his sentiments, but still she hadn't stayed. The distance she put between them she claimed was to protect Mason, but it was all really to protect herself. Mason was completely safe with him, and she had to know that. No, this was because Jess didn't trust him. Or maybe didn't trust herself around him. Either way, she was gone.

"Want to get something off your chest, son?" His dad sat down beside him.

Beckett huffed. "Like what? That my future just drove away without me, determined to never let me out of the present because of a past I had nothing to do with?"

"You can't change the past." His father slapped him

on the back. "But the good news is that the future is a little more malleable."

"I don't see how." He waved a hand toward the road. "Did you not see her drive away without a backward glance?"

"We haven't had the closest relationship, and I accept the bulk of the responsibility for that." His dad leaned back, stretching his legs out in front of him. "But I see how you look at Jess and her boy. Your mom is in love with that little guy already."

Beckett couldn't stop the rude reply that broached his lips. "All things I know, Dad."

"I'm going to let the disrespect in your tone slide this time because I know you're smarting at the loss of your lady. I won't sit here and be the target for your wrath though." His dad rose to his feet. "If you aren't going to do whatever you can to get her back, you'd better get that out of your system fast."

Beckett flashed his father an apologetic look.

His dad stopped him before Beckett could verbally acknowledge taking his frustrations out on him. "You want her back, right? Take care of her present needs, and the future will fall into line."

With those final words of wisdom, the man went back inside the house, leaving Beckett to think about the advice he'd been given. His dad seemed to think things with Jess could still be fixed. To Beckett, the future looked bleak. He didn't see a path forward that gave him a future with Jess. She didn't trust him, but once he thought about it more, it became clear that she was trying to consider Mason's best interests. How could he be mad about that?

Could his dad be right though?
Take care of her present needs.
What did she need most? And how could he provide that for her?

CHAPTER TWENTY-SEVEN

LOSING CLINT WHEN she was expecting Mason had hurt, but it was nothing compared to losing Beckett. Three days had passed since she'd walked away from him, her eyes filled with tears. It had taken her about an hour to realize that while she'd been infatuated with Clint, and at the time thought herself to be in love, it was Beckett who her heart truly desired.

She let out a deep sigh, filled with unrequited longing.

"If you miss him that much, why don't you call him?" Freya asked gently. They'd been staying with Freya since leaving the Wilders' home. The apartment was cramped. Even Mason had complained about the lack of space. Jess hadn't had the heart to argue about that, since she herself was sleeping on the couch. A very lumpy couch, at that.

The jab that really hurt though was when Mason had asked when they'd see Beckett again. In only a few interactions, he'd taken to Beckett easily. Her little boy had fallen for Beckett just like she had, and she hadn't had it in her to crush his hopes yet. She'd put him off, saying Beckett was busy with the storm cleanup.

"It's not that simple." Jess stirred her coffee, playing with it rather than drinking it. She wanted to explain, but the words just weren't there. Her mind told her that being with Beckett was an unacceptable risk, but her heart wanted him with every beat it took. And because of that, there was no explanation that fully sat right.

"Bull." Freya set her coffee mug down on the table. She reached across and put her hand on top of Jess's. "You're in love with him. He's clearly crazy about you." She glanced toward the spare bedroom where Mason was still sleeping and lowered her voice to a whisper. "And you can't think that Mason would be upset if you and Beckett got together."

Jess didn't respond. It sounded so easy when Freya could put it in such straightforward terms. But Freya hadn't seen the hollowness in Beckett's eyes when he'd thrown her out of his room, or felt the change in his touch when he'd helped her down the stairs to Freya's car.

"Well, if you aren't going to do the right thing, I can't make you." Freya poured out the last of her coffee and stuck the mug in the dishwasher. "I have some things to do this afternoon, but you mentioned going by your house to see what we could salvage. You want to get Mason up and ready?"

Jess slowly got to her feet. She doubted there was much that could be saved from that damaged house. The only thing worse off in her life right now than that storm-ravaged house was her broken heart.

They did need to see what could be recovered though. Maybe some of their clothes could be washed and would be usable, but Jess feared that all of the furnishings would be a total loss. Mason had expressed hope that some of his toys had survived, so he would be eager to get up and go with them to see what he could find.

An hour later, Freya pulled up to the front of Jess's house. A construction crew had started putting up new roof trusses. Stacks of shingles and supplies sat next to the fence. Another group of people seemed to be carrying her belongings out of the house and sorting them into bins. It looked like a beehive with all the activity buzzing in and out.

"What in the world?" Jess murmured as she got out of the car. "Did you do this?" she asked Freya.

"No, but I was aware of it, and I've been in contact with the man in charge," Freya said quietly. "Don't hate me too hard."

"Who then?" Jess made her way up the sidewalk slowly, taking care to balance on the uneven concrete walk. It had been on her list of things to fix, but after the tornado that list had grown exponentially, with the sidewalk slipping down near the bottom. "Where did all these people come from?"

As if in answer to her question, Beckett walked out the open front door. "We need to get the roof on quickly and—"

He stopped midsentence, his eyes greedily searching her face. She heated under his scrutiny, wishing she'd taken more care with her appearance.

The man he was talking to wore a hard hat and a T-shirt with the logo of a construction company on the front. "Roof is the top priority, of course, Mr. Wilder." As if sensing that he wouldn't get a reply from Beckett, he spoke quickly before walking away.

"Beckett!" Mason called from behind Jess. He rushed around her and flung himself into Beckett's legs. "I been asking Mommy when we could see you. She said you were busy, but she didn't tell me that you were busy here. Are you fixing our house? Was it supposed to be a surprise for me?"

"Was it a good surprise? I'd hoped to get it done before you found out." Tousling the boy's hair, Beckett answered him while keeping his gaze locked on Jess's. "As cool as lying in your bed looking at real stars might be, I couldn't let you and your mom have a house without a roof."

Mason, oblivious to the tension between the two adults, launched into a detailed description of the field trip his class had taken to the planetarium and all the things he knew about stars. Then he spotted a bunch of his things in one of the bins in the yard. He rushed over to check it out, leaving Beckett and Jess to awkwardly try to get through their first meeting since things went sideways.

Beckett gave her a grim smile. The normal lightness she associated with Beckett was missing from his eyes. Even when they'd argued, there'd been a happiness about him that had drawn her in. It was missing. Had her actions taken that from him?

"You didn't have to do this," she said quietly.

"A man takes care of his family." He gave that simple explanation with a shrug.

His family? Jess sucked in a sharp breath. Beckett considered them his family? That casual lift of his shoulders that implied everything he'd done here was no biggie frustrated her to no end. He brushed it off like he'd done virtually nothing, maybe brought them a pizza for dinner or something of little consequence. Providing them with a livable home was the biggest of deals in that moment, especially since he knew how much the house meant to her.

"Beckett, look what I found!" Mason squealed as he ran back up with a baseball and glove in his hand. "Can we play catch? Please!"

Beckett nodded and walked toward the backyard with Mason skipping along happily at his heels. When he looked over his shoulder at her, Jess nearly burst into tears.

Jess watched them go, her heart in her throat. He'd been the last person she'd expected.

Freya nudged her, almost tipping her over. "Weren't you going to go through your things?"

"Why would he do all this?" She waved a hand from the house to the yard and back. "He was so angry with me. He hasn't spoken to me in days."

"You really don't have a clue, do you?" Freya snickered. "Dang, girl, but you are blind if you don't see it."

Jess looked at her in confusion. "See what?"

"That my son is in love with you."

"Mr. Wilder!" Jess nearly tipped over as she spun to face Beckett's father. "I didn't see you there."

"Beckett's been insistent that we get this house livable for you and Mason." Mr. Wilder gave her a scrutinizing gaze. "I don't know what you fought over. But if you feel the same way, you might want to tell him. That boy of mine is stubborn. If he thinks you don't want him, he's going to stay out of your way. This is as close to a declaration of love as you'll get from him if you don't give him a sign that his attention is wanted."

Jess gaped at him, completely unsure of what to say.

"I hope you'll excuse me. I have an appointment." He walked over to the fence and called out to Beckett, tapping his fingers on the face of his watch.

Beckett came out of the yard with Mason at his side. "I'll play catch with you another day, if your mom says it's okay. She has my number. Just tell her to give me a time."

He made eye contact with Jess. "All she has to do is call."

Her breath hung in her throat. He really was just waiting for her to invite him back into her life. She hadn't believed it. Even given his father's open speech and Freya's teasing jabs, Jess had been convinced she'd ruined things permanently with Beckett. Now she was less sure.

Still, nothing had changed really. Beckett still wanted to go back to Lexington while she was firmly rooted here. She'd have to give up so much—her career, her family home and her hometown and all the memories of her parents. Moving to Lexington would mean putting her faith in Beckett, trusting him to provide for both her and Mason until she could find a job.

Was what she and Beckett could have worth that risk?

As she watched Beckett and his dad drive away, another idea came to mind. It would take some coordinating, but it might be the only way for them both to truly get what they wanted.

CHAPTER TWENTY-EIGHT

JESS IMPATIENTLY STRAIGHTENED the files on her desk. It had taken her a solid week and a half to put the proposal together. She'd checked and triple-checked the numbers before reaching out. Even though she was as prepared as she could be for this meeting, her nerves were completely shot.

She looked up at the sharp single knock.

"May I come in?" Richard Wilder stood in the open doorway.

"Please," she said, waving for him to take the empty chair across from her desk. "Thank you for agreeing to meet with me today, Mr. Wilder."

"Richard, please."

She nodded. "I wanted to talk to you about the emergency department proposal before I submitted it."

His eyebrows rose and she swallowed hard at how much the man across from her reminded her of Beckett. "My son is handling all of the proposals. Now, I know you've had a falling out—"

"Will you at least look at it?" She bit her lip as she waited for his answer. "And I know the ambulance service here in Woodvale is a bone of contention between you and Beckett, so I didn't want to have this come as a surprise or exacerbate the issues between the two of you."

He motioned for her to continue.

After handing him the folder, she gave him a quick pitch. He said nothing in response. She'd expected a few questions. Maybe some arguments. But she didn't expect silence. Did he hate it? Nothing in his expression gave her a hint either way. As the minutes ticked past while he flipped through the printed proposal, she grew more and more anxious.

This was the best chance she had to fix things with Beckett. She didn't have a backup plan really. Maybe she should reiterate some of her key points?

"You've really thought this out," he finally said.

She breathed a sigh of relief. That wasn't an instant no. Good sign, right? "I tried to consider all the angles. Some of the data Beckett and I worked on together. Not in this form, but he helped me with determining needs during our meeting before the tornado. As you know, he has far more experience in that area than I do."

"You've sold me on the concept, but I'm not in charge of this project."

"I was hoping you could still help me out." She blurted out the rest of her plan, the part that had little to do with funding, and everything to do with love.

CHAPTER TWENTY-NINE

It HAD BEEN three weeks since he'd last laid eyes on her. A busy period, thankfully, since it hadn't left him too much time to dwell on losing Jess. He hadn't initiated the fixing of her house as an excuse to bump into her, but he wasn't upset that he had run into her and Mason that day. He'd made it clear that the ball was in her court, hadn't he? She hadn't called though, and no matter how many times he looked at his phone, she hadn't texted either. So, what could he do but assume she had no interest in seeing him?

Beckett got to the hospital about thirty minutes before the monthly special committee meeting was due to begin. He had received all the proposals and was set to make some announcements which he considered a top priority. To his frustration, his father had stepped in and taken over the proposal and funding for the emergency department. Beckett wasn't sure if it was to take away the opportunity for him to fund the ambulances or to limit his contact with Jess.

He sat with his head in his hands trying to find a way to address the committee without making a fool of himself. It would seem rude if he avoided Jess but making eye contact might make him lose his train of thought. Every time she crossed his mind, he got distracted by the what-ifs and what-could-have-beens.

Lasting relationships had never been his strong suit. In the past though, his job had always played a role in ending things for him. Sometimes women romanticized dating a first responder, loving the idea of a man in uniform more than the actual reality. Things would be great for a few weeks, until she wanted to take a trip away only to realize he worked nearly every weekend. His odd hours would inevitably begin to chafe, and he'd never had a strong enough connection with a woman to fight past the schedule frustrations.

Until Jess…

Now his schedule wasn't the issue, but the location of his job. He'd have to give up being an EMT permanently if he moved here. Even with the requested budget that he and Jess had worked up, there wouldn't be much for him. The only EMT position open was on third shift, and he'd never see her and Mason. Still, he'd filled out the application and it was on hold waiting for him to click Submit.

When people started filing into the room, Beckett didn't look up. Even still, he knew the exact moment Jess walked through the door. She hadn't spoken, but he was aware of her arrival, nonetheless. He took a deep breath. This would be so much easier if she didn't want to be with him at all.

Being together should be easy. Love shouldn't mean choosing between your partner and your career though.

"Okay, looks like everyone is here." Freya kicked the meeting off. Beckett risked looking up at her as she filled everyone in on the current status of repairs to the emergency department and the estimated timeline to completion. She gave a brief rundown of exactly what their insurance was covering and how that affected the budget.

"Now, I think Beckett has some announcements to make regarding the funding his family's foundation is graciously donating." Freya gestured, indicating for him to begin when ready.

He took a deep breath. Eventually, public speaking had to get easier. While he'd never have his dad's eloquence in front of a crowd, he hoped he at least wouldn't get so flustered that he looked like an idiot.

Jess cleared her throat.

He glanced her way, looking down at the table before he could meet her gaze. Not looking at her took far more effort than he'd anticipated. "Do you have a concern before I get to the numbers?"

"I do, actually." He heard her chair squeak as she stood up. "We need more EMT funding, and we need it now."

Jerking his gaze up to her face, he stared at her in shock. His forehead wrinkled in confusion. Had he hallucinated? He waited for her to continue, sure that there had to be a catch or that she was about to completely contradict what she'd just said. She'd argued from the get-go that her emergency department came first, although she'd acknowledged that more ambulances were needed. And they'd come to the conclusion together that there would be no way to fund more ambulances unless they had more outside income.

"The problem I see is that this is beyond the scope of

what should fit into the budget of the emergency department. I've submitted a proposal for an all new department—call it the Department for Emergency Services for now, if you will. Ambulances and EMTs are outside the bounds of what should be considered as part of the ED. They need their own department, with a leader willing to advocate for his team's needs, no longer stuffed under the umbrella of the emergency department where they have to fight for funding against trauma surgeons and strep tests."

The room was quiet as the committee seemed to digest Jess's words. Beckett couldn't blame them for needing a moment. He was a little dumbfounded himself. Not only was she agreeing with him, she'd taken his plans and supersized them.

"Would you be in charge of this new department as well?" someone asked.

"No, not at all. I am not the ideal person for that role." Her lips upturned when she looked at him. That soft, shy smile made him sure that it would be ten times harder to move on than he'd imagined it would be. "But I think Beckett Wilder would do an admirable job as the head of the new department. Don't you?"

"Any opposed to giving this idea further merit?" Freya asked.

Beckett's dad stood and cleared his throat. "Jess has shown me her proposal. It needs a little more work, but I think we can make something happen. And Beckett's welcome to apply for the position, but he'll have to earn it fairly."

Beckett sank into his chair. His mind was a million miles from where it should be, focusing on where Jess had taken this meeting instead of where it was meant to go. If this went through, it would accomplish all that he'd been shooting for here in Woodvale. He'd fought so hard for it that he didn't know what to do with himself now that the issue was on its way to resolution and even his father seemed to be on board.

His dad placed a hand on his shoulder. "Do you think you could help Jess get that proposal cleaned up? She doesn't have the experience that you have with running an ambulance. I think you'd have a better idea of whether or not the proposed budget is viable."

He nodded slowly. Oh, man, getting that proposal together would mean working alone side by side to get it complete and ready to submit. Could she stand to be in his presence that long? More importantly, could he make it through even an hour alone with her without taking her in his arms and giving her a physical reminder of just how good they could be together?

He scrubbed a hand over his face and pondered the woman across from him. It was through her that his wishes were finally becoming reality, at least when it came to the hospital and their hometown. If only she'd make such an about-face when it came to a relationship with him, then all of his dreams would come true. When he looked up, their eyes met and there was a hint of something in her gaze that made it hard to breathe.

He sat up a little straighter and had to bite the inside of his cheek to stop himself from blurting out how much he missed her in front of all the members of the special committee. She'd captured his heart the way no other woman ever had and nearly broken him when she sent him away. The longing in her eyes sent a spark of awareness coursing through him.

She'd changed her opinion on EMT funding. Dare he hope she'd reconsidered their relationship?

CHAPTER THIRTY

BUTTERFLIES FLUTTERED IN Jess's stomach as the others filed out of the conference room. No, they were too big to be butterflies. More like pterodactyls. She took a deep breath and tried to quell her ragged nerves.

Beckett had made the first move when he had worked so hard to get her house ready to be lived in. He hadn't sought credit for his acts, and if she hadn't caught him, he'd probably have let her think it was a guardian angel who wanted to remain anonymous.

Freya was the last one to leave the room, and she gave Jess's arm a reassuring squeeze. "Get your man back," she whispered.

"So," she began. Briefly, she'd considered simply throwing herself into his arms, thinking he'd certainly see that as an apology. That wouldn't be fair though. She owed him an earnest apology and a verbal declaration of her love.

"So," he repeated when she didn't say anything besides that single syllable. "Thank you for finally seeing the merit in my idea. I appreciate your vote of confidence in recommending me to lead the new department too. If you want to let me know when a convenient time to work on the proposal would be, I'll make the timing work."

His words caused an ache deep in her chest. He hadn't completely dismissed her, but she'd held out hope that he might be a little more pleased. She had only herself to blame for Beckett's current attitude though. She'd hurt him. Maybe one day she could tell him about how badly she'd hurt her own stubborn self too.

"If you had been anyone else, life would be so simple." She winced as the words came out of her mouth. That was not what she meant to say at all. She'd rehearsed a speech, a true apology. She'd made enough mistakes with this man. She didn't need to make more with impetuous words.

"Am I supposed to apologize for being myself?" He pinched the bridge of his nose. "I can't change who I am, even if you want me to. We aren't talking about how my job frustrates you or how you might want me to break an annoying habit. The part of me you object to isn't something within my power to change."

"I don't want you to change. Well, other than your address. I really would like to stay here in Woodvale." She smiled sadly at him as she moved over to take the seat next to his. "I fully admit it might have seemed that I wanted you to be someone different. It wasn't you that was the problem though, and it took me a minute to wrap my head around the fact that maybe I was wrong."

"So, where does that leave us?" He flexed his hand like he wanted to reach for her but wouldn't allow himself to do so. "I can't change my background."

"I know."

"Do you?" He moved in closer. His scent was in

her nose, and she wanted to bury her face against his chest. But they still had some things to work out. The sparkle had returned to his eyes, and she swallowed hard at his nearness. "Because you've held it against me a few times."

"I was letting my past with Clint cloud everything about my life. I measured everyone against the hurt he caused me, and I used the memory of that pain as a shield for why I had to protect myself, as an excuse for why I should stay alone."

"So, you're okay with me being a Wilder now."

"Yes," she said with a sigh. It had been unfair of her to hold his upbringing against him to start with. She'd just been unable to see past the wall of hurt Clint had built.

"Did you plan this new department to try to get me to stay in Woodvale?"

"Yes."

"You are going to marry me then." His mouth descended on hers before she could process his words and she returned his kiss with great enthusiasm. Electricity arced between them and warmed her quickly. Reluctantly, she pulled back though.

"We're at work," she said. "And did you just order me to marry you?"

"I'm not giving you a chance to say no." He nuzzled her cheek. "The last few weeks have been torture."

"You are too forgiving." She sighed, relishing the feel of his hands on her. "But can you please give me a chance to properly tell you just how sorry I am for hurting you?"

Swiftly, he leaned back, putting his hands behind

his head. He looked so kissable that his actions didn't make it much easier to concentrate. She forced her eyes to his and focused on the apology she should have gotten out before allowing him to kiss her.

"I should have trusted you more." It still rubbed her wrong that she'd instantly assumed Beckett would run like Clint. But she had, and she'd let that fear control her and she'd nearly ruined the best thing that had ever happened to her as a result. "I'm really sorry that I didn't. And if it's any consolation, I've learned my lesson."

"Good." He brushed his fingers along her jawline. "I suppose since you've basically created a job just for me, I have to stay in Woodvale now, huh?"

"You've been wanting to get more ambulances in Woodvale, haven't you? I thought perhaps if I helped you accomplish that goal it would help you see that I'm truly on your side and supportive of you." She teased little circles on the smooth fabric of his suit pants. "I also think your talents are wasted here in this boardroom."

"Oh?"

She reached over and tugged his tie a bit. "I don't think these ties are quite right for you, are they? I'm dying to see you in an EMT uniform."

"And here I was wondering when I could get you out of some of your clothes."

"Beckett!" Her cheeks heated at his blatant flirting.

"It might not be easy, but I think if you're willing to give us a try, it will be worth it." He brushed the pad of his thumb over her lower lip. "You were in cahoots with my dad about this, weren't you?"

"I needed to find a way for us to work this out. I realized it wasn't fair for me to ask you to give up your career when I wasn't willing to give up my house and this town. I needed to find a way to compromise." She shrugged. "Plan B was that Mason and I would follow you to Lexington."

"You were actually considering moving to be with me?"

"If that's what I had to do, then yes." A tear trekked down her cheek. "This will always be home for me, but you told me once that sometimes the people you are with can change how you feel about a place. Not having you here with me would make it hard to stay here now."

"I just have one question—are you keeping any other secrets from me?"

"Just one," she said softly.

"What's that?"

She wrapped her arms around his neck. "Only that I am in love with you, Beckett Wilder."

"I'm in love with you too, Jessamine Daniels."

EPILOGUE

One year later

JESS STOOD ON the back deck at the Wilders' lake house watching Mason try to teach Richard and Elaine about Pokémon. The expressions on their faces were a mixture of concentration and confusion. They had become active parts of Mason's life from the moment that Beckett had announced his engagement to Jess.

"Is he jabbering on about his Pokémon again?" Beckett asked as he walked up behind her.

"Oh, yes." She tilted her head and murmured in pleasure as his lips sought the pulse point on her throat that he knew drove her insane. "Where have you been?"

"Picking up a little something that I ordered for you."

"Hmm?"

He pulled out a small jewelry box. "Open it."

She took the proffered gift from his hand. When she opened the lid, she found a small tornado charm on a delicate chain. "Oh…" she said, fingering the piece gently.

"It was one year ago today that the tornado hit Woodvale and threw you into my arms. We survived that storm by relying on each other, and I thought this might be a good reminder that if we lean on each other, we can survive any storm that life throws at us."

"I like that." She smiled broadly at him, trying her best to blink back tears. "Will you put it on me?"

She lifted her hair, and he fastened the clasp for her. "Should we go rescue them?"

"Nah. They can hold their own for a few more minutes, don't you think?" Beckett pulled her in for a searing kiss. It was several minutes before they ended the embrace.

"I suppose it wouldn't hurt for them to practice a bit before they become grandparents again in the fall." Jess looked up at him and waited for the news she'd just dropped on him to click.

"Are you telling me we are about to become a family of four, Mrs. Wilder?"

"I most certainly am."

Beckett put his hand tenderly on her stomach. "Really?"

She nodded. "You think Mason's going to want to be a big brother?"

"He's been asking for a brother since the day we got married—what do you think?"

"I think I am in awe at how much my life has changed in a year. I never imagined I could be this blissfully happy or that I could trust a man so implicitly again."

"You are the best thing that's ever happened to me too, Jess." His lips settled on hers again.

"Are y'all gonna kiss every minute of every day?" Mason asked, tugging on their arms.

"Only about seventy-five percent of them," Beckett

teased. "The rest I'm going to spend chasing you and your brother or sister."

Mason had prepared to run, but Beckett's words froze him in his tracks. Confusion on his face faded to excitement. "A brother or sister? Really?"

Jess nodded. "Around Halloween."

"Sweet. Now I don't got to use my Christmas wish on a brother!" He ran away laughing.

"I told you he'd be happy."

"Dad, are you going to chase me or not?"

"I love hearing that." Beckett kissed her nose. "Dad… It never gets old. Now, if you will excuse me, love, I have a son to catch."

* * * * *

COMING SOON!

We really hope you enjoyed reading this book.
If you're looking for more romance, be sure to
head to the shops when new books are
available on

Thursday 21st
July

To see which titles are coming soon, please visit

millsandboon.co.uk/nextmonth

MILLS & BOON ®

Coming next month

FALLING FOR THE VILLAGE VET
Rachel Dove

'I've really enjoyed our date. I wanted to say that before we start talking about Portaloos.'

She burst into guffaws of laughter. He watched her with a very amused smile on his face. His hair was a little messed up, making him look more casual than usual. Ruffled.

'You're a goofball deep down, do you know that?'

'Yep. Just like you.' He looked her up and down slowly. 'Minus the colourful clothing.' He bit at his lip. 'I'm not all bad. I wish you'd known me before, when I was younger. I was different then.'

'Things change us in life,' she soothed.

'Nothing's changed you.'

She laughed again. 'Not now, no. It took me a while after my divorce to lick my wounds. I bought this place and just hid away at first.'

'Doesn't sound like you.'

He spoke as if he'd known her much longer than he had, but it sounded right to her too. They had seemingly been studying each other. Judged each other, yelled at each other, but yet here they were laughing, working on the charity drive together and enjoying the evening.

'It wasn't,' she breathed. 'I'm glad you came to live here. I'm not sure if anyone's actually said that to you yet.'

'It is nice to hear.' He was so close now. His eyes were taking her in, and she felt the stirrings of attraction sparking. 'Especially from you.'

'Your harshest critic,' she near whispered. They laughed again. 'What a battle-scarred pair we are.'

He laughed softly again, and something changed. It was so slight, so minuscule that she could easily have missed it, but he tore his gaze from hers, and poured them both a glass of wine.

'We'd better get on with the planning, then—I need to get back to Hendrix.' He wasn't rude, or surly. He was the man she'd come to know. The man who was so buttoned-up, she didn't think he'd ever get free. She hid her red face behind her wine glass, taking a good long pull. Trudy was coming to sort the dogs tomorrow, so she could sleep all day and then hide in work. Then she hid her disappointment at the date that wasn't a date. The non-date that had turned into a hot date and then back into a non-date. Just as she was starting to feel... Well, it wasn't anything, obviously. She sat up on her couch, pulled a pen from the pile on the table, and flipped open her notepad. Closing her heart at the same time.

Continue reading
FALLING FOR THE VILLAGE VET
Rachel Dove

Available next month
www.millsandboon.co.uk

MILLS & BOON

THE HEART OF ROMANCE

A ROMANCE FOR EVERY READER

MODERN

Prepare to be swept off your feet by sophisticated, sexy and seductive heroes, in some of the world's most glamourous and romantic locations, where power and passion collide.

HISTORICAL

Escape with historical heroes from time gone by. Whether your passion is for wicked Regency Rakes, muscled Vikings or rugged Highlanders, awaken the romance of the past.

MEDICAL

Set your pulse racing with dedicated, delectable doctors in the high-pressure world of medicine, where emotions run high and passion, comfort and love are the best medicine.

True Love

Celebrate true love with tender stories of heartfelt romance, from the rush of falling in love to the joy a new baby can bring, and a focus on the emotional heart of a relationship.

Desire

Indulge in secrets and scandal, intense drama and plenty of sizzling hot action with powerful and passionate heroes who have it all: wealth, status, good looks…everything but the right woman.

HEROES

Experience all the excitement of a gripping thriller, with an intense romance at its heart. Resourceful, true-to-life women and strong, fearless men face danger and desire - a killer combination!

To see which titles are coming soon, please visit

millsandboon.co.uk/nextmonth

JOIN US ON SOCIAL MEDIA!

Stay up to date with our latest releases, author news and gossip, special offers and discounts, and all the behind-the-scenes action from Mills & Boon...

 millsandboon

 millsandboonuk

 millsandboon

It might just be true love...